SMALL
MERCIES

DENNIS LEHANE

SMALL MERCIES

abacus
books

ABACUS

First published in the United States in 2023 by HaperCollins
First published in the United Kingdom in 2023 by Abacus

1 3 5 7 9 10 8 6 4 2

Copyright © 2023, Dennis Lahane

The moral right of the author has been asserted.

*All characters and events in this publication, other than those
clearly in the public domain, are fictitious and any resemblance
to real persons, living or dead, is purely coincidental.*

A CIP catalogue record for this book
is available from the British Library.

HB ISBN: 978-0-3491-4575-4
TPB ISBN: 978-0-3491-4576-1

Printed and bound in Great Britain by
Clays Ltd, Elcograf S.p.A.

Papers used by Abacus are from well-managed forests
and other responsible sources.

Abacus
An imprint of
Little, Brown Book Group
Carmelite House
50 Victoria Embankment
London EC4Y 0DZ

An Hachette UK Company
www.hachette.co.uk

www.littlebrown.co.uk

For Chisa

To cut oneself entirely from one's kind is impossible. To live in a desert, one must be a saint.

—Joseph Conrad, *Under Western Eyes*

HISTORICAL NOTE

On June 21, 1974, U.S. District Court Judge W. Arthur Garrity, Jr., ruled in *Morgan v. Hennigan* that the Boston School Committee had "systematically disadvantaged black school children" in the public school system. The only remedy, the judge concluded, was to begin busing students between predominantly white and predominantly black neighborhoods to desegregate the city's public high schools.

The school in the neighborhood with the largest African American population was Roxbury High School. The school in the neighborhood with the largest white population was South Boston High School. It was decided that these two schools would switch a significant portion of their student bodies.

This order was to take effect at the beginning of the school year, on September 12, 1974. Students and parents had less than ninety days from the date of the ruling to prepare.

It was very hot in Boston that summer, and it seldom rained.

SMALL
MERCIES

1

The power goes out sometime before dawn, and everyone at Commonwealth wakes to swelter. In the Fennessy apartment, the window fans have quit in mid-rotation and the fridge is pimpled with sweat. Mary Pat sticks her head in on Jules, finds her daughter on top of her sheets, eyes clenched, mouth half open, huffing thin breaths into a damp pillow. Mary Pat moves on down the hall into the kitchen and lights her first cigarette of the day. She stares out the window over the sink and can smell the heat rising off the brick in the window casing.

She realizes she can't make coffee only when she tries to make it. She'd brew some on the stovetop—the oven runs on gas—but the gas company grew sick of excuses and killed their service last week. To get the family out of arrears, Mary Pat has picked up two shifts at the shoe warehouse where she has her second job, but she still has three more shifts and a trip to the billing office before she can boil water or roast a chicken again.

She carries the trash can into the living room and sweeps the beer cans into it. Empties the ashtrays from the coffee table and the side table and one she found on top of the TV. It's there she catches her reflection in the tube and sees a creature she can't reconcile with the image she's clung to in her mind, an image that bears little resemblance to the sweaty lump of matted hair and droopy chin dressed in a tank top and shorts. Even in the flat gray of the picture tube, she can make out the blue veins in her outer thighs, which somehow don't seem possible, not yet. Not yet. She's only forty-two, which, okay, when she was twelve seemed like one foot over the threshold into God's waiting room, but now, living it, is an age that makes her feel no different than she always has. She's twelve, she's twenty-one, she's thirty-three, she's all the ages at the same time. But she isn't aging. Not in her heart. Not in her mind's eye.

She's peering at her face in the TV, wiping at the damp strands of hair on her forehead, when the doorbell rings.

After a series of home invasions two years back, in the summer of '72, the Housing Authority sprang for peepholes in the doors. Mary Pat looks through hers now to see Brian Shea in the mint green corridor, his arms full of sticks. Like most of the people who work for Marty Butler, Brian dresses neater than a deacon. No long hair or bandit mustaches for the Butler crew. No muttonchop sideburns or flared pants or elevated shoes. Definitely no paisley or tie-dye. Brian Shea dresses like someone from a decade earlier—white T-shirt under a navy blue Baracuta. (The Baracuta jacket—navy blue, tan, or occasionally brown—is a staple of Butler crew guys; they wear it even on days like today, when the mercury approaches 80 at nine a.m. They swap it out in the winter for topcoats or leather car coats with thick wool lining, but come spring they all bring the Baracutas back out of the closet on the same day.) Brian's cheeks are shaved close, his blond hair cropped tight in a crew cut, and he wears off-white chinos and scuffed black ankle boots with zippers on the sides. Brian has eyes the color of Windex. They sparkle and glint at her with an air of mild presumption, like he knows the things she thinks she keeps hidden. And those things amuse him.

"Mary Pat," he says. "How are you?"

She can picture her hair splayed sodden on her head like congealed spaghetti. Can feel every splotch on her skin. "Power's out, Brian. How are you?"

"Marty's working on the power," he says. "He's made some calls."

She glances at the thin slats of wood in his arms. "Help you with those?"

"That'd be great." He turns them in his arms and stands the pile upright beside her door. "They're for the signs."

She seems to remember spilling beer on her tank top last night and wonders if the scent of stale Miller High Life is being picked up by Brian Shea. "What signs?"

"For the rally. Tim G will be by with them shortly."

She places the slats in the umbrella bucket just inside her door. They share space with the lone umbrella with the broken rib. "The rally's happening?"

"Friday. We're taking it right to City Hall Plaza. Making some noise, Mary Pat. Just like we promised. We're going to need the whole neighborhood."

"Of course," she says. "I'll be there."

He hands her a stack of leaflets. "We're asking folks to pass these out before noon today. You know—before it gets crazy hot." He uses the side of his hand to wipe at sweat trickling down his smooth cheek. "Though it might be too late for that."

She takes the leaflets. Glances at the top one:

BOSTON'S UNDER SIEGE!!!!!!!!

JOIN ALL CONCERNED PARENTS AND PROUD MEMBERS OF THE SOUTH BOSTON COMMUNITY FOR A MARCH TO END JUDICIAL DICTATORSHIP ON *FRIDAY, AUGUST 30*, AT CITY HALL PLAZA.

12 NOON SHARP!
NO BUSING! NEVER!
RESIST!
BOYCOTT!

"We're asking everyone to cover specific blocks. We'd like you to cover . . ." Brian reaches into his Baracuta, comes back with a list, runs his finger down it. "Ah. Like you to cover Mercer between Eighth and Dorchester Street. And Telegraph to the park. And then, yeah, all the houses ringing the park."

"That's a lot of doors."

"It's for the Cause, Mary Pat."

Anytime the Butler crew comes around with their hands out, what they're really offering is protection. But they never exactly call it that. They wrap it in a noble motive: the IRA, the starving children in Wherever the Fuck, families of veterans. Some of the money might even end up there. But the anti-busing cause, so far, anyway, seems totally legit. It seems like *the* Cause. If for no other reason than they haven't asked for a dime from the residents of Commonwealth. Just legwork.

"Happy to help," Mary Pat tells Brian. "Just busting your balls."

Brian gives that a tired eye roll. "Everyone busts balls in this place. Time I'm done, I'll be a eunuch." He tips an imaginary cap to her before heading down the green corridor. "Good to see you, Mary Pat. Hope your power comes back soon."

"Wait a sec," she calls. "Brian."

He looks back at her.

"What happens after the protest? What happens if, I dunno, nothing changes?"

He holds out his hands. "I guess we see."

Why don't you just fucking shoot the judge? she thinks. *You're the goddamn Butler crew. We pay "protection" to you. Protect us now. Protect our kids. Make this stop.*

But what she says is "Thanks, Brian. Say hi to Donna."

"Will do." Another tip of the imaginary cap. "Say hi to Kenny." His smooth face freezes for a second as he probably recalls the latest neighborhood gossip. He flashes her doe eyes. "I mean, I meant—"

She bails him out with a simple "I will."

He gives her a tight smile and walks off.

She closes the door and turns back into the apartment to see her daughter sitting at the kitchen table, smoking one of her cigarettes.

"Fucking power's off," Jules says.

"Or 'Good morning,'" Mary Pat says. "'Good morning' works."

"Good morning." Jules shoots her a smile that manages to be bright as the sun and cold as the moon. "I'm going to need to shower, Ma."

"So shower."

"It'll be cold."

"It's fucking ninety degrees out." Mary Pat pulls her pack of Slims back across the table from her daughter's elbow.

Jules rolls her eyes, takes a drag, directs the smoke at the ceiling in a long steady exhale. "What did he want?"

"Brian?"

"Yeah."

"How do you know Brian Shea?" Mary Pat lights her second of the day.

"Ma," Jules says, her eyes bulging, "I don't *know* Brian Shea. I know Brian Shea because everyone in the neighborhood knows Brian Shea. What did he want?"

"There's gonna be a march," Mary Pat says. "A rally. Friday."

"Won't change anything." Her daughter tries for a tone of casual apathy, but Mary Pat sees the fear swimming in her eyes, darkening the pouches underneath. Always such a pretty girl, Jules. Always such a pretty girl. And now clearly aging. At seventeen. From any number of things—growing up in Commonwealth (not the kind of place that produces beauty queens and fashion models, no matter how pretty they were coming out of the gate); losing a brother; watching her stepfather walk out the door just when she'd finally started to believe he'd stick around; being forced—by federal edict—to enter a new school her senior year in a foreign neighborhood not known for letting white kids walk around after sundown; not to mention just being seventeen and getting into who knows what with her knucklehead friends. A lot of pot around these days, Mary Pat knows, and acid. Booze, of course; in Southie, most kids came out of the womb clutching a Schlitz and a pack of Luckies. And, of course, the Scourge, that nasty brown powder and its fucking needles that turn healthy kids into corpses or soon-to-be-corpses in under a year. If Jules keeps it to the booze and the cigarettes with the occasional joint thrown in, she'll only lose her looks. And everyone loses their looks in the projects. But God forbid if she moves on to the Scourge. Mary Pat will die another death.

Jules, she's come to realize over the last couple of years, never should have been raised here. Mary Pat—one look at *her* baby pictures and childhood snapshots, all scrunched face and wide shoulders and small powerful body, ready to audition for the roller derby or some shit— looks like she came off a conveyor belt for tough Irish broads. Most people would sooner pick a fight with a stray dog with a taste for flesh then fuck with a Southie chick who grew up in the PJs.

But that's Mary Pat.

Jules is tall and sinewy, with long smooth hair the color of an apple. Every inch of her is soft and feminine and waiting on a broken heart the way miners wait on black lung—she just knows it's coming. She's fragile, this product of Mary Pat's womb—fragile in the eyes, fragile in her flesh, fragile in her soul. All the tough talk, the cigarettes, the ability to swear like a sailor and spit like a longshoreman, can't fully disguise that. Mary Pat's mother, Louise "Weezie" Flanagan, a Hall of Fame Irish Tough Broad who'd stood four-eleven and weighed ninety-five pounds soaking wet after a Thanksgiving dinner, told Mary Pat a few times, "You're either a fighter or a runner. And runners always run out of road."

Mary Pat sometimes wishes she'd found a way to get them out of Commonwealth before Jules finds out which she is.

"So where's this rally taking place?" Jules asks.

"We're going downtown."

"Yeah?" That gets a wry smile from her daughter as she stubs out her cigarette. "Crossing the bridge 'n' shit." Jules raises her eyebrows up and down. "Look at you."

Mary Pat reaches across the table and pats her hand so she'll look at her. "We're going to City Hall. They can't ignore us, Jules. They're gonna see us, they're gonna fucking hear us. You kids ain't alone."

Jules gives her a smile that's hopeful and broken at the same time. "Yeah?" She lowers her head. Her voice is a wet whisper when she says, "Thanks, Ma."

"Of course." Mary Pat feels something clench in the back of her throat. "You bet, sweetie."

This may have been the longest she's sat with her daughter, just talking, in months. She'd forgotten how much she likes it.

A tiny clap of thunder shakes the floor beneath their feet, rattles through the walls, and the lights come on above the stove. The fans start moving in the windows. Radios and TVs in the other apartments return to battle with one another. Someone whoops.

Jules shrieks, "I call shower!" and bolts from her chair like she owes it money.

Mary Pat makes coffee. Takes it into the living room with one of the freshly emptied ashtrays and turns on the TV. They're all over the news—South Boston and the coming school year. Black kids about to get bused into Southie. White kids about to get bused out to Roxbury. No one on either side happy about the prospect.

Except the agitators, the blacks who sued the school committee— been suing it for nine years because nothing was ever good enough.

Mary Pat has worked alongside too many blacks at Meadow Lane Manor and the shoe factory to believe they're bad or naturally lazy. Plenty of good, hardworking, upstanding Negroes want the same things she wants—a steady paycheck, food on the table, children safe in their beds. She's told both her children if they're going to say "nigger" around her, they better be sure they're using it about those blacks who aren't upstanding, don't work hard, don't stay married, and have babies just to keep the welfare checks rolling in.

Noel, just before he left for Vietnam, said, "That describes most of the ones I've ever met, Ma."

"And how many have you met?" Mary Pat wanted to know. "You see a lot of coloreds walking up West Broadway, do ya?"

"No," he said, "but I see 'em downtown. See 'em on the T." He used one hand to imitate someone holding a subway strap and the other to scratch under his arm like a monkey. "They's always going to Fo'-rest Hills." He made chimp sounds and she swatted at him.

"Don't be ignorant," she said. "I didn't raise you to be ignorant."

He smiled at her.

God, she misses her son's smile; she first saw it, crooked and wide, when he was on her breast, drunk on mother's milk, and it blew open a chamber of her heart that refuses to close no matter how hard she presses down on it.

He kissed her on the top of her head. "You're too nice for these projects, Ma. Anyone ever tell you that?"

And then he was gone. Back out to the streets. All Southie kids loved the streets but none more so than project kids. Project kids hated staying in the way rich people hated work. Staying in meant smelling your neighbors' food through the walls, hearing their fights, their fucks, their toilet flushes, what they listened to on their radios and record players, what they watched on TV. Sometimes you'd swear you could *smell* them, their body odor and cigarette breath and swollen-feet stink.

Jules comes back into the living room in her old tartan bathrobe, at least two sizes too small at this point, drying her hair. "We going?"

"Going?"

"*Yeah.*"

"Where?"

"You told me you'd take me back-to-school shopping."

"When?"

"Like fucking *today*, Ma."

"You doing the buying?"

"Ma, come on, don't fuck with me."

"I'm not. You notice we don't have a stove?"

"Who gives a shit? You never cook."

That gets Mary Pat off the couch with blood in her eyes. "I never fucking cook?"

"Not lately."

"Because the gas was turned off."

"Well, whose fault was that?"

"Get a fucking job before I break your head in," Mary Pat says, "talking to me like that."

"I have a job."

"Part-time don't count, honey. Part-time don't make the rent."

"Or keep the stove working, apparently."

"I will knock you into fucking next week, I swear to Christ."

Jules raises her fists and dances back and forth in her ridiculous robe like a boxer in the ring. Smiling big.

Mary Pat bursts out laughing in spite of herself. "Put those hands down before your punch your own head, end up talking funny the rest of your life."

Jules, laughing through her teeth, shoots her the bird with both hands, still doing the ridiculous dance in the ridiculous robe. "Robell's, then."

"I got *no* money."

Jules stops dancing. Puts the towel back over her head. "You got some. You might not have Boston Gas bill money, but you got Robell's money."

"No," Mary Pat says. "I do not."

"I'm gonna go to the spearchucker school looking poorer than them?" Her eyes well, and she runs the towel violently over her head to make the tears get no further. "Ma, *please?*"

Mary Pat imagines her there on day one, this trembly white girl and her big brown eyes.

"I got a few bucks," Mary Pat manages.

Jules drops into a crouch of gratitude. "*Thank* you."

"But you gotta help me knock on a bunch of doors first."

"Fuckin' what now?" Jules says.

They start in the Heights. Knock on all the doors that circle the park and the monument. A lot of people aren't home (or assume she and Jules are Christian Scientists spreading "gospel" so pretend not to be), but plenty are. And few need converting. They provide the outrage, the righteousness, the umbrage. They'll be there on Friday.

"Bet your ass we will," an old lady with a walker and smoker's breath tells them. "Bet your sweet ass."

The sun's in descent by the time they finish. Not setting so much as dipping into the brown ribbons of smoke in a constant drift from the power plant at the end of West Broadway. Mary Pat takes Jules to Ro-bell's and they pick out a notebook, a four-pack of pens, a blue nylon school bag, a pair of jeans with wide flares at the bottom but which run high on the hips. Then Jules, in the groove of it all finally, goes with her mother to Finast, where Mary Pat buys a TV dinner for herself. When she asks what Jules wants for dinner, Jules reminds her she's going out with Rum. They move through the checkout line with one TV dinner and one *National Enquirer*, Mary Pat thinking she may as well have *Lonely, Aging, and Pudgy* plastered to her forehead.

On the walk home, Jules, out of the blue, says, "You ever wonder if there's some different place?"

Mary Pat says, "What now?"

Jules steps off the curb to avoid a pile of ants swarming what looks like a broken egg. She pivots around a young tree before stepping back up on the sidewalk. "You just, you know, you ever have the feeling that things are supposed to be one way but they're not? And you don't know why because you've never known, like, anything but what you see? And what you see is, you know"—she waves at Old Colony Avenue—"*this?*" She looks at her mother and cants a bit on the uneven sidewalk so they won't collide. "But you know, right?"

"Know what?"

"Know it's not what you were meant for." Jules taps the space between her breasts. "In here."

"Well, sweetie," her mother says, with no fucking idea what she's on about, "what were you meant for?"

"I'm not saying it that way."

"What way?"

"The way you're saying it."

"Then how're you saying it?"

"I'm just trying to say I don't understand why I don't feel the way other people seem to feel."

"About what?"

"About everything. Anything." Her daughter raises her hands. "Fuck!"

"What?" Mary Pat wants to know. *"What?"*

Jules waves her hand at the world. "Ma, I just . . . It's like . . . Okay, okay." She stops and props a foot up on the base of a rusted BPD callbox. Her voice falls to a whisper. "I don't understand why things are what they are."

"You mean school? You mean busing?"

"What? No. I mean, yes. Kind of. I mean, I don't understand where we go."

Is she talking about Noel? "You mean when we die?"

"Then, yeah. But, you know, when we . . . forget about it."

"No, tell me."

"No."

"Please."

Her daughter looks her right in the eyes—an absolute rarity since her first menstrual cycle six years ago—and her gaze is hopeless and yearning in the same breath. For a moment, Mary Pat sees herself in the gaze . . . but what self? Which Mary Pat? How long since she yearned? How long since she dared believe something so foolish as the idea that someone anywhere has the answers to questions she can't even put into words?

Jules looks away, bites her lip, a habit of hers when she's fighting back tears. "I mean, where do we go, Ma? Next week, next year? Like, what's the fucking," she sputters, "what's the—Why are we doing this?"

"Doing *what*?"

"Walking around, shopping, getting up, going to bed, getting up again? What are we trying to, you know, like, achieve?"

Mary Pat wants to give her daughter one of those shots they give tigers to knock them out. What the fuck is she on about? "Are you PMSing?" she asks.

Jules hucks out a liquid chuckle. "No, Ma. Definitely no."

"So what?" She takes her daughter's hands in hers. "Jules, I'm here. What?" She kneads her daughter's palms with her thumbs the way she always did when she was feverish as a child.

Jules gives her a smile that's sad and knowing. But knowing of what? She says, "Ma."

"Yes?"

"I'm okay."

"You don't sound it."

"No, I am."

"No, you're not."

"I'm just . . ."

"What?"

"Tired," her daughter says.

"Of what?"

Jules bites the inside of her cheek, an old habit, and looks out at the avenue.

Mary Pat continues kneading her daughter's palms. "Tired of what?"

Jules looks her in the eyes. "Lies."

"Is Rum hurting you? Is he fucking lying to you?"

"No, Ma. No."

"Then who?"

"No one."

"You just said."

"I said I was tired."

"Tired of lies."

"No, I just said that to shut you up."

"Why?"

"Cuz I'm tired of you."

Well, that's a nice ax in the heart. She drops her daughter's hands. "Fucking buy your own school supplies next time. You owe me twelve sixty-two." She starts walking up the sidewalk.

"Ma."

"Fuck you."

"Ma, listen. I didn't mean I'm tired of *you*. I meant I'm tired of you giving me the third fucking degree."

Mary Pat spins and walks toward her daughter so fast Jules takes a step back. (*You never take a step back,* Mary Pat wants to scream. *Not here. Not ever.*) She puts a finger in her face. "I'm giving you the third *fucking* degree because I'm worried about you. Talkin' all this stuff that don't make sense, your eyes misting up, looking all lost. You're all I got now. Ain't you figured that out? And I'm all *you* got now."

"Well, yeah," Jules says, "but I'm young."

If she hadn't smiled right away, Mary Pat might have laid her out. Right there on Old Colony.

"Are you okay?" she asks her daughter.

"I mean, I'm not." Jules laughs. "But I am. That make sense?"

Her mother waits, her eyes never leaving her daughter's.

Jules gestures broadly at Old Colony, at all the signs—SOUTHIE WILL NOT GO; WELCOME TO BOSTON, RULED BY DECREE; NO VOTE = NO RIGHTS—and the spray-painted messages on the sidewalks and the low walls around parking lots—*Nigers Go Home; White Power; Back to Africa Then Back to School.* For a second, it feels to Mary Pat like they're preparing for war. All that's missing are sandbags and pillbox turrets.

"It's my *senior* year," Jules says.

"I know, baby."

"And nothing makes sense."

Mary Pat hugs her daughter on the sidewalk and lets her cry into her shoulder. She ignores the stares of passersby. The more they stare, the prouder she grows of this weak child she's borne. *At least Commonwealth hasn't erased her heart,* she wants to say. *At least she held on to that, you thickheaded, coldhearted Hibernian assholes.*

I might be one of you. But she isn't.

When they break the clutch, she wipes under her daughter's eyes with her thumb. She tells her it's okay. She tells her someday it *will* make sense.

Even though she's waiting for that day herself. Even though she suspects everyone on God's green earth is.

2

Jules takes another shower when they get back, and then her poor excuse for a boyfriend, Ronald "Rum" Collins, and her sidekick since second grade, Brenda Morello, come calling. Brenda is short and blond with huge brown eyes and a figure so full and fleshy that it seems designed by God to make men lose their train of thought whenever she walks by. She knows this, of course, and seems embarrassed by it; she continues to dress like a tomboy, something Mary Pat has always liked about her. Jules calls Brenda into her bedroom to ask about what she's wearing, so Mary Pat gets stuck in the kitchen with Rum, who, like his father and uncles before him, has the conversational skills of a baked ham. Yet he's mastered the art of saying very little around girls and his peers at Southie High, replacing the natural dullness in his eyes with a lazy contempt that a lot of kids take as a sign of cool. And her own daughter fell for it.

"You look, ah, nice today, Mrs. F."

"Thank you, Ronald."

He looks around the kitchen like he hasn't seen it a hundred times. "My ma said she saw you up the supermarket last week."

"Really?"

"Yeah. Said you were buying cereal."

"Well, if she says so."

"What kind?"

"Of cereal?"

"Yeah."

"I don't remember."

"I like Froot Loops."

"They're your favorite, huh?"

He nods several times. "'Cept when they're in the milk too long and they turn it, like, different colors."

"That'd be unfortunate."

"So I eat it fast." He gets a look in his eyes like he's putting something over on Kellogg's.

While her lips say, "That's quick thinking," her head says, *I pray you don't breed.*

"But, yeah, I don't like colors in my milk." He arches his eyebrows as if he just said something wise. "Not. For. Me."

She shoots him a tight smile. *And if you do breed, please don't breed with my daughter.*

"I like milk, though. Without colors."

She continues smiling at him because she's too annoyed to speak.

"Oh, hey!" he says, and she turns to see Jules and Brenda coming into the room behind them. Rum steps past Mary Pat and puts a hand on Jules's hip and kisses her on the cheek.

At least tell her she looks nice. Pretty.

"So let's get outta here," he says, and slaps her daughter's hip, lets loose a high-pitched cackle-yelp that immediately makes Mary Pat want to brain him with a fucking rolling pin.

"Bye, Ma." Jules leans in and gives her a peck on the cheek and Mary Pat gets a whiff of cigarettes, "Gee, Your Hair Smells Terrific" shampoo, and dabs of Love's Baby Soft just behind her daughter's ears.

She wants to grab Jules's wrist and say, *Find someone else. Find someone good. Find someone who might be dumb but won't be mean. This one will grow mean because he's only one or two elevator stops above retard, and yet he thinks he's kind of smart, and the ones who are like that grow mean when they realize the world laughs at them. You're too good for this boy, Jules.*

But all she says is "Try to come home at a reasonable hour," and returns the quick kiss to her daughter's cheek.

And then Jules is gone. Lost to the night.

When she goes to cook her TV dinner, Mary Pat is once again reminded that her gas is shut off. She puts the dinner back in the freezer and walks up the block to Shaughnessy's. In Southie, everything has to be given a nickname—it's like canon law or some fucking thing—so Shaughnessy's, which is owned by Michael Shaughnessy, is never referred to as Shaughnessy's but as Mick Shawn's. Mick Shawn's is known for its Saturday-night brawls (they keep a hose behind the bar to clean the blood off the floor) and its pot roast, which stews all day long in a pot in the tiny kitchen off the end of the bar, just past the hose.

Mary Pat sits at the bar and eats a plate of it. She drinks two Old Mil drafts and shoots the shit with Tina McGuiggan. Mary Pat has known Tina since kindergarten, though they've never been close. Tina has always made Mary Pat think of a walnut. As something hard and curled into itself, dry and difficult to break. Men have always found her "cute," though, maybe because she's small and blond and has a helpless look that men refuse to believe is just a look. Tina's husband, Ricky, is doing seven to ten at Walpole for an attempted armored car heist that went tits up from the get-go; bullets flew, but no one got shot, thank the good Lord. Ricky kept his mouth shut about Marty, who'd financed the job, so Ricky's doing easy time, which is nice for him, but doesn't help Tina make her rent, doesn't keep her four kids in Catholic school uniforms and dental checkups.

"But whatta ya gonna do?" she says to Mary Pat after finishing a brief rant on the subject. "Right?"

"Right," Mary Pat says. "Whatta ya gonna do."

It's a refrain they all hold dear. Goes alongside *It is what it is* and *Shit happens.*

They aren't poor because they don't try hard, don't work hard, aren't deserving of better things. Mary Pat can look at almost anyone she's ever known in Commonwealth in particular, or Southie in general, and find nothing but strivers, ballbusters, people who treat ten-ton burdens like they weigh the same as a golf ball, people who go to work day in, day out, and give their ungrateful-prick bosses ten hours of work every single eight-hour day. They aren't poor because they slack off, that's for fucking sure.

They're poor because there's a limited amount of good luck in this world, and they've never been given any. If it doesn't fall from the sky and land on you, doesn't find you when it wakes up every morning and goes looking for someone to attach itself to, there isn't a damn thing you can do. There are way more people in the world than there is luck, so you're either in the right place at the right time at the very *second* luck shows up, for once and nevermore. Or you aren't. In which case . . .

Shit happens.

It is what it is.

Whatta ya gonna do.

Tina drinks some of her beer. "How was your pot roast?"

"It was good," Mary Pat says.

"I hear it's slipping." Tina looks around the bar. "Like everything these days."

"Nah," Mary Pat says. "You should try it."

Tina gives her a long, slow look, as if Mary Pat suggested she burn her bra or some shit. "Why do you think I should *try* things?"

Mary Pat looks in Tina's eyes and sees in the dark swim of them that Tina was probably drinking harder stuff before Mary Pat arrived. "Then don't try it."

"No, I just want to know."

"What do you want to know?"

"Just what the fuck," Tina says. "Why do you want me to try the stew?"

"The stew"—Mary Pat feels the blood flush up her neck and flood her jaw—"is not stew. It's pot roast."

"You know what I'm saying. Don't pretend you don't know what I'm fucking saying."

"And," Mary Pat has to restrain herself from sticking a finger in Tina's face, "there's nothing new about it. It's the same old pot roast."

"So eat it."

"I just did."

"So what the fuck are you bothering me about it for?"

Mary Pat's surprised by the sudden weariness in her own voice. "I'm not bothering you, Tina."

Tina's been leaning forward, her mouth open, ripples running up her neck. But then, at Mary Pat's tone, her eyes suddenly soften. She slackens in her seat and takes a wet drag on her Parliament, exhales in a rush. "I don't know what I'm saying."

"It's okay."

Tina shakes her head. "I'm just *mad*. And I don't even know why. Someone told me—I can't even tell ya who, some guy—the pot roast wasn't as good here anymore, and I thought, *I can't fucking take this. I can't*." She puts her hand on Mary Pat's wrist so they lock eyes. "I mean, you know, Mary Pat? I can't fucking take it sometimes."

"I know," Mary Pat says. Even though she doesn't.

But, then again, she does.

She's back home half an hour when Timmy Gavigan drops off the signs. Timmy G is from a family of nine on K Street. He played decent hockey in high school but not decent enough to get a scholarship anywhere, so now, at twenty, he works at a muffler place on Dorchester Street and hustles for the Butler crew when they'll throw him a bone. It's what all the young guys around here aspire to these days—bag work for the Butler crew. But she suspects Timmy is too soft, too decent at his core, to ever ascend the ranks the way a hard case like Brian Shea or Frankie Toomey did. As she watches him walk back down the hall toward the exit door, she hopes he sorts himself out before a nickel in prison sorts it out for him.

She spends the next two hours attaching the signs to the sticks Brian Shea dropped off with the nails Timmy G provided. Someone clearly assumed Mary Pat owned a hammer, which she does. The nails are small and thin, the kind that make it hard to hold upright and not get your thumb in the way of the hammer, but she manages. For the first time that day, maybe the first time that week, she feels useful, she has purpose. She's doing her small part to stand up against tyranny. Nothing else to call it. Nothing else fits. The people in power are telling her where she's going to send her only living child to school. Even if that endangers her child's education and even endangers her life.

Which is bullshit. And it isn't about race. She'd be just as angry if they told her she has to send her kid across the city to Revere or the North End or someplace mostly white. The thought occurs to her that maybe she wouldn't be *as* mad, maybe she'd just be really annoyed, but then she hammers another sign to another stick and thinks, *Fuck that, I don't see color. I see injustice.* Just another case of the rich fucks in their suburban castles (in *their* all-white towns) telling the poor people stuck in the city how things are going to go. In that moment, Mary Pat feels a kinship with black people that surprises her. Aren't they all victims of the same thing? Aren't they all being told How It Is?

Well, no, because a lot of the coloreds want this. They've been fighting in the courts for it. And if you came from a shithole like Five Corners or the shoot-'em-up projects along Blue Hill Ave. or Geneva, of course you'd want to be in a nicer place. But Southie ain't a nicer place, it's just a whiter place. Southie High is just as big a mess as Roxbury High. Same exploding toilets, cracked heating pipes, water damage to the walls, mold, peeling paint, out-of-date textbooks with the pages falling out. She can't blame the coloreds for wanting to escape their shithole, but trading it for her shithole makes no sense. And the judge who ordered all this lives in Wellesley, where his own law won't apply. If the coloreds had sued to attend Wellesley High? Dover Middle? Weston K through eight? Mary Pat would march for *them*.

But then there's the Other Voice asking, *Would you? Really? How many names you know for black people, Mary Pat?*

Fuck you.

How many? Be honest.

I know "colored" and I know "nigger."

Get the fuck outta here. Tell the truth. And not just what you know, what you've used. What's escaped your chapped fucking lips.

But those are just words, she pleads to some imagined judge. *Poor people talking shit about poor people. Race don't come into it. They keep us fighting among ourselves like dogs for table scraps so we won't catch them making off with the feast.*

Once she finishes her work and all the signs are stacked along the wall on either side of the front door, she sits at the kitchen table with the window open and listens to the sounds of Commonwealth on a hot summer night and wishes her daughter were with her. They could've played hearts or watched TV.

Somewhere in the projects someone calls for Benny. A baby wakes up squawking. A single firecracker explodes. A few people walk below her window talking about someone named Mel and a trip to the Thom McAn in Medford. She can smell the ocean. And that single firecracker.

She was born here. Three buildings away in Hancock. Dukie grew up in Rutledge. (All the buildings in Commonwealth are named after signers of the Declaration of Independence: Jefferson, Franklin,

Chase, Adams, Wolcott, where she lives now, a few others.) She knows every brick, every tree.

A young couple walks under a streetlight the yellow of bile, and the boy says he's sick of it, just sick of it. The girl counters, "You can't just quit. You gotta try." He says, "That's a shit deal." She says, "That's the only deal. You gotta try."

Just before they're out of earshot, Mary Pat is pretty sure she hears the boy say, "Well, okay."

Her eyelids flutter with fatigue. She finally drags her ass to bed. She can still hear the girl's voice—*You can't just quit. You gotta try*—and she wonders where Ken Fen might be now (though she suspects she knows, even though she definitely doesn't want to). She wonders if he's still mad at her and why he doesn't seem to give a shit that she's just as mad at him, that he left her, that she never changed—he did. And who the fuck is he to change after almost seven years of marriage? Who the fuck is anyone to pull a stunt like that?

"Why'd you stop loving me, Kenny?" she asks the dark. "We made vows in front of God."

She finds herself hoping Kenny will somehow materialize out of the dark, at least his face, but there's nothing there but the dark.

And then she hears what could be his voice in her head, but all he says is: "Enough, Mary Pat. Enough."

She whispers, "Enough what?"

"Stop," he says. "Just stop."

The tears stream hot now. They slide from her eyes down her cheeks to her pillow and from her pillow down into the collar of her pajama top. "Stop *what?*"

Nothing. He doesn't say another word.

As she falls asleep, she can hear it. Or imagines she can. It's below the asphalt, below the basements and the subflooring.

The grid.

Of circuits and conduits and connections that channel the electricity and water and heat that rise up through the wiring and pipes and tubing to power her world. Or, as was the case this morning, choose not to. She can see it spreading across her dimming consciousness in a blanket of soft light. She can feel it fluttering under her eyelids.

It's all connected, she imagines mumbling to someone. *It really is.*

3

Jules never comes home that night.

Not so unusual. Not a big deal. (Though it gets a vein pulsing in Mary Pat's throat and throws her stomach off until lunch.) Jules is seventeen. An adult in the eyes of the world. If she were a boy, she could enlist.

Nonetheless, before she leaves for work, Mary Pat calls the Morello house. Brenda's father, Eugene, answers with a burrish "Hullo."

"Hey, Eugene," she says, "did Jules sleep over? She there?"

Eugene says he'll go check, comes back on the line a minute later. "Neither of them." She hears him gulp something she assumes is coffee, light a smoke, and take a deep drag. "They'll turn up when they need money. Gotta go, Mary Pat."

"Sure, sure, Gene, thanks."

"G'bless," he says before hanging up.

G'bless. They could add it to the list that includes *It is what it is* and *Whatta ya gonna do.* Phrases that provide comfort by removing the speaker's power. Phrases that say it's all up to someone else, you're blameless.

Blameless, sure, but powerless too.

She heads to work, arrives a minute before start time, still gets a look from Sister Fran, as if a minute early is as bad as a minute late. Sister Fran looks like she's thinking of whipping out one of her "God favors" nuggets of wisdom, like "God favors the pious for in the pious lives the wisdom of humility" or "God favors the clean because in cleanliness one better sees the reflection of God." (She uses that one on the window washers a lot.) But Sister Fran merely snorts as she passes behind Mary Pat and leaves her to start her day.

Mary Pat works as a hospital aide at Meadow Lane Manor in Bay Village, a neighborhood that can't decide if it's white, black, or queer, two subway stops from Commonwealth on the edge of downtown. Meadow Lane is an old folks' home (an "old fucks' home," she and her coworkers call it after a few beers) run by the Sisters of Charity of Saint Vincent DePaul. Mary Pat works the morning shift, seven to three-thirty, Sunday through Thursday, with a half hour off for lunch. She's been doing it for five years. It's not a bad job once you make peace with the humiliation that comes with cleaning bedpans, giving daily baths to grown adults, and maintaining an air of servility not just to crotchety old white people but a few crotchety old black ones as well. It certainly isn't the type of job she dreamed of when, as a child, she'd drift off to sleep. But it's predictable, and she can do it most days with her mind on other things.

She starts her day with the morning wake-ups, and then she and Gert Armstrong and Anne O'Leary deliver the breakfasts. They're behind the eight ball the whole morning because Dreamy banged in sick and the morning shift is a four-person job. Dreamy is the only black woman on their shift and, to Mary Pat's recollection, she's never been sick. Dreamy's real name is Calliope, but everyone has been calling her Dreamy, she told them all once, since first grade. It fits her—she always has a look in her eyes like she's someplace else, she has a light sleepy voice, and she moves like a soft summer rain. When she smiles, it breaks ever so slowly across her face.

Everyone likes Dreamy. Even Dottie Lloyd, who hates the blacks with a passion, allows that Dreamy is a "good nigger." Dottie said to Mary Pat once, "If they all worked as hard as her, were as polite as her? Shit. No one would ever have a problem with them."

Mary Pat considers herself kind of friends with Dreamy; they've spent many a lunch talking about their lives as mothers. But it's a white-and-black friendship, not the kind where you exchange phone numbers. Mary Pat asks Sister Vi, one of the decent ones, if she knows what's going on with Dreamy, Dreamy's never sick, and Sister Vi gets a weird look in her eyes, the kind of look you'd expect to get from Sister Fran. It feels judgy and distant. She says, "You know I can't discuss another employee, Mary Pat."

After breakfast, still behind the eight ball, they're on to bedpans or helping the ones who aren't quite at the bedpan stage get to the bathroom, which often involves wiping an ass, an indignity Mary Pat finds even less appealing than cleaning the bedpans. If the old folks need no help getting to the bathroom, then they need no help, and she and the other girls (all the aides are women) move on to the morning baths.

On her lunch break, she calls home, but Jules doesn't answer. She calls the Morellos again, gets Brenda's mother, Suze, this time. Suze says nope, she ain't seen either of them but figures they'll turn up.

"How many times, Mary Pat," Suze says, "how many times we been through this with these two? And they always turn up."

"They do," Mary Pat says, and hangs up.

Back at work, as they're prepping the trays for the lunch run, Dottie Lloyd mentions a "nigger drug dealer got hisself killed" at Columbia Station, ended up fucking up the morning commute. Why couldn't they just lift him off the tracks and let the trains through? He ruins people's lives selling his shit and now he's fucking up the morning commute? It's hard to say which sin is more unforgivable.

"Found him on the inbound track," Dottie says. "Least he could have had the decency to land on the outbound track. Then he would have only pissed off Dorchester and, you know, fuck Dorchester."

Mary Pat pulls the large aluminum tray of mini–milk cartons from the fridge and places it on the prep table, starts putting the cartons on the hard plastic trays they bring to the rooms. "Who are we talking about now?"

Dottie hands Mary Pat the afternoon edition of the *Herald American,* and she reads it over the prep table. MAN HIT BY SUBWAY CAR. The article goes on to report that Augustus Williamson, twenty, was found dead under the inbound platform of Columbia Station early this morning and that police have confirmed he suffered multiple head traumas.

It doesn't say anything about the dead black guy being a drug dealer, but it's a pretty safe assumption, or otherwise why would he be there? Why come into their part of town? She doesn't go into theirs. She doesn't know anyone who says they'll be spending the afternoon on Blue Hill Ave. to shop for clothes or go pick up a record at Skippy White's. She stays on her side of town, her side of the fucking *line,* and is it too much to ask that they do the same? Why do they have to antagonize? You go downtown, okay, fine, that's where they all intermingle, black and white and Puerto Rican. They work together, they bitch about their bosses, lives, the city together. But then they go back to their own neighborhoods and sleep in their own beds until they have to get up in the morning and do it all over again.

Because the truth is they don't understand one another. It's not a plan of Mary Pat's making, nor is it her desire, that they have different tastes in music, in clothing, in the food they put on their tables. But that's the way it is just the same. They like different cars, different sports, different movies. They don't even talk the same. The Puerto Ricans barely speak the language, but most of the blacks she knows have grown up here and still it's like they didn't. They speak that jive of theirs, which, truth be told, Mary Pat likes, loves the rhythm of it, loves the way they emphasize different words in a sentence than any white people she knows, have a way of punching out through the ends of their stories with big booming laughs. But it doesn't sound anything like the speech that leaves the mouths of Mary Pat or her friends. *So if you don't speak like us,* Mary Pat wants to ask, *and you don't like our music, our clothes, our food, our ways, why come into our neighborhood?*

To sell drugs to our kids or steal our cars. That's the only answer left.

Something about the newspaper article, though, bugs her the rest of the shift. She can't put a finger on it, but there's something in there that sets off an alarm. What? What is it? And then it hits her: "What's Dreamy's last name?" she asks Gert.

"Calliope," Gert says.

Mary Pat frowns. "Did you really just say that?"

"What?"

"Calliope's her real first name," Anne O'Leary says with a withering sigh.

"So what's her last name?" Gert says.

"You're her friend," Anne says to Mary Pat. "How do you not know?"

"I mean"—Mary Pat can feel her face pinken—"I just know her as Dreamy."

There's a quiet that feels not-quite-awkward-but-awkward's-on-the-way, and it's broken only when Dottie, of all people, says, "Williamson."

"What?"

"Dreamy's last name. It's Williamson."

"How the fuck would you know?"

"I'm a beast for the details."

Mary Pat moves down the prep table until she finds the *Herald*. She opens it to the article for the other girls, points at the dead drug dealer's name—Augustus Williamson.

"So?" Gert says.

Gert is dumber than a busload of retards on a bus driven by a retard.

"So," Mary Pat says, "Dreamy always talked about her son, Auggie."

It takes the other girls a minute.

"Oh, shit," Anne O'Leary says.

Dottie says, "That's why she didn't come to work."

4

On the way home, Mary Pat doesn't admit to herself that she's worried, but she doesn't dillydally either. No stops, no pop-ins at any of the bars. Just straight home.

Jules is not there. And Mary Pat can tell from a quick glance around their unit that she hasn't been there during the day.

She calls the Morellos a third time, gets Suze again, but Suze immediately says, "She's here. Let me get her."

Mary Pat feels herself slide down the wall but can't decide if it's relief or something else. Did Suze say "Jules is here"? Or "She's here"? In which case "she" could be—

Brenda. Whose voice comes over the line now. "Hey, Mrs. F."

"Hey, Brenda." A leaden dread fills Mary Pat's stomach. "Jules there?"

"I ain't seen Jules since last night." Brenda's words come out a little too fast, as if she's been preparing them.

"No? Who'd you see her with last?" Mary Pat lights a smoke.

"She was with, you know, Rum and, ah, you know, Rum."

"Rum and Rum? He comes in a pair now?"

"No, I meant just Rum. She was with Rum."

"Where was this?"

"Carson."

Carson is the local beach. Not much of one. No tide. An inlet of the harbor, not the ocean beyond. Mostly a place for kids to go and drink behind the old bathhouse.

"When did you see her and Rum last?"

"Like, midnight?"

"And they just wandered off?"

"Well, yeah, I mean, you know."

"I don't know." Mary Pat can hear the edge in her voice. Hopes Brenda doesn't hear it to the point that it shuts her down. She softens her voice. "I'm just trying to find her, Brenda." She lightens the mood further with an embarrassed laugh. "Just being a silly worried mom."

Nothing on the other end of the line but silence. Mary Pat bites down into her lower lip hard enough to taste blood and nicotine.

"I mean," Brenda says, "I mean, she walked off with Rum, and that's the last I saw her."

"Was she drinking?"

"No!"

"Bullshit," Mary Pat says. The gloves come off for a second. "Brenda, *do not* take me for a fool, and I won't take you for a fucking liar. How drunk was she?"

Hisses and pops on the line. A dog barking somewhere far off on Brenda's end. Then: "She was, you know, feeling no pain. She had a few beers, some wine."

"Pot?"

"Yeah."

"Was she stumbling drunk?"

"No, no. Just buzzed, Mrs. F. I swear."

"So, last time you saw her, she was with Rum?"

"Yeah."

"And you haven't heard from her since?"

"No."

"If you do?"

"I'll call you first thing."

"I know you will, Brenda." Putting some steel into the words before adding, "Thank you."

Brenda hangs up, leaving Mary Pat looking at the phone in her hand and feeling a screeching train of helplessness barrel through her. Jules is seventeen, able to do what she wants. If Mary Pat calls the cops, she knows they can't do a damn thing about it until it's been seventy-two hours. *At least.* And Mary Pat doesn't have that. So she's now in the position of sitting on her hands or chain-smoking until her daughter walks back through the door.

She tries it for a bit, finds herself thinking of Dreamy Williamson facing life without her child, and recalls that Dreamy sent her a beautiful card when Noel died. She roots around in a drawer where she put most things related to Noel's death—his dog tag and war medals, his laminated funeral card, the sympathy cards—and eventually finds the one Dreamy sent her. On the front is a cross and the words *May the Lord Grant You Strength in Your Hour of Need.* Inside the card, filling up both sides, she wrote to Mary Pat:

Dear Mrs. Mary Patricia Fennessy,

It's a terrible thing for a mother to lose her child. I cannot imagine the hurt you are feeling. Many times at work you have brought a smile to my face or made the day go quicker by telling me stories of your beloved Noel. What a scamp he was! What a rascal! He loved his mama, that was clear, and his mama loved him. I do not know why the Good Lord would ask something so painful of a fine woman such as yourself, but I know He makes our hearts so big so our dead can live in them. That's where your Noel is now. Living in his mother's heart like he once lived in your womb. If I can ever be of assistance, please reach out to me. You have always shown me every kindness and your friendship is something I value.

My sincerest condolences,
Calliope Williamson

Mary Pat sits at the kitchen table staring at the letter until the words blur. This woman wrote to her as if she were a friend. She signed her last name, which Mary Pat couldn't even recall this afternoon. She called Mary Pat a fine woman and spoke to a friendship that Mary Pat is hard pressed to grasp. Yes, she's *friendly* with Dreamy, but *friendship* is something else entirely. White broads from Southie aren't friends with black women from Mattapan. The world doesn't work that way.

For a minute or so, Mary Pat looks for a pen and paper to write a note of condolence to Dreamy, but she can find only a pen and some scrap paper. She resolves to find a proper sympathy card tomorrow and puts the pen back in the drawer.

She takes a beer, her pack of Slims, and an ashtray into the living room and turns on the TV, comes right in on the news and right in on the story about Auggie Williamson. Investigators believe he was fatally struck by the train between twelve and one a.m., and the impact threw his body under the platform. The conductor of the train never felt the impact. Trains raced by the body all last night until they stopped running, and a few went past it this morning before one conductor noticed the corpse in the crevice under the platform. Police won't confirm rumors that drugs were found on his person, nor will they explain how he came to be on the platform last night or why/if he'd jumped or been pushed into the path of the train.

They put a picture of him up on the screen and she can see Dreamy in his eyes, which were a brown so soft it's almost gold, and in his chin and lips. He looks so young. But the reporter announces that he graduated high school two years ago and was working in the management trainee program at Zayre.

High school graduate? Management trainee program? Do drug dealers enter management trainee programs?

But, oh, she thinks as she looks through the boob tube into his eyes, *you're just a baby.* Her mother used to say that from the time a child took his first steps, every step after took him farther and farther away from his mother. Mary Pat looks at the photograph of Dreamy's son in the last moment before it's wiped off the screen, and she imagines her own child's picture showing up on the same newscast, maybe tomorrow, maybe the next night.

Where the fuck *is she*?

She turns off the TV. She calls Rum's place, gets his mother. No love is lost between her and Mary Pat, so the conversation is brief: "No, Ronald isn't here, he's at work up the Purity Supreme until ten. No, I haven't seen Jules in, like, a week, maybe more. Anything else?"

Mary Pat hangs up.

She sits there. And sits there. She has no idea if it's for an hour or a minute.

Before she knows she's doing it, she swipes her smokes and her keys from the tray by the recliner and leaves the unit. She goes around the back of her building and then follows the path until she reaches her sister's door in Franklin. Big Peg has a daughter the same age as Jules; the girls aren't terribly close, but they do like to get high together. Almost the same thing could be said about Mary Pat and Big Peg—they're not terribly close, but it never kept them from drinking their weight together if they happened to cross paths.

Mary Pat, not much for travel, has still managed to see parts of New Hampshire, Rhode Island, and Maine in her life. Not Big Peg. Peg married Terry "Terror Town" McAuliffe two days after senior prom. They started dating freshman year at Southie High, and neither of them has an ambition known to anyone beyond the fact that they never want to leave Southie. It's a big day if they make it to Dorchester, and Dorchester is only six blocks away. And if the world finds their worldview narrow, well, Big Peg and Terror Town don't give a fuck about the world, they only give a fuck about Southie. They raised seven kids who took their parents' pride in their neighborhood like gospel from Christ (if Christ had been raised in Commonwealth and was prone, on general principle, to pounding the shit out of anyone who wasn't). Depending on their ages, those kids—Terry Junior, Little Peg, Freddy, JJ, Ellen, Paudric, and Lefty (who was given the birth name of Lawrence but has never been called it a day in his life)—rule the corners, the project stoops, and the playground sand pits with a pride so bright and unyielding it can't help but turn violent when even marginally challenged. As a project rat herself, Mary Pat knows all too well what happens when the suspicion that you aren't good enough gets desperately rebuilt into the conviction that the rest of the world is wrong about you. And if they're wrong about you, then they're probably wrong about everything else.

Big Peg opens the screen door in a faded housedress, a beer and a lit cigarette in the same hand. "You all right?" she asks her sister with suspicious eyes.

"I'm looking for Jules."

Big Peg pushes the door open wider. "Come in, come in."

Mary Pat enters and they stand there just inside the door, these two sisters who were never close. Peg's unit is a three-bedroom that currently sleeps nine people, the shotgun corridor running from the front door to the kitchen in back, the rooms off the corridor. The noise of the place is, as always, several decibels past the point where most human beings could hear themselves think.

"Oh my God, you so wore these pants."

"No, I didn't."

"Yes, you did, I can smell your farty ass in them."

"Fuck you."

"I will hit you with a baseball bat."

"No, you won't. You can't find one."

"Freddy has one."

"Mom, stop her!"

Jane Jo, aka JJ, comes bolting from one of the rooms and barges across the hall into another. Her little sister, Ellen, comes flying after her, both of them shrieking. And then the room they enter seems to explode. Things get upended in there, toppled, the walls give off dull thuds.

"The fuck you doing in my room?"

"I need your bat."

"What bat? Get out of my room."

"Gimme the bat."

"I'll hit you in the fucking head with the fucking bat."

"Just help me find the bat."

"Why do you want the bat?"

"To hit Ellen with it."

There's a pause and then:

"Cool."

Ellen starts wailing.

Big Peg leads Mary Pat to the kitchen, closes the door. Big Peg says, "When's the last time you saw her?"

"Last night. Right around this time."

Big Peg snorts. "I've lost Terror to two-*week* benders. He always turns up."

He/she/they always turn up. If Mary Pat hears that one more time to-night, she's going to stove someone's fucking head in with her bare fist.

"Jules isn't Terry," Mary Pat says. "She's Jules. She's seventeen."

"Little Peg!" Big Peg screams without warning, and twenty seconds later, her eldest daughter, a girl who's always managed to be twitchy and listless at the same time, comes through the doorway, going, "What's up?"

"Show some manners. Say hi to your aunt."

"Hey, Mary Pat."

"Hi, sweetie."

Big Peg asks, "You seen Jules? Look at your aunt when you talk to her."

"Not lately." Little Peg's listless/twitchy eyes twitch listlessly at Mary Pat. "How come?"

"Ain't seen her since last night," Mary Pat says. She can feel the helpless-hopeful smile she wears around her cigarette. "Just getting a little worried."

Little Peg stares back at her with nothing in her eyes, her mouth slack and half open. She could be a mannequin in a Kresge's window.

Mary Pat remembers when Little Peg was five and Mary Pat used to babysit her occasionally. *That* Little Peg was hilarious and sparked like a snapped electric wire in a storm. She was so aware of herself and the life around her, so *joyful*.

What takes that from them? Mary Pat wonders.

Is it us?

"So, you ain't seen her in a bit?"

"No."

"Like, how long?"

"I saw her up the park last night."

"Which?"

"Park? Columbia."

"When?"

"Like, eleven? Maybe eleven-forty-five. No later than that."

"Why no later?"

"Cuz Ma gives me a beating I don't walk through the door by twelve."

Mary Pat looks at her sister, who raises her eyebrows proudly in confirmation.

"So sometime between eleven and twelve?"

"Yeah."

"Who was she with?"

Now this dead-eyed fidgety girl with the stringy brown hair and acne-inflamed forehead grows cagey. "You know."

"I don't."

"You do."

"I swear to Christ, I don't." Mary Pat gets so close she can see her own eye reflected in her niece's. "Rum?"

A nod.

"And who else?"

"You know."

"Stop saying 'You know.'"

Little Peg looks to her mother, but Big Peg's nostrils flare and her breathing is heavy enough that they can hear it over all the other noise in the house. Always a sign, since Big Peg was a child, that volcanic eruptions are on their way.

"Answer my sister."

Little Peg turns her head back to Mary Pat but lowers her eyes. "Well, I mean, Rum was with George D."

Big Peg slaps her daughter on the side of the head. Little Peg barely flinches. "You fucking kidding us?"

Mary Pat says, "You mean George Dunbar."

"Yes."

"The drug dealer," Mary Pat says.

Another slap from Big Peg, same place, same velocity. "The guy who sold the shit to your cousin Noel that *killed* him? That guy? You're hanging out with that fucking guy?"

"I don't hang out with him."

"Watch your tone with me."

"I don't hang out with him," Little Peg whispers. "Jules does."

Mary Pat feels her insides seize up—heart, throat, even her guts, everything just clenches.

For all their power, the one thing Marty Butler's crew can't get their arms all the way around is the drug traffic in Southie. They try; there are all sorts of stories floating around about small-time dealers found in shallow graves on Tenean Beach or with needles shoved through their eyes in empty warehouses, but still the drugs get in. They come from the blacks, of course, in Mattapan and Jamaica Plain and the sprawl of Dorchester, but it's the whites like George Dunbar who sell it to their own people. And no one from the Butler crew is going to kill George, the story goes, because George's mother, Lorraine, is Marty Butler's girlfriend. Mary Pat has heard that Marty himself has knocked George around a few times, even gave him a shiner one time, but the kid keeps doing it. And he isn't the only one, so the drugs keep pouring in.

"It's like when the Japs used to send hordes of kamikazes at my old man and my uncles in Dubaya Dubaya Two," Brian Shea said to Mary Pat once. "If they send enough of them, a few of them are getting through. And not even the greatest navy in the world can stop it. And we're just a crew, Mary Pat, we can't keep it all out."

This was back when Mary Pat came to Brian (and by extension Marty) for justice in Noel's death. "But you *can* punish the people you know are doing it," she pleaded.

"And we do when we catch them. We punish them hard. Sometimes permanently."

But not George Dunbar. Because he's untouchable.

And now this untouchable merchant of poison is hanging around her daughter?

As gently as possible, she says to Little Peg, "Why does George Dunbar hang around Jules?"

"He's good friends with Rum."

"I didn't know that."

"And he's, you know—"

"If you say 'you know' one more fucking time," Mary Pat snaps.

"He goes with Brenda."

"What do you mean—'goes'?"

"He's her boyfriend."

"Since when?"

"Since, like, I dunno, beginning of the summer?"

"So you saw all four of them together at the park?"

"Yeah, no. What?" For a second, Little Peg looks completely confused. It's the look of someone, in Mary Pat's experience, who's lost the thread of the story she's trying to keep straight. "I mean, yeah and no, because Brenda and George were beefing, so she left, and then Rum and George and Jules left, and that's when I left."

"And this was at Carson Beach?"

"What? No. No, it was at Columbia Park, like I said."

"Cuz Brenda told me they were all hanging at Carson Beach."

"Then she's a fucking liar."

Her mother gives her another slap upside the head. "Watch your fucking mouth."

"We were at Columbia Park," Little Peg says. "That's where I saw her. If she went to Carson after, I don't know about it, because I went home."

Mary Pat and Big Peg exchange a look—the look of all parents when they know a kid has presented a story and will stick to it for now. No use in pushing further; then she might *really* start to lie.

"Okay," Mary Pat says. "Thanks, honey."

Little Peg shrugs.

"You can go," Big Peg says.

After Little Peg leaves, Peg gets them a couple beers from the fridge and they sit at the kitchen table and drink them. When the small talk runs dry in under a minute or so, the conversation turns to the neighborhood storm cloud everyone's obsessed with.

Of Big Peg's older kids, one's out of high school, and three are in it. All of them won the lottery and will be staying at Southie High. Sheer luck of the draw. No Roxbury for them. No fear of the bathrooms and the corridors and the classrooms for them.

Turns out that's not good enough for Big Peg. Oh, no.

"I ain't sending them," Peg says.

"What?"

She swallows some beer and nods at the same time. "Ain't sending them. We're joining the boycott. Weeze would roll over in her grave if she saw a pack of darkies walking down the same corridor as her granddaughter at *South Boston High School*, Mary Pat. Tell me I'm wrong."

"Weeze" (or "Weezie") was what they'd called their late mother, Louise. No one else had ever called her that, just her kids, and only while she was alive, in a conspiracy of silence.

"You're not wrong," Mary Pat admits, "but what about their education?"

"They'll get their education. I give this a month, two at the most. When the city realizes we won't bend and all we want is what's ours?" Big Peg winks in a knowing way. "They'll back down."

The words—and Big Peg's confidence—ring hollow. And when they do, the fear that's been eating away at Mary Pat's stomach lining all day returns.

Big Peg sees it, sees the tears that well up in her sister's eyes. "It's gonna be okay," Peg says.

Mary Pat looks her sister directly in the eyes for the first time in who knows how long and can hear the rawness of her own voice when she whispers, "I can't lose another one. I can't. I can't lose . . . anything else." She wipes at a single tear before it reaches her cheekbone, drinks some beer.

Big Peg says, "You gotta get ahold of yourself, hon. Nothing bad happens to kids from Southie as long as they stay in Southie."

Mary Pat brings her fist down on the tabletop hard enough to rattle the beer cans. "Noel OD'd in the playground *across the fucking street.*"

Big Peg is unfazed. "Noel went to some fucked-up country on the other side of the world and came back with his head all screwed up because he left the neighborhood." Peg's eyes implore her to see the basic common sense of her argument.

Mary Pat stares back across the table at her sister. Is that what people really think about her son? That it was Vietnam that turned him to drugs? Mary Pat tried thinking that way for a while, but then she faced the sobering truth that Noel didn't discover heroin in Vietnam (Thai stick, yes, heroin, no); heroin discovered Noel in the projects of South Boston.

"Noel never touched heroin in Vietnam," she says, and it sounds like a weak argument when it leaves her mouth. "He got hooked here. Right here."

Big Peg sighs in a way that suggests there's just no reaching some people, and her gaze clicks off Mary Pat's face. She stands, draining her beer in one long swallow, and says, "Well, I gotta be up for work in the morning."

Mary Pat nods. Stands.

Big Peg walks her down the noisy hallway, all seven of the kids fighting about something, paired off into mini-skirmishes with no ability to see the larger war.

At the door, Big Peg says, "She'll turn up."

Mary Pat feels too defeated to be annoyed. "I know."

"Get some sleep."

Mary Pat laughs at the idea of it.

"You can't let them rule your life," Big Peg says, and shuts the door behind her.

5

She finds Rum out on the loading dock behind the Purity Supreme. Ten at night and the heat still hits like a steamed blanket; the loading dock smells like wilted lettuce and bananas so overripe they split their skin. Rum's smoking a cigarette and drinking tallboys with the other supermarket punks who've just gotten off work from produce, deli, and bagging. The strength in numbers puts a brave look in his eyes when Mary Pat gets out of Bess, and that look turns to amusement when Bess's door creaks and the engine shudders to a stop.

Bess is Mary Pat's piece-of-shit station wagon that she has no choice but to drive until it gives up the ghost. Not that she drives much, but every now and then she can't avoid it. She could have walked here, but she obsessed on an image of the headlights sweeping the back of the loading dock and the punks scattering like rats, except for Rum, who she'd bump with a fender or the car door. What she forgot was that the effect of Bess on just about anyone is not threatening but comic. Bess is a two-toned 1959 Ford Country Sedan. Its rear end sags like an old dog's ass, rust and winter road salt have eaten away the rims of the wheel wells and the lower third of the paint job, the roof rack is long since gone (no one recalls where or when), both taillights are cracked (but operational), and the tailpipe hangs on with nothing more than Hail Marys and fraying butcher's twine. About the only thing you can say for Bess anymore is that she was a great car to transport the two kids around in, she has a 352 V8 under the hood that turns her into a rocket on the highway, and the radio works. Bess once sported two different shades of green—"April" and "Sherwood"—but at this point, both shades are so blanched you'd have to take Mary Pat's word for it.

When she gets out of Bess, the boys in her headlights cut up, except for Rum, who just watches her come with a cocked eyebrow she considers tearing off his face as he guzzles from his tallboy.

She doesn't go with any preamble. "Where's Jules?"

"Fuck should I know?"

"Don't let the beer give you too much stupid right now, Ronald. You might confuse it with courage."

"What?"

"Where's my daughter?"

"I don't know."

"When's the last time you saw her?"

"Last night."

"Where?"

"Carson Beach."

"And then?"

"And then what?"

"Where did she go?"

"She walked home."

"You let my daughter walk home in this neighborhood at one in the morning?"

"It was twelve-forty-five."

"You let my daughter walk home in this neighborhood at twelve-forty-five?"

He raises the beer toward his lips. "Uh—"

She slaps the beer out of his hand. "Alone?"

No one's cutting up anymore on the loading dock. She knows their mothers. They know her. Everyone's as quiet as a church pew waiting a turn for confession.

"No, no," Rum says quickly. "She wasn't alone. George gave her a ride home."

"George Dunbar?"

"Yes."

"The drug dealer?"

"What? Yes."

"Gave my daughter a ride home."

"Yes. I was too fucked up."

She takes a step back from him, makes a show of assessing him. "Where you going to be in an hour?"

"What?"

"I asked you a fucking question."

"I'm gonna be, like, home."

"*Like* home? Or home?"

"Home. I'm going home."

She notices his four-year-old orange Plymouth Duster in the employee parking lot. She's always hated the sight of that car, as if she's always known its owner was a sign of bad things to come.

"If George doesn't back up your story, I'm coming to see you again."

"Fine," he says in such a way that she knows he has something to hide.

"You can just tell me now."

"Nothing to tell."

"It'll be better for you if you do."

"I'm fine."

"Okay." She holds out her arms as if to say, *This was your choice, how it goes from now on.*

She catches his Adam's apple bobbing in his throat as he swallows, but then he looks at his shoes and the beer can she knocked out of his hand.

She gets back into Bess, and they all stare at her, wide-eyed, as she backs up and drives out of the parking lot.

"I don't give two shits what he told you," George Dunbar says to her half an hour later. "It isn't true."

She looks at this handsome kid with his smooth demeanor and his heartless eyes who sold her son his own death in a little plastic baggie. He stares back at her with a gaze so flat and stripped of emotion it would look weird on a Ken doll.

George was a part of the fabric of the Fennessy household for about ten years, always running in and out with Noel; in all that time, she never felt she got a clear view of him. It was as if a part of him, a core part, wasn't there when you went looking for it. She mentioned this to Ken Fen once and he said, "Most people we know are like dogs— there's loyal ones, mean ones, friendly ones. But all of it, good and bad, comes from the heart."

"What kind of dog is George Dunbar?"

"None," Kenny said. "He's a fucking cat."

She looks now at this cat who couldn't even be bothered to show up to Noel's funeral. "Why would Rum lie?"

"I have no idea what goes on in another man's mind."

George Dunbar did two years of college. Majored in economics. He didn't drop out because he couldn't hack it; he dropped out because he was making too much money selling drugs. His uncles run a cement mixing company, and George, she's always heard, has been promised a third of the business that once belonged to his late father. But he'd rather deal drugs. For a kid from Southie, he speaks like some rich people she's run into over the years—like his words and God's come from the same well, while your words come from a place off the map that no one can hear or see.

"So you didn't drive her anywhere?"

"No, I did not. She walked off to go home at around quarter to one."

"And you let a girl her age walk home alone through this neighborhood?"

George gives her a look of pure bafflement. "I'm not her keeper."

They sit in the gazebo in Marine Park. Across Day Boulevard, Pleasure Bay is lit in a gummy moonlight. George Dunbar was easy to find. Most nights he can be found sitting in the gazebo in Marine Park. Everyone in Southie, from cops to kids, knows it. Just more proof he's protected. If you want drugs, you go to the gazebo and see George Dunbar or one of the kids who works for him.

She finds herself wishing that his mother will get caught fucking around on Marty Butler, get her ass thrown to the curb. And that two days later, someone will mess up George Dunbar's perfect hair by pumping a bullet into his fucking head.

"What'd you guys get up to last night?" she asks him.

He shrugs, but she catches him looking off to the trees for a moment, a sign that he's thinking about his answer as opposed to just answering.

"We all had a few beers in the ring at Columbia. Then we walked on down to Carson."

"When?"

"Eleven-forty-five."

She's never known kids to be so precise. They always speak in rounded-up time: *I was there at noon. One. Two.*

But these kids—Little Peg, Rum, and now George Dunbar—keep saying "eleven-forty-five" or "twelve-forty-five." As if, on the night in question, they were all checking watches they don't own.

Two kids on bicycles and a hippie in a VW van wait outside the gazebo, watching them, waiting for Mary Pat to leave so they can score.

George notices them. "I gotta go."

"He was your friend."

"What?"

"Noel," she says. "He thought of you as his friend."

"I was his friend."

"You kill your friends?"

"Leave me the fuck alone," he says very quietly. "And don't come back, Mrs. Fennessy."

She reaches out and pats his knee. "George, if anything happened to my daughter, and you were involved?"

"I said, leave me the fuck—"

"Marty won't be able to save you. No one will be able to save you. She's my heart." She squeezes his knee a little harder. "So, pray—on your *knees* tonight, George—that my heart turns up safe, or I might come back and rip yours right out of your fucking chest."

She stares into his flat eyes until he blinks.

She rolls Bess past the Collinses' house, but Rum's orange Duster isn't there. No matter. Southie's small when you own an orange car.

She finds the Duster twenty minutes later, parked outside the Fields of Athenry (which, in true Southie fashion, everyone just calls the Fields). This is Marty Butler's stronghold. You don't walk in there unless you're from Southie, and you don't walk back out on your own two feet if you act even a little off. In its ten-year existence, it's never been crowded, even on Saint Patrick's Day, and there's never been a fight on the premises. The only person ever known to bump a line in the bathroom got his nose broken mid-snort by Frankie Toomey, aka Tombstone, aka the killer of killers on Marty Butler's crew.

She parks Bess in a spot on Tuckerman and walks back. She finds Rum sitting at the corner of the bar, drinking a beer with a whiskey back. They all hang out here—all the boys who've left high school with no plans and just enough balls over brains to be occasionally useful to Marty. She orders the same as Rum. As she waits for her drinks, she ignores him, though she can feel him staring at her and breathing shallow through his mouth. She takes in the rest of the bar. Tim Gavigan, the kid who dropped off her signs, is in here; she thinks she spots Brian Shea down the end, definitely notices Head Sparks, who did a couple jobs with Dukie back in the old times. There are a few other guys she recognizes but can't name off the top of her head, guys who are in the Life.

The bartender, Tommy Gallagher of Baxter Street, brings her drinks, takes her money, leaves her and Rum to themselves. She downs the shot. Turns to Rum. Sips her beer from the mug. "You lied to me."

"No, I didn't."

"Sure you did. George didn't drive Jules home."

"First I told you she walked home, but you got all pissy, so I said George drove her home to get you off my back." He raises and lowers his eyebrows as he slurps some beer.

"So, she did walk home alone?"

He looks at his beer. "What I fucking said."

"That's your story."

"Yeah, it's my story. Why don't you—"

When she breaks his nose with her right fist, it sounds like a cue ball shattering a tight rack. The whole bar hears it. He screams like a girl, and she hits him again, exact same spot, drives the punch through his hands, which are soft and covering that nose. Then she punches him in the eye, bringing her left fist to the party this time.

He says something like "Wait" and something like "Shit-fuck," but by that point she's blasting combos into his thick fucking woodchuck head—left eye, right eye, left cheek, right cheek, two quick punches to his left ear, and then a single blast to his jaw. A tooth—yellow with nicotine, red with blood—leaves his mouth.

They pull her off him. Their grips are hard, forceful. The grips send a message: *We're not fucking around.*

But once they have her arms, she uses her legs. As fast as she can, she kicks his face, his chest, his stomach. And then her feet meet air.

They drag her to a barstool.

She hears a voice she recognizes say, "Stop. Mary Pat, stop. Please."

She looks into the Windex eyes of Brian Shea.

"Come on," he says. "Huh?"

She exhales.

The men holding her loosen their grip but don't let her go.

"Tommy," Brian Shea says to the bartender, "give Mary Pat another of what she was drinking. Then give us all a round."

Rum tries to get to his knees but falls over.

"You can let me go," Mary Pat says softly.

Brian cranes his head down to look in her eyes. "Yeah?"

"Yeah. I'm good."

"You're good." He chuckles at that. "She's good!" he crows to the guys holding her, and the whole bar laughs way too loud.

He nods at someone, and the hands—there were at least six of them—leave her body.

Rum makes it to his knees this time, but he vomits, and the vomit is red.

"She mighta punctured a fucking lung," Pat Kearns says.

"Bring him to the doc on G," Brian says. "Make sure the doc knows he don't get the Cadillac treatment. This one's a Dodge. A used Dodge."

They start to drag him out.

Brian says, "The fucking *back* door, you dumb fucks."

They drag him in the other direction. Eventually, they reach the back door and beyond, and the bar noise returns to normal, which, as Mary Pat has always read it, feels itchy and fearful but gives off a pleasant hum nonetheless.

"This is no little thing, Mary Pat."

She downs her second shot of the night, looks Brian in the eyes. "I know."

"You started a fight in Marty's place. His sanctuary."

"That wasn't a fight," she says.

"Oh, no?"

She shakes her head. "That was a beatdown. That little pussy didn't get one shot in."

"You can't do *beatdowns* in Marty's place. If you were a fucking guy, you'd be dead. Or, you know, at least in a body cast."

"So put me in a body cast, but wait until after I find my daughter."

He narrows his eyes. Downs his own shot. "Jules?"

"Yeah."

"Where's she at?"

"That's my question. No one's seen her since last night."

"Why didn't you say so?"

"I did." She jerks her thumb at the blood and vomit Rum left in his wake. "To him."

He grimaces. "That fucking putz? Asking him for information is like asking a telephone pole for a steak and cheese." He points two fingers at his own chest. "*We* help. *We* provide services to this neighborhood. *We* coulda been looking for Jules all day if you'd asked. No one forgets what you did for us, what Dukie did for us—we're here for you, Mary Pat." He takes out a small notepad and a pencil. Licks the tip of the pencil as he opens the notepad on the bar. "Tell me everything you know."

After she finishes, he says, "I'll square what you did here tonight with Marty." He puts the notebook and pencil back in the pocket of his Baracuta. "But you gotta give us twenty-four hours."

"*Twenty-four hours?*"

"It's not gonna take that. It's probably gonna take, like, three, but you can't be running around like Billy Jack—fuckin' Mary Pat Jack— beating the fuck out of people. You can't do it. It's gonna bring attention."

"I can't sit on my hands for twenty-four hours."

He exhales loudly. "Then give us till, say, five tomorrow. A full day. Give us that long to find her for you. You don't rattle any cages, you sure as shit don't go to the fuckin' cops, you let us work for you."

She lights a cigarette, turns it between her fingers, round and round. Closes her eyes. "That's a lot to ask."

"I know it is. But with this busing bullshit and that spook getting himself killed last night, we don't need one more outside eye looking into this neighborhood. Because they might start asking how it really runs, how things really get done, and we cannot have that, Mary Pat. We absolutely cannot."

She looks around the bar, can feel that everyone was just looking at them and are now pretending they weren't. She looks back at Brian Shea. "Five o'clock tomorrow. That's my good-girl-behavior limit."

Brian signals Tommy for another round. "Fair enough."

6

She doesn't sleep more than three hours all night, and none of that sleep strings together but arrives instead in fifteen-minute blocks followed by alert anguish, staring into the black, fidgety and hopeless, followed by another fifteen-minute spurt of sleep two hours later, followed by staring into the black.

Lying in bed, staring up at the dark, she feels seen but not heard by whatever looks down upon her. Eventually, its eyes leave her, and she is alone in the universe.

At work she's a zombie, stumbling through her shift, hoping no patient codes on her because she won't be up to the task. Again Dreamy takes a personal day, so again they're shorthanded. Gossip flies up and down the corridors—Auggie Williamson committed suicide. No, he OD'd and fell in front of a train. There are witnesses, but they haven't come forward. He was chased onto the platform. It was a drug deal gone bad and he tried to run, slipped on the platform, and fell in front of a train. *Ker-runch*.

But none of the rumors addresses how it is that the train conductor never noticed the impact. Maybe he hadn't seen Auggie, but he must have *felt* the impact. It was in all the papers that Auggie died somewhere between midnight and one, but his body wasn't found until the morning commute, tucked under the platform. So, what's it like to get off your shift, go home and sleep eight hours, then wake to the news that you drove your subway car into someone's head? The poor guy, someone says, he has to live with that the rest of his life.

After work, Mary Pat changes out of her uniform in the locker room and puts on the clothes she arrived in, and then she does something she doesn't even admit to herself she's doing until she's crossing over the Charles River on the Red Line—she takes the subway to Cambridge.

Getting out at Harvard Station, she enters Harvard Square, and it's as bad as she suspected it would be—fucking hippies are everywhere, the air smells like pot and B.O., every twenty feet or so someone's playing a guitar and crooning about either love, man, or Richard Nixon, man. Nixon helicoptered off the White House lawn almost three weeks ago, but he's still their bogeyman, these pampered, over-educated, draft-dodging pussies. She loses count of how many of them are barefoot, tromping around dirty streets in their frayed bell-bottoms and their multicolored shirts with their beads and long hair, the girls without bras and their ass cheeks spilling out of their cutoff shorts, filling the air with cigarette smoke and clove cigarette smoke and pot smoke and every one of them a fucking embarrassment to their parents, who spent an ungodly amount of money to send them to the best school in the world—a school no poor person could ever get into, that's for fucking certain—and they return the favor by walking around with dirty feet and singing shitty folk music about love, man, love.

When she steps onto campus, the ratio of hippies to normal-looking college students drops to about one in three, which is somewhat comforting. The rest of the students look like the college students in movies—square jaws and square haircuts, the girls in dresses or skirts and blouses, hair straightened and shiny, the boys wearing oxfords and chinos and walking with the assured posture of the upper class.

What both groups have in common, though, is a deep-seated confusion about what *she* could be doing on their campus.

She's not dressed like a slob from the projects. She's dressed like many a housewife walking around South Boston (or Dorchester or Rozzie or Hyde Park) at this very moment—red polyester shirt, tan slacks, and a plaid shirt jacket in defiance of the heat. She wore the outfit to work this morning because she wanted to say to anyone who cared to look—*I am in control. I have my shit together. Ignore the cuts and bruises on my knuckles and see only the classy lady your eyes behold.* But some part of her must have also known that she might not be heading straight home after work, that she might be making a trip across the river into a world so alien she'd feel more at home in another country. Ireland, for sure. Canada, maybe. She'd thought she looked smart, put together, but judging by the sidelong stares she's getting from the snot-noses and the hippies in Harvard Yard, she sticks out for exactly who she is—a working-class broad from the other side of the river who came into their world in her laughable Sears-catalog best. They presume she took the wrong subway car, ended up wandering the Harvard campus like a child lost in a supermarket, before she'll return to her grimy world to tell her grimy kids about all the shiny things she's seen but was never allowed to touch.

She's visited here once with Ken Fen, just before Christmas two years back, the day after he officially got the job working in the mail room. It was a Saturday in the dead of winter, so there were only a few bundled-up students in the Yard, and no hippies loitered in the square on a 15-degree day. They'd met his boss, whose face she could no longer remember, and he'd given Ken Fen the keys to the room and the master key to the mailboxes and explained the duties of his shift, which would go from noon to eight-thirty every weekday. Then he left them to roam the room themselves.

The mail room was housed in the basement under Memorial Hall, a building so grand and imposing that it's hard to imagine someone like Ken Fen could work here, day in and day out, without some part of him trembling at the sheer majesty of it.

Kenny Fennessy grew up in the D Street projects, a place so fierce it made Commonwealth and Old Colony look like Back Bay and Beacon Hill by comparison. Huge guy. Six-three. Hands that turned into coiled rebar when he clenched them into fists. If you fucked with him, you better bring three of you because he would not stop fighting until a coroner called it. But if you *didn't* fuck with him, Ken Fen would never lay a hand on you. Never bully you or poke at you. He'd much rather listen to your story, hang out with you, find out what you liked to do, and do it with you. Since birth, Ken Fen had no choice but to buy into the violence. He just never bought into the hate.

When she met him, he was recently divorced, paying a king's ransom in alimony to an ex-wife who'd told him once with bitter pride that she wasn't capable of love, and if she were, she wouldn't waste it on him. He and Mary Pat dated for a year before getting married. Ken Fen never had a nickel for himself until he got a job working the mail room at Harvard, which made it look like maybe, in a couple years, once he'd caught up on all his debt, he could move them out of public housing.

As an added benefit of his job, he could attend Harvard lectures for free. Couldn't get credit, but he could sit in. That's where the trouble started. Suddenly, he's coming home with books (*Siddhartha* is one she remembers, *The Tin Drum* another), suddenly, he's quoting people she's never heard of. Not that she's heard of a lot of people, but suddenly, he's *quoting,* and Kenny was never a quoter.

She finds him sitting alone at a table in the middle of the mail room. She's timed it so she'll arrive at his lunch hour, but he doesn't have any food in front of him, is just sitting there reading (of course). He looks up with a beam of a smile when she enters. The smile dies fast, as if snatched from his face by the quickest of hands, and she realizes in that moment that he was expecting to see someone else.

"Hi," she says.

He rises from the table. "What're you doing here?"

"Have you seen Jules?"

He shakes his head. "Why would I have seen Jules?"

"I thought she mighta come to you. I can't find her."

"Since when?"

"Night before last."

"Jesus, Mary Pat." He comes to her. Takes her by the elbow. "Come sit down."

Even though he hadn't wanted to see her, even though he's still mad at her (or are his feelings for her worse than anger somehow?), even though he had been so irritated and impatient the last time they spoke—in her moment of need, he comes right to her. He's a rock, Kenny. Always has been. First one to give support, last one to ask for it.

She sags a bit as he leads her to the table and pulls out a chair. Her eyes fill. The fear she's kept tightly wrapped bursts through its wrapping, and a small moan escapes her lips as he helps her into the chair and pulls up another across from her.

It takes her a few seconds to catch her breath, and when she starts speaking, it's like she can't stop. It all just spills.

"I haven't seen her since the other night, and I have this *feeling*? I have this feeling, Kenny, and it's the worst feeling, it's worse than any I had that whole year Noel was in Vietnam, and worse than the one I had the day Dukie, God rest him, left the house and I never saw him again. It's like a part of her never left my womb, you know? It stayed in there and became something else, became, like . . . *molded* . . . to my body. The inside of it, with the blood and the organs and all the other shit you can't survive without? That's where part of her has always lived. But, but, but I can't feel her there for the first time since she was born." She thumps her own chest harder than she intended. "She's not *in here* anymore."

He hands her tissues he found somewhere, and she uses them, is surprised that they come back sopping in her hand. He takes the wet clump from her and hands her a couple of fresh ones and then a couple more after that until her face is dry and her nose is clear.

"So you haven't seen her or heard from her?" she asks.

His eyes are sorrowful. "No."

"She'd reach out to you if she was in some kinda trouble she didn't want me to know about."

"Probably, yeah."

"She loves you."

"I know."

"She has your number?"

"Yup."

That stings a bit. She doesn't have his number, but her daughter does.

"So, okay," he says, "let's back up. Tell me what you know."

It takes her five minutes.

"So," he says in that analytical voice he uses sometimes when he's explaining a play in a football game she didn't understand or, later in their marriage, when he was explaining what one of his quotes actually meant. "She's with the kids at the park until midnight. Then she's at Carson another forty-five minutes. She walks toward home. That's their story."

She nods. "And they're sticking to it."

"Sounds like horseshit."

"Why?"

"They're fucked up, right? Drinking and getting high and shit?"

"Yeah."

"But they all know the time."

"To the minute," she says. "That bothered me too."

He thinks for a bit, his eyes, as always, brimming with an intelligence he could never fully hide no matter how hard he tried, the thing she loved about him only a little less than she loved his kindness.

"Wait a minute," he says. "All this mystery—whatever we're calling it—went down between midnight and one Saturday night, right?"

"Yeah."

"Well, what's right across from Columbia Park, Mary Pat?"

She shrugs. "A lot of things."

"Columbia Station," he says. "Where that black kid got killed."

She's not quite following. "Yeah . . ."

"Between midnight and one," he says. "That's what the papers say."

"But what does one have to do with the other?"

"I don't know, maybe these kids saw something."

She tries to work that around in her head.

"Or," Ken Fen says, "maybe they were involved somehow."

She narrows her eyes at him, and in that moment, a black girl with an Afro the size of a toddler walks in the room carrying a bag of food. Mary Pat can smell the food—there's something fried in there—and she notices two bottles of Coke dangling from the fingers of the black girl's other hand. Sees the warmth in her smile as her eyes fall on Kenny.

So, Mary Pat thinks with a shock of disgust and embarrassment, *this is her.*

This is who you left me for.

This nigger.

The girl—*goddamn, she's gorgeous*, Mary Pat thinks before she can stop herself—is smiling uncertainly now at Mary Pat, and for some reason the first thing Mary Pat thinks to say is, "How *old* are you?"

"Jesus Christ." Ken Fen pushes his chair back from Mary Pat.

The girl is coming toward them now with a small private smile on her face. "I'm twenty-nine." She places the food down on the table and stands behind Kenny. "You?"

Mary Pat can't help but chuckle inside, but she doesn't let it show.

An odd silence settles into the room. The longer it goes on, the more uncomfortable it grows. And yet none of them breaks it for the longest time.

Until Mary Pat stands and says to Kenny, "Let me know if you hear from Jules."

Kenny grimaces. He indicates the black girl-woman, who has moved around to his hip. "Mary Pat, this is—"

"I don't want to know her fuckin' *name*."

The black girl-woman lets out a startled hoot of a laugh, and her eyes widen.

Mary Pat can feel the rage pulsing behind her eyes. She can feel them redden. She has an image of these two crossing the Broadway bridge, her small black hand in his big white one. It's almost unbearable to imagine—the looks they'd get! The humiliation that would crest like a wave and crash down on Mary Pat and Jules and even stain the memory of Noel, God rest his soul.

Kenny Fennessy of the D Street projects returns to Southie a race traitor, a fucking jungle-bunny lover.

Whether Ken Fen and Afro Girl lived or died on their little walk— and Mary Pat doubted they'd make it to C Street alive, definitely no farther than E—the shame that would follow Mary Pat and Jules, as long as they held on to the Fennessy name and probably for decades after, would be impossible to surmount.

But it's Kenny and the black girl-woman staring at *her* with contempt. How'd that happen?

"How you live with yourself," she hisses at Kenny, "is anyone's guess."

"How I live with *myself*?" Kenny says as the woman grabs at his arm, but he walks right through it to reach Mary Pat.

She feels suddenly at sea. She didn't want *this*. For a moment she can't think of anything to say, she just wants to slink out of here, she just wants to go back to searching for Jules. But it's been building up for so long, ever since Kenny left her, and the words just fall out of her mouth.

"We were happy."

He says, "We were *happy?*"

It hits her—they weren't. She was. But he never seemed to be.

"We hit a few bumps."

He says, "Those weren't bumps, Mary Pat. They were our fucking lives *shriveling*. From the time I could walk, all I ever saw was hate and rage and people pounding booze so they wouldn't feel it. Then they'd get up the next day and do the same fucking thing all over again. For fucking decades. I spent my whole life dying. Whatever time I got left, I'm living it. I'm sick of drowning."

The beautiful black girl is looking at them with a calm Mary Pat finds both admirable and insulting.

Mary Pat looks back at Kenny and can see past his anger (and her own) to the hope in his eyes—teeny-tiny but flaring—as if it's saying, *Live this new life with me.*

And some part of her almost says, *Yes, let's go.* Some part of her almost grabs his face and crushes her lips against his and says through gritted teeth: "Let's fucking *go.*"

But somehow the words that leave her mouth are, "Oh, so you're too good for us?"

A desperate *pop* escapes his lips. A sound caught somewhere between a soft scream and a loud sigh. Whatever micro-sliver of hope lived in his eyes hops the bus out of town, and now he's looking at her with dead pupils, dead irises, dead everything.

"Get the fuck outta here," he says softly. "If Jules shows up, I'll send her your way."

7

Five o'clock comes and goes without a word from Brian Shea.

Six and seven o'clock do the same.

She walks to the Fields. There's a sign on the door: *Closed for Private Function*.

What the fuck does that mean? she wants to shout. The whole bar is a private function.

Mary Pat knocks on the door. At least a dozen times. Enough to waken the aches in her right hand that have been there since she beat the shit out of her daughter's useless excuse for a boyfriend.

No one answers the door.

She tries Brian Shea's house next. Over on Telegraph Hill, it's one of the original redbrick townhomes that front the park. His wife, Donna, answers the door. Donna and Mary Pat (and Brian too) were in the same grammar school class, same class at Southie High too. At one point, Mary Pat and Donna were thick as thieves, but that was before their lives curved in different directions and Mary Pat ended up raising two kids in the projects while Donna Shea (née Dougherty) married a marine, traveled the world, and then came back when said marine got fragged by his own guys in a place called Binh Thúy. Donna came back childless, moved in with her senile mother, and looked to be staring at a long slow decline to her own senility when she hooked up with Brian Shea instead and changed the whole course of her life. Her mother died, Brian got bumped up to second in command of the Butler crew, they moved into a townhouse on Telegraph Hill, and Brian bought her a two-toned Mercury Capri right off the lot. No kids, no pets, no struggle. Donna Shea hit the trifecta. All she has to worry about now are canceled nail appointments and any unexplained lumps on her chest.

Donna looks at Mary Pat from the other side of the threshold and says, "What can I do for you?"

As if Mary Pat knocked on her door selling term life.

"Hey," Mary Pat says. "How you doing?"

"I'm okay." Donna looks bored. Glances over Mary Pat's shoulder at the street. "What's up?"

"I'm looking for Brian."

"He ain't here."

"Do you know where he is?"

"Why do you want to know where my husband is?"

"He was looking into something for me."

"What?"

"Where my daughter might be. She's been missing since the night before last."

"What's that gotta do with him?"

"He offered to look into it."

"So wait for his answer."

"He said he'd get back to me by five tonight."

"Well, he ain't here."

"Okay."

"Okay."

"So."

"So."

"I just . . ."

"What?"

"I'm just trying to find my daughter, Donna."

"So, find her."

"I'm trying," though what she wants to say/scream is *Why are you being such an asshole?* She can't think of anything more to say, so she turns and walks down the steps.

"Mary Pat," Donna says softly.

Mary Pat looks up the stairs at her. "What?"

"I'm sorry. I don't know what the fuck's wrong with me."

She invites Mary Pat into her home.

"I have no idea why I'm not happy," Donna says after she gets them each a beer. "But I'm *not*. I mean, I got everything. Right? Look at this place. Brian's a good guy, a good dresser too. He takes care of me. He's never hit me. Can't remember a time he even yelled at me. So what's not to be happy about?" She waves her arm at the dining room. The china cabinet as big as a butcher's freezer, the chandelier above them so enormous its shadows drizzle down the walls like vines, the table they're sitting at parquet-top with seating for twelve. She says it again: "Why am I not happy?"

"How the fuck would I know?" Mary Pat says with an uncomfortable laugh.

Donna sucks on a cigarette. "You're right. You're right, you're right, you're right."

"I don't know if I'm *that* right," Mary Pat says. "I just don't know why you're not happy."

"I'm getting laid good," Donna says. "I'm taken care of. He buys me anything I want."

Mary Pat looks at the antique grandfather clock standing in the corner of the room: eight-twenty. Almost three and a half hours past Brian Shea's promised deadline.

"Donna," she says, "I can't find Jules. And Brian promised to look into it. So I need to find him."

"You don't wanna fuck him?"

"No, I don't wanna fuck him."

"Why not?"

"Because I fucked him in high school and it wasn't that great."

Donna turns the color of boiled potato—a translucent white. Her eyes grow to the size of baseballs. "You fucked my Brian?"

"In high school."

"*My* Brian?"

"He wasn't yours then."

"We were friends then."

"Yeah."

She stubs out her cigarette, her eyes never leaving Mary Pat's. "Why didn't you tell me?"

"Cuz you had a crush on him."

"No, I didn't."

"Yeah, you did."

"But I was going with Mike Atardo."

"Right. But crushing on Brian."

"I never told you that."

"But I knew."

"So you fucked the guy you knew I had a crush on?"

"I was drunk. So was he."

"Oh."

"Yeah."

"And where was I?"

"At Castle Island with Mike Atardo."

She shrieks. "The night I lost my cherry?"

"Yup."

Donna shrieks again. And so does Mary Pat. It feels good for a moment to remember who they were before they again have to sit with who they are.

After a few soft chuckles, Donna says, "Oh, shit, Mary Pat, what the fuck? How did we get here?"

"Where?"

"Here. Where we're practically strangers. We used to be *friends*."

"You left."

"I did."

"Lived in Japan."

"Ugh."

"Germany."

"Worse."

"Hawaii, I heard."

Donna lights another cigarette. "That was nice."

"I'm sorry your husband died."

"I'm sorry yours did."

"No, he just left me."

Donna shakes her head. "The first one. Dukie?"

"Oh, right." Mary Pat nods. "That was a long time ago."

"Still gotta hurt."

"He hit me a lot."

"Oh. What about the second one?"

"Never. He was a gent."

"But he left you."

"Yup."

"Why?"

It takes Mary Pat so long to speak that by the time she finally does, Donna's finished her cigarette and the light in the room has changed.

"I embarrassed him."

"How?"

"I dunno."

"Your hair?"

I have bad hair?

"Your face? Your tits? Your . . . what?"

"My hate." Mary Pat lights a cigarette of her own.

"I don't understand."

"I don't either." Mary Pat exhales a long stream of smoke. "But that's what he said the day he left. He said, 'Your hate embarrasses me.'"

Donna snorts. "Sounds full of himself."

"He is that."

"So fuck him. And, like, what, he don't hate nothing? He's a fucking saint?"

"Exactly."

"You're lucky to be rid of him."

"Eh."

"No?"

"I'm alone. I'm fucking forty-two."

"You'll meet a guy."

"I liked him."

"A better guy."

Mary Pat shrugs.

"You *will*."

"I might meet a guy who's better for me, maybe, but I'll never meet a better guy."

They sit in silence for a bit. The house feels too large and cold—even in the middle of a heat wave—for Mary Pat to imagine joy occurring here. If she felt envy for Donna coming through the door, she doubts she'll still feel it by the time she leaves.

"Why are you wasting time with Brian?" Donna says abruptly. "Why don't you go right to the source?"

"Marty?"

"No. The source. Jules's boyfriend."

"I went to Rum twice. I kinda beat the fuck out of him the second time. I don't know if he'll be, uh, forthcoming from now on."

"Rum isn't Jules's boyfriend."

"What?

"Mary Pat, come on, you know."

"I don't."

"Shit. Shit, shit, shit. Fuck me. Shit." Donna turns a shade of white so pale it makes her pink lips appear scarlet.

Mary Pat watches her the way you watch a pot that's about to boil over. "Who is Jules's boyfriend, Donna?"

They listen to that big clock tick for a bit. The room picks up new shadows. Dry leaves scrape along the sidewalk outside.

"She's with Frank."

"Frank who?"

"Frank-are-you-fucking-kidding-me. Who do you think?"

Mary Pat doesn't even want to say his name. "Frank Toomey?"

"Uh, yeah."

"Tombstone Frankie?"

"Yes."

Frankie Toomey is married with four kids. His devotion to his family has long been considered his most redeeming quality outside of his good looks and his beautiful singing voice. (And he *is* good-looking, movie-star level; his resemblance to James Garner is noticeable.) More than his looks, he's got charisma to burn, but he only uses it on the kids of the neighborhood. Buys them candy, ice cream, slips the really poor ones a few extra bucks to "help out your ma." It's Frankie, not Marty, the boys want to grow up to be. And Frankie, not Marty, the girls want to grow up to be with, apparently. He walks the streets like he doesn't just own them; he built them. He calls out to everyone by name and has a hearty laugh that carries for blocks. That's the Frank Toomey all kids grow up seeing.

The adults know he's called Tombstone because he has more bodies on his résumé than the local chapter of the Hells Angels. When he's not killing for the Irish, he's loaned out to the Italians. During the McLaughlin war in the early '60s, Frankie whacked so many guys that when Al Coogan, a barber, saw Frankie approach his shop, he ran into traffic to escape him and ended up shattering a hip. Turned out Frankie just wanted a haircut.

"My daughter?" Mary Pat whispers.

Donna looks pained. "I thought you knew. Everyone knew."

"Who's *everyone*?"

"You know. Everyone."

"But me."

"I'm sorry."

"Are you, though?"

"Sorry? Yeah. It's like, when we're in Marty's world, Brian's world, we only live there. Only spend time with each other. Only know what we know."

"But what you knew is that Frankie Toomey was seeing my Jules, a girl seven years younger than *half* his age."

"Yeah."

"And that was okay?"

They hold each other's gaze and time falls away, and the girls they were once could maybe, just maybe, become the angels on the shoulders of the women they are now.

But Donna's eyes grow distant. "I'm no one's keeper, Mary Pat."

"You're the second person to say that to me this week." Mary Pat stands. "You know, we always say we stand for things here. We might not have much, but we have the neighborhood. We got a code. We watch out for one another." She flicks her fingers and overturns her beer can. She watches it flow across Donna Shea's parquet table. "What a crock of shit."

She lets herself out as Donna runs to get the dish towels.

8

The two guys leaning against the faded brown sedan parked out in front of her building look so much like cops they should have just stayed in uniform. The younger and taller of the two has a bandit mustache and long sideburns. His thick hair reaches the shoulders of his black pleather car coat, and a gold chain around his neck catches the streetlight and winks at her as she approaches. Mary Pat would bet he's seen *Serpico* at least three times.

The other one is shorter, fleshy and on his way to fat if he's not careful. He has the kind of face she usually associates with boxers and loan sharks. He wears a porkpie hat. His clothes are too tight on him, and his tie has been askew since the day he bought it. Divorced, she guesses, lots of TV dinners and drinking alone. A description, she quickly realizes (and just as quickly banishes), could describe her. Upon closer inspection, she puts his age at mid-thirties, ten years younger than her initial assumption, but hard years are baked into those decades somewhere.

They flash their badges. The young one identifies himself as Detective Pritchard. The older one is Detective Coyne.

"Is Julie around?" Coyne has a surprisingly gentle voice that doesn't match the rest of him.

"No, she's not."

"May I ask where she might be?" Again, his tone is almost courtly.

"I don't know. I've been looking for her myself."

"Since when?" This comes from the young cop in the car coat. His voice is curt and without a hint of kindness.

"Haven't seen her in"—something catches in her throat as she realizes it—"forty-eight hours."

"You report it to anyone?"

"To who?"

"To us?"

"What're *you* gonna do? Would you actively search for her?"

"Without clear evidence of foul play?" The older one shakes his head. "No, we don't do that."

"So what good would reporting it do?"

They look at each other and nod-shrug at the same time. Fair point.

"Can we come inside?" Coyne asks.

Mary Pat's not going to be seen voluntarily walking two cops into her building. That would be like bringing a pornographer to Christmas dinner. "It's a mess," she says.

Coyne smiles politely, but his eyes say he doesn't believe her.

"There's a bench over there." She indicates it with her head.

They sit on a bench facing a basketball court with no basketball hoops, just poles and backboards, under lights that turn the air the color of brown mustard. Every now and then a bat flies overhead in a crazed kilter, like a kite caught in a storm.

Coyne says, "So, the last time you saw Julie, she—"

"Jules."

"Sorry?"

"Nobody calls her Julie. It's Jules."

"Got it. Last time you saw her?"

"Night before last. Around eight o'clock."

Pritchard writes that in his notebook.

"Can we skip this back-and-forth shit?" she says.

"Of course," Coyne says easily, and she likes his easiness. Maybe he's the first cop she's ever met who's not a drunken, philandering ass-hole. Or maybe he's just perfected the art of resembling a decent man.

Mary Pat puts a cigarette in her mouth, and Coyne's there with a Zippo before she can find her Bic. The Zippo has the Marine Corps emblem on it—eagle, globe, anchor—and dates of service she can't make out. She nods once her cigarette glows, and he removes the lighter with a quiet click.

"My daughter," she begins, "didn't come home Saturday night. I been looking for her since. I figured out she was with several people who claim they were at Columbia Park and then Carson Beach be-tween eleven and twelve-forty-five. Those people were Ronald Collins, Brenda Morello, George Dunbar, and my niece, Peg McAuliffe."

She waits for Pritchard to get the names into his little notepad be-fore she continues.

"There were other kids there too, but I don't know exactly who. My niece left before midnight. George Dunbar and Ronald Collins claim my daughter left them at twelve-forty-five to walk home, and that's the last anyone ever saw of her."

"You believe that story?" Pritchard asks, still writing in his notepad.

"No."

"Is that why you beat the piss out of Ronald Collins in Marty But-ler's bar last night?"

"I have no idea what you're talking about."

Coyne laughs. "It's all over town, Mrs. Fennessy."

Pritchard says, "You snip his fucking balls while you were at it?"

"Hey," Coyne says sharply.

"What?"

"You don't swear around a woman. You don't talk about genitalia."

"Gena-what?"

Mary Pat shoots a look of gratitude at Coyne. It's a neighborhood thing—if you don't know a woman, you don't curse around her, even if she herself swears like a drunken trucker. It's considered discourteous. Same rule applies to discussing private parts.

"Where you from?" she asks Coyne, because now she knows he's a 'hood rat from somewhere.

He tilts his head toward Dorchester. "Savin Hill."

"Stab-n-Kill," she says.

"You got a nerve to talk," he says, looking around at the redbrick wasteland of Commonwealth.

She shoots him a touché smile. "Jules ain't contacted anyone, not me, not her stepfather, not her friends—at least according to her friends. A mother knows things about her kids."

"And what do you know?"

"She's in trouble," Mary Pat says through a wet exhale of gray smoke. "Why're you looking for her?"

"Why do you think?" Coyne's eyes never leave hers.

She looks out at the empty basketball court, can hear the bat up there somewhere pinwheeling desperately across the sky. She recalls what she's known since the moment Ken Fen raised the possibility. "It has something to do with Auggie Williamson. The kid who died at Columbia Station."

Coyne's face is unreadable. "Why would you say that?"

"Because she was in the area with some of her asshole friends, and now you're here asking about her. One plus one." She flicks her cigarette through the chain-link fence onto the empty court.

Coyne lights his own and places the lighter on the bench between them. She catches half the word—"Viet"—peeking out of the shadow that falls on the bench. "Where did you serve?"

He can't follow for a second but then notices the focus of her gaze. "I was all over. It wasn't a war yet. I was an 'adviser.'"

"Was it already a fucked-up place?"

"Oh, yeah," he says. "It was just prettier. We hadn't blown a lot of it up yet. Charlie neither. But you knew it was going to go sideways even back in 'sixty-two. You know someone who served?"

She nods. "My son." She catches Pritchard giving Coyne a *let's move her along* look, but Coyne just stares the younger man down.

"He make it home?" Coyne asks her.

"Kinda," she says.

"What's 'kinda'?" He looks around the basketball court as if Noel might be hanging out there right at this moment.

"He OD'd." She looks at Coyne. "So, he kinda made it home and he kinda didn't."

For a moment it seems like he forgot how to move. His chalk white skin manages to find an even whiter shade, and she suspects he's lost someone close to him—a son or a brother—to the brown powder. When he lifts his lighter off the bench and pockets it, she notices the faintest of tremors in his hand. He exhales a stream of smoke. "I'm sorry, Mrs. Fennessy."

She says, "You know what neighborhood sent the most kids to Vietnam?"

He guesses. "Southie?"

She shakes her head. "Charlestown. But Southie was second. Then Lynn. Then Dorchester. Roxbury. I got a cousin works for the draft board. She told me all this. You know who didn't send a lot of kids to Vietnam?"

"I can guess," he says with a bitterness so old it comes out as apathy.

"People in Dover," she says. "In Wellesley and Newton and Lincoln—their kids get to hide in college and grad school and have doctors who say they got fucking tinnitus or fallen arches or bone spurs or whatever other bullshit they can come up with. These are the exact same people who want me to bus my kid to Roxbury but wouldn't let a black guy take two steps into their neighborhood once the lawns have been cut and the sun goes down."

"I ain't arguing with you," Coyne says. "How does Jules feel about being bused?"

She stares at him for so long he finishes his cigarette and starts to look uncomfortable.

"Mrs. Fennessy?"

She sees where this is going now. "A black kid runs in front of a train, and you think some white kids were somehow involved because they were pissed off about busing?"

"I didn't say that."

"You didn't have to."

"And the kid didn't run in front of any fucking train," Pritchard says.

Coyne's jaw tightens and his kind eyes flash, cold and unkind, at his partner.

"How'd he die?" Mary Pat says.

"Still waiting on a final determination of that," Coyne says.

"Why don't you ask your daughter?" Pritchard says.

"Vince," Coyne says to his partner, "will you shut up, please? Just do me that courtesy."

Pritchard rolls his eyes and shrugs like a teenager.

Coyne turns back to Mary Pat. "We have witnesses who saw Auggie Williamson exchange words with a group of white kids on the outskirts of Columbia Park around midnight. Those kids then chased him into Columbia Station, where he died. We can't confirm whether your daughter was one of those kids, but it would be very smart for her to come to us before we come to her. So, Mrs. Fennessy, if you know where she is, do yourself a huge favor and tell us."

"I don't *know* where she is," Mary Pat says. "I've torn my hair out trying to find her."

He holds her gaze with his own. "I want to believe you."

"I could give a shit whether you believe me, I just want to find my daughter. So if you guys want to go on the hunt for her, please, be my fucking guest."

Coyne nods. "Do you know any place she could be hiding out?"

If Jules is hiding, she's hiding in her secret life. The one that may involve Frank Toomey. Which would, by association, involve Marty Butler. And saying anything to a cop that leads them to Marty Butler would be the same as sticking her head in an oven, turning on the gas, and firing up one last cigarette.

"I don't."

She's trying to keep the hope from her eyes and voice because something finally makes sense—if Jules was involved in some stupid shit that led to the death of that black kid, then she could very well be hiding somewhere within a ten-block radius of where Mary Pat sits right now. And if that's the case, well, Mary Pat can address any bad shit her kid may have gotten up to, she can deal with that.

Coyne hands her a business card—*Det. Sgt. Michael Coyne, BPD Homicide Div.*

Homicide. Hom-i-cide. This is not your everyday bad shit that would bring a cop calling. It's not a shoplifting beef or check kiting. This is as serious as a tumor on an ovary.

Coyne points at the card. "If she pops her head up, you call that number and have them put you through to that extension. Or you just ask for me by name."

"Detective Michael Coyne."

"Bobby," he says. "Everyone calls me Bobby."

"Why?"

He shrugs.

"What's your middle name?"

"David," he says.

"But everyone calls you Bobby?"

He shrugs. "This life. You know? Try and make sense of it."

"Okay, Bobby." She pockets the card.

He stands and brushes at the wrinkles in his trousers. Pritchard flips his notepad closed.

"If you see your daughter," Coyne says, "do the smart thing, Mrs. Fennessy."

"And what would that be?"

"Have her call us first thing."

She nods.

"Is that a yes?"

"It's a nod."

"As in you'll think about it?"

"As in I heard the words that left your mouth."

She scoops up her cigarettes and walks back to her building, lets herself in.

9

She falls asleep in the La-Z-Boy and wakes an hour later when someone pounds a fist against her door. She runs to the door and opens it without checking who's on the other side, her body throbbing with the scream of a hope that it's her, it's Jules, it's her.

But it's not Jules. It's not anyone. No one's there. She looks up and down the hall. Still no one. She looks back in at her apartment. It's empty in a way it was never empty after Dukie or Ken Fen or even Noel left. It's empty the way graveyards are empty—filled to bursting with the remains of what can never be again.

Back in seventh grade, Sister Loretta used to say that even if hell was not the firepit with the horned demons and the pitchforks that the medievalists supposed, it was, make no mistake, a void.

It was an eternal separation from love.

What love?

God's love.

Anyone's love.

All love.

The pain from a pitchfork or even from an eternal flame cannot compare to the pain of that void.

"Everlasting exile," Sister Loretta said, "the heart forever untouched and forsaken."

Mary Pat steps back inside long enough to grab her smokes and her lighter.

When she reaches the Fields, the sign is still up—*Closed for Private Function*—and the lights behind the single high window are dim, but she starts knocking and she doesn't stop. She uses her left hand because the right is still barking from the contact with Rum's woodchuck head. She's been pounding a solid minute when someone throws the locks on the other side of the door. Three of them. One after the other. And then nothing. It's her last warning—if you want in, you open the door. Final chance to walk away.

The fear is not small. Suddenly, it's the only thing she can feel. A full-bodied presence. As real and substantial as another human being standing on the sidewalk beside her. Other people have gone through this door, she knows, and never come back out. This door is not just the door to a building; it's a border between worlds.

She flashes on Jules dancing around the kitchen in her bathrobe the other morning, pretending to box, smiling that lopsided toothy smile of hers, and Mary Pat pushes the door open.

The guy standing behind the bar has a lit cigarette between his lips and squints at the smoke floating into his right eye as he pours himself a shot of rum. He's a guy everyone calls Weeds because he's skinny and unpleasant to look at. Has a harelip, a left eye that floats in the socket, and is rumored to have pushed his little brother off a roof when they were kids just to hear the sound of the poor bastard landing. He's not wearing his Baracuta jacket tonight, just a T-shirt that looks soiled in the dim light.

Larry Foyle sits at a table along the wall. Larry's body looks like a set of tires stacked atop one another, and his neck isn't much smaller. His head is enormous, like the head of a statue. His hands could cup a moose in one palm. He still lives with his parents and can often be found pushing his grandfather in his wheelchair along Day Boulevard. Larry is usually affable, a sly cutup, but tonight he looks at his beer and not once at Mary Pat. Like Weeds, he's stripped down to a T-shirt.

She can't make out the state of it, or even the color, but she can smell his body odor from twenty feet.

They're the only two men in the room. Down at the end of the bar, the back door is open; she looks at Weeds. His eyes pulse once in the poor light, an indication she's to head to that back door. Then he downs his shot and pours himself another.

During the walk down the bar, she waits to hear the scrape of chair legs, the rustle of limbs, footsteps rushing up behind her. A vein pulses in a part of her throat she never knew a vein to exist. The bar area gives way to a thin dark corridor that leads to the bathrooms and the back door. It smells of Lysol and urinal cakes. The night breeze feels damp and warm on her face.

Brian Shea is waiting out back. She's never been out here before and is mildly surprised they've made a kind of grotto out of it, with cobblestone covering the ground and lights strung from the exterior walls of the bar and the body shop next door. A few wrought-iron tables and chairs share space with potted plants and the occasional beer keg. At the far end stands a blue three-decker house with white trim. That house has been the subject of dozens of rumors over the years—it's Marty Butler's true residence; it's a stash house; it's a high-end casino; it's a high-end bordello; it's where they keep all those paintings that were stolen from the Fogg Museum back in '71. Until tonight she'd never seen it full-on, only the top floor from the street. It looks like nothing much, like every other three-decker in Southie and Dorchester, though the paint's been kept up.

Brian Shea doesn't offer her a seat, but she takes the one across from him anyway. The first thing he says, with a hint of cruelty in his tiny smile, is "You went to my *house*?"

"Yes."

"Why would you do that?"

"You didn't keep your word."

"My what?"

"Your word. You told me you would reach out to me by five o'clock. You didn't."

The smile grows a little larger, a little crueler. "You've been around long enough, Mary Pat, to know that someone like you doesn't make demands of someone like me."

"And you've been around long enough, Brian, to know I don't give a fuck what you think I've been around long enough to know."

He puts his palm to the back of his neck and stares at her with his Windex eyes. His T-shirt isn't as soiled as Weeds's was, but she notices streaks of chalky residue on his arms and a spot of it on his cheek.

Did these guys break into a schoolhouse? Or hot-wire a cement mixer?

"Did you know my Jules was having an affair with Tombstone?"

"He doesn't like that nickname."

"He'd prefer Child Molester?"

"She's seventeen."

"So you did know."

A small downward flick of the eyes. "I knew."

She feels light-headed for a moment. As if she might fall out of her chair. "Is she with him now? With Frankie?"

He shakes his head. "Frank hasn't seen her in days."

"How do you know?"

"He told me. I promised you I'd ask around, I did."

"I'll ask him myself."

"No, you won't," he says. There's a thin wisp of fury in his voice, and she knows it's a far bigger threat because it isn't a threat but a promise. "Frank has a wife and kids and probably twenty-four-hour BPD or fed surveillance on him. You are not going to go making a scene at Frank Toomey's house. You hear me?"

"So where is she?"

"I asked if you fucking heard me."

"I heard you."

The cords in his neck relax. He sits back.

"So where is she?"

"I don't know."

"You said you asked around."

"Yes."

"And what did you hear?"

"That the last anyone saw of Jules was when she walked home that night."

"I don't believe you."

"I don't care."

"Cops came by my place."

"You sure you didn't go to them?"

She grimaces.

He widens his eyes. "Well, I dunno, Mary Pat. I don't know who you are right now. You're off your fucking nut."

"My daughter is missing."

"Girls her age go missing all the time. Maybe she's hitchhiking to San Francisco or, I dunno, fucking Florida."

"The cops said—"

"You're quoting cops now?"

"They said she was mixed up in that thing where the boy got killed."

"What boy?"

"The boy at the train station."

"The nigger drug dealer?"

"How do you know he was a drug dealer?"

A snort. "Oh, okay, he was looking for the Peace Corps office and got lost. Make you happy?"

"The cops said—"

"Stop saying 'the cops said,' 'the cops told me.' Are you out of your fucking mind? We don't talk to cops around here."

"I didn't talk to them, they talked to me. They told me a group of white kids chased the black kid into the station. They think those white kids might have been George Dunbar, Rum, Brenda Morello, and my daughter." She lights a cigarette.

Brian is watching her with an expectant look in his eyes that gradually fades. "That's it? Cops tell you some white kids who *might* have been your daughter and her friends *might* have chased a nigger drug dealer into Columbia Station where he *might* have fallen on his spearchucker head and fucking died? And you want to do what with this information?"

"Find out if it's true so it'll help me find my daughter."

He notices the chalk on his arms and slaps it off with his hands. He indicates something she hadn't noticed before—a sledgehammer resting against a toolbox by the steps to Marty's three-decker.

"I been working my ass off all day, helping the boss renovate his house, and I'm fucking bushed. Exhausted. Meanwhile, you go to my house and disturb my wife and dump a beer all over my dining room table like a slob with no manners. Then you fucking come here— *twice*—while we're busting our asses to make the boss's living room look nice. And why, Mary Pat? Why? Because your fucking daughter is probably off getting high or getting laid and forgot to call? Or because she said, 'You know what? Enough of this shit, enough of this town, enough with them about to bus a bunch of fucking chimpanzees into my school, I'm going to Florida.' Because I will bet you a thousand bucks of my own money that that's where she's headed. So I suggest you think of your daughter in Florida, sipping drinks, getting a tan. I suggest you remember that kids leave, that's what kids do, but neighbors are forever. They shovel your walk when you're sick, tell you when someone's looking at your house funny, that kinda thing." He lights his own cigarette, his pale blue eyes holding hers through the flame. "But you, right now, *you* are not being much of a neighbor. And we're all getting pretty tired of it."

"You're getting tired of it?"

"Everyone is."

"Well, tell everyone I'm just warming up." She stands.

He flicks his cigarette into her chest. He does it casually, then stares at her blankly as she swipes at the sparks and pieces of coal before they can burn the fabric of her shirt.

"Shitty things," he says as he reaches for a fresh cigarette from his pack, "happen to shitty neighbors."

She can't think of a comeback—she can't really think of anything at this point; her brain swims—so she leaves.

10

The next morning, she goes into work feeling so jagged it's like she's got sharpened quills sticking out of her. By this point, all the other girls know she hasn't seen her daughter in three days, and they give her a wide berth. A few look like they're considering offering sympathies or . . . something, but are too wary to approach.

In the break room, over coffee, all the talk centers on Auggie Williamson.

By now, the reporters have pieced together some of the facts from that night. Auggie Williamson's car—a '63 Rambler—broke down on Columbia Road. That left Auggie a couple options, neither ideal. The first was to walk along Columbia Road for about a mile until he reached Upham's Corner and turned onto Dudley Street, at which point he would be among his kind. But that would be a long mile through a white neighborhood into a slightly mixed neighborhood before he reached a mostly brown one.

The second option, and the one he took, was to walk a few hundred yards to Columbia Station. There he could board the subway southbound, hope he didn't run into any white gangs in the four stops it took him to reach Ashmont Station, where he could transfer to a bus that would take him into Mattapan, where he could, again, find safety among his own kind.

That was the option Auggie Williamson chose, but within those few hundred yards, he either talked some shit to the wrong people or tried to pull some nigger bullshit like stealing another car to get himself home or sticking someone up for carfare.

And he got what was coming.

At least that's the sum total of the theories of the girls in the break room.

She reads the newspapers as the girls gossip.

Auggie Williamson had been returning from his job at the Zayre department store off Morrissey Boulevard. He'd worked until midnight because they were taking inventory that weekend and he was in the management trainee program. According to the papers, Auggie Williamson was twenty. He had lettered in baseball at Boston English, where he carried a consistent B-minus average through all four years. After graduation, he worked for a year at a pizza joint in Mattapan Square before being accepted to the management trainee program at Zayre.

Some of this information, Mary Pat suspects, she's half heard from Dreamy over the years. Half heard because she was only half listening.

Dreamy has two daughters, Ella and Soria, who Mary Pat knew about, though she could never quite recall their names. Raised in the same household as Auggie, created by the same man, Dreamy's husband, Reginald, a sweet, respectful, polite man. Dreamy works with Mary Pat, Reginald works as a clerk at the DPW, Ella's in high school, Soria's in seventh grade. The whole family sounds like a straight-up working-class family on the rise. Auggie had no criminal history.

She comes across a picture of Auggie in his baseball uniform in yesterday's *Herald American*.

"Look how they try to make him look like a saint." Dottie's suddenly standing over her, a butt sticking out of her mouth, unlit. She lights it now. "Keep talking about how he was a hard worker, his father's a hard worker, blah blah blah. We'll see." She nods at the rest of the girls. "We'll see."

"But," Mary Pat says quietly.

"What?" Dottie leans down to hear her.

"But he's Dreamy's kid. And we all know Dreamy, all know what a hard worker she is."

The other girls murmur and exchange looks of possible agreement.

Dottie's having none of it. "The mothers can be saints—you see that on the ten o'clock news all the time. But the sons, the sons, Mary Pat, we all know, are born to crime. They have no fathers, so they—"

"He had a father."

"And look where it got him." Dottie snorts and takes in the rest of the room. "As nice as Dreamy might be, who would leave her son in here alone with their purse? Anyone?"

All the girls shake their heads.

Dottie turns on Mary Pat. "How about you?"

"Let her be, Dot," Suse says. "She's going through something."

Dot smiles warmly at Mary Pat. "I'm just asking—would you leave your purse unattended with this Auggie Williamson?"

"No," Mary Pat says. But before Dot can crow, she adds, "I wouldn't leave it alone with anyone."

"Okay. Would any of us leave our *daughters* alone with him?"

A round of headshakes. Dot looks at Mary Pat in triumph. Takes a step back when she sees what lives in Mary Pat's eyes.

Mary Pat stands, a crumpled paper in her hands that she doesn't remember crumpling. "I can't leave my daughter alone with anyone, because I can't fucking *find* her."

Dottie holds up a hand. "Mary Pat, I'm sorry."

Mary Pat cocks her head at that. "Are you? Because you run your mouth a lot, Dottie, about the niggers and how they're all lazy and from broken homes and how the men all fuck around and don't stick around to raise their kids."

A nasty little smile finds Dottie's little green eyes. "Because it's the truth."

And a question that's been nagging at Mary Pat for a while—

maybe her whole life, who knows?—finds her tongue. "It's your truth too, though, ain't it?"

A few of the girls make audible noises, something between gasps and moans.

"What'd you fucking say?" Dottie asks.

"Aren't you from a broken home? Didn't your husband fuck around and then leave you to raise the kids by yourself? I've noticed the people who bitch most about the coloreds and their bad qualities, they usually *have* those qualities themselves. I mean, when's the last time you did even *half* the amount of work around here the rest of us do?"

Dottie clenches her fist and steps hard up to Mary Pat. "You listen to—"

"Dottie, you're gonna unclench that fist before I snap it off at your wrist and shove it straight up your fat fucking ass."

Dottie looks at the rest of the girls. After a few seconds, she tries a laugh. But when she looks back at Mary Pat, her little green eyes swim with fear.

"I am not going to repeat myself," Mary Pat says.

Dottie's fingers unfurl slowly from her palm. She wipes the palm on her slacks. "You're not yourself." She turns to the girls. "She's not herself. And who can blame her?" She takes a drag off her cigarette, her elbow cupped in her palm to steady the shakes. Turns her eyes back on Mary Pat. "Who can blame you?" She crinkles her face in something that's supposed to resemble sympathy. Her eyes pulse once—just once—to let Mary Pat know this moment will not be forgotten. Or forgiven. And then she smiles sadly, playing to the room. "You poor dear."

After the break is over, Mary Pat lingers to smoke another cigarette and read the papers. If the nuns got an issue with it, they can take it up with her. In her present mood, they better be awfully brave fucking nuns.

Unnamed witnesses saw a black man running into Columbia Station at twelve-twenty, followed by at least four white kids. One witness thought it was four males with long hair, another witness thought it was two boys and two girls. (*Was one of those girls mine?* Mary Pat wonders. But she doesn't really wonder. *Jules. For fuck's sake. Jules.*) One witness distinctly heard someone whistling, the way one whistles to a dog. Another heard someone call, "We just want to talk."

Police have ascertained that there were other people on the platform when Auggie Williamson and his four pursuers arrived. They are asking those people to come forward. It's believed—though not proved yet—that Auggie Williamson fell or was pushed into the path of the train. That the impact to his head spun him around on the platform and he somehow, from there, fell to the tracks and rolled under the platform.

It all sounds fishy as hell. If Mary Pat can buy that someone could extend his head into the path of a moving subway car and not end up getting the rest of his body knocked onto the tracks ahead of the car, she certainly can't accept that Auggie then staggered in place long enough for the train to pass before conveniently falling forward onto the tracks and then rolling backward under the platform.

No drugs were found on his person. The papers make sure to mention that. All that means to Mary Pat's neighbors (and most of the whites in West Roxbury and Neponset and Milton and everywhere else in or around the city that's stayed uniformly white) is that whoever killed Auggie Williamson—whether with intent or by accident—stripped him of the drugs he was carrying.

And if this didn't have such a personal aspect for her—if Auggie wasn't Dreamy Williamson's son, if Jules wasn't a "person of interest" in his death—Mary Pat would have written it off the same way.

But reading through the papers, chain-smoking one Virginia Slim after another, she allows a picture to emerge in her mind of an Auggie Williamson who might *not* have done drugs, who most certainly was not from a broken home, who possibly didn't try to steal a car or rob someone for cab fare but was, instead, a twenty-year-old kid whose car broke down in the wrong neighborhood.

And what neighborhood is that, Mary Pat?

My neighborhood.

When she walks out of work at the end of the shift, Marty Butler's butterscotch AMC Matador is parked at the curb. Weeds stands by the back door, and as soon as Mary Pat has exited Meadow Lane Manor, he opens that door and she spies Marty sitting in the back.

She doesn't move for a moment, just stands on the sidewalk pretending she has options. Once that little fantasy runs aground, she gets in the car with him.

He smiles and kisses her cheek and tells her she still looks as lovely as the day she married Dukie, thereby reminding her that he was at her first wedding, reminding her that Dukie worked for him, reminding her that he doesn't just own the present, he owns history too.

Marty looks like he stepped out of a JCPenney circular. The Dad Model, wearing cardigans with a football cocked in his hand or fake-laughing with the other Dad Models. Square haircut, strong jaw, cleft in his chin. Eyes that smile without a shred of joy. Never has a hair out of place, a whisker or shadow on his cheeks. His teeth are white and straight. He's handsome in the blandest of ways and hasn't seemed to age for at least twenty years.

It's a mystery what made Marty Marty. Some say it was the tour of duty in Korea. Others whisper ever so quietly that Marty Butler was always fucked in the head. A guy Dukie used to drink with, who grew up with Marty on Linden Street, told Dukie, "In high school, 'member he had a sister died from TB? He skipped her funeral to play basketball. Scored twenty-four points."

As Weeds drives them back toward Southie, Marty asks Mary Pat, "Will you be at the rally Friday?"

"Oh, right." In truth, Mary Pat had forgotten. The busing outrage, which seemed to consume everyone in Southie right now—and had consumed her up until three days ago—had slipped from her mind.

"'Oh, right'?" Marty chuckles. "It's only the future of our way of life at stake, Mary Pat."

"I know," she says. "I know."

"You know who the truly happy countries are? Denmark, Norway, New Zealand, Iceland. You never hear a bad thing about those places. They don't fight wars, they don't suffer unrest. You never see them on the news. They have unity and prosperity because they stay whole. They stay whole because the races don't mix because there are no races to mix." He sighs, blowing it out through his lips. "First they'll tell us where our kids can go to school, next they'll tell us which god we're allowed to pray to."

"You pray?" She doesn't mean to insult him, but it's never occurred to her that someone like Marty Butler takes to prayer.

He nods. "I pray every night."

"On your knees?" She just can't picture it.

"On my back. In bed." He shoots her an amused grimace. "Mostly for wisdom, sometimes for special dispensations for members of our flock."

Our flock. His and God's. That explains it.

"Do you recall when little Deidre Ward had the cancer? Sure, she was only seven or eight. I prayed hard those days, and wouldn't you know the cancer went into remission. The Lord listens, Mary Pat. The trick is to have a pure heart when you ask Him for something."

"Will that bring my Jules back to me?"

He gives her a distant smile and pats her leg. Gives the flesh above her knee a firm squeeze. His thumb and index finger dig all the way into the tissue. And then he pats lightly again and removes the hand as they cross over the bridge into Southie.

"How's that car of yours?" he asks. "Still running?"

She nods. "As unlikely as that may seem."

He gives his own reflection that distant smile of his. "Some things don't know when to quit."

"Why should it?" she says. "As long as it's still getting me where I need to go."

He looks at her and wiggles his eyebrows up and down like they're in on a joke together. "And your apartment there? At Commonwealth?"

She shrugs. "The same."

"Because I came into some cans of paint, Mary Pat. Crates of them. They're all sitting in a warehouse over on West Second. Every color of the rainbow. Would you be interested in sprucing up your walls? Adding some color?"

"If you have a few cans I can take off your hands, sure, Marty, that'd be nice."

He waves at the absurdity of the proposition. "No, no, hon. We would never expect you to do your own painting. You take a few days somewhere and we'll pop in and paint them walls professionally for you. You'll come back to a place so pretty you won't even recognize it."

"What's with all the renovation lately, Marty?"

"What now?"

"Well, first your place and now mine?"

He looks at her with such bafflement that she knows he has no idea what she's talking about.

"The house behind the Fields," she says.

He stares back at her. Still no clue.

Weeds, from the front seat, says, "She's talking about the work we're doing on the kitchen, boss."

"Ah!" Marty says. "Of course, of course." Another pat for her knee. "The thing of it is, I don't think of that house as 'mine,' Mary Pat. I still live in the same spot I always did over on Linden."

She smiles and nods and tries not to let him see into the part of her brain that knows he's lying. Brian Shea claimed they'd been working on the living room. Weeds claimed it was the kitchen. And Marty had no fucking clue about any of it until Weeds tipped him off.

"Well, think about the paint, at any rate," Marty says.

The car pulls to the curb in front of Kelly's Landing. A takeout place going back to Prohibition times—best fried clams in the city—it closed a month back. Mary Pat's parents went on their first date at Kelly's; her mother remembered her own father taking her there as a child, as she took Mary Pat, and Mary Pat took Jules and Noel. And now it's boarded up. A place that provided food and memories for generations. The owners, it's said, decided it was time to try something new, time for a change.

Change, for those who don't have a say in it, feels like a pretty word for death. Death to what you want, death to whatever plans you'd been making, death to the life you've always known.

They get out of the car and walk past Kelly's onto the causeway.

"I miss the smell," Marty says. "That fried-food smell? My entire life, I walked past here, the air had that smell. Now it just smells like low tide."

Mary Pat says nothing.

"How did we get here?" Marty Butler wants to know.

He's not talking about the causeway they're walking along. He's talking about this point in their relationship, such as it is. It's been cloudy all day, the sun taking the day off behind a wall of woolen gray. No hint of rain but no hint of sun either. She and Marty walk toward the Sugar Bowl, a small oval park surrounded by benches. The Sugar Bowl sits a half mile out in the bay where the two causeways meet. People fish from the causeways. Mary Pat and Marty pass men and a few women casting their lines, some out of boredom, some for their dinner. Ken Fen used to fish out here, came home a couple times with flounder that was gamey. Most of the time, he admitted, he just went there to check out of his own head for a little bit. The fishermen and fisherwomen all acknowledge Marty with nods, but nobody speaks and nobody approaches.

"How did we get here?" Marty asks again. As if he didn't know. As if he hasn't known every move she's made since her search for Jules began.

"I don't know," she says. "I'm just trying to find my daughter."

"It feels so unnecessary," Marty says. "All this . . ." He searches for the appropriate word in the clouds, comes back with "conflict."

"I'm not after conflict," she says. "I'm not looking for a fight."

"Tell me what you need," he says to her.

"I need Jules. I need my daughter."

"And we need peace around our thing," he says. "Peace and quiet and nobody looking our way."

"I understand that."

"You understand that, but you beat the snot out of a kid in my bar? You understand that, but you run around the neighborhood causing a fuss?"

"She's my daughter, Marty."

He gives that a quick flick of his head, his lips pursed, as if it's an entirely different subject matter, as if he's speaking English and she's speaking Mandarin.

"What it is, Mary Pat, is a matter of order. Everything works when everything works a predictable way. Look at this bay." He waves his arm at the water around them. Pleasure Bay. Walled in by these causeways and the tiny park where they intersect. "No waves. No surprises. Not like out there." Now he's gesturing at the ocean beyond. "Out there, you've got waves and swells and undertows." He turns his bland face to her. "I don't like oceans, Mary Pat, I like bays, I like harbors."

They pass a woman feeding the seagulls. She flicks hard pieces of bread at the birds from a white paper bag dotted with grease spots. She's surprisingly young for a bird feeder, no older than Mary Pat, but her eyes burn with loss. Loss of love, loss of hope, loss of mind—it's impossible to tell which. But loss. The gulls caw and tread the air in front of the woman in terror. Afraid to get close, too hungry not to risk it.

"I'm not going to cause any trouble," Mary Pat tells Marty.

"You're already causing it." He fishes a pack of Dunhills from his Baracuta and lights one with a slim gold lighter, turning away from the mild breeze to do so. She gets a look at the crown of his head and notes that his brown hair is orange up there, which tells her he uses hair dye, which makes her wonder for a moment if he's a closet fag. Were that the case, so many things about Marty Butler would finally make sense.

"If I'm causing trouble," she says carefully, "it's not because I want to cause *you* trouble. It's because I want to find my daughter."

"But what does that have to do with me?"

"She was Frank Toomey's mistress."

He makes a face as if he just bit into something unpleasant. He turns the grimace to the sea for a moment and then sighs softly. "I'm aware."

"Marty," she says, "you're fucking *aware?*"

He holds a hand up to his ear, a man who loathes when women use profanities. "Frank assures me he hasn't seen your daughter in a couple weeks. I asked all my men. She hasn't been around Frank, she hasn't been around the Fields."

"So where is she?"

"That's not the issue at hand."

"It very much *is* the fucking issue at hand."

He shakes his head. "Your daughter is missing. My heart breaks for you. But her leaving to wherever she went does not overrule my right to conduct business in this neighborhood."

"No one's stopping you from conducting business."

"You are." He doesn't raise his voice, but it definitely grows tighter. "You are."

"How?"

"Everyone's watching us. If this busing abomination happens? Cameras will be on this neighborhood like it's the moon landing. And now with this colored kid getting killed and your daughter maybe being mixed up in it, they're going to bring more cameras in here. And the one place those cameras can't point? Is at me. And mine. But if you keep acting the way you're acting, hon? I fear they may have no choice."

"I just want to find my daughter."

"So find her. But look someplace besides my organization."

"But what if someone in your organization knows something they're not telling you?"

"They wouldn't dare."

They near the Sugar Bowl, and Mary Pat is surprised to realize it's almost empty. Just one man sitting on the center bench watching them come. The Sugar Bowl is never empty on a summer day. But here's this one man and no one else.

Do I die here? she wonders. *Is my crime already that big?*

It wouldn't be, she knows all too well, the first time (or the fifth) that Marty Butler made a problem vanish by making a person vanish.

They reach the end of the causeway, and the man who rises from the bench is a man she's never seen before. He's wearing a blue leisure suit with a white turtleneck. His brown hair is combed back tight against his scalp. He holds a doctor's satchel in his right hand as he stands and looks down at Mary Pat. He's very tall.

Marty says, "This is a friend of mine from down Providence. You can call him Lewis. You see that bag in Lewis's hand, Mary Pat?"

She nods. Lewis stares at her the way ravens stare at worms.

"I want to give you the bag," Marty says. "Lewis wanted to give you something else. Because it's not merely my business you're affecting with all your noise. You're affecting Lewis's. And the people he works with down Providence."

"I'm just—"

"Don't say you're *just looking for your daughter*. There's more to this.

And you know it. Now, Lewis would like to end this his way. But I convinced him to try my way first."

Lewis hands her the satchel.

"Open it," Marty says.

She notices, with no shortage of humiliation, that her hands shake as she unsnaps the clasp over the center of the satchel, then pries the bag open. It's half filled with money—stacks of well-used hundreds, all rubber-banded together.

"Brian tells me Jules went to Florida," Marty says.

The man from Providence stares at her and never blinks.

"Brian feels pretty sure of this."

"I don't know that she did," Mary Pat manages.

"Ah," Marty says, "but that's where you have to take a leap of faith. Your friends have looked for her on your behalf, those friends of yours that people don't lie to. And those friends have not found her. So you must put faith in their opinion that she is no longer to be found in this general area. But it's not just faith I'm asking for. I'm saying you go prove it to yourself."

"How would I do that?"

"Take the money in that bag and use it to fly to Florida, stay in a nice hotel, and spend your days looking for your daughter. Kinda money that's in that bag, Mary Pat, you could stay down there for a few years."

Lewis lights a cigarette, considers her through the flame.

Marty stands in front of her. His eyes are very still. "I'm going to walk my friend Lewis back the way we came. You stay here for a bit and collect your thoughts and make a final decision. If you decide to keep the bag, I hope you use its contents in good health and with my blessing. If you decide to return the bag, you know where to find me. Whatever decision you make, this topic we've been discussing? We'll never speak of it again. Do you understand?"

She doesn't trust herself to speak. She manages a nod.

"We understand each other, then, hon." Marty squeezes her shoulder once before he and Lewis walk back up the causeway toward land.

Once they're out of earshot, she stops constricting her face, and the sob leaves the back of her throat like a ball of bile and exits her mouth. She looks down at the money in the bag as her tears stream onto the paper.

And she knows her daughter is dead.

She knows her daughter is dead.

11

Bobby Coyne and Vincent Pritchard drive through Southie to interview the final witness on their list—thus far—to the last night of Auggie Williamson's life. The witness, a tower crane operator named Seamus Riordan, agrees to meet them at Boyd Container Terminal along Summer Street during his lunch break.

The moment they cross into Southie, Bobby feels a difference in the air. Bobby grew up only a few miles south in Dorchester, in a parish that was wholly white and predominantly Irish; he presumes that in most places in America, a distance of a few miles between two enclaves that share identical ethnic characteristics doesn't represent a seismic difference in culture. But crossing the border into Southie always gives him the feeling that he's just entered the rain forest of an unknowable tribe. Not specifically hostile, not dangerous by their nature. But, at their heart, opaque.

Driving along Broadway, he sees a young guy exit a bus and then turn to help an old woman who was waiting to board that bus. In his entire life, Bobby's never seen more people help little old ladies cross streets, avoid puddles or potholes, carry their groceries, or find their car keys in purses overstuffed with rosary beads and damp tissues.

Everyone knows everyone here; they stop one another in the streets to ask after spouses, children, cousins twice removed. Come winter, they shovel walks together, join up to push cars out of snowbanks, freely pass around bags of salt or sand for icy sidewalks. Summer-time, they congregate on porches and stoops or cluster in lawn chairs along the sidewalks to shoot the shit, trade the daily newspapers, and listen to Ned Martin calling the Sox games on 'HDH. They drink beer like it's tap water, smoke ciggies as if the pack will self-destruct at midnight, and call to one another—across streets, to and from cars, and up at distant windows—like impatience is a virtue. They love the church but aren't real fond of mass. They only like the sermons that scare them; they mistrust any that appeal to their empathy.

They all have nicknames. No James can just be a James; has to be Jim or Jimmy or Jimbo or JJ or, in one case, Tantrum. There are so many Sullivans that calling someone Sully isn't enough. In Bobby's various incursions here over the years, he's met a Sully One, a Sully Two, an Old Sully, a Young Sully, Sully White, Sully Tan, Two-Time Sully, Sully the Nose, and Little Sully (who's fucking huge). He's met guys named Zipperhead, Pool Cue, Pot Roast, and Ball Sac (son of Sully Tan). He's come across Juggs, Nicklebag, Drano, Pink Eye (who's blind), Legsy (who limps), and Handsy (who's got none).

Every guy has a thousand-yard stare. Every woman has an attitude. Every face is whiter than the whitest paint you've ever seen and then, just under the surface, misted with an everlasting Irish pink that sometimes turns to acne and sometimes doesn't.

They're the friendliest people he's ever met. Until they aren't. At which point they'll run over their own grandmothers to ram your fucking skull through a brick wall.

He has no idea where it all comes from—the loyalty and the rage, the brotherhood and the suspicion, the benevolence and the hate.

But he suspects it has something to do with the need for a life to have meaning. Bobby is a child of the '40s and '50s. When, as he recalls, you knew who you were. Without question.

And it's the "without question" that's bothered him ever since. While he tromped through Vietnam. While he danced with the needle. While he worked patrol in the heart of the city's black communities— Roxbury and Mattapan, Egleston Square and Upham's Corner.

He wants to question. He *needs* to question. A Vietnamese hooker he'd thought was a friend once walked up to him in a club in Saigon and tried to cut his throat with a razor blade in her teeth. Bobby thought she'd been leaning in to give him a kiss until the last microsecond, when he felt a voice in his chest scream-whisper, *No. Fuck no.* Even as he chucked her off his lap, he felt an odd sympathy for her—if he were a Vietnamese bar girl, he'd want to kill his ass too.

Looking out at Southie now, as the bustle of Broadway passes by in its uniform whiteness—white baby pushed in a stroller by white mother as three white muscle-heads in their straining white T-shirts exit the drugstore and pass an old white couple sitting on a bench and a gaggle of white girls runs along the sidewalk past a white boy sitting on a mailbox looking forlorn, and all around them, in the background and in the foreground, are other white people—Bobby recalls a taxi girl in Hué telling him she could never go back to her village now that it was known she'd slept with a white man. (Not Bobby; some guy way before Bobby.) It shocked him, this idea that she could be looked down upon because she'd slept with a *white* man. That made no fucking sense, where Bobby came from. He told her that. He said, "We're the people who solve problems. That's why we're here."

His taxi girl, Cai, said, "People should be left to themselves."

Is that the key? he wonders as he looks out on Broadway. *Should everyone just leave everyone else the fuck alone?*

Seamus Riordan seems to think so. Those are the first words out of his mouth when they meet up with him in the break-room trailer at Boyd Container Terminal: "Couldn't you've just left me be?"

Seamus Riordan is from Southie, so he's a hard case. He'll bust their balls as a matter of course.

"Why were you on the platform that night?" Bobby asks.

"Coming home."

"From?" Vincent asks.

"Being out."

"Out where?" Bobby wonders.

"Of the house."

"So, you're out of the house," Bobby says pleasantly. "Any place specific?"

"Yup," Seamus says, and folds his arms.

"Where?"

"Specifically?"

"Yes."

"I was, ya know."

"I don't."

"Hanging out with someone."

"A friend?"

"Sure."

"Hey!" Vincent says. "Why don't you cut the shit?"

Vincent looks ready to pop out of his skin. Like a lot of guys who try too hard to act like they deserve respect, he has very low tolerance for people he correctly perceives don't respect him. This leads to Vincent getting in a lot of confrontations, which has led to two excessive-force complaints being leveled against him in the last eighteen months. So the fact that, at a relatively young age, he's reached Homicide, the very tip-top of the career ladder, means he's inexplicably failing upward, which can only mean he's connected to someone with major juice in the department. He's someone's nephew, someone's cousin, someone's rent boy.

He doesn't play Bad Cop well, though. He comes off more as Bitch Cop or Whiny Cop or Embarrassing Teenage Son Cop.

Which is what elicits Seamus Riordan's black hole of a smile. "Cut the what?"

"The shit." Vince lights a cigarette and exhales the gray smoke through his nostrils, which is why his nose hairs are more prevalent than they should be on a guy in his late twenties.

Seamus Riordan looks at Bobby. "Am I a suspect in something?"

"Not at all."

"I'm just a potential witness?"

"That you are."

"So if I don't like this dickhead's attitude, I can just walk away, go climb back up in my crane, am I right?"

Bobby places a hand to a surging Vincent's chest. "You can."

Seamus Riordan gives Vincent a *fuck you* glare. "Then you should check your fucking attitude, Serpico."

Now Vincent's torn—between embracing the comparison to his idol (not Serpico the man, whose ethics he doesn't share, but Al Pacino as Serpico, his fashion hero) or taking the comparison for the insult Bobby is sure Seamus Riordan intends it to be.

Vincent leans into the former. "Check *your* fucking attitude, little man."

Seamus gives Bobby a wry smirk of the eyes, as if to say, *Kids these days, am I right?*

Bobby lights his own cigarette. Offers Seamus the pack. Seamus takes one and Bobby lights it for him and then lights Vincent's and suddenly they're all friends. Ready to go to the bar together once they're done, that kinda vibe.

"It was over by the time I got out of the train," Seamus says.

"Tell me," Bobby says.

"There were these four kids . . ."

"White?"

"Yeah."

"Male or female?"

"Two boys, two girls. The inbound train had just left and they were standing on the edge of the platform and the boys were screaming at each other, one of them calling the other a retard, I heard that. And one of the girls was, like, just screaming? Like losing-her-fucking-mind screaming. And then the other girl slapped her and she shut up."

This is now as far as Bobby and Vincent have gotten into the timeline of the night. The other witnesses have taken them through:

1. Auggie being chased into the station.

2. Auggie jumping the turnstiles.

3. Four white kids—as of yet not positively identified but suspected to be George Dunbar, Rum Collins, Brenda Morello, and Jules Fennessy—immediately jumping the turnstiles behind him.

4. Auggie running onto the platform as the inbound train neared the station.

5. The kids charging after him.

6. One of the white boys calling, "We just want to talk to you."

7. A white girl calling, "You run slow for a nigger."

8. One of the four kids (no one could say which kid) throwing a beer bottle.

9. The beer bottle landing by Auggie Williamson's right foot, causing Auggie to look back over his shoulder. Causing his feet to tangle.

10. The train entering the station.

11. Auggie Williamson stumbling.

12. One of the four kids (a female) yelling, "You're in the wrong fucking neighborhood."

13. A thump. Every one of the first five witnesses heard the thump. The sound of impact—object meets human. (The conductor, meanwhile, possibly drinking on the job and a year short of his pension, claims to have seen and heard exactly nothing.)

14. Auggie Williamson spinning in place and falling in a heap to the platform.

From that point, all recollections of the first five witnesses grew hazy. Those were four loud, violent kids on that platform. No one wanted to catch any of their eyes by mistake. No one wanted to be dragged into this. Be the next person to hear they were in the wrong neighborhood.

So they looked away.

Then three walked off. Left the station. Took their chances hailing cabs.

Two waited for the outbound train that Seamus Riordan arrived on. Kept their eyes focused on the tracks until they could see the lights of the incoming train. But neither looked back at those four kids and whatever they were doing to the kid they'd been chasing.

The outbound train arrived. The two witnesses got on.

Seamus Riordan got off. At twenty past midnight, he was the only passenger to exit.

"And that's when I seen the five of them."

"You mean four."

"The four of them and the spook kid."

"Wait," Bobby said, "what?"

"The four white kids and the black kid," Seamus said. "Four plus one makes five."

"But he'd fallen off the platform by then."

Seamus Riordan narrows his eyes. "He was lying at their feet."

"*After* the train left the station?"

"Yeah."

"You're not making this up?" Vincent says.

"Who the fuck would *make that up*? Your parents raise any kids who aren't fucking retarded?"

Bobby Coyne watches Vincent for signs of impending violence, but by now he's like a ball-snipped dog. If Seamus gives him much more abuse, he'll roll on his back for a belly rub.

"So," Bobby says, "the train's gone, the victim's still on the platform with the kids standing over him?"

"Yup."

"And then?"

Seamus's eyes bug. "I don't fucking *know*. I didn't make it to forty-three in this fucking town because I linger when I see four people standing over a body."

"So he was dead?"

"I didn't say that."

"You said 'a body.'"

"Yeah, like, someone lying on the ground. He was kinda moving from side to side. I could see that much. Then I left."

"But he was *on* the platform."

"How many times I gotta say it? You wanna try a new language? Fucking, I dunno, Flemish, that be better? He was on the platform. Rolling back and forth a bit. Wait, not rolling. More like . . . flapping." He shrugs. "Like a, I dunno, a fish just came off the hook."

Vincent peers at Seamus Riordan. "But what kind of fish?"

"A black cod," Seamus says. And he and Vincent laugh their asses off.

Not for the first time in his life—or even the eightieth—Bobby hates humanity. Wonders if God's great unforgivable crime was creating us in the first place.

"And then you left?" he asks Seamus Riordan.

Seamus Riordan's laughter trails off. "Yeah, I left."

"And a kid died."

Something catches in Seamus Riordan's eyes. A glint of shame, perhaps. Or maybe Bobby's just being hopeful.

Because in the next breath, Seamus shrugs and says, "Wasn't my kid."

12

After his shift, Bobby has a few pops with a couple of Robbery detectives at JJ Foley's and then heads home to the house on Tuttle Street where he lives with his five sisters and his brother, Tim, the failed priest. None of the Coyne siblings is married. Three, Bobby among them, tried and failed. Two came close to the altar but didn't make it the whole way there. The other two have never even had a long-term relationship.

This is a source of great mystery in the extended family of Coynes and those families the previous generations married into—the McDonoughs and Donnellys and Kearneys and Mullens—as well as to the neighborhood at large, because several of the Coyne girls were real lookers, or had been in their youth, anyway.

The house is one of the last of the sprawling single-family Victorians that's stayed a single family on Tuttle Street. Most of the rest of them, built for large Irish families between the big wars of the first half of the century, have been converted into two-family houses. Some have even been cut up into multiple-unit buildings. But not the Coyne house. It remains exactly as it was when they all grew up here, learning its creaks and hiding places and the source of its sad groans on heartless winter nights.

He finds Nancy and Bridget sitting at the kitchen table, nursing their nightly highballs and smoking their cigarettes—Parliaments for Nancy, Kents for Bridget. He grabs a beer from the fridge and a fresh

ashtray and joins them at the table. Nancy, who works in urban planning, is bitching about a coworker to Bridget, who's an ER nurse at
City. Nancy, still a stunner in her early forties, can talk paint off a wall;
Bridget, meek and mousy and perpetually pickled when not working,
barely utters a full sentence in a given day.

Nancy finishes her rant about someone named Felix and the coffee
maker in the break room and flicks her eyes at Bobby. "You need to
lose a few pounds, Michael. Don't you think he needs to lose weight,
Bridge?"

Bridget looks down at her knees.

"That's a rather unkind way to greet a man." Bobby peels back the
tab on his beer.

"I want you to live a long life."

"You used to tell me I was too skinny."

"But that was the heroin."

The word "Oh!" pops out of Bridget's mouth in horrified surprise.

"Well, it's not a secret!" Nancy says.

"Actually," Bobby says, "it kinda is."

"To the outside world." Nancy waves at the windows. "Not in
here."

Claire comes through the side door off the driveway and hangs her
umbrella on a hook. "What's not in here?"

"We're talking about Michael's problem."

"The drug thing?" Claire pulls the cork from a bottle of red, pours
herself a glass. Kisses Bobby's head lightly as she comes around him
to take a seat.

"Yes, the drug thing," Nancy says. "He thinks we're going to blab it
to the world."

"Why would we do that?"

"No one said you would," Bobby says. "I just find it uncomfortable
to talk about."

"You're a fucking hero," Claire says, and Bobby is touched to see

Bridget look at him with wide eyes and an emphatic nod. "You know how many people kick that shit?"

"Very few," Bobby admits.

"But you did." Claire raises her glass to him and drinks.

"I was just telling him he could lose a few pounds," Nancy says, "and it turned into this thing."

"What *thing*?" Bobby says.

"See, he's getting upset."

"I'm not getting upset."

"Yeah, you are."

"Jesus Christ."

"Like I just said. Upset."

Bobby sighs and asks Claire how her day was.

"We," Claire says, turning her wineglass in a small circle on the table, "have a real storm of shit coming. I don't think anyone realizes yet."

Claire is a secretary at the Metropolitan District Commission Police barracks in Southie. MDC cops work the beaches and the parks and leave the project crime to city cops. So most city cops think MDC cops are pussies, but Bobby's always found them to be the most knowledgeable source of information for all things Southie.

"This the busing thing?" Bobby asks.

Claire nods. "We're getting some ugly intel. Mass-unrest kinda ugly."

"It'll blow over," Bobby says, just to be optimistic.

"I don't think so," Claire says. "You're working that colored kid's death, right?"

"I am."

"Was he a dealer?" Nancy wants to know.

Bobby shakes his head.

"Well, what was he *doing* there?"

"Car broke down."

"He shoulda taken better care of it."

"Oh, so it's his fault," Claire says with a roll of her eyes.

"I'm not saying it's his fault," Nancy says, "just that if he'd taken better care of his car, it wouldn't have broken down and he wouldn't have died."

Claire says, "Sounds like you're saying it's his fault."

"I said the exact opposite!"

Claire turns to Bobby. "You making arrests soon?"

"Not unless we catch some big breaks. Pretty sure we know who did it. But knowing it and proving it, you know, big difference."

"Well, give us a heads-up if you think you're gonna bust anyone white from Southie anytime near the first day of school. Cuz this city is about to go *boom*." She refills her glass of wine.

"I dunno," he says, suddenly weary.

"You don't know what?" his sister Diane asks. Coming down the front hall now, just off her shift at the public library in Upham's Corner. Goes immediately to the stove and turns on the kettle for her tea.

"We're talking about the kid got killed at Columbia Station," Nancy says.

"You caught that?" Diane asks Bobby.

"I did."

"I heard Marty Butler's guys were involved," Claire says.

"Eh. More like wannabe–Marty Butler guys. But"—Bobby thinks of George Dunbar for a second—"if he takes a personal interest, he could cause headaches, sure."

The Butler crew has a lot of cops on their payroll. At both a local and a state level. Even if you're not a dirty cop, you're reluctant to cross or expose the ones who are (or could be; you rarely know for sure). If you do go forward and make a case against Marty or one of his boys, evidence has a way of vanishing, witnesses contract acute amnesia, and the cases tend to die a quick death in open court. Whereupon the cops at the center of them have a history of being demoted or reassigned.

So, if you take a run at the Butler crew, you cannot fucking miss. Not if you're fond of the little things—a living wage, a pension at the end of it, or a roof over your head. Shit like that.

Claire knows the ins and outs of police culture the way the rest of them don't. She pats Bobby's hand and says, "Be careful. No one's life is worth your own."

Bobby has fought a war—okay, a "police action"—in a country nine thousand miles away trying to prove the opposite.

Nancy, always the first to go for the jugular, chimes in. "And you gotta think about Brendan."

Brendan is Bobby's son. He's nine and lives with his mother except on weekends, when he comes here and spends forty-eight hours with his father, five crazy, doting aunts, and gentle, bleak-hearted Uncle Tim, the failed priest. Bobby loves Brendan in a way that defies every notion he ever had about love before his son entered the world. He loves him beyond all capacity for rational thought. He loves him more than he loves all other people or things or dreams—including himself, including his own—combined.

"Nobody," he says to his sister, "not even Marty Butler, is crazy enough to come after a cop. And even if he was, he sure as shit wouldn't come after a cop's kid. Not if he wants to see the next day of his life. Where do you come up with this shit, Nance?"

Nancy, never one to admit a mistake, pivots. "I wasn't talking about physical harm, *Michael*, I was talking about you losing your job, your pension. And then what will that treacherous cow you used to be married to do to our weekends with Brendan?"

"It's a fair point," Diane says, and even Bridget nods in agreement.

Bobby's family loves his son almost as much as Bobby does. Even Tim, floating in a fog of bitterness and the most esoteric reading material Bobby's ever come across, manages to visibly lighten on weekends. And it's not just because Brendan is the sole nephew (or niece). Brendan is, simply put, a wonderful individual. Nine years old and he's thoughtful, empathetic, profoundly curious, funny as fuck, and warm. It's as if he somehow inherited the best traits of his blood relatives but none of their damage. Yet, anyway.

His sisters would say, "That's only because Shannon doesn't have him all to herself," but the truth is that Shannon is a good mother. Terrible wife and didn't come highly recommended as a daughter or sibling, but she loves her son, and she's dedicated herself to his upbringing in a way she never dedicated herself to anything or anyone in her life.

"I won't lose my job or my pension or my boy," Bobby tells his sisters now.

"As long as you don't fuck with Marty Butler."

"He's a fucking criminal," Bobby says. "I'm a cop."

"He's a *connected* criminal," Claire reminds him.

It isn't just fellow cops Marty Butler has in his pocket. There are judges for sure, probably at least one congressman or state senator, and maybe, just maybe, the darkest of the dark whispers say, someone or maybe a half-dozen someones in federal law enforcement. Over the years, far too many potential witnesses against Marty or his associates—whose identities were kept under lock and key, mind you—have vanished or been killed.

"I know," Bobby assures them all. "It was kids chased Auggie Williamson into the station. And no matter what I find out, it's not looking like first-degree murder. Might not rise much higher than involuntary manslaughter." He yawns into his fist, exhausted. "I'm gonna hit it, ladies."

He puts his beer can in the trash, gives each sister a peck on the cheek, and heads up to bed.

After a shower, he sits by his window and smokes and looks out at the night. He told his sisters the truth—he doubts the kids who were instrumental in the events that led to Auggie Williamson's death will face serious prison time. And that fact, he realizes, was what created the sudden wave of exhaustion.

He'd stood with the parents, Reginald and Calliope Williamson, as they identified their son in the morgue. They didn't cry or wail. They took in the breadth of their son lying on the metal table and each ran their hands down one of his arms—Reginald on the left, Calliope on the right. Then they did the same to his cheeks. With their hands there—each pressed to their son's face—Reginald said, "I love you, my son," and Calliope said, "We are always with you."

Bobby's seen a lot of parents identify their dead offspring. It stopped getting to him some time ago. But the way the Williamsons beheld their son, how they'd caressed his arms and face, as if doing so might provide warmth on his journey to the other side, stuck with Bobby for most of the day.

If four black kids had chased a white kid into the path of a train, they'd be facing life. If they entered a plea, the best offer would be a minimum of twenty years hard time. But the kids who chased Auggie Williamson into the path of a train won't, Bobby knows, face more than five years. If that.

And sometimes that disparity wears him the fuck out.

Bobby finishes his cigarette and climbs into bed.

When he closes his eyes, he can see Reginald and Calliope's palms gliding ever so slowly along the bare arms of their dead son.

Not how you ever imagined it would end twenty years after you first burped him and changed his diapers.

Bobby's killed two people in his life. Neither could have been older than eighteen. One may have been fifteen, sixteen. Bobby has no way of knowing for sure. He killed them both in Vietnam on the same day while he defoliated bush near his base. The VC hid in vegetation. They harvested food from vegetation. So Uncle Sam sent Bobby and his platoon out with a South Vietnamese platoon to poison the fuck out of the countryside around their base. They had hand sprayers and spray trucks. Farther south they were using helicopters. Someday soon, Bobby had heard, they planned to drop the shit out of planes.

The kids who came out of the bush did so from both sides of the road, skinny little fuckers with square heads and rifles or machetes bigger than they were, firing or swinging away like it was do or die, now or never. Which, as it turns out, it was. Bobby shot one of them in the face with his M14, was tackled right in the road by another who had a fucking machete but didn't think to use it until Bobby was on the ground. Bobby put the muzzle of his .45 into the kid's abdomen and fired up twice. Blew the kid's esophagus to shreds. Was looking into the boy's eyes as those bullets ripped through his body. Was looking into his eyes a few seconds later when the boy died, Bobby thinking, *Why didn't you use the machete before you tackled me?*

That was back in the days when the VC was still figuring it out. That morning Bobby and the other guys killed fifteen of them, the whole gang. The corpses lay on the road afterward, and it was clear from their rib cages that none of them had eaten a full meal in months.

Two of them were dead because they'd tried to kill Corporal Michael "Bobby" Coyne of Dorchester, Massachusetts. But he knew they were really dead because they were in the way. Of profit. Of philosophy. Of a worldview that said rules apply only to the people who aren't in charge of making them.

Call them gooks, call them niggers, call them kikes, micks, spics, wops, or frogs, call them whatever you want as long as you call them something—anything—that removes one layer of human being from their bodies when you think of them. That's the goal. If you can do that, you can get kids to cross oceans to kill other kids, or you can get them to stay right here at home and do the same thing.

Bobby lies in a soft comfortable bed nine thousand miles and twelve years removed from those dead boys on the road and decides that tomorrow he's going to haul all four of those Southie kids in.

13

The next morning Bobby sends out four cruisers to pick the kids up. The uniforms come back with only two of the kids, though. Julie Fennessy still seems to be in the wind; no one's seen her since the night Auggie Williamson died. The rumor on the street is that she's down in Florida, but nobody knows where specifically. It nags at Bobby— the mother was clearly worried about her daughter's whereabouts. But if the girl was involved in a death, taking off to Florida might make sense, particularly to a seventeen-year-old.

The other miss is George Dunbar, the drug dealer. He's the son of Marty Butler's main piece of ass, which might mean the patrolmen didn't look too hard for him or maybe didn't even look at all.

Which means when Bobby and Vincent go down to holding, the only two assholes waiting for them in the interview rooms are Ronald Collins and Brenda Morello. Ronald Collins, a Southie kid from a line of Collinses who go back to the potato famine, is as dumb as his older brothers, his father, and his three uncles, most of whom, per Bobby's recent research, have done time. He's a hard case not because he's particularly hard but because he's too fucking stupid to know there's any other way to be.

Brenda Morello, on the other hand, with her wet eyes and her shaky chin, is the jackpot. She's been ready to blab since the moment she was picked up walking to her summer job at Sullivan's on Castle Island. When Bobby and Vincent enter the interview room, she looks up at them with her tear-streaked face, and the first words out of her mouth are "Can I please go home?"

Bobby takes the seat across from her.

Vincent remains standing, which, of course, makes Brenda more nervous.

Bobby gives her his friendliest smile. "Just want to ask you a couple of questions."

"And then I can go home?"

She can walk right out the door right now—she hasn't been charged with anything—but she doesn't grasp that, and it's not part of their job description to enlighten her.

"Can you tell us what you did Saturday night?"

Brenda pretends to think about it, looking up at the ceiling for a moment. "I dunno. Hung out."

"Where?"

"You know."

"We don't."

"Around."

"Around Columbia Park?" Bobby says.

She stares back at him, her mind working furiously now that his question confirms all her fears about why she's there.

"You were there with Ronald Collins, George Dunbar, and Jules Fennessy."

"Maybe?" she tries.

"No fucking maybe about it," Vincent says as he walks behind her.

Her eyes fill. Vincent walks behind her again and she tenses, expecting a slap.

"Brenda," Bobby says gently, "look at me."

She does.

"We know you were there. And then something happened."

"What happened?"

"Why don't you tell us?"

Bobby can see it consuming her suddenly—this terrible knowledge she's kept inside of her for almost a week now.

But she replies, "Nothing happened. Nothing I remember."

Bobby pops open his briefcase, removes a photo of Auggie Williamson, and places it on the table. It's not just any photo. Bobby goes for the jugular—it's the morgue photo.

It has the desired effect. Brenda's face half crumbles, and she puffs air like a fish in a bucket.

"No," she says. "Nothing happened."

Now Vincent does hit her. Just a quick flick of his fingers off the back of her head. She yelps. In outrage more than pain.

Bobby puts a finger on the photo. "This young man is dead. And we have it on good authority, Brenda, that you were one of the last people to see him alive."

She shakes her head several times. "No."

Vincent stands directly behind her. "Say no again, you little twat, and see where it gets you. You ever spent time in an ICU?"

Bobby flicks him a *dial it back* glance and then waits for Brenda to look at him again before he asks her, "Were you the one who said, 'You run slow for a nigger'?"

Brenda's mouth forms an O of shock. "I never said that."

"No?" Bobby looks at Vincent for a moment. "We heard you did."

"Well, then someone's fucking lying, cuz I didn't say that."

"But you were on the platform at Columbia Station when *someone* said it."

"I—What? No, I was—No, I was not on any platform. I was at Columbia *Park* with my friends, and I got in a fight with my boyfriend and I left. And they went to the beach."

"We have witnesses who place you on the subway platform."

"Well, they're lying."

"Why would they do that?"

"I dunno. Ask them."

"We can put you in a lineup."

That puts a fresh quiver in her chin.

"If we put you in a lineup, this lady you knocked down, she's gonna remember you, Brenda."

"I didn't knock any lady down," Brenda says with clear indignation.

"That's not what she said," Vincent says.

"Well, she's lying."

"Everyone's lying, aren't they, Brenda?"

"Maybe not, but she is."

"She was pretty convincing," Bobby says. "Has her elbow all scraped up. Says she stepped off the outbound train and you slammed into her."

"We weren't on the outbound side of the platform," Brenda says. "We were on the inbound." She realizes her mistake a second too late. Lowers her head, stares at her shoes.

When she raises her head, Bobby can see in her eyes that they broke her. She'll tell them everything now. She won't stop talking until sunup.

There's a soft rap on the door, and Vincent opens it on Tovah Shapiro, attorney at large. Even before Tovah Shapiro crosses the threshold, she's already telling Brenda, "Don't say another fucking word."

Tovah Shapiro is the worst kind of defense attorney—she used to be a prosecutor, so she knows how cops think. Plan. Act.

"Did they read you your rights?"

Brenda has no idea who this woman is.

"Did they?"

"No," Brenda manages.

"My name is Tovah Shapiro. I'm your attorney." She sits at the table by her "client."

"Don't you mean you're Marty Butler's attorney?" Bobby asks.

Tovah cocks her head at him. "Hey, Bobby. How you been?"

"Been good, Tovah. You?"

"Never better. Still living at Mommy and Daddy's house?" Before

Bobby can answer, she turns back to Brenda. "So you weren't Miran-dized."

"What?"

"Did anyone say the words 'You are under arrest' to you?"

"No."

"Then we can go."

"Right now?"

"Right now, sweetheart."

As Brenda stands, she chin-gestures at Vincent. "He hit me."

Tovah whistles slowly, says to Vincent, "With complaints already pending against you? Oh, Vinny, you make it so easy."

Bobby holds up the photo of Auggie Williamson in front of Brenda. Brenda looks and then quickly looks away. "He was a human being, Brenda. You know what happened to him. We can offer you a deal."

Tovah gives that a sharp laugh. "You have to be able to charge some-one with something, Bobby, before you offer a deal."

"We'll make that happen real soon."

Tovah rolls her smoky eyes at him. Everything about Tovah is smoky. Smoky and sexy as hell—the way she moves, the way she laughs, the way she chews her bottom lip before she delivers one bomb or another.

"You've got nothing." She searches his eyes for confirmation.

Bobby hopes he's giving her dead eyes in return. He's trying like hell. "We've got plenty."

Her eyes keep searching his. Roving. If she keeps it up much longer, he'll need a cold shower. "I repeat—you've got nothing."

They exit the interview room and find Rum Collins standing in the hallway alongside Boon Fletcher of Fletcher, Shapiro, Dunn & Levine. Boon gives Bobby a withering roll of his eyes, as if to say he expected better of him, and Bobby uses his middle finger to scratch the bridge of his nose.

He and Vincent stand in the hall and watch the two Southie kids walk out with two lawyers they couldn't afford if they hit the number every day for a month straight, and Bobby knows that if they want to close this case now, it just got a hell of a lot fucking harder.

After he punches out, Bobby can feel the eels creeping into his blood, starting to itch. In the past, the primary way to scratch that itch was the needle, the spoon, and the brown powder. Now he recognizes it as a sign that it's been too long since he went to a meeting.

He finds one in a church basement in Roxbury. He walks down the steps into the basement room that smells the way all Narcotics Anonymous meeting rooms smell—of coffee and cigarette smoke and donuts.

He takes a seat in the circle. Sparse attendance tonight—eleven bodies for thirty chairs—and no one's too chatty. A white businessman with a briefcase looks really pissed off; a Puerto Rican woman dressed like a maid seems embarrassed. There's a chunky black guy wearing construction boots caked with the same plaster dust that salts his hair. A woman who looks like a grade school teacher, a middle-aged guy with the sad eyes of a dog in the pound, a twenty-year-old who's probably court-ordered and looks like he could be high right now. Three of them Bobby's crossed paths with at other meetings for sure—the black Pan Am stewardess, the Polish truck driver, the birdlike woman who lost one of her kids in a fire. But no one's in a sharing mood tonight. Finally, the guy running the group, Doug R., looks to Bobby and says, "How about you, friend? Care to share?"

It's been months since Bobby shared at a meeting. He's been warned by his sponsor, Mel, a retired cop, that this is another sign a slip could be coming. Walling oneself off into one's own bullshit is its own form of dishonesty.

After a few dry coughs and a few false starts, he manages to get out a couple of sentences. "I had this dream the other night. My mother and a friend of mine from the marines were looking for me on a street in Hué."

"In Way?" asks a woman with frizzy blond hair and sharp green eyes. She's the one Bobby guessed might be a teacher.

"Hué. It's a city in Vietnam. I was stationed around there for a while. So, yeah, my mother, who died when I was a kid, and my buddy Carl Johansen, who died when I was over there, they're walking up this street looking for me. And I can see them because I'm in this, like, empty storefront with windows that stretch the entire block. And I'm running right alongside them yelling, 'Hey, it's me! It's me!' But they can't hear me. I start banging on the windows and they still can't hear me. Then I reach the end of the building. And I can't get out. My mother and Carl just keep walking and calling my name until I can't see them anymore. And then, after a while, I can't hear them anymore. So, so I turn around in this empty store, and there's a table with my lighter and my spoon and my powder on it. The syringe is brass-plated. Really comfy-looking chair for me to sit in. So I do. And I, ya know, get my works in order and shoot up. I won't lie—it felt fucking great."

People shift in their chairs. He can feel Doug R. watching him carefully, wondering if he made a mistake asking Bobby to share.

"I think," Bobby says, "that Carl was in my dream because, for a long time, I used the war as an excuse to shoot up. 'I saw this terrible thing, I saw that terrible thing, so I got lost.' But war didn't make me lost. I came back without a scratch. But I did get lost over there. Because I was like a child again. I knew nothing, not even the language. I didn't know their gods, I didn't know their customs, what was the right or wrong way to behave. I was just a twenty-two-year-old with a gun." He looks out at the group, can't tell from their eyes or their body language if he's going on too long, if he's connecting with any of them. But he plows forward, stumbling into each sentence like a toddler learning to walk. "This city here, it's kinda gray all the time. You know?" He looks up at the ceiling. "Right now the sun shines during the day, but it's pretty gray seven months out of the year. Or maybe, I dunno, it was just gray in my house growing up. I think of my house after my mother died—maybe even when she was still alive—and it just feels like everything was the color of the sidewalk, even the air.

"But in-country? Vietnam?" He looks around the circle. "You've never seen the color green until you've seen Vietnam. I've been trying to describe it for years and just fucking failing—the rice paddies in the morning with the mist coming off them and the blood-orange sky at night and birds flying low over the deltas and, I dunno, it looks like a place gods would choose to go on vacation. Filled with wonder. But that beauty got all tangled up with death, and fucked up my head once I realized that *I* was death, walking around with my big gun. I was the one killing all the beauty." He notices he's involuntarily hung his head and corrects it. Looks them all in the eyes. "But when I shot up, that went away, and all I could feel was the wonder. When I shot up, it felt like, like . . ." He fixes on the face of the blond woman, sees something in her eyes that feels desperate and hopeful at the same time. "Like all that beauty spread through my veins. It found a home in my body. And I was perfect. I was whole."

The blond woman blinks. A single tear falls from her eye and breaks as it crests her cheekbone into three tinier tears that feel, for Bobby, like a trio of sacred C-words—communion, consecration, consummation.

The woman looks away, but Bobby can feel the eyes of the rest of the room on him. He shrugs, suddenly embarrassed to have gone on for so long.

Doug R. says, "Thanks for sharing."

There's a smattering of polite golf claps.

The angry-looking guy in the business suit says with precise enunciation, "I am a heroin addict because God, if not dead, is certainly on sabbatical."

Bobby can feel everyone trying not to groan.

• • •

On the front steps, as Bobby's leaving, the blond woman comes down the steps alongside him. She says, "Do people in there know you're a cop?"

He considers her, realizes there's something vaguely familiar about her. "It's not something I advertise."

"You arrested me once. Two years ago."

Shit. This is exactly why Bobby doesn't admit his profession in the meetings.

"I've never forgotten you," she says. "The hard face but the kind voice." She lights a cigarette and stares through the smoke at him when she exhales. "Were you using then?"

"Two years ago?" He nods. "That would have been right before I kicked it."

"So, you were using, but you were busting addicts like me."

Bobby tries not to hide from his ugly truths anymore. "Yes."

Everyone else has gone to their cars. It's just the two of them in front of the church. A slight breeze slides through the trees and fingers the strands of their hair. In the distance, they can hear the traffic on the southeast expressway—a quick horn beep, the rattle-and-thump of truck tires.

She smiles. It's warm and sudden. "You arrested me, but you never charged me."

"No?"

She shakes her head. "You put me in a car and drove me toward the station house. But then you asked me who I used to be before I got hooked on junk, and I told you I was a *functioning* druggie, thank you very much. Had a good job as a—"

"Social worker." He smiles, remembering. "Your hair was different."

"It's naturally kind of a mousy brown, so I color it now. Got a perm."

"It's becoming," he says, and immediately wants to shoot himself in the fucking head. *Becoming?* Where the fuck did that come from?

"You drove me to a clinic on Huntington Avenue," she says. "You remember?"

"A bit."

"You walked me in and said, 'You can still go back to who you really are.'"

"Did it take?"

"Not for another six months. But I've been clean for four hundred and eighty-one days now."

"Good for you."

"It's still scary. Is it scary for you?"

"Oh, yeah."

She holds out her hand. "Carmen."

"You don't look like a Carmen."

"I know. But my mom was into opera."

Bobby smiles like he knows what the connection between the two things could be. He shakes her hand. "Michael. But everyone calls me Bobby."

"For God's sakes, why?"

"It's a long story."

"Could you tell me on the walk to my car? I'm several blocks away, and it's a little dicey around here."

"Sure."

They turn up the sidewalk together.

It's a soft summer night that smells of imminent rain. Bobby walks Carmen toward her car. He glances sideways once, catches her glancing sideways right back at him with a secretive smile, and he considers the possibility that maybe the opposite of hate is not love. It's hope. Because hate takes years to build, but hope can come sliding around the corner when you're not even looking.

14

The phone rings and rings. Mary Pat stares at it, no idea how long she's been sitting on the couch in the living room, no idea how long that phone's been ringing. It stops. And then, a minute later, it starts again. Stops after nine rings. A minute of silence. Maybe more. Maybe five minutes. And then the phone ringing. Once. Twice. Three times. It's halfway through the fourth ring when Mary Pat gently removes the cord at the back.

It must be Meadow Lane. She's supposed to be at work right now. That realization almost breaks through the numbness that has defined her since she opened the bag Marty Butler gave her. But the numbness is still too strong. It's head-to-toe Novocain. It's numbness with weight—there's nothing gentle or calming about it. It clamps down on her skin, blood, brain, and nerve endings. Like a hand gripping the back of her neck and pressing her face against the ground because it fears what will happen should she ever get to her feet.

It needn't fear. She can't imagine regaining her feet. Not in any way that matters. She definitely can't imagine going back to work for a while. Doubts there'll be a job still waiting for her by the time she's ready to return. And that's fine.

She's found a station on her radio—WJIB—that plays only classical music, and she can't stop listening to it. She doesn't turn it off even when she goes to sleep (not that there's much sleep happening in her life these days). She's been a Top 40 girl her whole life, never into any particular band, just always liking the music of the day. This summer it's been "Rock the Boat" and "Billy Don't Be a Hero" and her favorite, "Don't Let the Sun Go Down on Me." But all that music sounds silly to her now, because it wasn't made with someone like her in mind. Even that lyric "Losing everything is like the sun going down on me" feels insufficient, because losing everything doesn't feel like the sun going down on her, it feels like an atom bomb went off inside her and she's now part of the mushroom cloud, a thousand little pieces of her breaking apart and floating out into space in a thousand different directions.

With classical pieces, she doesn't know the song names or the names of the composers (unless the DJ chimes in at the end of a four- or five-song block, at which point the early songs are too far back to place a name to the appropriate tune), but the music speaks to her grief in a way nothing else can. It slides *through* the Novocain. Not enough to find her heart but enough to find her head. She floats through the notes as if the notes are currents in a larger body of water—a dark body of water, she's sure, a wide river at night—and travels into a space in her mind where her entire history and that of her family before her and the family she's made are all intertwined. She can sense—though not feel or articulate—a connection between all who have lived and died in her bloodline. Of course, part of the connection is ethnic heritage—they were all Irish and all married only other Irish since the first of them, Damien and Mare Flanagan, stepped off the boat at Long Wharf in 1889—but the other part of the connection is more elusive. And yet, riding the current of Beethoven or Brahms or Chopin or Handel, she can touch a part of herself that feels far more true than factual, an Original Mary Pat, a Mother Eve Mary Pat, a Mary Pat rooted so far back she may have breathed her last on a peat bog in the village of Tully Cross in the townland of Gorteenclough back in the twelfth century. And that Original Mary Pat understands something in the music about the ties that bind them all in this family—from the firstborn American Flanagan (Connor) to the lastborn American Fennessy (Jules) that gives meaning to the story of the bloodline. Present-Day Mary Pat can't put her finger on what that is, but she listens to the notes in numb belief that she might one day.

A bust goes down outside her window. Two cops chase one of the Phelan brothers (who knows which one; there're like nine of them, all heading to jail from the moment they left the maternity ward) into Commonwealth and tackle him on the asphalt in front of the Morris Building. A Phelan brother getting busted is no big deal—like a leaf falling from a tree—but one of the cops is black. That brings out the neighbors with their loud mouths screaming nigger this and nigger that, and then some kids get up on the roofs, and the bottles and the rocks rain down. Pretty soon, black-and-whites and paddy wagons pull down the small lanes that twist between the buildings. They screech to a stop. Car doors snap open and closed.

The parents back off, but the kids on the roofs find some bags of garbage somewhere and start pelting the cops with rotten lettuce and empty cans of Dinty Moore, soft potatoes that explode when they hit cars or heads. After a while, the kids bolt, and it all settles down. One of the cops looks around at the off-white splatter of potato everywhere and the windows pocked with fresh cracks and splinters from rocks and the shattered bottles all over the ground, and he calls out to all the window screens surrounding the spot where the melee took place: "You can clean this yourselves. We ain't sending Sanitation, you fucking animals."

And they pull out of there like an occupying army disgusted by those they're forced to govern.

Later, the women and the kids who did it (several with fresh abrasions or black eyes courtesy of the men who fathered them) come out with brooms and dustpans and buckets and set to cleaning up the mess. Normally, Mary Pat wouldn't blink before she hopped to and helped them—that's what community is based on, she's always thought, pitching in—but she just can't get off the couch. It's like she's nailed to it.

And where is that community for her? By this point, she knows the gossip has to be all over the neighborhood—no one has seen Jules Fennessy in six days. Word will also be out that it's best no one ask about her either. So everyone knows, as she does, that her daughter is dead.

But no one visits. No one checks in.

Big Peg came once. Banged on the door a few times, but Mary Pat didn't answer. She knew no matter what evidence she presented to Big Peg that Marty Butler's crew had killed Jules, Big Peg would reject it. Marty isn't just Southie's protector. He isn't just Southie's favorite son. Marty isn't just the rebel for them all who thumbs his nose at the outside establishment. Marty *is* Southie. To believe Marty is evil—not merely criminal, not a practitioner of hijinks and shenanigans, not just running an underworld that needs to be run by *someone*, so why not him?—is to believe Southie is evil. And Peg could never do that. So, instead of baring her soul to a sister who would turn her back to that soul and ask it to put its clothes back on in the name of common decency, Mary Pat didn't answer the door.

She finally does answer the door when the SWAB Sisters come calling. There're half a dozen of them, unrelated by birth or marriage, but so called because they've been friends for at least twenty years and were the first group to form against the school committee's decision to even *hear* the case of the colored families who sued in *Morgan* v. *Hennigan*. SWAB stands for Southie Women Against Busing. Mary Pat attended one of their earliest meetings, way back in '71, long before anyone truly believed this could turn into anything real; she'd just shown up for the donuts and the Riunite Lambrusco. Back then, SWAB consisted solely of the six women who now show up at her door on the seventh day since she's seen Jules—Carol Fitzpatrick, Noreen Ryan, Joyce O'Halloran, Patty Byrnes, Maureen Kilkenny, and Hannah Spotchnicki (née Carmody).

Mary Pat agreed to become an actual member in 1973, when it was starting to appear like, holy shit, this busing bullshit might actually *happen,* but she isn't what you'd call an avid member. She'll do something if asked, but she never seeks them out. Most of the women in SWAB—and there are a couple hundred now—are like Mary Pat, but the SWAB Sisters, the original six, those bitches are evangelical.

The face of their leader, Carol Fitzpatrick, looms in the eyehole in Mary Pat's door, the other five fanned out behind her. Mary Pat is fresh from a shower she can't remember taking, standing there in a robe that saw better days before the Kennedy-Nixon debates, and feeling number than ever. The women on the other side of the eyehole look like something from a cartoon—if not harmless, certainly comical. Carol has to knock only a few times before Mary Pat opens the door.

They seem taken aback, as if they didn't truly expect to see her. Or, if they did, they expected her to look better.

"Mary *Pat!*" Carol says, and claps her hands joyfully. "Where have you been?"

"Here." Mary Pat steps aside to let them in.

No one seems to notice the overflowing sink and overflowing ashtrays, the empty beer cans everywhere, the glasses sticky with liquor sediment, the takeout pizza boxes, the takeout fish-and-chips box, the McDonald's bags crumpled on the kitchen counter.

"We need to get you ready," Joyce says.

"Ready for what?" Mary Pat asks, and they all laugh.

"Ready for *what!*" Patty Byrnes says. "Oh, you're a caution."

"Come, come." Maureen Kilkenny leads her down the hallway toward her bedroom.

A second later, or so it seems, Carol has joined them in there, and the two women are going through Mary Pat's meager closet. They toss one dress on the bed, followed by another. Then a blouse-and-skirt combo. Next come the shoes—Mary Pat has only two pairs of dress-up shoes, one heels, one flats, so that immediately narrows it down to a 50/50 choice.

They hold each dress and then the blouse-and-skirt combo up to Mary Pat's body, and she watches herself let them, can hear them chirping about which one looks best and which could go with the shoes—Has to be the flats, Carol says, no one can wear heels as long as they'll be standing, plus it sends a conflicting message. Mary Pat sees herself standing in her bedroom but it's not her, it's Novocain Mary Pat, the lost, the numb, the beaten. Carol and Maureen decide on the blouse and skirt. The blouse is the red of wine and the skirt is a plaid number, vaguely tartan. The flats are black. Once the clothes are on, they work on her hair and makeup in the bathroom, and Mary Pat catches sight of herself in the mirror and feels a strange pride in acknowledging that she looks like a ghoul, like something that has been siphoned of all blood but nonetheless walks among the living.

They whisk her back out to the main room, where the other four wait. The fast-food boxes and beer cans are gone, the ashtrays are emptied, the glasses are drip-drying in the dish rack.

"Where are we going?" Mary Pat asks.

Again, they all laugh at the absurdity of the question.

But then Hannah Spotchnicki bursts out with "The rally!"

"At City Hall," Carol says.

"Oh," Mary Pat manages. "Right."

"Can't go there without you, silly!" Noreen Ryan says way too chirpily when you consider the fear in her eyes.

"We need everyone," Carol says. "Everybody we can lay our hands on."

The absurdity of the sentence in her present circumstances is not lost on Mary Pat. She smiles at Carol. "Every body you can lay your hands on?"

"Uh-huh."

"What if you can't?"

"What?"

"Lay your hands on the body?"

Mary Pat has no idea how long everyone just stares at her—could be a second, could be five minutes—but most of them seem like they'd prefer to run right out the fucking door.

Maybe, Mary Pat thinks, *I'll become one of those women who pushes her belongings around town in a shopping cart and sleeps in playgrounds.*

"You need fresh air," Carol says. "You need to be a part of something meaningful. You need purpose, Mary Pat. Now more than ever."

Now more than ever.

So they do know.

"Okay," Mary Pat hears herself say.

They move her out that door like she's on a hand truck.

Along the roadway just outside the projects, a school bus waits. If anyone grasps the irony, they don't mention it. The bus is a faded denim blue with the ghostly words *Franklin Middle School* still visible under a layer of old paint. The tires look bald. About twenty women have been waiting on the bus the whole time. They've got the windows down and their cigarette arms out the windows. Several fan themselves. It's not boiling yet—no sun, a cloudy morning—but it's humid as hell.

Mary Pat knows most of the women. Almost all of them have bee-hive hairdos, which is hardly unusual for Southie. What is unusual is that most of them have placed small American flags or what appear to be tea bags in the center of the hives. They barely meet her eyes as she takes her seat near the front with the SWAB Sisters, but she looks at them long enough to confirm that, yes, those are tea bags. As the bus lurches out onto the roadway, Mary Pat looks down the length of it, sees Mary Kate Dooley, Mary Jo O'Rourke, Donna Ferris, Erin Dunne, Tricia Hughes, Barbara Clarke, Kerry Murphy, and Nora

Quinn. Old friends all. And not one looks back at her. Stacked at the rear, taking up the final four seats and the space behind them, are the signs—some, Mary Pat is sure, she assembled herself a few nights ago on the floor of her apartment.

They drive out through South Boston in the humid gray. They smoke and make small talk, and the center of the city looms closer with every intersection they pass through.

"I don't want to talk about her," Joyce O'Halloran is saying to Carol, her hands up by her ears.

"So why are you talking about her?" Carol asks.

"I'm not. She's just a fucking, ya know, an embarrassment. She's what you get with the spoiling and the TV and the music they listen to, everybody glorifying the drugs and the free love. That's sure as hell not how we were raised, but she thinks it's okay to mouth off about everything. Like, fucking *everything*. If I believe in something, she believes the opposite. And not because she believes it. But because she wants to hurt me."

"She wants to hurt you," Carol agrees.

"She wants to hurt you," Hannah chimes in.

"Who's this now?" Mary Pat asks.

"My daughter," Joyce says, waving airily. "Cecilia. Little bitch. Me and my husband are raising five kids, and four of them aren't bad, but this one? The middle one?"

"The middle one's always a trial," Noreen Ryan says.

The Swab Sisters all nod in agreement.

"She's just a teenager," Maureen says. "They go through their phases."

"Mmmm," Joyce says, clearly not convinced.

The bus bounces across the Northern Avenue Bridge and takes a right on Atlantic, and now they're officially out of South Boston and into Boston proper. City Hall is only a mile away.

"Time for us, girls." Carol reaches into her purse and comes back with a palmful of small flags and tea bags.

Mary Pat takes a flag. Instead of sticking it in her hair, she slips the little wooden stake into a buttonhole of her blouse.

Joyce, Carol, and Noreen choose flags. Patty, Maureen, and Hannah go with the tea bags.

Mary Pat watches them help one another place them in their hair and has to ask, "What's with the tea bags?"

"You don't remember? We discussed it at a meeting."

"I must have missed that one."

"The tea party, Mary Pat. The Boston Tea Party?" Hannah says. "When they chucked all the tea into the harbor?"

"I know about that," Mary Pat says.

"Well, we're throwing our own rebellion against tyranny," Patty says. "Hence tea bags."

"Is anyone going to get that?" Mary Pat says.

Several of the women blanch, and Mary Pat can hear murmuring behind her, but it's too late for debate because now they're turning off Sudbury Street onto Congress, the JFK Federal Building canting in the window at the northeast edge of City Hall Plaza, and Mary Pat getting a look now at the sea of people streaming into the plaza from what seems like every direction. The traffic is reduced to a crawl. As they creep along, the concrete edges of City Hall come into view. It's an ugly building, colorless except for some brick at the base of it, graceless from head to toe. Inside, it's worse. It seems constructed solely to make anyone who has to do business with the city realize before even entering the building that the house always wins.

"How many people are we expecting?" Mary Pat asks the group.

Carol says, "Maybe fifteen hundred?"

They reach the curb. As they exit the bus, the bus driver hands everyone another tea bag.

They open the back door and each grabs a sign. Mary Pat's says END JUDICIAL DICTATORSHIP. The woman next to her lifts one that reads

BOSTON UNDER SIEGE. Mary Pat finds herself wishing she'd grabbed that one—it's a better acronym.

They climb the stairs leading from the back of the building to the plaza. The clouds are gone. The sun, bright and blistering, immediately bores into the back of Mary Pat's neck. The crowd moving up the stairs—so thick that Mary Pat and her bus companions seem but specks in the larger throng around them—is already sweating, several faces pink with heat. There are a lot of flags—American flags, Irish flags, sheets tied to poles with neighborhood names: Southie, mostly, but also Dorchester, Hyde Park, Charlestown, and East Boston. Halfway up the stairs, the crowd starts shouting the Pledge of Allegiance, and Mary Pat has to admit it feels good as the words leave her mouth, particularly at the end, when the crowd kicks it up several notches and shout-spits the final words: "liberty and justice for *ALL*!"

She's starting to suspect there're more than fifteen hundred of them, and when they reach the top of the stairs and spill into the plaza, she's overwhelmed to realize there are *thousands* of them. She can't see to the end of them. They have to be nine thousand strong, maybe ten.

Carol leads the group to a fountain where they add their tea bags to hundreds more, the tea staining the water a rusty brown. Mary Pat once again wonders if anyone will get it. She imagines an old flatfoot standing over the fountain later, saying, "Ah, now, don't these morons know that tea tastes better when the water's properly boiled?"

Along the far edge of the crowd—most of them safely across the street at 3 Center Plaza—she notes the counterprotesters. Hippies, mostly, white and scraggly and living on their trust funds; a few blacks with confrontational Afros and dashikis; and finally, a cluster of men and women who look like Mary Pat and the people she knows—working-class Irish, Polish, and Italian. There's not too many of them, but they're there, holding signs that say things like END SEGREGATION NOW (not much of an acronym there either) and EDUCATION IS A CIVIL

RIGHT. Among the group, Mary Pat is shocked to see a few older folks she recognizes—Mrs. Walsh from Old Colony; old Tyrone Folan from Baxter Street; the entire Crowley family from M Street.

Before she can identify anyone else, they're in the sea, buffeted along by some unseeable North Star that leads them to a spot maybe ten feet short of the stage. Here there are no counterprotesters. *Who would dare?* They're packed in hundreds deep—not just Southie, white Dorchester, Hyde Park, Charlestown, and East Boston but the whole fucking *city*—Revere, Everett, Malden, Chelsea, Roslindale—except for (obviously) Mattapan and Roxbury and the sections of Dorchester that are fully black now. In what's come to be called Phase 1, the city will be desegregating fifty-nine of the two hundred schools in the public school system, starting in less than two weeks. Within two years, all two hundred schools will be affected. And that explains the crowd—this will be a problem for *all* of them eventually.

The first three speakers are members of the Boston School Committee, those who fought hardest, for almost a decade, to keep the schools the way they should be. The first speaker, Shirley Brackin from St. William Parish in Dorchester, reiterates what all the people there already know—that none of those in charge of desegregating the schools in a manner as fucked up as busing actually live in the neighborhoods they've decreed must change; that not one of those people sends their kids to public schools; that not one of those people—the white ones, anyway—live in integrated neighborhoods (because there pretty much are no integrated neighborhoods in Boston). The next speaker, Geraldine Guffy of St. Augustine Parish in Southie, rips at the inevitable destruction of their way of life: Theirs is a village life within a city, where neighbors know neighbors because they all grew up together, went to the same schools, played in the same playgrounds and sports leagues, knew one another's parents and grandparents so well, why, if one of those kids got out of line, those other parents and grandparents were free to step in and discipline—with a smack to the head or the backside or just a stern tongue-lashing—as if that kid were their own. "They say this will change the neighborhood in a good way," Geraldine Guffy says, and then has to wait for the roar of boos to die down, "that in some sugar-sweet fairy-tale land, our kids and the colored kids will become friends. But our kids and the colored kids are going to return home every day to their friends and their families in their neighborhoods. They're not going to become friends, just schoolmates. And our traditions, our way of life, our feelings of safety and security? We won't be able to buy those back. You can't buy back something when it's already gone. And all those things will be gone the moment you see that very first bus roll down the street toward *our* high school."

The crowd erupts in a mixture of euphoria and threat. Mary Pat looks back over her shoulder and can't fully grasp the size of it. She's in the center of the plaza, yet the crowd is so immense she can't see any of the streets that surround them.

She can feel their power and their outrage and their sadness, and she's surprised to suddenly feel it with them. For the first time since she opened that bag of money and understood what it signified, she feels *something*. She thought that after losing her daughter, she had nothing, and she mostly does, but she needn't forget that she still has her way of life. She still has her neighborhood and all the people in it. She still has community. And what these social engineers and limousine liberals are doing is taking a wrecking ball to that. To her way of life. To the only life she's ever known and the only thing she has left to defend in this world.

By the time the third speaker, Mike Dowd of Most Precious Blood Parish in Hyde Park, takes the stage, he can get out only a sentence or two before he's drowned out by the roars of the crowd. He waits them out, goes another two sentences, and they roar again. Mary Pat and the half-dozen SWAB Sisters are right there with them, screaming themselves hoarse.

"God made us," Mike Dowd bellows. "God made us women and God made us men and God doesn't make mistakes, right?"

The crowd is a little less sure how to answer, but they mostly cry out, "Right!"

Mike Dowd leans into the mic. "And God made us white and black and brown and Oriental. And was *that* a mistake?"

Again, a bit of hesitation, as if the crowd's confused because no one told them there'd be a quiz, but eventually, a roar of "No!" roils up into the sky.

Mike Dowd shouts, "Exactly! No. God did not make a mistake. He chose to make us white and black and brown and Oriental and even red Indian. Those were the colors he wanted. If He wanted us to mix, then He would have mixed us. Made us half yellow, half blue. Purple and white." Chuckles of approval roll through the crowd. "He didn't make us mixed. Because He doesn't want us to mix."

Well, isn't it the truth? Mary Pat thinks. *Isn't that just the bottom line? We have our way of life, the coloreds have theirs. The Hispanics, theirs. The Orientals have Chinatown, for God's sake, and you don't see anyone trying to force them to disband and disperse across the city. No, they know their place. And as long as they keep knowing it, they will be left in peace to manage their own affairs. And that's all we want.*

But as the morning moves along and the speakers grow louder (and a lot more repetitive), Mary Pat has begun to feel her outrage thin when she catches sight of a woman with the same hair as Jules move through the crowd. The woman's face is rounder and older than Jules's, but the hair is near identical. And suddenly, it's like she's lost her again. Like she's losing her over and over and over. Like she can see the baby Jules cupped, naked and squawking, in her hand, and then she's rushing straight through her daughter's life, observing it the way you observe a train blasting past you—teething, first step, first flu, scraped knees, missing front teeth, first-grade pigtails, second-grade ponytail, a permanent broken heart in fourth grade after Mary Pat tells her Daddy's

never coming home again, acne at twelve, breasts at thirteen along
with apathy for *everything*, eighth-grade graduation, high school dance
nights, the end of the apathetic stage coinciding with Noel's final decline, the return of her spunk, her humor, her loud, goofy laugh—and
then she's gone, her daughter's gone, she's left this life, she's stepped off
into a void. Chambers of Mary Pat's heart she was certain she'd shut
tight fly open, and a sea of loss rushes in. She suddenly can't remember
what she's doing here or why she should give two flying fucks why
blacks or Jews or Orientals cross the bridge into Southie.

Jules.

Jules.

Why'd you leave me?

Where'd you go?

Has the pain stopped, baby?

Is your world warm?

Will you wait for me to find you there?

Please wait.

For a moment she wants to drop, just fall to her knees and wail her
daughter's name. And she might have if, at that moment, the crowd
hadn't surged to the right as though it were a single organism, and
Carol, beside her, hisses one word:

"*Teddy.*"

Mary Pat looks through the throng, and now she can see him, flanked
by security personnel and two MDC cops, his black hair slicked back
and matching his black suit. Edward M. Kennedy. Brother to the dead
president who gave his name to the federal building fifty yards away.
Senator Edward M. Kennedy on the national stage, but here, in Boston, he's Teddy. Mostly it's because he's Irish and the Irish don't put
on airs, so President Kennedy was always Jack, and Attorney General
Robert F. Kennedy was always Bobby, but maybe he's also Teddy because of the three, he's the one they all take a little less seriously. So
clearly the youngest, so clearly the needy one, desperate for approval.

And, of course, they all know he was kicked out of Harvard for cheating and abandoned his mistress in a sinking car in a Martha's Vineyard lagoon and still has an eye for other ladies who aren't his wife, particularly when he goes on his benders in the pubs of Beacon Hill and Hyannis Port. And all of that would be fine for his constituents, the good people of Southie and Charlestown and half of Dorchester, he's one of them, after all, a Hibernian, a mick, a Paddy—except that Teddy's bona fides have been suspect of late. Particularly in matters of race and even more particularly on the matter of busing, which he came out in full support of during several recent interviews.

Mary Pat can feel the crowd turning on him before he even opens his mouth or they theirs. Who is he to stroll down here in his fine suit and slick haircut and expensive tie and shoes and explain to them what's what? They know what's what.

"Hey, Teddy," some guy shouts, "where do your kids go to school, Teddy?"

Teddy ignores the voice, even though the guy keeps asking the question about every fifteen seconds.

By this point, Teddy's almost reached the stage, but the crowd swarms the steps so he can't walk up. He turns to one of the organizers, Bernie Dunn, who wears a brown suit far less expensive than Teddy's, and says, "Are they going to let me up?"

"Doesn't look like it," Bernie says. "Listen to me, Teddy. I—"

"They need to let me up on the stage," Teddy says.

"No, they don't. You're not hearing us. It's despicable what's going on, Teddy."

"I understand your point, but—"

"But nothing. We're not going to have some judge tell us how to run things, tell us where our kids are going to go."

"I understand, but you have to agree something had to be done."

"They're gonna rip our neighborhoods apart, parish by parish, and you're letting them. Hell, you're helping them."

"Are you going to let me talk?" Teddy asks.

"No." Bernie seems a little surprised himself. "We've heard all you have to say."

And Bernie Dunn turns his back on a Kennedy.

Everyone adjacent to him does the same. The next cluster of people follows suit. And on and on through the crowd. When the surge reaches the SWAB Sisters and Mary Pat, Mary Pat feels light-headed as she turns her back on Senator Edward M. Kennedy of the Commonwealth of Massachusetts. It's like turning her back on the pope.

Those who don't turn away from Teddy turn toward him, and Mary Pat can hear it getting ugly quick.

"Where do your fucking kids go to school, Teddy?"

"Where do you live, Teddy?"

"You're an embarrassment to your brother and to your people."

"Go back to Brookline, you fucking faggot."

"You're not one of us anymore!"

"Fuck you, nigger lover! Fuck you! Fuck you! Fuck you!"

They hear the commotion and turn back to see the MDC cops and the security guys hustling Teddy toward the building named after his brother. Mary Pat is baffled by the back of Teddy's suit. It's almost completely white now, as if he's been shit on by a flock of birds. It takes her a second to realize it isn't bird shit.

It's spit.

The crowd is spitting on a Kennedy.

Mary Pat feels ill. *Isn't there a line we don't cross?* she wants to ask the crowd. *Isn't there a place we don't allow ourselves to go?*

The crowd keeps spitting on the senator until his guards and the two cops get him into the federal building. The front of the building is clear glass, so Mary Pat can see them hustling him toward the elevators, and that should have been the end of it—everyone should have regained their sense—but then a pane of glass the size of a semitruck shatters.

The crowd lets out a roar of approval. Joyful shrieks split the air like birdshot.

Half a dozen police officers rush into the crowd from the edge of the plaza. It serves as a reminder that an entire police station sits less than a block away, so no one rushes the building. The cops don't swing their clubs or anything stupid, they just hold their hands at arm's length so the crowd will take a few steps back. They say a lot of "Now, now, we understand" and "We get it, we do," as if they're talking to children having a tantrum.

The crowd keeps yelling—at least a hundred voices screaming about Garrity and Kennedy and hell no we won't go—but the violence stays confined to that one pane of glass, unless you count the spitting.

"Well, they heard us," Carol says to the other SWAB Sisters. "They sure as hell heard us."

Joyce O'Halloran's daughter, Cecilia, approaches the group of women with a scowl on her face. She's got her mother's sharp cheekbones, thin lips, and lack of chin. Her eyes are red with recent tears.

Joyce seems to notice her without really *seeing* her because her tone stays light. "Look what the cat dragged in."

"Can you hear that?" Cecilia says, pointing at the crowd, her eyes growing redder.

Joyce lights a cigarette and stares at her problem child. "Hear what?"

"*That.*"

Mary Pat notices now. The chants of the crowd have coalesced. At first it was a smorgasbord of "Re-sist!" and "End dic-tator-ship!" and "Southie won't go!" but now it's one unified chant:

"Nig-gers suck! Nig-gers suck! Nig-gers suck!"

"I still don't know what you're talking about," Joyce says.

The child's eyes widen. "You don't hear that?"

Joyce's thin lips grow thinner, and she blows her smoke almost directly into her daughter's face. "I hear a lot of things. I hear people laughing at you and your nipples poking through your hippie T-shirt.

When you wear that to the colored school next week, let me know how they treat you."

"I'm not afraid to go to Roxbury High, Ma. It's you parents making it a nightmare, not us kids. *We're* fine."

"Put on a bra," Joyce says, and this time her smoke goes directly into her daughter's face.

Cecilia's face tightens. Her jaw clenches and unclenches and her eyes grow cold. "I can put on a bra no problem. What's your cure for being an asshole?"

Joyce punches her daughter in the side of the head. Joyce is big, her daughter is small, and the punch knocks Cecilia to the ground. When she starts to stand, Joyce grabs her by the hair and swings at her neck with a closed fist, but Mary Pat hooks her arm around Joyce's and stops the punch.

She looks into Joyce's eyes. There are two doses of rage in there—one for Cecilia, one for Mary Pat.

"No," Mary Pat says. "Stop."

Behind her, Cecilia scrambles to her feet.

Mary Pat separates from Joyce, and now they face each other from three feet apart.

The rest of the SWAB Sisters are frozen in shock.

"Mary Pat," Joyce says, "step aside."

Mary Pat shakes her head.

"Step aside!" Carol says.

"Step aside!" Maureen shrieks.

"Mary Pat," Joyce says, breathing shallow, "I will discipline my child as I see fit."

Again Mary Pat shakes her head.

"Get out of her fucking way!" Hannah Spotchnicki screams.

"No one touches this girl," Mary Pat says.

Joyce charges and immediately comes up short when Mary Pat buries her fist in her solar plexus. Joyce hits the ground on her hip, lies there with her mouth open and gasping desperately for breath that's still a good ten seconds away.

Three of the five remaining SWAB Sisters—Hannah, Carol, and Patty—attack as one. They must think they're tough, Mary Pat reasons, because they're from Southie and they've waged reigns of terror over their husbands and children for years. But being from Southie is one thing; being from Commonwealth Housing Development is quite another.

Mary Pat keeps her head down like a bull and hits whatever's nearest. Doesn't just hit—she squeezes, she scratches, she yanks. It's pure street fighting like she hasn't done since she was jumped by three girls at Old Colony back in high school. She rips off earrings, punches pussies, yanks on sagging tits as though milking a cow. She stomps ankles, kicks knees, bites a set of fingers that claw at her face. She loses some hair, gets her face and ears all scratched up, but pretty soon three more bitches are on the ground moaning, and Mary Pat is still standing—no one even got her off her feet—wiping at the blood in her eyes.

She looks around for Cecilia, but the girl is long gone. Noreen and Patty hold up their hands so she knows not to attack them. Both appear petrified and revolted.

Mary Pat turns back to her victims, sitting or lying on the pavement amid torn scraps of clothing, little plastic flags, splatters of blood, and flattened tea bags. Carol is the one nursing the freshly bloody fingers and staring up at her in a kind of dumbfounded fury. The flesh around her right eye is already turning stone blue. It takes her a bit to form a proper sentence, but when she does, it comes out as clear as a bell.

"You're dead to us," she says. "And when word gets out what you did here today, you'll be dead to everyone in Southie."

Mary Pat shrugs. The time for talk has passed. She turns and makes her way out of the crowd, which parts before her every step.

15

The first thing Mary Pat thinks when she reenters her apartment is that her place got robbed while she was at the rally. Nothing looks familiar. She wonders if she somehow let herself into the wrong unit—same layout as hers, yes, but the kitchen counters are clean, the floors have been swept, the ashtrays emptied. Not a beer can or sticky glass or pizza box in sight.

But in the next breath, she remembers . . .

Those bitches cleaned my home.

Was that why she took such pleasure in pounding the fuck out of them?

Possibly. Quite possibly.

She wanders down the hall to her bathroom and stands over the sink and looks in the mirror. She's got a mouse growing under her left eye, scratches on her forehead (none deep), one on her neck (very deep; the blood soaks the collar of her blouse), a fat upper lip. In addition, what the mirror doesn't show is the deep ringing in her right ear, like a fucking phone that won't quit. She's also twisted her left knee pretty good, and someone stomped the ankle of the same leg.

She goes to work first on the scratch in her neck with a series of cotton swabs and hydrogen peroxide, catches her reflection smiling even as she winces from the pain. "Pain means the peroxide's working," her mother always said. "Getting clean hurts."

Mary Pat applies a large flesh-colored bandage to the cut once it's clean. She's got a basketful of Band-Aids, bandages, gauze, iodine, surgical shears, and antiseptic under that sink. It's like the ER at City down there. Back when Dukie was in the Life, she needed it, of course. After he passed, she kept it around for Noel, who never met a conflict he couldn't escalate into a fistfight.

Like mother, like son.

She smiles again. The truth is, she's loved fighting ever since she can remember. Literally. Her first concrete memory of any length is of Willie Pike riding his bike through a puddle in front of the spit of lawn where four-year-old Mary Pat sat fussing over the hair of her Raggedy Ann doll. She saw the gleeful look in the little fucker's eyes as he aimed the bike for the puddle. And he saw that she saw it. He pedaled faster, the little shit. Smashed his tires through the puddle and covered Mary Pat and Raggedy Ann in the slimy water that probably hadn't come from rain—those puddles just sprang up all over Commonwealth, even during weeks of dry weather, and smelled of sulfur and bleach. She chased Willie Pike past four buildings before he wiped out on a turn. And when she got to him, she didn't pause—a harbinger: she *never* paused in a fight—she unleashed. He was six and a boy, so there was no way she was going to win, but he was bleeding from both nostrils and crying like a pussy by the time he did get on top of her. He got a few licks in before Old Lady McGowan pulled him off and slapped him a few times around the head for good measure. Sure now, Old Lady McGowan told him, his father needed to strap his bottom black and blue for hitting a little girl. Old Lady McGowan thumb-poked him in the shoulder a few more times for emphasis before she walked Mary Pat back to the puddle to get her Raggedy Ann. When Mary Pat picked the doll up, it felt like lifting a trophy.

She'd have at least twenty more fights before she reached sixth grade—and those were the ones outside her door. Inside the Flanagan home, it was Rock 'Em Sock 'Em Robots from seven a.m. wake-up to ten p.m. shutdown. The boys—John Patrick, Michael Sean, Donnie,

Stevie, and Bill—lived in one room. At one point, John Patrick's senior year at Southie High and Bill's first year in second grade, all five
of them were living in there at the same time. Mary Pat's father, those
times she could remember him actually being home, would say the
room smelled like a fish's asshole. After John Patrick left—hitching a
ride west; no one had heard from him in twenty years—a battle en-
sued for his top bunk. Donnie, who was stronger than Michael Sean,
got it for the first six months, but Michael Sean spent all that year
working out at L Street until *he* was stronger. About a week of fist-
fights and two broken noses later, Michael Sean got the top bunk, but
Stevie hated the sound of Michael Sean snoring through his broken
nose, so he tried to smother his brother with a pillow—Stevie, pos-
sessor of the scariest glare Mary Pat had ever seen, was always fucked
in the head—and their mother had to break it up. Stevie, who was
thirteen at that point, small and feral like their mother, slammed their
mother's head against the window and broke the pane. That it was
it for Stevie, they shipped him off to St. Luke's Home for Troubled
Boys and never spoke of him again, even when they saw his name in
the papers ten years later for that stickup that went horribly wrong
in Everett.

The stitches—black, thick, and hard as metal, all seven of them—
remained in the back of their mother's head for three weeks, and when
they came out, it wasn't much better. For the rest of her life, Louise
Flanagan's hair grew around the scar and refused to fall over it, so it
looked like all her thoughts, secrets, and shames could be accessed by
pulling down on a red zipper in the back of her skull.

Not that her mother couldn't dish it out as well as she took it.
To this day, Mary Pat can't look at a wooden spoon without recall-
ing the sting of one against her wrist, her cheek, the poke of the tip
in her stomach. And that was for the minor offenses. For the major
offenses—Weezie's shoe. She had three pairs, all prewar, all built to
last. Every five or six years, she'd get the soles replaced, and then

everyone walked on eggshells for weeks, hoping to not be chosen as the one she'd use to break them in.

If the old man was around, you had to watch out for his hands—the backs of the knuckles as hard and pointed as lug nuts, the flick of his index finger springing off his thumb into your temple, the grip of his fingers in your hair to drag you across the floor toward his belt (as he had the night Mary Pat got all Ds on her report card). Jamie Flanagan loved that belt most of all. He hung it on a hook just outside the bathroom door for that purpose only, used a different one to hold up his pants.

Then there were the internal skirmishes—between brother and brother, sister and sister, brother and sister, or, the worst of them all, two siblings against one. After Stevie and his faulty-hand-grenade temper were removed from the house, Donnie and Big Peg were given the widest berths because you never knew where you stood with them. But Mary Pat and Bill, once he grew up, were the ones everyone avoided getting *really* mad because neither had an off switch.

Her last fight with Big Peg, Mary Pat had spent two nights in the hospital with a concussion and compound fractures to the head because Big Peg had hit her full in the face with a brick, but what no one ever forgot was that before the ambulance arrived, Mary Pat returned to consciousness and *finished* that fucking fight before passing out again.

"I hit you with a brick," Big Peg said when they wheeled her into the hospital room to visit Mary Pat. "A brick."

"Next time use a cinder block," Mary Pat said.

She hasn't seen any of her brothers in years. Michael Sean joined the Merchant Marines and drops occasional Christmas cards from ports of call she otherwise would be unaware of—Cabo Verde, Maldives, South Sandwich. Donnie lives in Fall River and installs gutters. There's no bad blood between them, just the unspoken acknowledgment that blood itself is all that ever tied them together. Last anyone heard of Bill, he was doing ten years for a stabbing in New Mexico, which was a surprise. Not the stabbing, the New Mexico part. Hot weather always made him irritable, which, come to think of it, might explain the stabbing.

Mary Pat finishes cleaning up and tosses all the bloody swabs in the wastebasket and wipes down the sink with a splash of rubbing alcohol. She considers herself in the mirror. Her face looks like she was dumped from the back of a truck into a pile of gravel. Her hands are screaming—not just the knuckles but the wrists. Her ribs ache. Ear still ringing away. Knee and ankle in need of ice.

She gets some from the freezer. Props the leg up on a kitchen chair, puts one napkin full of ice on the ankle, another on the knee. Outside the window, Commonwealth is eerily quiet. Everyone must still be at the rally or in the bars around City Hall. She sits there and smokes, flicking the ash into a spotless ashtray. She can't believe how *clean* her kitchen is. They really did a nice job. *Professional grade,* she thinks with a smile.

For the first time in a week, she loves how she feels—bruised and scabbing up, the taste of blood in her mouth that some describe as bitter but she's always felt was kind of buttery. She reaches behind her and turns on the radio, and the DJ, just coming out of commercial, welcomes her to settle in and listen to some Mozart, a boy genius who started composing at five.

"The Piano Sonata Number Eleven," the DJ says in a voice as smooth as toffee, "is also known as the *Rondo Alla Turca.* Composed as a trifle, it has, over time, become one of his most popular pieces the world over."

The DJ's voice feels as if it's coming from the darkest of rooms. She pictures him in the black, surrounded by the inky shadows of bookshelves.

The music begins and Mary Pat closes her eyes, floats in the light dance of the piano keys.

Mozart knew what he was supposed to do. He didn't hunt down what he was good at—at five, he wasn't searching. *It* found him. Greatness. Just as it found Ted Williams's arm and eyes and legs. Just as it found James Joyce's pen. (Not that she'd ever read Joyce, but she knows he's the greatest Irish writer of all time.) Work only gets you so far. You have to lean into what you were born to do.

Mary Pat, since as long as she can remember, has been getting slapped, sometimes lightly, sometimes hard. She's been punched, tripped, hit with hangers, hit with broomsticks, Wiffle-ball bats, those wooden spoons, her mother's shoes, her father's belt. Donnie once threw a bar of brown soap at the back of her head and knocked her completely off her feet. On the streets, she fought girls, boys, and packs of both. Anytime one person attacked her, she fought back against all of them, throughout her history, who'd ever hit her or twisted her hair or ear or nipple, anyone who'd ever screamed at her or snapped at her, hit her with a belt or a shoe. Everyone who had ever made her feel like a frightened little girl wondering what kind of fucked-up fire she'd been born into.

She can't remember that girl, but she can *feel* her. She can feel her bafflement and terror. At the noise and the fury. At the storm of rage that swirled around her and spun her in place until she was so fucking dizzy from it, she had to learn to walk in it without falling down for the rest of her life.

And she learned well. She's happiest when she's opposed, most ecstatic when she's been wronged.

She's lost the last four days of her life to mourning.

Okay.

The mourning is not over—not by a long shot—but she decides, as she rises and tosses the ice into the sink, that it can be paused for a bit.

She opens every beer can in the fridge, one by one, drains them in the sink, and tosses the cans in the trash. She follows the cans with the bottles—of whiskey, of vodka, of—*who the fuck brought this into my house?*—peach schnapps. She rinses the sink until the smell is gone and wipes it down with the napkins that held the ice and throws those in the trash too.

She looks at the counters and resolves for them to stay that way. From here on out, it's clean counters. Clean counters and a clear head.

She refills the liquor bottles with water from the tap and puts them in a cardboard box. Adds toilet paper and bags of chips and peanuts, a loaf of bread. She goes through the apartment with another box and adds any clothes she'll want to wear over the next few days. She removes the basketful of medical supplies from under the bathroom sink. She takes the two boxes and the basket out to Bess and loads them in the trunk.

Back inside, she digs Dukie's kit bag out of the corner of her closet. That's what he always called it—his "kit" bag. It's dark green canvas and, if caught on his person, could have added years to a burglary sentence. It contains the tools of his trade: lockpicks, a glass cutter and suction cup, electrical tape, a stethoscope, two bolt cutters (one small, one large), several watches (the batteries long since dead), nylons to use as masks, several pairs of gloves, a lock punch, duct tape, binoculars, and a pair of handcuffs and key.

Jesus, Dukie, she wonders, *why the handcuffs?*

"Never mind," she says out loud. "I don't wanna know."

She leaves the dead watches behind, goes into the kitchen, and sweeps all the sharp knives into the bag. She gets Marty's bag of money from the dresser drawer and walks those two bags out to Bess's trunk too.

Her last trip to the apartment, she stands inside, taking it in for a minute. She's lived here since she was twenty-two. Maybe she'll see it again.

Maybe she won't.

16

Bobby comes out the back of the BPD headquarters to find Mary Pat Fennessy sitting on the hood of the ugliest fucking car he's ever seen, just past the back of the parking lot. Bobby takes the T to and from work, and the exit of the parking lot leads to an alley that unwinds in a lazy curve to the rear of the subway station. Mary Pat and her "car" are parked right at the mouth of the alley, clearly waiting on him.

Bobby stops by the car and lights a cigarette. "Is this thing street-legal?"

"Hundred percent," Mary Pat says.

Bobby walks once around the car. It has the look of something that if you blow on it, even slightly, it'll come apart like in a cartoon. He smiles at the tailpipe—cooking twine is definitely not legal to secure a tailpipe—and marvels at the complete lack of tread on the tires. A baby's ass was never so smooth. He bends, looks under the chassis, can't see any engine parts or brake pads dangling down there. So, that's something. He returns to the front and Mary Pat. "Hundred percent, huh?"

She gives him a tiny smile. "Maybe ninety."

"Try sixty," he says.

As he gets closer, he sees her face looks like she was attacked by live trees in a fairy tale. They just whacked at her with their thin branches until she reached the other side of the haunted forest. She sports a large flesh-colored bandage that almost blends in with her neck. Her hands are bruised, the knuckles swollen. She wears a sleeveless white-and-yellow-checked blouse over blue jeans rolled up at the cuffs and low-top canvas Converse sneakers. When she looks back at him, her eyes are a little too bright for Bobby's taste. It's a brightness he's seen before in the eyes of people who can't be reached.

He eyes her cuts, her bruises and bandages. "Happened to you?"

She shrugs. "You should see the other girls."

"Plural?"

She nods. "Never could respect bitches who forget that if you start a fight you should damn well fucking know how to finish one."

He feels the smile find his face a second before he thinks to pull it back. "What can I do for you, Mrs. Fennessy?"

"Call me Mary Pat."

"What can I do for you, Mary Pat?"

"I was wondering if you were still looking for my daughter."

"You betcha. Happen to know where she is?"

Something dislodges in the brightness of her eyes for a moment, a flash of uncertainty and pain, but then it disappears, and the brightness returns.

"I don't," she says.

"So why are you here?"

"It might help me find her if I knew—really knew—why you were looking for her."

He cocks his head at her, waits her out.

"What?" she asks.

"You know why I'm looking for her."

"Because you think she was on the platform when Auggie Williamson died."

"It's gone a little beyond 'think.'"

"Okay," she says. "So how come no one has been arrested?"

"Because there are laws against just arresting people willy-nilly without hard evidence."

"But you can bring them in for questioning."

"Who says we haven't?"

"If you had, you would have gotten some evidence."

"Is that how it works?" He chuckles as he flicks his cigarette into the alley. "Wasn't your first husband Dukie Shefton?"

She cocks her head at him. "Someone's been doing his homework."

"And Dukie was in the Life. I mean, man was a legend among thieves."

Mary Pat feels a small flush of ancient pride well up in her at the memory of her first husband and his street rep. "He was."

"And he was an independent, correct?" Bobby says. "Wasn't affiliated with a crew."

"He was independent, all right." Mary Pat lights her own cigarette.

"But," Bobby says, hitting the word for emphasis, "he still kicked up a percentage of his take to Marty Butler."

She shrugs. "That's the way it is in Southie."

"'That's the way it is in Southie.' We're in agreement then, Mary Pat. So, if I bring people in for questioning but can't get any evidence at all out of them because they don't even get to talk to me for five minutes before a lawyer raps on the door, what does that tell you?"

She looks at him for a long while, rolling the cigarette up and down between her fingers. "Tells me those people are a lot less afraid of you than they are of someone else."

"Yup."

She takes a thoughtful drag, exhales a series of smoke rings that drift toward the alley before dissipating one by one. "So you're saying the crime will go unsolved?"

"Hell, no," he tells her. "No one's letting this one drop."

"Because a black kid died?"

"Because a black kid died on the dividing line between Southie and Dorchester on the eve of busing. It makes for the kinda story line newspapers tend to squeeze a lot of mileage out of."

"Yet no one's in jail."

"Because we haven't broken the logjam. But we will. And when we do, the dominoes will fall."

"Or the bodies will."

"Excuse me?"

She shifts on the hood, pulls one leg up there with her, grips the ankle. "You know as well as me that if any of this leads back to Marty Butler, *all* the kids on that platform that night are as dead as Auggie Williamson."

"Why'd you say it that way?"

"What way?"

"You said 'all' the kids like some of them are gonna be dead regardless."

"If Marty Butler doesn't have success paying your legal bills," she says eventually, "he'll cut bait and pay for your funeral."

"Which could be why we're not turning up the heat too quickly."

"But if you wait too long, they'll get their stories straight, Marty will pay off people to be their alibis, and you'll get nowhere at all."

"That's the risk." He puts a foot on the fender.

"You think my daughter was involved, and I know she wasn't. If we can prove what happened, I can prove her innocence."

"And then maybe she'll come out of hiding?"

She drifts on him for a moment. Like she just—*poof*—leaves her body, and he's left staring at a statue perched on the hood of a car.

Then she comes back, but her voice is small and thin. "Yes. Then she'll come out of hiding."

He's been watching her face as close as he can. "She *is* in hiding? Yes?"

She plucks at one of her sneaker laces. "She's in hiding for sure."

"Then," he says, "you'll just have to be patient, Mrs. Fennessy."

"Mary Pat."

"You'll have to be patient, Mary Pat. If I want this to stick, I have to do it right."

He can tell from the look on her face that she thinks he's not only lying to her, he's lying to himself.

"What if I talked to them?" she says.

"To who?"

"The people who don't want to talk."

"No," he says. "Bad idea."

"Why?"

He indicates her hand and face. "Your type of negotiation is called coercion under duress. It doesn't stand up in court."

"Only *if*"—she strikes the air with her cigarette—"an officer of the law had prior knowledge of it."

"What'd you read a law book?"

"I was married to Dukie. He managed to stay out of prison most of his life and rob everything of fucking value that wasn't nailed down in this city at one time or another. He *was* a law book."

"What ever happened to Dukie?" Bobby asks.

"He didn't take a knee."

"To who?"

"The person you're supposed to take a knee to."

Standing there, taking her in, he gets a sudden whiff of her utter solitude. Of the series of traumas, big and small, that's passed for her life.

"Mrs. Fennessy, please go home."

"And do what?"

"Whatever you do when you're home."

"And *then* what?"

"Get up the next day and do it again."

She shakes her head. "That's not living."

"It is if you can find the small blessings."

She smiles, but her eyes shine with agony. "All my small blessings are gone."

"Are you sure?"

"Oh, I'm sure."

"Then find new ones."

She shakes her head. "There aren't any left to find."

Bobby is struck by the notion that something both irretrievably broken and wholly unbreakable lives at the core of this woman. And those two qualities cannot coexist. A broken person can't be unbreakable. An unbreakable person can't be broken. And yet here sits Mary Pat Fennessy, broken but unbreakable. The paradox scares the shit out of Bobby. He's met people over the course of his life who he truly believes existed as the ancient shamans did, with one foot in each world: this one and the one beyond. When you meet these people, it's best to give them breadth the length of a football field, or else they may suck you right into that next world with them when they go.

Because they're going. Make no mistake. They are fucking going.

"Mary Pat," he says gently, and she looks up at him, "do you have someone you can talk to?"

"About what?"

"About whatever you're going through right now?"

"I'm talking to you."

Fair enough.

"And I'm listening."

Mary Pat studies his face for a bit. "But you're not hearing."

"What am I not hearing?"

Sitting on the hood of that ugly car, her eyes still far too bright for Bobby's liking, she points a finger at the sky, twirls it, and answers him. "The silence."

Bobby tries to formulate some kind of response, but nothing occurs to him.

Mary Pat comes off the hood, walks to door of her heap, and gets behind the wheel. She backs up, then pulls forward, and gives no indication she even sees him as she drives away.

17

A few hours later, Bobby has dinner with Carmen Davenport at Jacob Wirth, a German restaurant in the theater district. Bobby picks it because it's just upscale enough to feel special for two civil servants, but not so upscale he'll have to go to a loan shark to cover the tab. His mind keeps drifting, though; he can't shake his odd encounter with Mary Pat. This is not where he wants his head to be on the first date he's managed to get in ten months. But he can't quit thinking of that finger of hers, twirling, as she pointed it at the sky and spoke of "the silence."

What fucking silence?

"So, out with it," Carmen says.

"What?"

"Whatever's got you distracted."

"Maybe I'm just nervous."

"Mmmm, nah." She places her napkin on her lap, settles her chair in relation to the table. "You're not here. In this restaurant. With me. And I look kinda nice, in case you overlooked it."

She wears a white peasant blouse over a denim skirt and knee-high boots the same mahogany color as the bar. Her hair is combed a little different than the night they met, falling a bit more into a curve over her eyes, and she's wearing more jewelry—a silver choker that matches the bracelet on her left wrist, thin white-gold hoop earrings. The green of her eyes is so pale it's almost translucent; it gives Bobby the impression she can see straight through the back of him.

Bobby tells her she looks beautiful.

"About time," she says. "Okay, you can stop squirming—what's on your mind?"

"You."

She chuckles and shoots him the bird. "I would rather you tell me what's preoccupying you than you stay preoccupied and eventually piss me off."

Their drinks come—red wine for her, a draft for Bobby—and they pause to toast their first date before they drink.

Bobby tells her about Auggie Williamson and all the witnesses who saw the four kids chase him near the train. And how Auggie ended up being found dead on the tracks the next morning. And how some of the witnesses corroborated who those kids could have been—four kids from Southie, two girls and two boys. And how, just when they had two of them in their hands, lawyers associated with Marty Butler showed up and bailed them out.

"What about the other two kids?" she asks.

"One's a hard case. The hardest case of the four, actually, and he's got a personal connection to Marty, so he's not gonna say shit."

"And the other one, the girl?"

"No one knows where she is."

"Is she dead?"

"Rumor is she's in Florida."

"You don't sound like you believe it."

"I'm wavering on the theory," he admits. "Of the four kids, I don't see why she would be singled out as a threat. That's what I keep bumping against."

Carmen thinks on that as she takes a sip of wine, staring at him with a calm intensity that he finds so attractive he immediately wants to duck from it. It's a Coyne family trait—if you feel happiness, duck. Because the only thing that could possibly follow happiness is pain. *Thanks, Mom*, Bobby thinks. *Thanks, Dad. What an outlook you gave your children. What a pair of fucking pips you were.*

Carmen says, "You have this girl who may have witnessed a murder."

"May have been *involved* in it."

"Or not." Her pale eyes widen to emphasize the idea. "She's just with them when they do it. Then maybe she got an inconvenient attack of conscience."

"That would do it," he agrees. Bobby flashes on Mary Pat today. That too-bright light in her eyes, those sudden micro-bursts of despair and agony.

The silence.

"You got kids?" he asks Carmen.

She nods. "I got one. He's in college now. One thing I didn't fuck up. I got him all the way through high school before the wheels came off."

Bobby reappraises her. "Did you *have* him when you were in high school?"

She smiles. "Such a silver-tongued devil, you are. No, Bobby, I didn't have him in high school. I was nineteen. And now he's nineteen, so do the math."

Bobby opens his mouth in mock horror. "You're four years older than me."

"Yeah, but I've clearly taken far better care of myself."

Bobby laughs. Can't remember the last time he did that so freely. After a second, Carmen laughs too. She takes his hand in hers, runs her thumb down the center of his palm.

"Should we order?" she says.

"Sure."

But they don't for a bit. They just sit there, taking each other's measure.

"Do you have kids?" she asks.

"One. He's nine. Lives with his mom weekdays."

"Well, let me ask you—what would you do if someone hurt your child and the police refused to do anything about it?"

Bobby can see Brendan and his hopeful eyes and hopeful smile, his kind demeanor and clear desire for everyone around him to be happy, a desire that frightens Bobby as much as it moves him. If the world hurt him—*really* hurt him—would there be anything left of Bobby to pick up and put back together?

He says to Carmen, "I'm not sure what I'd do. I mean, I'll be honest—I know what I'd want to do—but I'm a man who obviously believes in law and order. If we were, I dunno, out in the wild, part of the wagon-trail west a hundred years ago, and someone hurt my son? Then, yeah, they'd be fucking deader than Abe Lincoln."

She nods. "I think the same thing most days—how easy it is to say you'd kill someone who hurt your child. But there are laws. And consequences. You kill someone, you go to prison. Your kid grows up without you."

"The rule of law is all that separates us from the animal kingdom."

"Do the parents of this girl feel that way?"

"It's just her mother."

"And what's she like?"

Bobby chuckles. "She's a piece of work. If I'd had half a dozen of her in my platoon at the beginning of Vietnam, we probably would have staved off the whole fucking war."

"This is a *woman* we're talking about?"

"Project chick from Southie. They breed them a little different there."

"You like her."

"I do," he admits. Then, seeing her eyes, "No, no, no. Not like that. Not like I like you."

"So how?"

"She's . . ." He thinks about it. How to describe Mary Pat Fennessy? "Nobody ever told this woman how to quit. Probably nobody ever told her it was okay."

"To quit?"

"To ease up. To, I dunno, cry? Feel?" He thinks about it. "Feel something besides anger, anyway. Every time I see my son? I hug him so tight he complains. I smell his hair and his skin. I put my heart to his back sometimes, just so I can hear his blood and the beat of his heart. I mean, he's of the age he's gonna get sick of it soon, so I'm just getting it in while I can."

She nods, her eyes gone soft, her thumb even softer against his palm.

"I'll bet you money," he says, "Mary Pat Fennessy was never held like that in her life."

"I suspect you're a good father," she says.

"Call no man a good father until after he is dead."

She rolls her eyes. "That's *not* the quote."

He smiles at her. "You know ancient Greek?"

"I know my classics," she says. "The nuns made sure of it."

"I don't like nuns," he blurts out.

"I don't like 'em either," she says. "Though they've got a raw gig. The priests get all the booze and all the credit, the nuns get, what? A convent?"

The waitress appears and they withdraw their hands so they can look at their menus and order.

After the waitress leaves, Carmen puts her hand back on the table and raises an eyebrow at him. He gives her his hand, and she places her other hand over it.

"Does this woman have other kids?"

"She had a son, but he died."

"Husband?"

"She's had two. Both left her, one by getting legally declared dead."

She removes a hand to take another sip of wine. "So, if something terrible did happen to her daughter, what does she have to live for?"

In that moment, a ghost walks straight through Bobby. It's perfectly sized to his body and touches every inch of him from the crown of his head to the soles of his feet before exiting through his chest.

"I don't have an answer for that," he tells Carmen.

After dinner, he walks her home. She doesn't live far—about a ten-minute walk—but they stroll, drawing it out. They walk under trees thick with leaves that smell of the day's heat, and after they pass through Park Square, the streets spread out before them in canyons of light and dark.

Over dinner, he learned more about her work running a halfway house in Roxbury for battered wives fleeing their spouses, often with kids in tow. Now, walking through the city on a still summer night, he asks why she does what she does.

She tells Bobby she dreamed of being a lawyer as a little girl, she even remembers dreaming of becoming a cop at one point, but when she reached college on a full academic scholarship, she still had to make ends meet for room and board. Someone hooked her up with a job at a shelter for runaways. And there, she tells Bobby, she discovered she had a knack for convincing people—some people, not all by a long shot—that they had the ability to change the course of their lives.

"And you were hooked," Bobby says.

She slaps his arm in agreement. "I *was* hooked."

"Gotta be a lot of pain in that job," he says. "Battered women? *Shit.*"

"Look who's talking."

"Nah nah nah," he says. "I see a lot of crap, of course, but my job is mostly clear-cut. Someone dies, I go find who was responsible. Sometimes I get them, sometimes I don't, but I don't live with the hope that someone's life could get better because of me. You, you gotta put your faith in these women who half the time go back to these assholes willingly or get chased down by them and talked into going back. How many times does one of those outcomes happen?"

"More than fifty percent of the time," she admits. "It gets dark, I won't lie. For a while, I searched for the light in the needle. But that eventually killed all the light."

"Where do you find it now?"

"Faith."

"In God?" he asks.

"People," she says.

"Oooh." He winces. "That's a bad bet."

"You don't believe people can change?"

"I do not."

She cocks her head at that and strolls a few steps ahead of him. "How will you ever get me into bed with a shit attitude like that, Bobby Whose Real Name Is Michael?"

"I'm just not sure where hope gets anyone," he manages.

She walks back to him. "You don't believe that. You had enough hope in me to bring me to rehab instead of jail. I still have my career because of that. You have enough hope in this mother from Southie that you obsessed about her all night on a date with *me*. And I look spec-tac-u-lar."

"You do," he admits.

She steps close and pulls him by his lapels toward her and kisses him for the first time—a light, slightly chaste/slightly moist kiss on the lips. "You wish you weren't hopeful, but you are. That's why I like you."

She drops his lapels and is on the move again.

"You like me?" he says.

Another look over her shoulder. "Tell no one."

• • •

They stop in front of her building on Chandler Street, a brownstone halfway down a block full of brownstones in a neighborhood that's not one Bobby would characterize as high-crime but not one he'd call low-crime either. Like the rest of the city right now, it's riven by tectonic shifts, caught between what it once was and what it hasn't yet become and might never be. Carmen points out a light on the third floor, tells Bobby that's her living room.

Their first kiss aside, it's understood, without ever being said, that he won't be coming up tonight, and he's okay with that. His time in Vietnam scrambled his brain when it came to women—all he'd known were bar girls and taxi dancers and the hookers who walked the broad sidewalks outside the Imperial City in Hué and shouted their come-ons in a nearly indecipherable mix of Vietnamese, French, and the hard-boiled English they'd learned from American gangster movies. When he got back stateside, he stuck to strippers and barmaids for his first few years on the force. Then he met Shannon, a woman he was pretty sure, in hindsight, he'd never loved. Shannon was cold and imperious and noticeably unfond of humanity, and Bobby mistook the shine she took to him with his being a person of value—if someone who doesn't like anyone likes you, doesn't that render you peerless? It gave him pride, but no pleasure, to have a woman that beautiful and heartless on his arm. To be fair to Shannon, it wasn't long into the marriage before she grasped that he didn't love her. Problem was, she loved him (insofar as Shannon could love anyone), and the realization that he'd never really loved her back turned her already selfish heart into a granite nugget. Only Brendan could get in there (and Bobby wondered if that would hold once he started talking back). After Shannon, Bobby went back to wholly meaningless sex. Not with hookers, necessarily, but with women who expected sex to be just as transactional as he did.

When he got clean, he stayed away from anything that triggered his twin predilections for self-destruction and self-loathing, and for a long time that meant steering clear of the kind of women with whom he'd most often kept company.

Now, standing in front of Carmen Davenport's building, holding both her hands by the fingers as she tells him she had a nice night and he agrees that he did too and they both smile goofily and wonder if they should try another kiss, he realizes that what scares him about her is what scares him about all intelligent women—that she's smart enough to see, very quickly, how completely full of shit he is. He doesn't know what he's doing; never did. Doesn't know where he's going; never had a clue. He feels, at his essence, that he is a baby who was dropped by a stork and is still falling toward a chimney. Everything else he shows to the world is costume.

They try another kiss, deeper this time, longer. Bobby is embarrassed to feel a slight tremor rippling through his body and hopes Carmen can't feel it too. What is he, fucking twelve?

When she breaks the kiss, her eyes are still closed. He watches them open, and the pale green looks back at him with that calm intelligence that scares the fuck out of him.

"Call me tomorrow." She heads up the steps.

"When?"

"Surprise me."

He waits for a bit after she gets inside before he heads to the subway.

At home, he's barely through the door when his sister Erin, the actuary, comes down the hall wanting to know where he's been.

"I been out. Why?"

"Work called, like, five times."

"They leave messages?"

"Yeah."

He waits, but Erin just stares at him.

"What did the messages say?"

More staring. Erin's never forgiven Bobby for introducing her to her ex-husband. Or for staying friends with the poor guy after she left him.

She walks away. "Said to call them back."

He goes to the phone table by the stairs and squeezes into the little seat as he dials. When he gets through to Pritchard, he says, "What's up?"

"You know that kid, Rum Collins, we brought in the other day?"

"Yeah."

"He's here."

"What do you mean?"

"I mean he limped in here, blood all over his pants, and said he wants to tell us what happened to Auggie Williamson."

"So take his statement."

"He'll only talk to you."

"I'm on my way."

"Hey, Bobby."

"Yeah?"

"This kid's pissed his pants. I mean, literally. He says the one thing we gotta promise him is we won't send him back out on the street."

"Okay. He say why?"

"Yeah. Because *she's* out there."

18

Around the time Bobby and Carmen Davenport are ordering their first round of drinks at Jacob Wirth, Mary Pat Fennessy is watching Rum Collins and another stoner supermarket employee share a joint on the back of the loading dock of the Purity Supreme. Mary Pat is parked next door under a tree in the lot of a Henry's Hamburgers that went under in '72 when someone took a couple of the burgers to a lab and discovered they were a whole lot of horse and very little cow.

Two cars in the Purity Supreme lot—Rum's Duster and a Chevy Vega that Mary Pat presumes belongs to his dope-smoking buddy. Everyone else is gone, including the security guard. They set the alarm inside, pulled the grates down, and locked them; that's the full extent of the night security for the Purity Supreme.

Rum's buddy produces a roach clip, and they huff the remainder of the joint, looking like a pair of fish as they do it, then swipe five with each other and walk to their cars. This is the tricky part. If Rum's buddy lingers by his car or takes too long to start it, the whole plan falls apart. Everything depends on Stoner Pal pulling away before Rum starts his engine.

Stoner Pal gets in his car first, but he doesn't start it right away. And now Rum is opening his own door and about to get behind the wheel. Mary Pat scrambles out of her car and searches around until she finds a rock the size of a Matchbox car. She hurls it high, like a pop fly, and for a moment she's not sure if she threw it with any accuracy. But then she hears the distant *whap* of it hitting the roof of Rum's Duster.

Rum gets out of his car. Stoner Pal, oblivious, guns his engine to life. He rolls down the window and asks Rum something. Rum is looking at his car roof. He looks around for any nearby trees. He holds up a hand to tell his friend it's all okay.

And Stoner Pal drives off.

Rum looks around the parking lot. For a moment he even seems to be looking beyond the Purity parking lot into the old Henry's Hamburgers parking lot. But he doesn't look hard and he doesn't look long.

He gets back in the Duster. Turns the key in the ignition. The engine rumbles to life.

And dies.

He tries again. This time there's a noticeable lag before the engine kicks over.

And it immediately dies.

His next four tries get nowhere. Just a high-pitched whirring noise as the engine tries to engage with an empty gas tank. After she siphoned out all the gas, Mary Pat poured in a pound of brown sugar for good measure. The only way Rum Collins's orange Plymouth Duster is leaving that parking lot is by a tow truck.

Rum gets out of the car. Looks under the hood. After a while, he closes the hood. Sticks his head back in the car. After a minute or so, comes back out. Goes to the back and slides under. He puts his ear to the gas tank, then raps his knuckles against it.

He stands, frowning. Does that for a bit. Looks back and forth at the gas tank a couple times.

He looks across at Henry's Hamburgers. Boarded up. Driveway sporting weeds. Weeds under the phone booth by the old front door too. But it *is* a pay phone, and it is lit up.

Rum reaches into his pocket. Glances at what she presumes are coins in his hand.

He trudges across the Purity parking lot, cuts through the missing partition of sagging fence, and makes his way toward the phone booth. Mary Pat's been idling the whole time, and she slips the gearshift into drive, rolls Bess slowly out of her parking spot, headlights off, depressing the gas pedal with increasing pressure, so that she's almost on top of Rum by the time he hears the car and thinks to turn and look. She punches the gas and shoots around to his right, the front tire missing him by no more than a foot but the driver's door swinging wide and hitting his body hard enough to lift him off his feet and chuck him over a patch of grass into the old drive-through lane (a first in the neighborhood; huge deal at the time).

By the time he gets to his feet, she's bunched his shirt in her hand. He stumbles and wobbles as she drags him over a curb and through the side door of the restaurant, which she'd jimmied hours ago. She throws him to the floor in the remains of the old kitchen. When he tries to get up, she delivers a one-two-three-four combination to his face, relying on the vicious speed of it over any real force to break his spirit. Which it does. He lies back and groans and covers his face and drops the hands only when he feels her unbutton his jeans. Before he can stop her, she's pulled his jeans and his Fruit of the Looms down to his knees and straddled him with a box cutter in her hand, one of the thin ones that looks like a large stick of Juicy Fruit but, he must know from his supermarket experience, can slice the top off a carton of canned goods like the cardboard's made of tissue.

Before he can believe she's really pulled his pants off, she's already yanked his ball sac toward her and flicked the blade along the underside.

She's going to venture a guess he's never screamed so loud or so high in his life. The blood flows freely from the cut.

"Tell me everything about the night on the platform at Columbia Station."

He tells her. Doesn't stop until she's fairly confident he's told her everything he knows. He even tells her the parts that don't reflect well on Jules, don't make Jules look good at all.

When he's done, she places her knees on his shoulders. Looks down at him for a bit. Casually, almost as if she's curious what could happen, she flicks the razor blade off his throat and neck a few times. The tears, hot as tea, she presumes, flow from the corners of his eyes and down into his ears.

"You're gonna kill me."

"Thinking about it." She shrugs. "Where's Jules?"

"I don't know."

She flicks the razor off the flesh beneath his chin. "But you know she's dead."

He scrunches his eyes and the tears flood from them. "*Yes.*"

"How?"

"Everyone knows," he says simply.

"Open your eyes."

He does.

"You're gonna call the police. And you're gonna tell them what you told me. If you don't, Rum, you listening? Say you're listening."

"I'm listening."

"If you don't, I'll come back for you. Nothing will stop me. Nothing will save you. No matter what happens, Rum, no matter who you think you know or who you think can protect you, they can't. Not against me. I'll get to you just like I got to you tonight. And I will cut off your balls. Then I will cut off your dick. And I will throw them down a sewer for the rats to eat while you bleed to death where I leave you." She stands. "Go out to that pay phone and call the police and tell them you want to confess to Auggie Williamson's death."

She starts to walk out and then stops. Turns back. Of all the beliefs she holds chambered in her heart, the one she holds dearest is the one she could now put at hazard simply by asking a question. It's the belief that Jules was the best part of her. That Jules was better than her or Dukie or Noel. And that wherever her soul ended up, it ended up where the good souls go.

She clears her throat. "Those things you said Jules did—did she do them?"

Rum gets a look on his face like he knew he should have changed that part of the story.

"Did she do them?" Mary Pat repeats, enunciating every word. "Don't fucking lie or I'll know it."

"Yes," he says.

She stands in the doorway a long time, her lower lip quivering.

"Well, I raised her, didn't I?" she says. "So I guess that's my sin."

She lets herself out.

19

Bobby's not even through the door of the station house when Pete Torchio, the duty sergeant, holds a phone aloft and says, "For you."

"Who?"

Pete winks. "Says his name is Special."

"What?"

"*Special* Agent Stansfield."

Pete thinks he's hilarious. That's why he's on his third wife and he's only thirty-two.

Bobby points at his desk as he passes through the gate. "You can put him through."

"Fills me with a deep pleasure, Bobby. Tickles my warm parts. You know that."

Bobby gets to his desk and the phone is ringing, the button for line two blinking. He presses it and puts the phone to his ear. "Giles?"

"Bobby. How's tricks?"

"Oh, you know. You?"

"You hear the busing protesters busted up one of the windows to our building?"

"I did."

"They were chanting 'Niggers suck' for over half an hour, Bobby." There's a tone in his voice that suggests somehow Bobby either a) is responsible or b) can explain the behavior. "I mean, half an *hour*."

"That's a long time for one chant," Bobby says. "You'd think they would have mixed it up."

"Should be kept in cages, people like that."

Giles Stansfield grew up in Connecticut. Went to Brown, then Yale Law. Until he joined the Bureau, he probably never met a black person who didn't work a service job for the Stansfields or for Yale. Same went for poor whites.

"What's up, Giles?"

"I hear you're sniffing around the Butler crew." His voice is suddenly convivial, as if they're chatting over a bowl of punch at a garden party.

"Where'd you hear that?"

"I'm just thinking you might want to communicate with us, so no signals get crossed."

"What signals could get crossed?"

"Just, well, signals." Giles's voice is still convivial but also a bit fretful, like the conversation is playing out differently than it had played out in his head.

"Why don't you tell me what those signals could be, and I'll know whether I could cross them with my own?"

He can hear Giles trying not to sigh. "I blame Nixon."

"I don't know what you mean." Bobby puts his service revolver in his desk drawer, adds his car keys for good measure.

"He created that Drug Enforcement Administration horseshit. Took the Bureau of Narcotics and folded them in with the ODEA. Then they grabbed a bunch of cowboys and rejects from precincts all over the Northeast, and now they call it an agency."

"I thought they called it an administration." Bobby doesn't know why he loves to fuck with Bureau guys so much, but he does.

"Whatever they call it, those little worms with guns, those little gerbils with badges, they're up on the Butlers too, apparently, which we didn't know until they busted one of his guys."

"What's wrong with that?"

"He was *our* guy. Been working one of Marty's chop shops for six months, and DEA went and cocked the whole thing up."

"That's too bad." Bobby pats his pockets for his cigarettes, gets a bolt of panic when he realizes they're not there. He looks around wildly, spies them right there on his desk, where he laid them about thirty seconds ago.

Across the bullpen, Vincent sticks his head out of Interview Room B and bulges his eyes at Bobby with a clear *Get in here* message. He scowls and closes the door again.

"Yeah, it is too bad," Giles is saying. "Duplication of effort doesn't help anyone. The solution is to just pick one team to run point."

Bobby scoops up his cigarettes and matches. "Great idea," he says, grinning from ear to ear. "We'll take it."

"Oh, no," Giles says quickly, "you guys got enough on your plate. Why don't you let us run point?"

"Why don't we schedule a meeting over it?"

"Sure, but until then we could just have a handshake deal that—"

"I'll have my girl reach out to your girl. We'll get a meeting on the books."

"Okay, but Bobby—"

"Gotta go, Giles." Bobby hangs up.

My girl reach out to your girl. Where does he come up with this shit?

In Interview Room B, Ronald "Rum" Collins is sitting on the far side of the table looking like someone used his face for golf practice. Some of the damage is older, and Bobby recalls that Mary Pat got to the kid in a bar about a week ago. The new damage consists of a torn right eyebrow, a swollen left ear, a black, bulbous right eye socket (on top of the older yellowed bruising from a week ago), teeth blackened with blood, and cuts to his neck that look like they came from a razor blade or the flick of an extremely sharp knife.

But as Vincent warned Bobby, the worst of him is just below the waist. He smells like piss and even some shit, and his jeans are stuck to him with blood.

"What's up, Rum?" Bobby sits across from him, trying not to smile at the absurdity of the sentence he's just uttered. Why is everything so funny tonight? Then it hits him: *Because—for the moment, anyway—I've got someone in my life. Makes everything a little brighter.*

And the next thought: *Christ, let this one last.*

Rum is biting the inside of his lip like it's his job. Bobby doesn't even want to think what it looks like in there. "She's gonna kill me."

"Who?"

"I can't say."

"Let me take a wild guess—Mary Pat Fennessy."

"I *can't* fucking say! I *won't* fucking say!"

Bobby leans over the table, gets a good look at the bloody crotch of Rum's jeans. "What'd she do to you, kid? She cut it off?"

"No!" Rum looks away for a bit, chewing on his lower lip like a rabbit now. "Said she would, though."

"So where's the blood from?"

"She, like, sliced at it."

"Your dick?"

"Under my balls."

"This is Mary Pat Fennessy we're talking about?"

Rum almost nods and then snaps to, and a wave of fear smell—rank and metallic—pops through all his pores. "I'm not going to fucking say, no matter how much you ask."

"Okay." Bobby offers him a cigarette. "Well, what will you say?"

Rum takes the cigarette and the light Bobby offers next. "I'll tell you what happened on the platform that night."

Behind Rum, Vincent raises his eyebrows at Bobby as if to say: *See?*

Bobby places an ashtray in front of him. "You mind if my partner takes notes?"

Rum shakes his head, his eyes on the table. "Sure."

Behind Rum, Vincent beams, his eyes the size of headlights.

When the group of kids broke up at Columbia Park around midnight, Rum, George Dunbar, Brenda Morello, and Jules Fennessy started for Carson Beach. But just before they reached Day Boulevard and prepared to cross to the beach, Brenda realized she'd left her keys back in the park somewhere. They were on a ring along with a white rabbit's foot and a bottle opener, the latter of which had come into play a few dozen times that night.

So they went back to the park to search for the keys. They were just about to give up when Jules spotted something white under one of the bleacher seats and—voilà—Brenda's keys. Columbia Park was empty now, so they sat back down and opened four more beers, and George passed around a joint. This was the good shit, he assured them, not the Mexican colitas he sold to schmucks but real Southern Californian sinsemilla. Truth was, Rum Collins couldn't tell the difference, but he figured all the booze was clouding his taste buds.

That was when George Dunbar, looking out at the road, said, "That's right—don't even fucking look at me."

At first no one knew who he was talking to, but then they all got a look at the car passing them, its exhaust belching, nigger kid behind the wheel looking at them.

"Drop those fucking eyes, spook," George said in a voice so low they could barely hear it. "Or I won't be responsible for what I do."

The black kid did drop his eyes—either by coincidence or due to some sixth sense for imminent danger—and the car belched and sputtered its way past them, going so slow it almost seemed to be floating. It passed under the expressway, where they lost it in the vast shadow cast by the overpass, and they didn't hear it anymore.

Jules was talking to Brenda in harsh, desperate whispers. She said, "I'm calling him."

Brenda said, "No. Wait till tomorrow. Cool off."

"He doesn't have to call it his own, he just has to pay for it."

Bobby stops Rum for a second. "You're saying Jules Fennessy was pregnant?"

"What?"

Bobby says, "She said, 'He doesn't have to call it his own, he just has to pay for it.'"

Rum thinks about it. "She coulda been talking about anything."

"Like *what*?"

"I dunno. Like a pet. Or a car."

This moron can fucking vote, Bobby despairs. *And breed.*

"All right," he tells Rum, "after she says she's gonna call him—and who's 'him,' by the way?"

Rum pauses quite a while before he gives it all up: "Well, Frankie."

It takes Bobby a few seconds, but then somehow he knows, out of all the Frankies in the world, who the kid's referring to. "Frank Toomey?"

"Yeah."

Holy fuck. Bobby turns in his chair, meets Vincent's eyes. Vincent looks as flabbergasted as Bobby feels.

"Jules Fennessy was seeing Frank Toomey?"

"Yeah."

"And you're telling us this now because . . . ?"

"Because she said she'd fucking kill me if I didn't."

Bobby looks down the table at Vincent to make sure he didn't write that last exchange into the record. Vincent is holding his pen aloft, so Bobby knows he didn't.

No more questions to Rum about why he's talking, Bobby reminds himself, *just let him talk.*

"Go back to your story," Bobby tells the kid.

Jules decided she was going to call Frankie at home. Where he lived with his wife and kids. At quarter past midnight. Nobody thought this was a good idea. They all tried to talk her out of it. But she marched across Columbia Road, a dime in her hand, and stopped at the pay phone just outside the subway station and dropped the dime in the slot. The boys stayed where they were, but Brenda jogged across the road to Jules and stood by her while she talked into the phone, ended up screaming something that sounded like "Well, you spend the money!" She slammed the phone down so hard on the cradle that they heard it on the other side of the road.

Rum and George Dunbar considered moving toward the girls, but they could tell by the way Jules was waving her hands and making ugly scrunch-faces that she was crying, and who the fuck wanted any part of that? Then the same spook kid who had driven by in the dying car walked out of the block of shadow thrown by the overpass, and who knew what he had in mind because he seemed to be staring at the girls, so Rum and George jogged across the street in time to hear him say, "Are you okay?"

"We don't have any money," Brenda said.

"Who asked for money?" Bobby asks Rum now.

"What? No one."

"So why did Brenda say she didn't have any money?"

Rum shrugs. "Why else was he talking to them?"

Even Vincent, no friend to the black man, is bewildered. "To see if she was okay?"

"Fuck that," Rum says. "He's not supposed to ask that."

"Why not?"

"Because it's none of his business. Look, we all get how it works. Maybe you don't, but we do. You don't talk to each other. It's that simple. I don't want no trouble in my life—I really don't—but if I was stupid enough to roll up on some colored girls in Mattapan Square and start talking to them and their boyfriends showed up? I would fucking *expect* them to beat the ever-living piss out of me. Nothing personal. Just the way it works. But here's the difference between me and that dumbass spook—I am *not* gonna roll up on a pair of spook girls and start talking to them. About *anything*. Because I'm not looking for trouble."

"But Auggie Williamson was?"

"Well, yeah."

Bobby and Vincent exchange a look.

Bobby says, "Keep talking."

"This nigger asking you for money?" George Dunbar asked Brenda.

Brenda looked into George's eyes and immediately sensed a major shift in mood on that sidewalk. "Just get the fuck outta here," she said to the colored guy.

He tried to take her advice, but George blocked his path. "You trying to get money from my girl?"

"No," the guy said quietly with a tiny smile that he might not have been aware of. "I was asking if her friend was okay."

"Why do you care about her friend?" George's voice was so quiet you could barely hear him. And they all knew what that meant.

"I don't anymore." The black guy held up his hands and tried to edge past George.

"Just fucking let him go," Jules said.

"You're right," George agreed. "You'll probably see him in school next week."

Jules snapped her head up, and something unreasonable found her eyes. "I told you to fucking go."

The black kid said, "I'm trying."

He sounded so afraid. Terrified. Of them. It surprised Rum. And offended him at the same time. Maybe they all felt the same way, because the next thing that happened was—

"You happy?" Jules screamed. No one knew at first who she was screaming at. "You got your buses, you got our fucking school, you're gonna move on to our neighborhood next?"

The black kid started walking a lot faster.

George got a big smile on his face and drained his beer. Practically in the same motion, he threw it at the black guy. It made a loud pop when it shattered.

Brenda laughed. So did Jules. Rum had never seen a person laugh and look so hopeless at the same time. The look stuck with him for days.

"Hey, wait up," George said just as the black guy reached for one of the doors to the station. "Wait up."

Now the black guy started to really move.

"We just want to talk to you," George said.

And they all fell in behind George as he kind of half skipped toward the station doors. Whatever was going to happen, it was now in motion. No turning back.

And who would want to? Rum hadn't felt this alive in years. Maybe ever.

Inside the station, the spook had already jumped the turnstiles. They all jumped them right after him.

Brenda called, "You run slow for a nigger."

Jules said, "Yeah, I thought you were all track stars and shit."

"Hey," George called to the guy again, "we just want to talk to you."

On the platform, as they all heard the train barrel down the track toward the station, George threw another beer bottle. It exploded at the black guy's feet, and the black guy turned with his hands up and said, "Let's just forget all about this."

"About what?" George said.

The black guy tripped over his own feet and fell on his back, and George and the two girls found this hilarious. Then—

"Hold up," Bobby says to Rum Collins. "Where the fuck are you in all this?"

"Huh?"

"Where are you in this story?"

"I'm, like, watching?"

"Then who threw the second beer bottle, numb nuts?" Vincent asks.

Rum stares back at them, a blank slate.

"George threw a beer bottle at Auggie Williamson outside the station, right?"

A nod.

"So that bottle's gone. Now you want us to believe he threw another one at him *inside* the station."

"Yeah."

"Where'd he get it?"

Rum turns a shade or two whiter. His lips part, but no words leave his mouth. Somewhere back in that pebble of a brain of his, he's backhoeing like a motherfucker.

"*You* threw the second bottle," Bobby says.

"No."

"Then you threw the first," Vincent says.

"No."

"Pick one."

"No."

"Fucking pick one!" Vincent flings a black ashtray made of hard plastic right at the kid's head. The ashtray misses, but the message lands.

"I threw the second one," Rum says.

"Now we're getting somewhere," Bobby says.

"Forget about what?" George Dunbar asked, standing over Auggie Williamson.

"Whatever," Auggie said, and they could all hear the shakes in his voice and see them in his hands. "Forget this ever happened."

"We can't," George said, "because you keep coming into our fucking neighborhood."

It was Jules who delivered the first kick.

"Jules Fennessy kicked him?"

Rum nods. "She was pissed, man. Just out of her head. It was like you could tell she felt bad for him? And the worse she felt for him, the madder she got. It made no sense."

Brenda kicked the guy next. Then George.

"Then you," Vincent says to Rum Collins.

Rum stares at them for a bit, eventually nods.

When Rum kicked the spook lying on his back, it felt better than anything he could remember feeling since maybe his ninth birthday, when he got that three-speed bike he'd been asking for since he was seven. Rum knew what he was staring down—the rest of life in Southie with every day looking exactly like the last. Maybe he'd move up at the supermarket, make his way from produce to deli, but after that, where would he go? He didn't have a head for numbers, he wasn't a leader, he knew that much. That meant any type of management position was off the table. So he'd spend his life in produce or deli or dairy. His life. From now to sixty-five. Find some dishrag hag for a wife and pop out four or five little Rums and watch them lose the only good thing about the life their father had known—at least, when Rum was a kid, you knew your neighbors. You shared your food and your rituals and your music. Nothing changed. It was the one fucking thing they couldn't take from you.

But they could. They would. They were. Forcing their notions and their ways and their lies on you. Lies because they told you change was going to make you happier, it was going to make you richer, it was going to brighten your world.

It wasn't bright. It was fucking dark. He kicked and kept kicking until he missed, which caused him to fall on his own ass, and then his "friends" were laughing at him and the black guy was on his feet and running—

Straight into the oncoming train.

"So the train hit him." Vincent's pen is poised over his notepad.

"More like he hit the train," Rum says.

"Explain."

"He bounced off it. Like, he probably thought he was gonna jump onto the tracks to get away? Well, one second the train wasn't there. Next second it was. And he ran right into it. Snapped around and bounced off the wall—you know where the sign is with all the train routes?—and then, yeah, he hit the platform."

"And rolled over and fell under the tracks?" Bobby says helpfully.

"Yup."

Bobby and Vincent nod at each other. Makes perfect sense.

Bobby smiles at Rum. "You know how much space lies between a subway car and the platform edge?"

Rum shrugs, sensing the boom even before it drops.

"Eight inches. Apparently, there's an industry standard. Plus, we measured."

Rum seems to have stopped breathing. He's that still.

Bobby holds up a hand to Vincent so he'll stop writing. "Now, Rum," he says, "judging by your face and the fact you walked in here to tell us the truth, I don't think now is the time to segue into bullshit. You're not smart enough to sell it, whatever it is, and if you don't come clean with us—"

"Like right fucking now," Vincent says.

"—then we're going to kick you loose and make sure everyone knows you were uncooperative with us. Which, hey, will buy you some street cred up and down Broadway. But will it endear you to Mary Pat Fennessy?"

Rum goes back to chewing on his lip as if his teeth are clock gears.

"Which nut will she take first?" Vincent asks Bobby.

Bobby says, "Depends on if she's right- or left-handed."

Vincent asks Rum, "Is she a righty or a lefty? Did you notice?"

Rum says nothing. It's like he's slipping into shock.

"He didn't notice," Vincent says.

"If she's right-handed," Bobby says, "we gotta assume it's the left side of his ball sac that's easiest to, you know, grab and then chop into."

Vincent winces and crosses his legs.

"If she's left-handed, she goes for the right nut."

"What about his dick?"

Bobby says, "Well, that's where you'd really have to get in her head. I mean, does she want to just grab it and yank it like some taffy and chop it off right at the root?"

"Stop," Rum whispers.

"Or would she start at the top and slice it right down the middle like a banana?"

Rum makes a gagging noise, and when they look over, his tongue thrusts out of his mouth and his head surges far ahead of his neck. He gags some more.

But he doesn't puke. Which is a relief. Because the shit and piss are enough. Add one more disgusting bodily fluid to the room, and no amount of cigarette smoke will help.

Now the tears come. They well up under his eyes and de-age him five years. "If she cuts off my dick," he says, "it's not like I'll just be walking around with no dick. I mean, I'll fucking die, won't I?"

"Depends how close you are to a hospital," Vincent says.

"And what you have on hand to stanch the blood flow," Bobby says.

"Well, that goes without saying," Vincent says.

"Does it? Kid's never had his dick chopped off before, so he might not know these things."

Another series of gags. They wait him out.

"Can you stop her?" The tears fall.

"We can arrest her," Bobby says. "Sure. You just give us a statement, swear she threatened you. And we'll pick her up."

"And then what?"

Bobby pushes a box of tissues across the table to him. "She'll go to court."

"Will she go to jail?"

Bobby looks at Vincent for his opinion.

"Doubtful," Vincent says.

"Why the fuck not?" The kid's half bawling now. "She said she'd cut off my balls. *And* my dick. She beat me up."

"Well, *if* we're talking about Mrs. Fennessy, she has no priors."

"Model citizen," Vincent says.

Bobby decides to slather it on. "Pillar of the community."

"So she'll get a low bail."

"If she gets bail at all."

"True. She's an ROR if ever there was one."

"What's an ROR?" The sobs have diminished to sniffles.

"Released on one's own recognizance."

"What's that mean?"

"Means she won't have to pay bail."

"And won't spend a night in jail."

"But she threatened my balls."

"Who did? Who is this 'she' you're so scared of, Rum? Give us a name."

He shakes his head.

"Then finish telling us what happened the night Auggie Williamson died."

"And don't shovel a bunch of shit at us about him bouncing off a train and then bouncing off a wall and dropping onto the tracks, because we know that's bullshit."

"How?"

"Witnesses. And the medical examiner's report. And ten years of fucking police work."

"You can tell us the truth." Bobby gives Rum another cigarette and lights it for him. "Or you can take your chances back out that door."

"And if I tell you the truth and it turns out I did something bad?"

"Then we'll arrest you."

"And I won't have to walk back out that door?"

"Not until you make bond."

"You'll be safe and sound in a nice comfy jail cell. We'll even throw in a pillow."

Rum takes a long drag and a longer exhale, staring up at the ceiling. Then he says, "He did run into the train, he did bounce off the wall. It knocked him out and he, like, laid on the platform all shaking and shit, and then he stopped shaking, so we thought he was dead."

"But he wasn't?"

He shakes his head. "I mean, we thought he was, but . . ."

They wait.

After a while, Bobby says, "Help us out with 'but.'"

When the black guy banged his face into the train, they all laughed, George Dunbar the loudest. When the guy bounced back into the wall and then dropped to the platform like he'd been dropped from a helicopter, they laughed harder. But then, as the car doors opened, they noticed he was having this weird seizure, as if he'd been electrocuted. His heels hammered the ground, his arms flung out and back to his sides, his head rolled from side to side, and his eyes pinned themselves so far back into his skull they looked like egg whites.

The four of them stood over him so that it would be hard for anyone passing by to get a clear glimpse of what they were standing over.

The train left the station.

George said, "Fuck you looking at?" to one couple, and they hurried off the platform.

The black guy went still. A single strand of white foam trickled out of the side of his mouth. Blood leaked from his ears.

Rum noticed an outbound train departing from the opposite track and saw one guy walking away from it with his head down. Big guy, not one you'd want to fuck with, but he clearly knew the score around here—if you don't see it, no one can ever make you say you did.

Suddenly, they were all screaming at one another. Rum can't, to this day, tell you what exactly was said, but he knows George was worried about witnesses, and Brenda was worried about her parents finding out, and Jules was screaming—really screaming—about how this is their fault, they're going to prison. Rum remembers pointing out that aside from kicking him, they hadn't really hurt this guy. He hurt himself. Rum had beat up a couple kids in his life, and he knew the difference.

Brenda slapped Jules to get her to stop screaming. Then George called Rum a fucking retard and said, "Let's book."

They left the colored guy on his back on the platform and climbed the stairs to the Columbia Road exit, and when they pushed open the doors, Frankie Toomey was standing against his car, waiting for them. Frank didn't acknowledge any of them but Jules. That was par for the course. Jules claimed to Brenda that he could be funny and surprisingly tender but, if so, he saved that part of himself for private or for the little kids he charmed up and down Broadway. Otherwise, he was as cold and hard as the nickname Tombstone implied. His body was hard, his face was hard, his eyes were as dead as a GI Joe doll's. He opened his car door and Jules got in. That's where

they split up—George and Brenda left in George's car, Frankie and Jules left
in Frankie's car. And Rum, odd man out as always, walked home.

"Let's back up," Bobby says.

Rum gulps from the cup of water they brought him, a look on his
face like he knows he's never gonna sell this bullshit to anyone. "Sure,
sure."

"How'd Auggie Williamson end up *under* the platform?"

"I don't know. Maybe he, like, rolled?"

"Okay . . ."

"We left him where he was."

"On the platform with white foam coming out of his mouth?"

"Just one side of his mouth."

"So, you go upstairs," Vincent says, "and find Frank Toomey waiting?"

A nod.

"What's his mood?"

A shrug.

"Come on. What's the groove coming off the man?"

Rum looks extremely uncomfortable, as if maybe the cut under his
balls is showing the first signs of infection. Either that or he's accli-
mating to a new source of terror. "I don't know. I don't know him. I
can't judge his 'groove.'"

"You know him," Bobby says. "You grew up seeing him around. He's
famous for walking into candy stores and buying a round of sweets for
all the kids. He's like every kid's favorite uncle on Broadway."

"Yeah, well, that was then."

"Plus, you're his beard," Vincent says.

"Good point," Bobby says.

"His *what*?"

"His beard." Vincent explains, "You covered for him by pretending to be Jules Fennessy's boyfriend so his wife wouldn't know Frank was fucking a sixteen-year-old."

"Jules is seventeen."

"Ah." Bobby wags a finger at him. "She wasn't when she started up with Frankie, though, was she?"

Rum's eyes zip in the sockets like marbles flung into a bowl. "I'm not here to talk about fucking Frankie."

"Yet here we are, talking about him."

"You want his 'groove'? He's death. That's his fucking *groove*. He's the coldest, scariest motherfucker I ever met." Rum holds up his hands. "I'm not saying nothing about Frankie Toomey."

"Nothing?"

Rum gives them his best tough-guy impression—hooded eyes, small sneer—and shakes his head slow. "Not one fucking thing."

"Then you," Bobby walks to the door and opens it, "are free to go."

Rum watches Vincent close his notebook and return the pen to the inside of his pleather sport coat.

"Chop-chop," Bobby says to Rum. "I wanna get home."

Rum says, "You guys said you'd charge me."

"For what?" Vincent lights a cigarette with his imitation gold lighter that works only a third of the time.

"For what happened."

"You didn't tell us what happened," Bobby says. "You told us some bullshit about Auggie Williamson running into a train, which, since you were chasing him, would maybe lead to a third-degree involuntary manslaughter charge . . ."

"Which no DA's gonna waste his fucking time on." Vincent reaches the door alongside Bobby. "I'm gonna pop down to JJ's. You?"

"I might join you."

"Nickle 'Gansies from midnight to two."

"Draft?"

"Yeah."

Bobby makes a face. "Draft Narragansetts give me the shits the next day."

"Me too. But hey, I'm off tomorrow."

They leave the interview room. Wander into the bullpen. Bobby sees he has three messages taped to the shade of his small banker's lamp. He checks them.

"Come back!" Rum calls from the interview room.

"Are you really going to JJ's?" Bobby asks Vincent.

"Thinking about it. Hungry too. Might grab a spuckie somewhere on my way. You?"

"I was supposed to be off tonight," Bobby says. "I just want to go home."

"Come back!"

Vincent lowers his voice slightly. "You know that chick in Property? One with the big brown eyes? The lips?"

Bobby laughs.

"What?" Vincent's already half indignant. "You know who I'm talking about?"

"Deb DePitrio?" Bobby says.

"Come on! Come back!" Now Rum is standing in the doorway of the room.

"Yeah, Deb."

"She only dates doctors."

"She's a *clerk*."

"Who looks like Raquel Welch. Are you fucking kidding me? You got a better chance dating the real Raquel than you do dating Deb."

"What, she's a friend of yours?"

"Kinda, yeah."

"So you think *you* gotta shot with her."

Bobby snorts at the notion. "I'm an out-of-shape cop ten years older than her. I got zero shot. And I know it. Which is why she doesn't mind chatting with me. You, on the other hand, I bet you slap on some

Aqua Velva, go leaning into her counter all 'What color lipstick you wearing?'"

"Fuck you."

"'You do something with your hair?'"

"No, really. Fuck you."

"Officers, please!"

"We're fucking *detectives*," Vincent shouts. Then to Bobby: "No chance, uh?"

Bobby shakes his head. "Two of you stranded on a desert island, she'd still probably hold out two, three years—at least—in case of a rescue."

"You're such a prick."

Bobby gives it some thought. "You're not wrong."

"Please!"

They both look over at him. He's leaning on the doorjamb, not wanting to risk stepping into a room of heavily armed people who, if they glance at him at all, do so with contempt. His blood-encrusted jeans are definitely stuck to his thighs and groin. His eyes are leaky again. "I can't go back out there."

Bobby and Vincent stare back at him with vacancy signs in their eyes.

"Please don't make me."

"We have nothing to hold you on," Bobby says.

"Go with God," Vincent says.

"Arrivederci," Bobby says.

"Vaya con dios," Vincent says.

"You just said that," Bobby tells him.

"No, I didn't. I said, 'Go with God.'"

"Frank Toomey," Rum says, "made us go back into the station."

Someone in the squad room whistles, low and long. Everyone's looking at Rum Collins now.

Rum looks at Bobby like a guy who knows his life will never be the same again. "He told us we had to finish the job."

20

According to Rum, after Frank Toomey told them to go back and "finish the job," he stayed where he was. Leaning against his car.

"So he didn't go with you?"

"No."

"And he didn't elaborate on what 'finish the job' meant?"

"No."

"He didn't get any more specific?"

Rum shakes his head. "Uh-uh."

Bobby can already see Frank's defense attorney going, "So, 'finish the job' could have meant going home for the night, cleaning up the bottles you broke, *or* could have even meant helping get Auggie Williamson to a doctor."

Finishing the job, Bobby knows, could mean fucking *anything*.

When it came down to what they did do when they returned to the platform, Rum was sure that someone rolled Auggie Williamson onto the tracks but was somehow unsure who that someone could have been.

And how could that be?

"I was taking a piss," Rum informs them.

This fucking job, Bobby thinks. You have them, they're on the ropes, ready to talk, and then some pestilent germ of a polluted idea works its way into their hamster brain and they think, *I can get out of this*.

And you're back to square one.

Bobby's too tired—and on his night off—to go back to square one.

"Rum," he says, "it takes two people to roll a body. Otherwise, the body goes right when you want it to go left, or left when you want to go right, it's a whole thing. So, you and George, you rolled Auggie Williamson off the platform. And he fell and hit the back of his head and died. You didn't mean it, but it happened."

Rum says, "That's not what happened."

"Yes, it is."

"Okay, we rolled him off the platform, okay, we did that."

Bobby nods.

"But then he got up."

"He what?"

"He got up. Like he rose to his feet?"

Vincent stops writing. They watch Rum Collins. He's not looking up and to the right anymore—a sure sign someone's lying. He's looking in—a sure sign someone's remembering.

"He got up. And then he fell back down. And then he kinda got to his knees. And the girls were crying cuz it was, like, pathetic? So we climbed down there with him?"

"All of you?"

Rum looks at them. Nods.

"And then what happened?"

"Someone found a rock."

"Who?"

Rum looks at them and says nothing.

"Who found the rock?"

Rum says, "It wasn't me."

"So who was it?"

Rum grits his teeth. "It wasn't me."

Bobby watches him for a bit. Looks at Vincent, who gives him a tiny headshake—they're at the part of the dance where they could lose this kid.

"Let's forget about who has the rock for a minute," Bobby says. "Just tell me what they did with it."

Rum turns that over in his brain for a bit. He's too stupid to know at this point that he's already copped to half a dozen felonies, including attempted murder.

He opens his mouth and, in a sentence, ties himself to it for life. "They—the person—hit him in the back of the head with the rock."

"Hit Auggie Williamson."

"Yeah."

And this was the piece that has never lined up with every story they've heard or every theory they've surmised about what happened that night—how did Auggie Williamson get the fracture at the base of his skull?

Now they know.

"And what happened to Mr. Williamson then?"

"Mr. Who?"

That gets to Bobby for some reason. If you're going to kill someone, at least know their fucking name. "Williamson," Bobby says through gritted teeth. "The black guy."

"He went down on his face. Never moved again." Rum stares at his thumbs for a bit before he looks up at Bobby and Vincent, blinking under the fluorescent. "Now that I told you what happened, can you square things with her?"

"With who?"

"The, uh, ya know, the broad who threatened to cut off my dick."

Bobby says, "I don't think you gotta worry about her anymore."

Rum lets out a loud sigh. "Fuckin' A."

Vincent says, "Ronald Collins, you're charged with murder in the second degree in the death of Augustus Williamson."

Rum, chewing a hangnail, says, "What?"

"You have the right to remain silent. Anything you say—"

"Wait a minute! Fucking *what* now?"

"—can and will be used against you—"

Rum looks at Bobby. "I didn't do it."

"You were there," Bobby says, "and you didn't stop it. In the eyes of the law, that makes you just as guilty as whoever swung that rock."

"No," Rum says. And then more emphatically: "No."

Vincent says, "Your only shot of walking the streets of Southie again before, I dunno, two thousand and four? Is to tell us who swung that rock."

"I want my lawyer."

"Tell us."

"I want my lawyer."

"Tell us!"

"I want my lawyer." He looks at them, tears streaming down his face but eerily calm. "Right fucking now."

Bobby and Vincent stand. "Okay."

"You're a hard guy?" Vincent says. "That's good. Cuz you're gonna do hard time with lots and lots of hard guys." He grabs his crotch. "Hard as drill bits."

"Over a nigger?" Rum stares at them in utter disbelief.

Bobby nods. "Bet your dumb white ass, motherfucker."

21

George Dunbar's two main dealers—Joe-Dog Fitz from H Street and Quentin Corkery from Old Colony—are working the gazebo at Marine Park for him. But George himself never shows up. Midway through the second day, after a big noontime rush from construction workers and some truckers from Boston-Buffalo, Joe-Dog and Quentin have an urgent discussion with their runners, all of them talking fast by the base of the gazebo. Mary Pat, with Bess's window down, can hear a few words and phrases from twenty yards away, the most important of which is "low on beauties and Pepsi," which she presumes means they're running out of speed and cocaine. *Heavens,* she thinks, *I hope you're still well stocked on heroin, dear ones.*

Quentin Corkery leaves the roost. He walks down the slope of Marine Park and hops in a yellow Datsun Z parked near the statue. He peels off the curb with a long screech. Mary Pat follows him back down Day Boulevard where, after less than two miles, he pulls off into Old Colony. The two housing projects in this section of Southie—Old Colony and Old Harbor—are sister projects to Commonwealth. They were all built within ten years of one another, all laid out with similar footprints. Mary Pat hangs back, puttering slowly up the thin road Quentin took to a rear parking lot. He pulls up directly in front of a small black stoop, hops out of the car, and runs inside the building. Mary Pat once dated a guy who lived here—Paul Bailey, doing eight to ten at Walpole, last she checked—and remembers the layout's the same as Commonwealth: shotgun hallway going straight up the center, doors to the units branching off that main vein. She can't get into position in time to see which unit Quentin enters, but she's set up on the little stoop with a clear view through the yellow door glass when he exits, and she clocks him coming out of the fourth door down on the left. She puts her butt on the top of the short railing and swings her body around, drops down off the railing, and is already tucked along the side of the building by the time Quentin exits, hops in his Datsun, and drives off, once again laying enough rubber to make Mary Pat wonder if he deals drugs just to keep himself in tires. Mary Pat walks back to Bess, sitting in the corner of the parking lot where she left her. She pops the trunk and rummages through Dukie's bag until she finds what she thinks she'll need, then closes the trunk.

She puts on gloves before she reaches the main door. Once she's inside, she notices the hallway smells a bit different from the ones at Commonwealth. Still smells of Lysol, spilled beer, and the potatoes, cabbage, and corned beef boiled inside at least a quarter of the units every Sunday. But there's something else, a hint of mold, maybe? The scent of a damp April sidewalk or a nearby swimming pool, but there aren't any swimming pools around here, that's for sure. Four doors down on the left is number 209. She knocks and waits, her ear against the door. She hears nothing. She knocks a second time to be sure. She's got the lock punch tucked under her shirt against her spine, just in case, but Dukie's pick goes through the lock as if it's a key. It takes less than thirty seconds, and she's in.

The unit smells of pot smoke, cigarette smoke, and poor hygiene. In the back room, she finds a flop bed with no sheets and a single pillow, dark with old sweat. In the living room, there's a torn couch, several plastic beach chairs, and a black-and-white TV sitting on top of a stack of five Yellow Pages, four of them still wrapped in plastic.

The bathroom looks like it's never been cleaned; it's possible the whiff of mold she got in the hallway stems entirely from this one bathroom, because the wall behind the sink is black, and woolly gray mold-fingers sprout up the tile from the edge of the tub.

She checks the toilet tank, but there's nothing stashed in there. Checks under the sink, the same. Bedroom yields nothing and neither does the kitchen sink. But on the fifth try—using a broomstick on the drop ceiling in the hallway closet—Ziploc bags plop to the top shelf or plummet all the way to the floor. She finds a chair and steps up to get her hand all the way in there and scoop the other bags out. Once that's done, she feels something else back there, just the edge of it, something hard. She extends her body and then her fingers, and she knows it's a gun the moment she wraps her fingers around the grip. She pulls it out—a .38 Smith & Wesson snub nose with a heavily nicked grip that's beginning to shed rubber. She steps down off the chair and opens the cylinder. It opens easily, so at least the gun's oiled and maybe even properly cared for. Six bullets nest inside.

She climbs back up, reaches in there a final time, and comes back with a small cardboard box that rattles. She opens it to find another half a dozen bullets inside.

She places all the bags on the kitchenette table, a greasy Formica top with more chips in it than her own. The extra-large Ziplocs contain weed, some of it green and pungent, some of it less green and crumbly, littered with stems; the large Ziplocs contain brown powder she recognizes immediately, with a pang in her heart, or white powder she assumes is cocaine. She knows a bag of black beauties as such right off (Dukie loved his amphetamines) and presumes the other pills are, respectively, ludes, LSD, and mescaline. It's not a lot of drugs, not for a dealer; if she had to guess, she'd say they've sold maybe two thirds of their latest stash by this point. Losing it isn't going to hurt them in the long run, but it will hurt them tomorrow.

She takes it all.

And the gun.

A few hours later, one of the runners shows up, lets himself in, and then comes back out with a desperate look on his face and tears off out of there.

Fifteen minutes later, both Quentin and Joe-Dog show up in Quentin's Datsun Z. They run inside. They're in there a while longer than the runner was. When they come back out, they look exhausted. And scared. They sit on the hood of Quentin's car and smoke cigarettes and don't say a word.

About half an hour later—*What took you so long, George?*—George Dunbar pulls up. George drives a beige late-'60s Impala. An absolutely forgettable car. George is clearly the only member of his crew with some idea of the benefits of escaping notice if you get up to criminal shit on a regular basis. George and his two dealers get into some finger-pointing—George at Quentin and Joe-Dog; Quentin and Joe-Dog at each other.

George storms inside. The other two follow.

Mary Pat starts Bess while they're in there. Once Bess is idling, she'll be all right, but when her engine first kicks over, it's not pretty. The exhaust coughs out puffs of smoke that rise in the rearview, and the motor clears its throat half a dozen times before it calms down. When they come out this next time, she's pretty sure, they'll be on the move. It's best to have Bess primed to move too.

She hears the door swing back against the building when they exit. They stop at the Datsun, where George unleashes a final tongue-lashing, followed by a strident finger pointed first at Quentin and then at Joe-Dog.

He hops in his Impala and peels out of there. Quentin and Joe-Dog stay where they're at longer than Mary Pat had hoped they would.

When they look down to light their cigarettes, she goes for broke and rolls along the back of the parking lot, eyes fixed straight ahead.

If they notice her, they don't seem to think much of it.

She finds George Dunbar pulled over three blocks away, using the pay phone in front of a liquor store. His lips don't move much; he's mostly nodding. A lot. And his eyes are wide. Mary Pat thinks it's a safe bet he's getting his own tongue-lashing.

He puts the phone back as if the receiver might bite. He gets in his car and drives off, with Mary Pat tailing him from three cars back.

It's not long before he pulls onto the Southeast Expressway and only a few miles farther before he pulls off and leads her along the edge of Dorchester and then over the Neponset River Bridge. From there, he leads her into Squantum, a spit of land that juts off the hand of North Quincy like a thumb that suffered an industrial accident. Squantum is surrounded, everywhere but the base of that thumb, by ocean, and she follows George and his nondescript Impala to a house on Bayside Road, just north of Orchard Beach. It's a small Cape with dark brown shingles and white trim, with a small yard and a terrific view of the harbor directly across the street.

George parks in front, and before he's out of the car, there she is— his mother. Lorraine Dunbar herself. Not much of a looker, to tell the truth, a face thin and hawkish under an abundance of fire-red hair, eyes too close together, a chin so violently squared off it looks like what's left behind after an amputation. But she still has the body of a sixteen-year-old cheerleader—firm legs, an ass that looks like you could play the conga on it, and tits that defy gravity, logic, and time. Lorraine tells everyone who will listen that it's her diet—lean meats and veggies, she crows, and no sweets—and her jogging. Where she came up with "jogging," no one fucking knows, but Mary Pat's seen her dozens of times running along Broadway or around the Sugar Bowl loop with her knees pumping so high they almost hit her chin, her cheeks puffing and lips pursed, wearing these zippered tops and pants of matching color with white piping and usually a matching headband to boot. Every time the topic comes up for discussion among the women of Commonwealth, someone offers the opinion that maybe, for tits and an ass like that, they could all do some jogging, but the idea lasts no longer than the smoke from the next cigarette.

Lorraine hugs her son and then looks out at the street. Lorraine is Marty Butler's woman, so she's been trained to look for threats in anything that looks out of place. She probably would have made Mary Pat and Bess if Mary Pat hadn't backed up as soon as she saw George pull over. She sits at the start of a curve about thirty yards back up the street, under a tree that throws a nice late-afternoon shade. To see her, Lorraine would have to stand in the road and catch the light just right.

Lorraine and George head inside.

Mary Pat settles in.

At one point, she turns her head and sees Jules sitting beside her in the passenger seat. Jules yawns and gives her a sleepy smile.

It's the sound of the outboard that wakes her.

It's dark. Bugs mass under the lone streetlight. At the sound of a screen door creaking open and then snapping shut, she turns her head to see George Dunbar exit the house and walk across the road to the small cup of shoreline. He wears shorts and no shoes.

Mary Pat takes the binoculars from Dukie's kit bag and trains them on the boat as it cuts its engine and bobs toward shore. Brian Shea jumps out of the boat as George half waddles in to meet it, and the two of them tug it to shore. Brian kills the light on the boat, and now the binoculars are no good.

Mary Pat turns off her dome light and exits Bess. She softly pushes the door shut behind her and crosses the road. Only one tree to hide behind and then just a beach wall that doesn't even reach her knees.

The tree stands at least twenty yards from Brian and George. But there's no one else around and not much to muffle the sound, if only they'd speak the fuck up. She settles in behind the tree and strains to hear.

Brian Shea tells George, "You gotta . . ." and "We didn't fucking . . ." and ". . . no free lunches."

George's back is to her, and his words travel upwind. He's a lot harder to understand. She thinks she hears him say "I know" a couple of times. And something that could be "concrete" but she somehow knows isn't. She knows that it's also not "discreet" but "creet" is said for sure.

A sudden breeze carries Brian Shea's three clearest sentences to her: "You already owe. Now you owe more. No one's gonna grow a sense of humor about this."

The breeze dies.

"I—" George says.

". . . move it . . . Blue Hill Ave. . . . I don't fucking care."

". . . just sayin' . . ."

". . . excuses are your own. Come on."

They lift something out of the boat. They carry it through the dark, each man about four feet from the other. As they cross the road, they pass under the edge of the streetlight, and Mary Pat sees they're carrying a duffel bag. It's dark green, similar to the one Noel returned home from the army carrying, except she's pretty sure this one has a zipper running up the center. George opens the trunk to his Impala, and they place it inside.

The car is only five or six yards away; Mary Pat can hear them pretty well now as Brian puts his hands on George's shoulders.

"You tell those stoned-up Moreland monkeys I expect maximum bang for my buck."

George nods.

Brian slaps George's face. Not lightly. "You listening?"

"I am, I am."

"You make damn sure they know they don't do something makes the front page, we'll dry up their entire fucking pipeline."

"Okay."

"And then you move the rest of the shit."

"Yeah, yeah."

"Not next month, not next year. Now. We clear?"

"We're clear."

"You're not family, kid." Brian steps in close and makes like he's going to slap George in the face again, but at the last moment, he pats his cheek instead. "You're just the son of the broad my boss fucks."

"I know."

"You *what*?" Brian's voice is sharp.

"I said I know. I know."

Brian Shea stares at him for a bit before walking back across the street. He drags his boat into the water with a few splashes and a few grunts, then engages the outboard and motors off.

An hour later, when George exits the expressway, Mary Pat thinks he must have made a mistake—instead of turning right toward Southie, he turns left toward Roxbury. She figures he's distracted and will bang a U-ey soon, but he takes them deeper and deeper into the heart of Roxbury, down streets she's never visited before, subsections of the city that feel as alien to her as Paris. But Paris is on the other side of the Atlantic; these streets are less than five miles from Commonwealth. It's midnight on a Sunday, but some streets are as lively as a block party—coloreds mingling on their porches or gathered on the sidewalk around their cars. Other streets are dead quiet, not so much as an alley cat's meow to break up the stillness. She feels eyes on her everywhere. Wonders if someone will just step in front of her car and scream, "White woman!" before they descend and tear her limb from limb.

That's what they do around here, isn't it? Wait for the unsuspecting honky, the disoriented whitey, the naive ofay? So they can show her who really owns these streets and how angry they truly feel.

She has no idea why they hate her so, but she feels their hate, in the looks she won't acknowledge, the looks she doesn't exactly see but knows are there, the looks that come from under the hoods of thick, sullen eyelids that clock her every movement.

Look around, a voice dares her.

She accepts the dare. Looks at the porches and stoops. No one's looking at her. No one's even aware she's there.

And they're not looking at George. Because . . .

George isn't there anymore. An intersection glows yellow a block ahead, but George's car isn't at it. She accelerates, the fear suddenly overtaking her chest with the pounding of cymbals: *I have no idea how to get out of here.* She reaches the intersection and looks up at the street signs to her left—she's on Warren Street, intersecting with St. James. She can't tell if George went right or left. Can't see his taillights. She looks up at the street signs again, this time to her right, and she wants to thank Jesus and the Holy Ghost and Saint Peter too that in a neighborhood this shitty, the street signs are actually intact, because it appears Warren Street splits two streets up the middle—to her left, St. James, but to her right, Moreland.

You tell those stoned-up Moreland monkeys I expect maximum bang for my buck.

She turns right on Moreland and accelerates. After one block, no George. After two blocks, no George. Resisting the urge to stand on the gas pedal, she keeps Bess at a steady pace. At the next stop sign, she looks to her right and sees the Impala. It's parked on the other side of a playground a half block over. Parked beside a white van with its left rear door open. Three black guys stand with George at the back of the van. One's tall and fat, another is skinny and short, the third is average height and build. They all have tall Afros and facial hair. They all wear glasses and turtlenecks. George is handing them items from his trunk, one after another after another.

Mary Pat's no expert, and her vision is limited, but she knows a rifle when she sees one.

Why is a white drug dealer from Southie giving rifles to three black guys in Roxbury on the eve of forced busing?

Mary Pat presses her head to her seat back.

What the fuck is going on?

22

Back in Southie, George leads them down the dark, empty blocks of cab companies and trucking depots. It's past one now, and Mary Pat kills her lights so George won't notice her behind him. There's no one down here, it seems, just the two of them bumping along old cobblestone streets in the dark. Few functioning streetlights, one bar that caters to Teamsters and closes at eleven. Mary Pat slows to a crawl. Even with her headlights off, if he rolls down his window, George will probably be able to hear her lurching along the cobblestones behind him. She hangs back a full two blocks and does her best to avoid potholes.

He pulls into a parking lot in front of a low-slung stretch of one-car garages. Gets out. Unlocks the third garage from the right and pulls up the door. He fishes in his pockets before entering the garage and walking to the back of a Chevy Nova. He opens the trunk. Comes back out, grabs the duffel bag from the Impala trunk. Without the rifles, it's much lighter than it was when he and Brian Shea lugged it across Bayside Road, but it's still heavy enough that his right shoulder dips a bit and his head tilts along with it as he carries the bag to the Nova and deposits it in the trunk.

He closes the trunk, locks it. Closes the garage door. Locks that too. Gets in the Impala.

And off they go again.

• • •

It's a short trip. George parks the Impala on East Second, up the street from his mother's official house. Mary Pat watches him cut between two houses and then, she presumes, he hops fences through backyards until he reaches his mother's house and slips in through the back. This suspicion is confirmed a few minutes later when a light goes on in the corner room of the second floor of Lorraine Dunbar's house.

Half an hour later, the light goes out. Mary Pat stays where she is for another ten minutes in case he's coming back out, but he doesn't. He's gone to bed, she's pretty sure. It's two in the morning. Anyone with common sense is asleep by now.

She drives Bess up East Second and heads back to that garage.

The parking lot and surrounding streets are as dark and quiet as when she left them, so she parks in the lot on the assumption that anyone else who rolls up here at this time of night won't be up to any good either, so she may as well keep Bess close in case she needs to make a quick getaway.

The padlock George attached to the garage door is as basic as they come, but it's nevertheless resistant to Dukie's picks. Or to her use of them, at least. This is a shame—she was just starting to get cocky about her ability to pick a lock; was, in her mind, giving Dukie posthumous shit for his common refrain that there was a "skill" to picking a lock that the average person didn't appreciate. After her fourth unsuccessful try, she gives up and goes with the bolt cutters.

As the bottom of the lock clatters to the ground and the top of it sits clamped in the blades of the bolt cutters, she thinks, *Fuck skill*.

But then changes her mind again when she picks the lock of the Nova's trunk on the first try.

"I still got it, Dukie," she tells him as she opens the trunk and shines her flashlight in.

The bag is unzipped and she can see right into it, but what she sees there doesn't compute. It *should*—what else had she thought could be in there?—but still it doesn't. There was a code in Southie. There were things you didn't do:

You didn't rat.

You never turned your back on a family member (even if you hated him).

You never told anyone outside the neighborhood what was going on inside the neighborhood.

And . . .

You never sold drugs.

Never.

Not ever.

The bag was filled with drugs. Kilos of brown powder, kilos of white powder, bricks of pot, plastic tubs filled with pills.

These aren't George Dunbar's drugs. They've been given to him. Entrusted to him. By Brian Shea.

These are Marty Butler's drugs.

All these years, everyone has wondered why Marty and his crew can't keep the drugs out of Southie.

And now she knows the answer—because they're the ones bringing the drugs in.

They've been killing their own.

They've been enslaving a whole generation of kids—to the pills, to the mirror and the rolled-up bill, to the needle and the spoon.

Drugs didn't kill Noel.

The Butler crew killed Noel. Just like they killed his father. Just like they killed his sister.

The Butler crew killed Mary Pat's family.

She leans against the wall at the back of the garage and considers that. For some reason, instead of tears or rage, all that exits her mouth is a dry chuckle.

She can see Marty Butler's bland catalog-model face floating in front of her own.

"You killed my family," she whispers in the silence of the garage.

He smiles back at her.

"I'm going to kill yours," she promises him.

George Dunbar arrives at the garage at eight a.m. He notices the missing lock first thing. He stares at the space where it was.

He looks around the parking lot. She can see through Dukie's binoculars that he's putting something together—the drugs that were stolen yesterday and now this. He's realizing that 1 + 1 = *someone's targeting him.*

He puts his hand against the outside wall of the garage.

He throws up. Twice.

When he finishes, he wipes his mouth. He bends and slowly rolls the garage door up.

His face relaxes a tad when he sees the Nova in there, just as he left it. He rushes to the back of it.

Mary Pat puts Bess in gear and rolls her up to a point about twenty feet from the garage door. She gets out. Leans against the hood. Waits. She can hear him in there as he rummages around the mostly empty trunk. He makes frantic squeaky sounds.

He closes the trunk. He comes toward the garage door with his lips moving, mumbling to himself. And then his eyes fall on her.

And he knows.

He doesn't know how he knows yet, but he knows.

He charges. He runs straight for her with his arms out like Frankenstein.

She pulls his own gun on him and places the muzzle to the center of his chest. "I can pull this trigger right now, and no court in the country will convict me. Probably give me a fucking medal. So, George, how would you like to proceed?"

He lowers his hands.

In the garage, with the door down, she pats him down for a weapon, but he's not carrying this morning. She notices a work light encased in orange plastic hanging in one corner and plugged into an extension cord. She gets it and hangs it from a hook above the hood of the car and watches George regain some of his confidence. It shows in his eyes first—and it's less a flowering than a recession—the way they go flat, stripped of everything but self-regard. Confidence was a quality she noticed in him way back, when he was best friends with Noel and used to come over their apartment all the time, back before drugs, before girls, even. Back when they talked about sports nonstop and argued over trading cards. Even then George had a self-possession that was noticeable. He seemed unconcerned what anyone thought about him and felt no need to express himself. An inability to express oneself wasn't uncommon in kids from Southie, but George's reticence didn't stem from inability; it stemmed, Mary Pat always felt, from will. And an internal arrogance. George, since as long as she could remember, seemed secure in the knowledge that he was better than anyone else—smarter, shrewder, less sentimental. With his lean features and close-cropped blond hair, eyes as green and cold as the land of his ancestors, George Dunbar's innate stillness gave most who knew him the disconcerting feeling that he *was* smarter and shrewder. He *was* better.

George has been doing the act so long, she can see that he believes it himself.

George says, "This must have been fun for you."

She gives him a quizzical look.

"The fantasy you had of how this would play out."

"And how did I think it would play out?"

"You'd steal my product, and I'd tell you what I know about your daughter."

"That's my fantasy?" She makes a show of considering the idea.

"But here's how it's really going to go."

She waits, an agreeable smile on her face.

He leans back against his car, not a care in the world, head tilted toward the ceiling. "You're gonna give me back my product, or my suppliers will kill you by the end of the day. And then it won't matter what you find out about your daughter."

"You keep calling her 'your daughter,' like you don't know her name."

He sighs. "But if you give me back my product, I won't say a word to my suppliers." He comes off the car, his eyes open yet unkind. "And you can go back to your . . . life."

"By 'suppliers,' you mean Marty."

He grimaces. "Whatever."

"So your deal is you let me live and you don't tell Marty I jacked your drugs because . . . you're a nice guy?" She closes some of the distance between them. "Or because if Marty or any of his crew found out you lost two loads in *one* day, well, George, I mean"—she chuckles—"your life will be fucking done."

George meets her chuckle with his own, his gaze darting a bit, though. "Okay, I'll grant you my job would go away. But I'll just go back to college."

"Oh, George. George." She shakes her head softly. "You failed Marty twice. Plus, you can help the police prove he's the *reason* drugs are getting into Southie. You know his routes, his suppliers, I'll assume. You probably know at least a few of the cops on his payroll." She can see her words have landed like body blows. She gets close enough for him to feel her breath on his face. "George, if you live for twenty-four hours after word gets out that you lost Marty's latest supply, I would lose all faith in the way the world works."

"My mother is—"

"Marty's piece of ass, yes. I know. It won't be enough to save you. Marty likes pussy but not as much as Marty *loves* money."

He says nothing for a minute. He looks down at her hands. "If you didn't have that gun . . ."

She steps back. Holds it up. "This gun?" She places the gun in her waistband at the small of her back. "No more gun."

He looks at the door behind her. Doesn't move.

"All you have to do is go through me," she tells him.

He considers his options.

"Just push me aside, George."

"Think I can't?"

She laughs loud. She can't help herself. "That's exactly what I think, George. You're running out of time."

"Wait."

"No," she says. "Make your move. Get me out of your way."

"Give me my product."

"Fuck your drugs."

"Give me—"

She steps close to him again. "You will not get your drugs until I walk out of here with everything I want. So either try to fight me right now, or drop the act and let's move this along."

George goes back to the dead eyes. She can see him practicing it in the mirror over the years in his mother's house.

"I'm a businessman," he says. "Let's negotiate."

"You're a fucking boy," she says. "Did you notice what was in your trunk?"

"It wasn't my product."

"The drugs are what's *not* in your trunk, yes. Did you notice what was in there, though?"

He thinks about it. "There was a gym bag."

"What'd you do with it?"

"I dunno."

She indicates with her head. "You tossed it aside, George. It's right behind you. Go get it."

His face scrunches in contempt. "You go get it."

She pulls the gun from behind her back and hits him in the forehead with the butt.

His eyes water and he stumbles backward. "Holy fuck!"

"Next time it's your perfect nose."

He gets the bag.

"Put it on the hood and open it."

He does. Stares inside. Can't compute what he's seeing. After a bit, she's pretty sure the hesitation on his face stems from understanding what the items in the bag mean, as opposed to any confusion.

Under the sudden harsh light, the items in the bag pick up a sallow, garish glow—

A needle, a spoon, a lighter, a length of rubber tubing, an eyedropper filled with water, and a small plastic baggie with brown powder inside.

"I assume you recognize your own supply."

He looks at it. "So?"

She sighs. "I've always given you credit for a brain. Maybe not a heart but a brain." She indicates the items with a flick of the gun. "You sell it. Now you're gonna try it. Or you will never see your 'product' again."

He laughs. It's supposed to sound derisive, but it sounds scared. "No fucking way."

She fires at his feet. He jumps. Grabs his ears.

She doesn't grab her own, but now she can't hear shit. That's what happens when you fire a round in a seven-by-four box with a metal door. *Stupid, Mary Pat. Stupid, stupid, stupid.*

Maybe the time for talk is over, though, because George is reaching into the bag. He wraps the rubber tube around his bicep, ties it off. He slaps the flesh around the inside crook of his elbow, looking for a vein. He's not very good at it because he's not acting from experience, only from years of observing the poor saps from whom he made his money.

Eventually, the ringing in her ears subsides enough for her to speak. "Lemme help."

She puts the gun back by the base of her spine. Prepares the powder on the spoon, adds the water, and cooks it with the lighter. She watched Noel do it once, near the end, after she'd thrown him out of the house before there'd be nothing left to steal. At that point he was beyond caring and sat on the bench in the playground under the half-broken streetlight. She watched him from the other side of the playground, out of his sight line as she leaned against the Jefferson Building, aware that she was watching suicide. Might take months, might take weeks (it took somewhere in between), but it was premeditated murder of the self nonetheless. He'd been in and out of rehab by that point, had robbed from her, robbed from his sister, robbed from Ken Fen, robbed from every friend he had until he had no friends left.

Except George. His supplier.

She sees George patting the flesh around the inside of his elbow again, and she reaches out and pinches the flesh so hard he yelps. "Hey!"

"That's how you get a vein."

He takes the needle and draws the mixture off the spoon. Once the syringe is full, he holds it out to her.

She shakes her head. "I'm not helping you shoot yourself up with your own poison."

It takes him four hesitant pokes before he hisses and drives the needle into the vein. He meets her eyes, his thumb over the plunger, and she waits him out.

He depresses the plunger.

He pulls the needle out. Hands it to her. "What now?"

"We wait."

Noel would talk about anything in the early stages of a high, back when he still lived with them and would use the bathroom to shoot up. He'd come out all dreamy-eyed and relaxed, sit at the kitchen table with her, and shoot the shit about anything—no defenses—for about ten minutes before she'd lose him. It's that sweet spot—about five minutes in but no longer than fifteen—that she waits for.

"What happened to Jules after you killed Auggie Williamson?"

He shrugs.

"George," she says, "what happened?"

Another shrug. "Dunno. She left with Frank."

"And after that?"

"Told ya—dunno."

She stares at him. Is he slick enough to lie under the influence of his first hit of heroin? Does he—does anyone—have that kind of will-power?

He smiles at her. A dreamy, distant smile. Knowing but not arrogant.

"You know how to pour concrete?" he asks her.

"You mix it, you pour it."

He sighs. "You've never done it, have you?"

"No, George, I haven't."

"Most people think it's easy. You grab a bag of it, mix it with some water, lay it down with a trowel, wait for it to dry."

She can sense this is not a random topic between them. She's aware that his family business—started by his uncles and his late father shortly after World War II—is cement.

"But it's *not* easy?" she offers.

A long slow shake of his head. "Not if you've never done it before, not if you don't know what you're doing. Not if your basement is eighty-five fucking degrees on a summer day and you mixed it wrong anyway, so it's already cracking five minutes after it fucking dries, and it fucking dries five minutes after you lay it down. What you got then is a mess. You can't get to what you're trying to seal over, but you haven't totally sealed it over either. I mean, it's there, what you tried to cover, like a fucking bug trapped in ice. And the fumes will knock you out."

He slides down the side of the car and sits against the tire and looks off at nothing. "I had this tricycle once. Metal. Heavy. It had a red seat."

She waits for more—a point, perhaps—but that's all she's getting.

"George," she says.

"Hmmm?"

"What were you trying to seal over?"

"Hmmm?"

"You said you were trying to seal something over in a hot basement."

He drifts, and then it's as if her words finally reach him at the other end of a long tunnel. "I wasn't the one who fucked up."

"No?"

Another slow headshake. "I don't fucking make mistakes with cement. *They* did."

"Who?"

He licks his lips several times. "You know."

"No, I—"

"Marty and Frank." He stares at her through half-mast eyes.

"What about them?"

"They tried to bury her in the basement, but they mixed the cement wrong, so they had to do it all over again."

Two thick veins, one on either side of Mary Pat's larynx, start to throb. "Say her name."

"Jules." A lazy smile for her as the heroin bathes his inner body from head to toe. "They had to bury her twice."

23

It's a few moments before she can speak.

She remembers the day she forced her way into the Fields. Larry Foyle and Weeds sported dirty T-shirts, their bodies sweaty and ripe with B.O. And then Brian Shea, his skin speckled with chalky residue, claimed he'd been helping "renovate" Marty's house. A sledgehammer rested against a toolbox in the rear grotto. Brian had been indignant because she'd gone to his house and questioned his wife in the disappearance of her daughter. He'd been threatening. Flicked a cigarette at her.

Insinuated that she was a bad neighbor.

Acted *self-righteous.*

And all the while, her daughter's body lay just twenty feet away in a cellar.

Brian Shea, with whom she'd had clammy, forgettable high school sex in his mother's bedroom.

Brian Shea, for whom Dukie had put in a word when he was just another kid on the make, trying to get in with Marty Butler.

Brian Shea, to whom Dukie once loaned money, only to have to chase him down to get it back.

Brian Shea, who was at the party they threw after Jules's christening.

Had been in their home, had eaten at their table, had drunk their liquor and beer.

Brian Fucking Shea.

"Why you crying?" George Dunbar, his back against the Nova, is watching her with a loose, sleepy gaze.

"Am I?" She dabs under her eyes with the heel of her hand.

He doesn't even hear her. He's already floating again.

She squats down by him and snaps her fingers in front of his face. "Did you see her?"

"Who?"

"Jules."

"When?"

"When you reset the basement floor?"

"Whose?"

"Marty's."

"Nah, nah, nah. We, um, we brought in the Quikrete. It's the stuff they should have used from the start. Concrete but sand too. It's good shit, dries fast . . ." He lowers his head, seems to fall asleep.

She slaps his face. His eyes snap open, meet hers. "You never saw Jules?"

"No, no. She . . . I mean, there was a hole in the floor, and it had been patched over, and then they poured the bad cement mix over that. So they busted up all the bad cement, and we came in and laid the Quikrete down, and that's where she is."

"Under the Quikrete."

He doesn't answer. He's into another nod.

She slaps him again.

"George! Is she under the Quikrete?"

"Yeah. She's there." His words are a muddy slur at this point. "She's there."

"George," she says before she loses him, "does anyone come to this garage besides you?"

He smiles and rolls his head on his neck. "No one knows it's here."

"No one?"

"Not a soul," he slurs.

If he notices when she handcuffs him to the handle of the car door, he doesn't seem to mind.

She gets some sleep in the backseat of the Nova.

When she wakes, it's hot as hell in there, the garage's metal door serving as a conductor for the rays of sun pounding the other side of it. George is rattling his handcuff against the door handle. She looks at her watch—two-thirty. Heroin begins to leave the bloodstream after six hours. George is right on schedule.

She loops the seat belt once around the back of the passenger seat. She uncuffs George, leads him over, and pushes him down into the seat. He groans a few times, asks her what she's doing, but she ignores him. She has to pull hard on the belt to get the latch plate up near his hip, but once she does, she slaps the cuff into the latch plate hole on the first try.

"You know what I don't get," she says.

He shakes his head, still a little foggy.

"You and Brenda. You don't seem like a couple." It's something that nagged at her while she was falling asleep in the back of the car.

"We're not."

She closes her eyes for a moment, wondering if there's any bottom to this.

"So if Rum was a cover for Frankie Toomey, who were you the cover for?"

"Who do you think?"

In the dark swelter of the car, she says nothing for a bit. And then: "Marty."

He doesn't nod. But he doesn't shake his head. He just holds her gaze.

"And George? One last question—when did they really take up with the girls?"

He takes a minute to formulate his thoughts. "Frank liked to say the reason they call it freshman year is because that's when it's freshest."

This is one of the moments she'll look back on and wonder how it was she managed not to kill him.

She drives them downtown.

"What do you know about how she died?"

George is out of sorts and grumpy. He keeps trying to raise his cuffed hand to block the sun from his eyes. He switches to his left hand, but it's still too much sun for one hand. "Frankie was pissed because she called his house after midnight and threatened to tell people."

"Tell people what?"

He gives her a careful look.

"Rum already told me she was pregnant," she tells him.

"Then, yeah, that's what she was threatening."

She drifts into oncoming traffic and has to swerve hard to avoid an oncoming cab. It's not anything George said. It's a fragment of memory from the last day she spent with Jules. They'd been walking along Old Colony, and Jules had spiraled into that weird dark mood which grew so exasperating that Mary Pat had asked her if she was PMSing. To which Jules replied:

No, Ma. Definitely no.

She was trying to tell me, Mary Pat thinks. *And I couldn't hear. I couldn't see and I couldn't hear. Because I didn't want to. Because truth hurts, truth costs, truth upends your world.*

They have to divert at the Broadway bridge because an anti-busing demonstration has shut down the bridge. As they follow the detour down along A Street, they pass throngs walking toward the bridge with anti-busing signs, anti-Garrity signs, anti-black signs.

They stop at an intersection and wait out the passing of a thick line of protesters.

"Why'd he kill her?" she says softly, surprised the words left her mouth because, in the end, no reason could be good enough.

"She wanted money to raise her kid."

"He has plenty of money."

"Doesn't mean he wants to share any. Plus, I heard she was asking for a lot. Said she didn't want to raise her kid the way she was raised."

Mary Pat tries to keep the wince in her heart from appearing on her face. "And if she didn't get the money?"

"She'd tell people it was his."

"Who told you this?"

"Larry Foyle. He was pretty down about it. Said it wasn't right. Said, 'We're killing little girls now?'"

"How'd you feel about it?"

"Really sad."

She looks over at him. He's still trying to dodge the sun, moving his head below his hand.

"No, you didn't," she says.

He sighs. "No, I didn't."

"Do you feel things, George? I've always wondered."

He frowns at his own reflection in the window. "I think it's a pretty idea, but no. Honestly? Outside of my mom, I never felt anything for anyone."

"At least you're honest."

He points at the protesters, stragglers now, but still a decent number of them working their way up A Street. "Look at these fucking morons. Whether niggers walk the halls of Southie High this year or not, you've all already lost. The towelheads just told us to go fuck ourselves and get used to walking until *they* decide to let us have more oil. But you'll pick a fight with the niggers, who are just as poor and fucked as you are, and tell yourselves you stand for something."

The traffic moves. They make it through the intersection just as the light turns from yellow to red.

"If you don't care about any of it, George, why'd you pick a fight with Auggie Williamson?"

He lowers his hand and looks at her, and the sun bathes the side of his face in harsh yellow that bounces and refracts as she drives.

"He was weak," he says. "You could see it in his eyes."

"Maybe he was just scared."

"Fear's a weakness." He holds his hand back up to the sun. "I don't like weakness."

"Maybe it's not weakness. Maybe it's just a kind heart."

He checks to see if she's serious. Once he decides she is, he lets out a bark of a laugh. "Well, I mean, fuck that, then."

She looks over at him for a bit and finally understands him after all these years. "I get it now. You don't have the anger, George. You just have the hate."

Neither says anything for two traffic lights.

As she turns onto Congress Street, Mary Pat says, "Why did they keep her body?"

"Huh?"

"If Frank Toomey did kill my daughter in that house, why did he leave her body there?"

"It's being watched." He shrugs. "That's what Marty's been told, anyway."

"Watched by who?"

"DEA."

"How does Marty know?"

"He's got someone in the FBI."

"No shit?" She can feel her eyes widen and hear an involuntary whistle leave her lips.

"Yup," George says. "That why he's untouchable."

She turns that over in her head a bit.

"Where we going?"

"I'm taking you to your drugs."

"Yeah?" He only half believes her.

"We had a deal. I'm holding up my end."

"I didn't promise I wouldn't say anything."

"You mean to Marty? About me jacking your drugs?"

"Yeah."

"I know you didn't. It's all fine, George."

He can't seem to compute that.

"Here we go," she says, and pulls over on the Congress Street Bridge by the harbor.

He looks at the red clapboard building that overlooks the water. At the gangway that descends to the harbor. At the yellow boat at the bottom of the gangway. "What're we doing here?"

"Do you know what that boat is?"

"Yes," he says irritably.

"Tell me."

"It's a replica of the ship."

"What ship?"

"What're we, in grammar school?"

"Humor me, George."

He gives her teenage-girl eye rolls. "It's a replica of the ship the Sons of Liberty boarded when they chucked all the British tea into the harbor back in seventeen seventysomething."

"Very *good*!" She claps his knee. "And why did they do that, George?"

"To protest taxes. Can you just—"

"Not taxes," she says. "Taxes without representation. That was the key part, George. They paid the British, but the British just took the money and didn't do a damn thing for them. So they chucked their precious limey tea right into the harbor. The point they were making, George, is if you take from me, then I fucking take *from you*."

He looks across the seat at her. "What are you on about?"

She gestures with her chin at the water. "That's where Marty's drugs are, George."

He doesn't get it. "On the boat?"

She shakes her head. "In the water."

George's mouth opens in a wide O. He stares through the windshield and blinks repeatedly. People walk by on the sidewalk outside the car, oblivious to the destruction going on within.

George finally speaks. He says, "Come on. No." His voice is small and pleading and cracks on the final word.

"I stood right up there in the middle of the bridge last night . . ."

"Please?" George stares through the windshield at the harbor.

"And I cut open the bags, one by one."

"Just . . . stop," he whispers.

"And I rained all those pills and powder down into the water."

He whispers something.

"What, George? I can't hear you. Speak up."

He makes a sound that falls somewhere between a grunt and a moan. "I'm dead."

"Without your drugs?"

"I'm fucking dead."

"Yeah," she agrees, "you certainly are."

She places the muzzle of the .38 into his midsection and reaches across his body to unlock the handcuff from the seat belt latch plate. She digs the muzzle farther into his abdomen, looks in his eyes, their noses only half an inch apart. She takes his wrist and swings it across their bodies and snaps the cuff into the driver's wheel.

She sits back and places the gun back under her shirt. "I look at you now, George, and I see a little boy who's scared, who wants a second chance. But they don't hand out second chances when you're an adult. Not around here. As a mother, I want to hold you in my arms. I want to whisper 'Shh' in your ear and tell you everything will be all right."

He's looking at her wildly, like maybe she'll do these things. "So, so, *help me*, Mrs. Fennessy. *Please*."

"I'd love to, George. I would." She caresses the back of his head and presses her forehead to his for a moment. When she speaks, her voice is kind and motherly. "But then? Then I remember that you sold my son the drugs that killed him, you murdered that poor black boy who just wanted to get home, and you helped bury my daughter in a basement." She removes her forehead from his, holds his hateful gaze with her own. "So I don't give a flying fuck, really, whether you die tonight or live a long hellish life in prison. I just know if I never look on your face again, it'll be a blessing from God Himself."

He repeatedly yanks the handcuff against the wheel as she exits the car.

She stops at a pay phone beside the Tea Party Museum and dials the number on the card she was given last week.

He answers on the third ring. "Detective Coyne."

She tells him where to find George Dunbar and hangs up.

24

Though the OPEC oil embargo officially ended five months earlier, a major side effect of the gas shortages of '73 is that no one drives around with a tank that's any less than half full. You never know when the Arabs are going to hold the oil hostage again, and no one wants to get stuck sitting for hours on end in those fucking lines.

So the cars parked out front of the Fields of Athenry that night are all sitting on gas tanks at least two thirds full. Most, including Marty Butler's AMC Matador, are topped up all the way. When someone tears a man's shirt—what arson investigators will later determine was the dress uniform of a U.S. Army corporal—into strips, ties the bottom of each strip to a small stone, and drops those strips into the gas tanks of every car parked in front of the Fields, it would take only a match, a firm hand, and balls the size of fucking ostrich eggs to light one hell of a fire.

Which is what happens.

The men in the bar notice the light playing off the windows. It almost seems like Christmas lights, maybe strung in a garland between two streetlamps and lifting in the winter breeze. But it's not winter, and those aren't Christmas lights. By the time they all get out to the sidewalk, it's like the end of the world or some fucking thing. Six cars in a row—half a block of them—are bonfires. Smoke and heat roil off the shells in oily waves.

They pull the hoses out from behind the bar and grab every fire extinguisher they can lay their hands on to keep the flames from hitting the bar itself, but the heat is like the heat of hell, and when the car windows start to blow out, guys get blasted with pebbles of glass. Poor Weeds catches a bunch of it in his right ear, enough to turn it into ground pork, as if his face weren't already bad enough, and they drag him back into the bar and someone goes looking for tweezers.

By the time the firemen show up, sparks drizzle off the roof and fat blue flames dance along the exterior walls of the bar. Everyone's evacuated. So they're standing there on the street—Marty and Frankie and Brian Shea and about fifteen other guys in the most feared crew on the south side of the city—and they're all sooty and bewildered, and the firemen push them back like they're regular citizens, everyday fucking schmoes.

It's Brian Shea who looks beyond the roof of the bar to the top of the building behind it and says, "Oh my God."

The firemen see it too, and they start shouting and pointing and calling for backup.

They'd all thought the bar was on fire, but the bar has just a couple of sparks and flames to deal with, flames that are already dying under the weight of the water smashing into them. But the house behind the bar—the house where Marty has done his deals and run his girls and his casino nights for wiseguys all across New England—that's got towers of flame shooting twelve feet high off the top of it.

They try to get to it, but the firemen push them back. Now the police are there and EMTs and, fuck, even reporters from 4, 5, and 7 and the *Globe*, the *Herald*, the *Argus*, and the *Patriot Ledger*.

Marty watches it all burn and says to Frankie, "If this is who I think it is, it falls on you, Tombstone. All on you."

Bobby finds a message taped to his desk lamp the next morning:
To: *Det. Sgt. M. Coyne*
Fr: *Some Southie Broad*

Message: *Sorry I burned the toast. She never got to Florida. She never left the cellar.*

Bobby can tell from the handwriting that Cora Sterns took the message. He finds her coming out of the women's locker room in street clothes. She doesn't want to stand around work one second longer than she has to, so Bobby has to hotfoot beside her toward the parking lot.

"When did the call come in?"

"Three in the morning."

"She called herself 'Southie Broad'?"

"Called herself '*Some* Southie Broad.'"

"And she said she burned the *toast*?"

Cora pushes out through the door into the parking lot. "She *in-sisted* I put that in the message. I was like, 'Lady, you fucking up the detective's breakfast sounds like personal business you don't call in on a department line.' But she made me write it down."

"Thanks."

"Don't give your chippies your work number, Detective, let your sisters deal with them."

"Yes, Cora."

She shoots him a kinda friendly/kinda not middle finger as she walks to her car.

Twenty minutes later, Bobby hears about the fire in Southie last night, and the penny drops.

The arson investigators, tracing the point of origin, determined that the blaze started in the basement. They hand Bobby an oxygen mask and tank, tell him the basement flooring was recently done over with cement that's still settling, so the fumes are toxic. They lead him down a blackened set of stairs and shine a light on a dark brown oval in the center of the floor. The rest of the floor is a goopy blue-gray. There's a film of it over the brown oval, but it's thin.

The arson investigator's voice comes through his mask as if up from a bathtub. "Is this what you're looking for?"

Bobby nods.

It takes them half the day to get the body up. They're all down there, sweating their balls off in masks and hazmat whites and the firemen trying to shore up the whole basement and make sure it doesn't collapse on their heads. To dig up the body, they have to send someone out to the special-equipment warehouse in Canton to get the right tool, which looks like a jackhammer with a putty-knife blade, but it cuts a perfect rectangle in the floor that looks, appropriately, like a coffin.

They keep taking trips upstairs to the grotto outside because, even with the masks and oxygen, it's easy to get dizzy down there. Brian Shea and half a dozen Butler guys watch them from the little tables out back of the bar, ask them why they're not somewhere fighting real crime, maybe busting the niggers before they can come in here and fuck up the schools and every other fucking thing by Thursday.

Gregor, one of the crime tech guys, has a smoke with Bobby, and Bobby asks why they're choosing to bring out the body with the soft cement and dirt still encasing it.

"Evidence," Gregor says. "We don't know what mighta leached in there."

Guys with the ME's office carry the body out in a black bag while they're sitting there, and Bobby and Gregor step aside while the guys load it into the morgue van. Bobby catches Brian Shea watching from across the way. Brian's a cold fish, a hell of a poker player, Bobby's always heard, but he looks pretty sick right now, like his stomach is filling with acid.

Bobby shoots him a broad smile and a big salute.

· · ·

Down at the morgue, they cut away the cement and dirt around the body and bag it all. Then they clean the corpse and straighten the legs and arms as best they can.

"Cause of death?" Bobby says.

Drew Curran, the medical examiner for this shift, grimaces at him. "This is my first look. Can you give me a second?"

Bobby sighs and reaches for a cigarette.

"You can't smoke in here, Detective."

A few minutes later, Drew says, "Oh, yeah, we got it."

Bobby comes out of his seat.

Drew peels back a puckered hole just below the left rib cage. "Someone shoved a five-inch blade right under her ribs and straight into her heart. Could've been looking in her eyes when he did it."

Bobby looks at her now, this child who came out of Mary Pat Fennessy's womb less than eighteen years ago. Even with the early stages of decomposition settling in, he can see what a pretty girl she was. Not just pretty but . . . soft. The mother is all hard edges and angles, a jawline set in permanent opposition, thin lips usually one curl away from a sneer. The mother is built for battle. The daughter, on the other hand, seems, even in death, to have arrived from a fairy tale. As if she's not dead but merely awaiting the restorative kiss of the prince, who, even as Bobby and Drew stand there, nears this building and the end of his quest.

We're not built for princesses down here, Bobby thinks.

"What'd you say?" Drew asks.

"Nothing," Bobby says. "Nothing."

"You got what you need?"

"Yeah," Bobby says, and leaves.

Next time she calls is halfway through his shift.

"We went by your place looking for you."

"I'm not there right now," she says.

"That's probably a good thing."

"I understand you may have taken a body out of a burned building recently."

"We did, yes."

"Has it been identified by next of kin?"

"We're waiting on next of kin to arrive."

"Would next of kin have to worry about arrest?"

"For what?"

"You tell me."

Neither speaks for a bit.

"My dad," Bobby tells her eventually, "was the best housepainter you ever saw. Inside, outside, didn't matter. He was a magician with a brush or a roller. People would ask him questions, though, about wood rot and load-bearing walls, even the electrical. My father would say, 'I do one thing better than anybody by *not* concerning myself with anything else.'"

"Sounds like a cool guy," Mary Pat says.

"When he was sober, yeah, he was." Bobby realizes how much he misses the old bastard in that moment. "I'm a homicide investigator. I don't investigate arson. That's what arson investigators are for. I don't investigate assault and battery. I don't concern myself with someone, say, who claims he was forced at gunpoint to shoot heroin into his veins."

"Well, *that's* a crazy tale," Mary Pat says.

"Right?" Bobby chuckles. "You should hear the one about the kid who was threatened with castration."

"Here?" Mary Pat says. "In the United States of America?"

"We suspect so, yes."

"What is happening to this world, Detective?"

"I don't know, Mrs. Fennessy. I really don't."

The silence on the line is comfortable until Bobby rips the Band-Aid.

"Can you meet me at the city morgue, 212 Hester Street, in two hours?"

Her tone darkens to pure black. "I'll be there."

He stands beside her in the corridor as Drew Curran wheels the gurney up to the viewing window, the sheet covering the body, head to toe. Drew comes around to the side of the gurney closest to the window and puts his finger on the corner of the sheet, looks through the glass at Bobby.

"You ready?" Bobby asks her.

"No one's ready for this." She sucks in some air. "Okay. Okay. Do it."

He nods at Drew.

Drew pulls back the sheet, stopping at the shoulders.

"Oh," Mary Pat says. "Ohhhhhhh. Ohhhhhhhh. Ohhhhhh."

First her face crumbles, then her body, and Bobby catches her before she can hit the floor. She keeps saying that one plaintive "Oh" over and over.

She stares through the glass at her daughter's corpse and then presses her face to the glass, the movement so fast and Mary Pat so strong that she drags Bobby to the glass with her in a single lurch. She shrugs him off her and places her palms to the glass and weeps and whispers her daughter's name.

Bobby never sees her leave. She fills out the paperwork and excuses herself to the bathroom, and after a while, he realizes he hasn't seen her come out. They send in a female lab tech, but she's not there. Her car's no longer in the back lot.

He can hear that "Oh" ringing in his head. Wonders if he'll ever get it out.

Turns out the house behind the Fields of Athenry isn't in Marty's name. It's in the name of a guy whose body was found in the trunk of a car in long-term parking at the Amtrak station in Pawtucket in 1969. The guy's name was Lou Spiro, and he left no surviving relatives, so no one ever looked into his estate. But Lou was sitting on some gold mines—a Southie liquor store, a Medford car wash, a metal compacting company in Somerville, and two strip clubs in Revere—that everyone has long assumed belong to Marty Butler.

While the BPD can't directly tie Marty or Frank Toomey to the body they found in the basement, they can freeze all the assets of the late Lou Spiro and begin taking steps to seize all his properties. That makes the burning of the home behind the Fields of Athenry the most disastrous calamity—by a huge fucking margin—to ever befall the Butler crew.

"You need to get out of town," Bobby tells Mary Pat the next time she calls him. "Maybe the country."

"But why?" she asks, all mock innocence.

"You're a marked woman."

"Eh." She takes a drag on a cigarette.

"Rum and George confessed," he tells her. "It'll be in the papers tomorrow or the next day. We're running around confirming all their details now. You won."

That brings a wet, angry laugh over the line. "I didn't win shit. They're walking around free."

"We have George Dunbar saying Frank and Marty hired him to repave the basement floor with Quikrete."

"So?"

"So it puts them by the body."

"They'll have twenty fucking alibis—minimum—for the night she died. They'll have witnesses placing them in Persia. You don't have anything on them."

"We got Frank giving an order on Auggie Williamson."

"I heard about that 'order,'" she says. "'Finish the job' could mean anything. That's what they'll say in court. You know that."

He does.

"They're gonna walk from this just like they walk from everything."

"Mary Pat," he says, "don't wreck your life trying to do something that is doomed to fail."

"My life," she says, "was my daughter. They took my life when they took hers. I'm not a person anymore, *Bobby*. I'm a testament."

"What?"

"That's what ghosts are—they're testaments to what never should have happened and must be fixed before their spirits leave this world."

"Mary Pat, you need help."

A dark chuckle. "It's not me who's gonna need help, believe you me."

"You've already dented their drug business, taken a blowtorch to their headquarters, and fucked up at least five businesses they own, by my latest count. Worse than all that, you embarrassed them. Made them look like fucking dunces."

"They're still walking the streets!"

Her voice is so loud he has to hold the phone away from his ear for a moment. When he puts it back, she speaks calmly:

"George tell you about the rifles he handed off to some black guys in Roxbury?"

Bobby grabs his notepad. "He did not."

"They were on Moreland Street not far from Warren, by a little park and playground. Three guys with big 'fros and goatees."

Bobby knows those assholes. It's a schizo-political group calls themselves the Global Liberian Liberation Front but go by the street name the Moorlocks. They're a batshit brew of conflicting ideologies—

Stokely Carmichael and Malcom X crossed with Back-to-Africa crossed with the Weather Underground and the West German Red Army Faction, all of it needing to be financed, so they deal a shitload of drugs to the very people they claim to want to "liberate."

"You know what the guns are for?"

"Brian Shea said they damn well better make some noise with them."

Damn, Bobby thinks, *if I'd met Mary Pat five years ago and she worked the street like this? I'd have made lieutenant by now.*

"Leave town," he tells her.

"Oh, Bobby," she says in a mildly baffled tone, "no one's gonna chase me out of my hometown."

And she hangs up.

25

Bobby and Carmen's first time together is awkward and fumbling at the outset. There's no sense of rhythm; it's like trying to dance after someone turns off the music. He has no idea what her body will respond to, and he makes a few poor guesses. But then he gets a whispered "Yeah, right there" and a quickening of her breath in his ear. Her heel glides along the back of his calf, and he moves his hip just a tad to his left, and she says "Yup" in such a way that *yup* becomes his favorite sound that week.

In the end they find a groove that works. It's not fireworks, but it's promising. The fireworks could be just up around the next bend. They'll find out next time.

After, they lie in her bed and listen to the sounds of Chandler Street three stories below on a humid night in early September, and Bobby embraces a sentiment he's never grown sick of since he returned from the war—*It's wonderful to be alive.*

She gets out of the bed. "Would you like some water?"

"Love some."

She walks naked into the kitchen. When she returns with two glasses of water, he notices that one of her breasts is slightly larger than the other, and her green eyes carry a shimmer in the half dark. She sits on the bed and hands him his water, and they look at each other for a bit, saying nothing.

"I like how considerate you are," she says.

"When?"

"In general," she says, "but in bed too. You listened to my body. A lot of guys don't do that."

"You've had a lot of guys?"

"For sure," she says easily. "You?"

"Guys? No. But women, yeah."

"So we won't judge each other's histories."

"Nothing good ever comes of that."

She slides down in bed beside him and holds her water aloft as she gives him a long kiss. Her hair tickles the side of his face. The kiss is warm and unhurried. *Another of life's blessings,* he thinks, *the leisurely kiss.*

When Carmen pulls out of the kiss, she glances at the clock on the bedside table. "Didn't you say you were on TV tonight?"

"I said I *could be* on TV. They filmed us walking those kids into their arraignment."

She crawls down the bed and turns on the small black-and-white on top of her dresser.

WCVB is wrapping up its intro. They cut to the studio and then cut in close on the anchor desk, and suddenly, there's Bobby in a little box to the right of Chet Curtis's shoulder. (*Lead story,* he thinks. *Damn.*) Bobby and Vincent and Rum Collins and George Dunbar, the latter two trying to keep their heads down, are frozen in the shot as Chet talks about the big break in the death of a young Negro on the eve of the city's controversial desegregation of two public high schools.

And just like that, they cut away from Chet and run footage of the latest anti-busing protest, this one over by Broadway Station.

"My new boyfriend," Carmen says, "a TV star."

"I'm your new boyfriend?"

"You're not?"

"I just wasn't sure I'd achieved that status."

"Oh, you got the status, m' man."

On the screen, the protest turns predictably violent. The camera jerks a few times. A fleshy guy from the school committee talks into a bullhorn, throws around words like "tyranny" and "subjugation."

"If the school committee had just acted in good faith years ago," Carmen says, "instead of trying to throw a wrench in things from the start, maybe we wouldn't be here."

"You're definitely not wrong," he says. "But how come it's always the poor who are expected to eat the food that's good for them no matter how it tastes? You don't see anyone in the rich neighborhoods dealing with this."

"Because they're not part of Boston Public Schools."

"Right. They don't want to be part of the public school system, and they don't want subway lines or bus lines coming into their towns because they don't want to mix with poor people in general and black people in particular. Or so it would seem."

"Not all the suburbs are white."

"Name one that isn't. Just one."

She tries. "Um . . ."

He waits.

"I can feel your look," she says. "It's very smug."

"Our suburbs," he says, "are designed to escape the melting pot. But now they're telling all the people they left behind precisely how they should go about rubbing elbows."

"But the schools *are* segregated," she says.

"Yes," he says. "And they shouldn't be. You'll get zero argument on that from me. It's racist bullshit, and it's unforgivable. But this is not the solution."

"What is?"

He opens his mouth, still caught up in the rhythm of the debate. Then freezes. "I have *no* idea."

"And that's the problem. If no one can come up with a solution, but a solution has to be found, then this—by being any kind of solution at all—is the best solution by default."

He says nothing for a bit.

"You don't look convinced," she says.

"No matter what we claim in public, in private we all know that the only law and the only god is money. If you have enough of it, you don't have to suffer consequences and you don't have to suffer for your ideals, you just foist them on someone else and feel good about the nobility of your intentions."

"Phew," she says. "You're cynical."

"I prefer skeptical."

"You can't compare the public schools here to the private schools in the suburbs. It's not apples and oranges."

"Why not?"

"Because people pay for the right to . . ." She turns in the bed and looks at him. "Ooooh, you bastard."

"Right?"

"You set me up."

"I did not."

After a bit, she says, "But something *had* to be done."

He flashes on Mary Pat Fennessy in the morgue the other day. *Talk about someone who believes something has to be done, no matter what the fallout is. Jesus.*

"Yeah, something had to be done," he agrees.

"Because if not now, when?" she asks.

He sighs and stubs out his cigarette. "There's the rub."

"Can I ask you something . . . delicate?"

"I'll gird my loins."

"You're an Irish cop from Savin Hill," she starts.

He knows exactly where this is going. "How come I'm not a racist? Is that the question?"

"Kinda. Yeah."

He drinks some water. "My parents were, let's say, difficult people. They'd both given up their dreams when they married, so to be their kid was, uh, not fun. They were angry and hated each other and couldn't admit to themselves that they were angry and hated each other. So they drank and they fought and they found a million different ways to make us kids proxy soldiers on their battlefield. Then my mother got sick and died. And my father realized he'd loved her as much as he'd hated her. And that fucked him up even worse. So, when I say my parents weren't saints, probably weren't even good people, you can believe me."

She's watching him with a curious half smile. "Okay."

"But they also weren't racists. Something about the idea of it—the pure irrationality of it—offended them. They didn't think black people were necessarily good, don't get me wrong, they just thought everyone—regardless of what color they were—was probably an asshole. And to say you were less of an asshole because your skin was lighter was reprehensible to them. It just made you a bigger asshole." He smiles, remembering their utter core *contrariness*. "There were only two big sins in the house on Tuttle Street—feeling sorry for yourself and racism, which, when you think of it, are two sides of the same coin."

"I think I might have liked your parents."

"Until the fifth drink," he admits, "they could be a lotta fun."

"What were their dreams?"

"Hmm?"

"You said they'd given up their dreams."

"My father was a painter. Not a housepainter—well, he was that too—but a genuine artist."

"And what did your mother want to be?"

"Anything but a mother. Or a housewife. I think she just wanted to be free." He can feel her looking deeper into him than anyone's cared to look for a long time. "What about your parents?"

"They wanted me to marry well. And live in the suburbs. And not need a job. I was always fairly certain I'd been a disappointment to them. But just before my mother died, she told me, 'We never ap-proved, but we were always proud.' Isn't that a weird thing to tell your kid?"

He thinks about it. "It's nice, actually. She's saying you took your path, and it wasn't what she would have chosen, but you did well." He finds himself flashing on Mary Pat Fennessy again, a woman robbed of both her children. Christ, he wonders, what could possibly give her the strength to get out of bed in the morning?

Fury.

Anguish.

Rage.

"You come from the upper middle class," he says to Carmen, "but you left it all behind to help people. To actually fucking matter in this world. If I was your parent, I'd be proud of you."

She taps his nose with her index finger. "If I was your mom, I'd be proud of you."

"This is a weird conversation to have naked."

"Ain't it?"

She rolls on her side and he tucks in tight behind her and they fall asleep with the windows open to the night and the TV still on.

26

Mary Pat spends a night in a motel on Huntington Avenue, just across from the Christian Science Mother Church. The motel accepts cash and doesn't ask for ID and, most importantly, has an underground garage where she can tuck Bess away in a dark corner that smells of oil. She sits in the motel room in the near dark and looks across the street at the church plaza. She doesn't know much about architecture or anything about Christian Scientists, but the mother church is an impressive structure. Two buildings—the smaller, sharper one with a pointy granite steeple is something she'd expect to see in Paris, maybe; the larger one behind it makes her think of pictures she's seen of Rome: a big dome at the top, presiding over wide arches and thick columns, all of it mirrored in the long, narrow reflecting pool that stretches the length of the plaza.

If Jules had come to her just two weeks ago and said she was converting to Christian Scientology, or whatever they call it, Mary Pat would have disowned her. Fennessys and Flanagans were Roman Catholics. Always had been, always would be, end of story. But now Mary Pat finds the whole idea—of disowning someone for choosing to believe in a different interpretation of God—ridiculous. If Jules lies right now in the embrace of the Christian Scientist God or the Buddhist God or whatever the Episcopalians believe in, Mary Pat cares only that it's an embrace. And that her daughter no longer knows anything of fear. Or hate.

She turns on the small TV on the dresser and, after fiddling with the antenna, finds the clearest picture on Channel 5. She catches the last half hour of a *Harry O* episode she's seen before, floats away sitting there, has no idea where she goes or that she went anywhere at all until she snaps back from wherever she was to find that the news is now on.

This has been happening a lot lately, these little episodes of vanishing within herself. She doesn't fall asleep or even doze, but time vanishes nonetheless. And she seems to vanish with it.

Halfway through the news, just before sports, they mention that "Funeral services will be held tomorrow morning at Third Baptist Church for Augustus Williamson, the young Afro-American man who died tragically at Columbia Station, further inflaming racial tensions on the eve of desegregation of our schools."

She recalls the note Dreamy wrote to her when Noel passed. If Mary Pat could write half as well as Dreamy, maybe she'd consider writing a note of her own. But she can't. Not only is her grammar bad, her handwriting is atrocious.

She finds herself staring across the street again at those remarkable buildings reflected, along with several other local buildings, in the long pool of water. *We pass on and the buildings remain. And eventually, even buildings as magnificent as these crumble.*

I'm not afraid to die, she tells those buildings, the room, God. *Not even a little bit.*

Then what are you afraid of?

Living in a world without her.

Maybe she feels the same way.

Jules?

No, you idiot. Dreamy.

Third Baptist Church of the Blue Hills sits on a small plot of land on Hosmer Street in the heart of Mattapan. When Mary Pat was very young, Mattapan was where the Jews lived in uneasy truce with a contingent of poor Irish. Then the blacks showed up, and the Jews headed for the suburbs or parts of Brookline while the Irish pushed into Dorchester or wandered into Southie. Synagogues and bakeries gave way to chicken joints and hair salons—as she drives along Morton Street looking for parking, Mary Pat loses count of how many hair salons. Not to mention army-recruitment billboards, menthol-cigarette billboards, and liquor stores. Southie's got Mattapan beat when it comes to bars, but Mattapan has the edge when it comes to purchasing your booze for home consumption. Parking's just as hard to find as it is in Southie, though, and people here love to double-park just as much. The walls and storefronts are more colorful, however—lots of vibrant murals, something you never see in Southie; plenty of bright awnings and clothing, on both men and women, that runs to tropical colors: bright yellows, mango greens, cotton-candy pinks. Before she can start feeling too kumbaya, like she could move here and be happy if she could only change skin color, she notices how many grates they have above their storefronts and how many of their windows have bars on them, how many of the side streets are cracked and ridden with potholes, and how many yards are so overgrown it would be impossible to see the fences if the fences didn't sag and poke out through the growth.

Have some self-respect, she thinks with a sudden defiant pride.

We're not the same. She pleads her case to some unseen judge as she backs into a parking space. *We're just not.*

As she turns off her ignition, a thuggish hulk of a young man stares in at her as he passes, maybe thinking about what she might have in her purse or entertaining even darker thoughts.

She has no idea why she does what she does next—terror?—but she does it: She smiles. A big friendly one and follows it with a small wave.

The young man—actually not all that big, not all that thuggish, just poor, his clothes not fitting him right—smiles back. It's maybe a slightly confused smile, a tad hesitant, but it's gentle, and he even returns her wave with a nod. And then he moves on, a boy really, couldn't be older than fourteen.

She sits there, overcome suddenly with a fresh horror of the self. Her daughter is dead, Auggie Williamson is dead, the lives of several teenagers on the platform that night are ruined, and her mind *still* grasps with grubby desperation for ways to feel superior to them.

To feel superior to someone. Anyone.

Inside the church, she steps into a pew at the very back. She's mildly surprised to discover she's not the only white person to attend Auggie Williamson's funeral; there are nine or ten others among the crowd of about a hundred. It's an impressive turnout, though she gets a sense from looking around at the clothing that a lot of the mourners are politicians or activists. It's all over the papers, how what appeared at first to have been an accident now looks to be a race crime perpetrated by four racist teens from the racist hotbed of South Boston.

The head of the Urban People of Color Action Committee has questioned whether Auggie Williamson's death was just the first of the "lynchings" they could expect once their children were bused into South Boston come Friday. A prominent community organizer asked if there was any end to the hate, and a spokesperson for the Roxbury Crossing Small Business Cooperative drew up a petition to rename Columbia Station Augustus Williamson Station or, at the very least, put up a plaque in his honor by the station doors.

The church continues to fill, and a lot of the folks look solidly working-class or lower-middle, dressed in clothes they bought at Sears or Zayre, not Filene's or Jordan Marsh. Mary Pat has chosen the last pew on the right in case she needs to make a quick, unnoticed exit, but a group approaches and asks with their eyes for her to move down the pew, as an elderly woman with a walker takes up their rear. Mary

Pat does so, and almost immediately, another five people enter the pew from the other side, and she's stuck in the middle. When she looks around again, the entire church is full. Some folks even stand in the back, fanning themselves with hymnals or the program for today's funeral.

Right before the service starts, Detective Bobby Coyne makes his way up the left side and takes a place against the wall between two stained-glass windows. He catches her eye and blinks in surprised acknowledgment, throws her that kindly smile of his, his eyes narrowing at her—a look that says, *Don't go anywhere when this is over.*

The family enters with the coffin. Mary Pat pictures the boy in that coffin and her daughter at the morgue, and she feels awash in loss and grief but also in sin she can't name or even fully define. But it's sin all the same. For a moment she fears she might pass out. The air has somehow grown too thin and too dense at the same time. She grips the back of the pew in front of her and steadies herself until the light-headedness passes.

In the Catholic church, funerals are second only to weddings and Christmas when it comes to the length of the mass, but even with that exposure, Mary Pat is unprepared for just how long a Baptist funeral can go. There're four spirituals before they even get to the readings. And after the readers, the minister, a Reverend Thibodaux Josiah Hartstone III, reminds the congregation that he was named after the town of Thibodaux, Louisiana, where, less than a hundred years ago, white militias descended on the homes of Negro sugarcane workers (including Reverend Hartstone's grandfather and grandmother) who were striking for a fair wage, and those white militiamen killed upward of a hundred and fifty Negro men, women, children, and elders (including Reverend Hartstone's grandfather and grandmother) for the sin of asking for fair treatment and a living wage. Mary Pat hears a chorus of "Amen" and a smattering of loud moans and "Help us, Jesus!" and "Help us, Lord!"

"And who were these four white children of South Boston if not another militia?" the Reverend Thibodaux Josiah Hartstone III asks his flock. "How is that militia of old any different than these four misguided thugs who murdered our cherished son, Augustus, for the crime of trying to get home? For the crime of driving a car that broke down? For the crime of trying to better himself in the management program of Zayre? For the crime of crossing *their* streets, treading *their* sidewalks, using *their* subway platform? Is this the milk of human kindness of which our good Lord Jesus spoke?"

Mary Pat feels light-headed again. And sick to her stomach. The eulogy for Auggie Williamson is turning, in some ways, into a eulogy for Jules. Into a eulogy for Mary Pat's legacy as a parent.

"No!"

"No!" he roars, one hand raised to the rafters. "No! Because, brothers and sisters, it's not *their* world. It's our world. It's God's world. And they had no right to take one of God's children out of God's world because they didn't like the color of the skin God gave him!"

Mary Pat lowers her head and swallows repeatedly against hot bile. Beads of sweat slide down behind her ears and into the collar of her shirt. One continues on down her spine. She keeps her head lowered. She takes deep breaths.

"But God is good," he says.

"Amen!"

"God is just!"

"Mmm-hmm!"

"God says Augustus is with Me now!"

"Praise Jesus!"

"And *I*, the Lord and Savior, *will* pass judgment on those who have hurt our brother Augustus! Because I am the Lord!"

"Praise the Lord!"

When Reverend Thibodaux Josiah Hartstone III wraps up his fire and his brimstone, he launches into a rendition of "The Day Is Past and Gone," and the congregation joins in with a kind of fever—a mix of joy and rage and God-love, heartbreak, and passion—that is unlike anything Mary Pat has ever witnessed. The floor shakes, the pews shake, the *walls* shake.

After "The Day Is Past and Gone," Auggie's father, Reginald, rises from the front pew and takes a place behind the lectern. He's a tall, elegant man. Mary Pat has met him several times over the years and has always been struck by his mix of deference and gravity. Now what strikes her, even from the back of the church, is the unreachable despair in his eyes. It's not the despair of the hopeless, it's the despair of the forsaken. The first is weakness, the second is a knife blade. Those who quit are victims, but those who are abandoned grow vengeful.

"Auggie was a typical kid," Reginald begins, his voice hushed against the microphone, "rebellious at times as a teen but never to the point where we truly worried. Loved his momma. Fought with his sisters. Oh, did he ever." He chuckles a bit. "Graduated high school but not with the kind of grades would get a black boy a scholarship to any colleges, so he went to work for that department store, was on the management track, hoped to run the whole New England district of the chain someday." He looks out with a gaze that rides above the congregation by several feet. "Loved his clothes, Auggie."

A soft chuckle hums through the crowd.

"Right?" Reginald says. "'Threads,' he called them. Even as a little boy, he was so *fussy* about his clothes. Liked his hats, his shiny shoes—had to shine like a brand-new dime—them big-collared shirts of his. He snagged a pair of pants on a doorjamb coupla weeks back? Was stitching up the tear himself. I said, 'Boy, why don't you buy a pair of dungarees so that don't happen?' He said, 'I wouldn't be caught dead in dungarees, old man, you know that.'"

Reginald says nothing for a bit. Mary Pat can feel the whole church waiting, wondering where this is going.

He leans into the microphone. "He wouldn't be caught dead in dungarees." He breathes heavily through an open mouth. "Instead, he got caught dead in South Boston. Well, he got *caught* alive. But then they killed him. And the Lord says forgive the sinner, if not the sin, but, ya know, *fuck* the sinner."

Lots of murmuring in the pews, people looking around. Up on the altar, Reverend Thibodaux Josiah Hartstone III sports a tight smile but leans forward like soon he might just make a dash for the mic.

Reginald Williamson says softly, "What's gonna change? When's it gonna change? Where's it gonna change? How's it gonna change? Human beings don't kill *fellow* human beings. Not easily. They just don't." He steps back from the lectern and runs a hand over his mouth. He freezes that way for a moment, the hand covering the mouth, as if to keep the words in forever. Then he steps back to the lectern and says, "They only kill *other* human beings easily. So, so, so, it can't change if they don't see us as fellow humans. Can't change if they only see us as others." He hangs his head. "It just can't."

But you are *others,* Mary Pat thinks before she can kill the thought. And even as she's trying to stanch the words barreling into her brain, the follow-up plows through. *You just are.*

The bile she's pushed back down to her stomach surges once more, a series of hot pebbles climbing up her esophagus. She lowers her head again, takes slow breaths.

When they escort the coffin back down through the church, the pews empty out in order behind it, front to back, so by the time Mary Pat exits the church, the coffin is already in the hearse and Dreamy and Reginald are in one of the limousines behind it and Mary Pat realizes that her plan to express a brief condolence to Dreamy and move on quickly was a fantasy. She sees Bobby Coyne talking to his partner, who's parked an unmarked haphazardly by the curb and is speaking urgently to him. Bobby is nodding and at one point looks around, possibly for her, but she uses the milling crowd to her advantage, and he soon speed-walks away with his partner and they drive off in the unmarked.

At the cemetery, Reginald, Dreamy, their family and closest friends, and the political activists stand up front by the coffin. Mary Pat and most of the other white people stand all the way back by the road.

The Williamsons own their own home in Mattapan. A small Dutch Colonial on Itasca Street. It's set up the way white homes Mary Pat aspires to live in are set up. Tidy. Well-kept lawn, recent touch-up on the trim. The floors are shiny blond oak. The entire house smells of wood soap. Front hall arrayed with photographs of Auggie and his sisters and some white-haired people Mary Pat assumes are grandparents. Living room off to the right past an arched entryway. Off to the left, a small dining room with stained-glass windows which leads into the kitchen. Beyond the kitchen, a brown wooden deck overlooking a small yard. The deck and the yard are where most of the mourners congregate.

Mary Pat, reaching the kitchen, looks around for Dreamy. She just wants to express her condolences and get gone. But the first person she runs into is not Dreamy, it's Reginald.

"I just want to say—" she begins.

"Fuck you want to say to me?" he says.

She looks closely at him to be sure he's the same Reginald she's met several times before. She's honestly not sure. Until his eulogy, she never heard him use profanity of any kind. Assumed he might be the type who didn't believe in it.

"Bitch, I said what do you want to say to me?"

She locks on his tie—she noticed it when he passed her pew on his way out of the church with his son's coffin. It's dark blue with light blue crosses on it. Definitely him.

Did he just call me a bitch?

"I, um, I wanted to express my condolences."

"Oh," he says kindly. "Oh. Thank goodness. That means a lot." He touches her arm with his big black hand. Gives it a light squeeze.

"What did you think I wanted?" she asks.

He squeezes her arm a little harder. "Thought you wanted to explain why your moron, nigger-hating daughter killed my intelligent, pure-hearted son."

"Can you let go of my arm?"

He squeezes even harder. "Am I holding your arm?"

"Yes."

"You sure?"

"Yes."

"Sure it ain't just a *circumstance*? Like, say, you went and put your arm in my hand and I ain't got no choice but to squeeze what you put in my hand? Ain't that a possibility?"

"No."

"No?" He cocks his head at her. "Well, I say it is. I say that whatever thought crosses my mind, Mrs. Fennessy, is the rule of fucking law in this house. You want to complain? Take it up with me right here, right now. You don't think I look in your eyes and know a tough bitch when I see one? I know you're a tough bitch. I know you could fuck many a man up, but I ain't that man, and you ain't in a place where you can afford to find out. Because if I were to—right fucking now—crush the windpipe of the mother of one of the demons who killed my child? A woman who trespassed into my home on the day of the funeral of my only son? If I were to do that, Mrs. Mary Pat Fennessy, I wouldn't go free, but I would have enough credit in prison for killing your ass to ensure I would live like a goddamn king for the rest of my days."

Far worse than the pain of his fingers gripping her arm like the teeth of five socket wrenches is the hate in his eyes. She's a bit of an expert on hate—she's been around it her whole life—and his hate *for her* is truly depthless.

"Reginald!"

They turn to see Dreamy entering the kitchen.

"You let her go right now."

Mary Pat will always remember these as a few of the most dangerous seconds of her life. She knows Reginald will choose one of only two roads—listening to his wife or doing something extremely violent extremely fast. Mary Pat is certain in that moment that if this man decides to kill her, he will succeed.

He drops her arm. "Get her out of my home," he says, and walks past his wife toward the deck.

In front of the house, some mourners mingle, so Dreamy walks Mary Pat to the end of the block. They stop by a mailbox, its blue paint faded and chipping from exposure to the elements.

Dreamy says, "I'm sorry for—"

"You don't have to apologize for that. He's angry. He didn't know what he was saying."

Dreamy's eyes narrow at her. "I'm not apologizing for Reginald. I stopped him from hurting you so my girls could have their father at home, not in some shithole prison."

Mary Pat can't help think, *Dreamy cusses too?*

"I was expressing my regret for your loss," Dreamy says. "However I feel about your daughter or about you, Mrs. Fennessy, I don't think any mother deserves to lose a child, never mind two."

"And I'm sorry for your loss," Mary Pat manages.

"Don't." Dreamy holds up a hand. "Do not speak of my son. He's dead because of you."

Whoa, Mary Pat thinks. *Hold on one fucking second there.*

"I didn't kill your son," she says.

"No?" Dreamy says. "You raised a child who thought hating people because God made them a different shade of skin was okay. You allowed that hate. You probably fostered it. And your little child and her racist friends, who were all raised by racist parents just like you, were sent out into the world like little fucking hand grenades of hate and stupidity and, and, and *you can go fuck yourself,* Mary Pat, if you think for one second I'm okay with that. Or that I forgive. I do not forgive. So go back to your neighborhood and sit with your monster friends and get yourselves all worked up to stop us from attending your precious school or whatever. But bitch, we're coming whether you like it or not. And we're going to keep coming until *you* quit, not the other way around. Until then, get *the fuck* out of my neighborhood."

And that's it. She's gone. Mary Pat stands by the mailbox and is mortified to realize she's crying—hot actual tears stream down her face—as she watches Calliope Williamson walk back up the block and disappear into her neat, well-tended home.

27

The headquarters for the Global Liberian Liberation Front sit inside a former synagogue on Dudley Street in a section of Roxbury that looks like the ash heap of the Urban American Dream. The three leaders of the GLLF sport horn-rimmed glasses and tower-of-power Afros, black turtlenecks and checked pants, matching Vandykes and airs of intellectual pretension, but Bobby knows all their reading matter was encountered first in a prison library. Whether the GLLF ventured into drug dealing as a means to finance a "higher end," or the "higher end" was conceived as a cover for the drug dealing, is irrelevant. They're fucking drug dealers, first and foremost.

The guys and girls who work under the main leadership are representative of the truth of the organization and rumored to be the ones who gave them the more authentic gang-sounding nickname, the Moorlocks. They're kids, mostly, who don't go in for turtlenecks or Vandykes or horn-rimmed glasses. They wear black leather car coats and wide-brimmed hats and shoes with three-inch heels. They deal drugs all over Roxbury, Mattapan, and Jamaica Plain, and they fuck up *anyone* who gets in their way. They're cowboys (and cowgirls) who don't give a shit. This recklessness makes them dangerous but, conversely, predictable if anyone decides to take a real run at them.

Vincent, who watches way too many movies and reads *Guns & Ammo* the way other guys read *Hustler,* wants to stage a pseudo-paramilitary raid on the GLLF building. Just go in there blasting and call it a plan.

Several of the major weapons companies have been sending urban police departments amped-up military-grade weapons for years. New law enforcement philosophies coming out of L.A. and New York have begun to advocate for special teams of combat-ready police cells. In L.A., the first of these has been given a name, SWAT, and they took on the Black Panthers and the SLA in sustained firefights that armchair John Waynes love to believe put the order back in law and order. In reality, Bobby knows, those gunfights led to limited results, a shitload of property damage, and a new micro-generation of substandard cops who think they can compensate for bad instincts, poor people skills, and limited intelligence with high-powered weaponry.

One day, Bobby knows, the Vincents of the department will get a chance to prove their theories correct or not. Whether they're proved right or wrong, the genie will be out of the bottle, and it will be probably hard, if not impossible, to put it back in. Until that day, though, Bobby outranks Vincent. He comes up with a plan for Operation Moorlock that involves a team in Narcotics while an ad hoc group of detectives from across Division handles surveillance on GLLF head-quarters to make sure no one goes unaccounted for until Operation Moorlock has its shit locked down tight.

Thursday morning, after Bobby gets all he needs from Narcotics, he and Vincent and two other detectives, Colson and Ray, knock on the front door of the GLLF and are welcomed inside by Rufus Burwell. The other two who take up the masthead, Ozzie Howard and Simeon Shepherd, are waiting in a large study that has only a few books on the shelves and smells of incense and pot.

"We're here for the guns," Bobby says once they're all seated.

Rufus strokes his Vandyke like he watched too many Charlie Chan movies as a kid. "We have no guns."

"Yeah, you do," Bobby says. "Look, we can go back and forth and then drag you down to the station and lose your booking slips for a few days while we toss the shit out of this place and any other places you're associated with. We can go that route. Or you can just give up the guns that Brian Shea and Marty Butler gave you and tell us why they gave them to you, and we'll never speak of it again. You won't do a night in jail, you won't get charged with anything."

Rufus, Ozzie, and Simeon exchange smug, lazy looks before Rufus turns back to Bobby. "I remain unconvinced of your sincerity or, frankly, your power."

"Okay." Bobby reaches into his pocket. He removes the booking photos of Rufus's nephew, Ozzie's girlfriend, and a yellow-eyed kid rumored to be Simeon's boyfriend. He lays the photos down amid the coke dust on the coffee table. "Those were taken half an hour ago. We've got every single one of them dead to rights on narcotics trafficking. Not possession, Rufus. Not possession with intent, Ozzie. Not intent to distribute, Simeon. Straight-up, good, old-fashioned, made-in-America motherfucking trafficking. That's a nickel each hard time before we even consider their priors. So you want to spend the rest of this decade visiting your nearest and dearest in prison? Keep telling me you got no guns."

Rufus and the other two share a few looks.

"They're in the basement," Rufus says.

While Vincent, Colson, and Ray go to the basement with Ozzie and Simeon, Bobby has a chat with Rufus.

"What were you supposed to use the guns for?"

"We still in the realm of no pending charges, Detective?"

"We are."

"You wouldn't be the first cop to break his word."

"Be the first time I broke mine, though. Rufus, I knew you back when you were running numbers for Red Tyler. I ever do you the wrong way?"

Rufus says, "Always a first time."

Bobby already owns this asshole for sitting on a box of illegal automatic rifles, and Rufus thinks Bobby needs more to send a black man with a record up the river?

"What," Bobby says very slowly, "were the guns for?"

Rufus sees something in Bobby's gaze that speeds up his answer. "They want us to shoot up the high school."

"Which high school?"

"South Boston High School."

"When?"

"Tomorrow." Rufus chews a hangnail for a bit. "Said to shoot some white kids if we're of the mind."

"Were you gonna do it?"

"Ain't answering that, Detective."

"And what were they gonna pay you?"

"Two kilos Mexican brown."

"And who was it who hired you for this job?"

Rufus snorts. "Gonna pretend you didn't even ask."

"I can apply plenty of pressure to get my answer."

"You go right ahead, Detective. I'd rather die, go to Walpole for ten, you name it. I ain't saying shit about it."

"We witnessed one of his employees hand you the weapons."

"And that employee, what's he say about who he works for?"

Bobby says nothing.

Rufus says, "Uh-huh."

Colson, Ray, and Vincent come back up the stairs, each carrying an M16.

"Those them?"

"Yup," Vincent says. "Serial numbers filed off, fully automatic. What were they supposed to use them for?"

"To start a race war," Bobby says, his eyes on Rufus, who tries not to look ashamed.

"Shit," Vincent says, "if we ain't already in a race war, what the fuck are we in?"

28

The line about Frank Toomey you always hear around Southie is that
he's not all that hard to find because who, in their right mind, would go
looking for him? But now, with everyone on high alert for a sighting
of Mary Pat, her milling about anywhere near Frank Toomey's known
hangouts or places of business is out of the question. And she has to
figure if they assume she's coming for him, visiting the street where he
makes his home is out of the question too.

But his wife, Agnes, a thin woman with a birdlike face and shoulders, is quite active in ROAR, the sister group of SWAB. Restore Our
Alienated Rights was formed by Louise Day Hicks, a member of the
Boston School Committee, to protect the "vanishing rights of white
citizens." The only reason SWAB and ROAR haven't folded into
the same organization yet is because Carol Fitzpatrick, the leader of
SWAB, and Louise Day Hicks, the leader of ROAR, hate each other,
dating back to some spat they had in kindergarten. Rumor has it the
source of the lifelong animosity is a broken crayon, but that's never
been confirmed. SWAB is in disarray at the moment anyway, in no
small part because Mary Pat knocked out some of the members' teeth
and broke at least one nose, so the ladies of SWAB don't look particularly "match fit," as her grandfather used to say, for a rally. But ROAR
has been planning their rally for a month. And Agnes Toomey has uti-
lized the manpower of all her husband's underlings in the Butler crew
to get the word out. So Agnes, who's spent her life in the shadow of

her fearsome husband, is taking her place front and center at tonight's rally. And since the Butler crew has spent endless man-hours getting the word out, it's possible—not probable, mind you, but possible—that Frankie will show up to support the Cause.

Mary Pat uses some of the blood money Marty gave her to go shopping at Filene's Basement. She buys a pair of large oval sunglasses that remind her of Jackie O's. She adds a black wig and a tan kerchief to her cart. She buys a powder blue gabardine pantsuit, a white blouse, and a pair of white nursing shoes. She treats herself to some lipstick, rouge, foundation, and false eyelashes that match the black of the wig. She splurges on a new purse for her gun.

After purchasing everything, she takes it to the dressing room and transforms herself. She's a little surprised the nursing shoes bite at her heels; the whole point of nursing shoes, she's always heard, is that they're comfortable and you don't have to break them in. Other than that, her shopping spree is a grand success. She looks in the mirror of the ladies' dressing room at Filene's Basement, and a stranger stares back at her. It's a bit disconcerting how easily she vanished. She takes the glasses off, and okay, there she is, if someone got up close and personal, those are Mary Pat's blue eyes for sure. But with the glasses back on, she has to peer hard at her profile to identify herself. And straight on, forget about it—she's another person entirely.

Last year, right before they ended, she and Ken Fen went to the movies at the Bug House on Broadway and saw a spaghetti western, *My Name Is Nobody*, with Henry Fonda and Terence Hill.

That's who she is now as she looks in the mirror: nobody.

A ghost.

With a gun.

After Filene's, she walks a few blocks and turns onto West Street for her appointment at the law offices of Anthony Chapstone, better known as Tony Chap. Tony Chap had been Dukie's attorney and did well by him, never billed him for so much as a paper clip unless he could point to the papers he'd clipped with it. It was Tony Chap who'd helped her get Dukie declared legally dead so she could marry Ken Fen in the church and, just as Dukie had said, his rates proved reasonable and without any hidden surprises.

Seeing him in his little office after the passage of half a dozen years, she's struck once again by what an odd and solitary figure he has always cut. She knows of no wife, no family. The only framed photographs in his office are of small dogs and places she presumes he's visited—leafy, mountainous places. He is, as always, impeccably dressed, but in a style at least fifteen years out of date—narrow lapels on his suit jacket, suspenders underneath, a silk bowtie. He's a courteous man, kind-eyed, and she's long since stopped questioning whether he has integrity, but knowable he is not. She doesn't even know how old he is—somewhere between forty and fifty-five, his face still as smooth and unlined as a light bulb.

He guides her to a chair and expresses his condolences for Jules. He assures her that all the paperwork is prepared and brings in his secretary, old Maggie Wheelock, been with him his entire career, to witness and notarize everything.

When it's all done—everything signed and initialed in triplicate—she removes some pocket change for herself from the bag of blood money and leaves the bag with Tony Chap.

She would have thought it would have given her pause to leave that bag of cash behind. In truth, she feels a hundred pounds lighter. And cleaner. Like she just took a bath in a baptismal font.

The Rally Against Tyranny takes place at seven o'clock, as the sun is beginning to set outside the Suffolk County District Courthouse on East Broadway in South Boston. The courthouse is just east of where

East and West Broadway meet, and that intersection is already clogged with people. With no traffic getting through, they line the street and sidewalks outside the courthouse, and the various leaders speak from the courthouse steps.

The fifth speaker, Agnes Toomey, a woman few have ever heard speak above a whisper, has no trouble finding her voice with a bullhorn. It goes against God's plan, she tells the crowd, to force a neighborhood, a culture, a place of pride and honor, to change its ways to accommodate those who are too weak or too lazy to help themselves.

Mary Pat, moving along the fringe of the crowd on the far side of the street, catches herself thinking that a woman whose husband kills people for a living might want to lay off the God talk.

The crowd doesn't get the irony. They're eating it up.

"If they want better schools," Agnes calls through the bullhorn, "let them build them. No one's stopping them."

Up and down Broadway, people honk their horns.

"If they want a better life," Agnes says, "let them get off their heinies and work for it."

Heinies?

The crowd cheers. The horns continue to honk.

"The American Dream is no handout."

The crowd goes fucking *wild*.

"The American Dream is roll up your sleeves and make your own way. Without welfare!"

A tidal wave of applause.

"Without government help and government orders!"

A group of men walk by Mary Pat, carrying pale white bodies under their arms, or that's what it looks like until Mary Pat looks close and sees they're life-size dolls, clearly as light as air in the big men's arms. The crowd lets the men pass. One of the men, she realizes, is Terror McAuliffe, Big Peg's husband. He looks right at Mary Pat, checking her out—face to breasts, breasts to face—and then he moves on.

No recognition.

"Francis and I have four children," Agnes is saying, "three of them at Southie High. But they're not going to school tomorrow. Because I won't let them go. Southie won't let them go! Am I right? Southie won't go!"

The chant rolls up and down Broadway: "Southie won't go! Southie won't go! Southie won't go!"

Agnes stands back, beaming, and her eyes drift to someone in the crowd, off to her right, about fifty yards from where Mary Pat stands. Mary Pat catches a glimpse of curly black hair in that section of crowd.

Mary Pat moves through the crowd. All her cockiness about her disguise suddenly feels like false confidence. Barroom bravado. Anyone, at any point, could turn, see her profile an inch away from their nose and . . .

What?

Scream her name.

That would do it.

Tom O'Rourke has the bullhorn now. Tom is also on the school committee. But he's a dry speaker, a cure for insomnia is ol' Tom, and even though he cycles through the usual greatest hits—tyranny, reverse racism, disruption of community and culture—he's got everyone's eyelids drooping when a cheer rips through the crowd. Mary Pat follows dozens of turned heads to see the men with the dolls swinging ropes over the streetlamps and flagpoles up by the courthouse. They're not practiced at it—only one rope holds fast on the first try—but the crowd gives them so much vocal support that Tom O'Rourke calls it a day. Which brings another round of cheers.

Mary Pat nears where she thinks she saw Frank Toomey, but the sun's gone down at this point. It's not yet full dark, but deep shadows have fallen across the crowd in jagged swaths. This makes it harder to discern faces than it would be in full dark, where your eyes tend to adjust. And the sunglasses sure don't help. Someone with black hair passes close to her, but when he emerges from the other side of the couple between them, he's got a beard and a double chin, and she recognizes him as one of the Clarks from I Street. She turns in the crowd and he's coming toward her, his eyes locking with hers, Frank Toomey himself, all brute force and Old Spice as he works his way through the crowd with a gruff "'Scuse me, 'scuse me" that sounds less like a minor plea and more like a major command. He comes right for Mary Pat; she can't move. They're packed in there too tight, people jostling and turning to see whatever's going on by the courthouse at the moment, but Mary Pat's realizing too late she should be reaching into her purse, which is twisted to the back of her right hip, as Frankie is almost on her, his mouth curving into a cruel smile as he gets in close enough for her to smell his breath and says, "'Scuse me, hon, I just gotta get by."

She pivots to her right as best she can and then he's brushing past her, his big bearish body sliding against her own, close enough for her to notice the smallest flecks of gray beginning to find his sideburns, and then he's moved on. And right behind him, hands in their jacket pockets on a summer night, are Johnny Polk and Bubsie Gould, two headbreakers who run South Shore Sand & Gravel and several porn shops in the Combat Zone.

Before the crowd can close, she steps into their wake, staying right on their heels, as Frank, two steps ahead of them, parts the crowd like the prow of a boat. She wishes she hadn't chosen a powder blue pantsuit—it seems the kind of detail people will remember later—but then she reminds herself she has no other endgame. Her primary objective is not to kill Frank Toomey and escape. It's simply to kill Frank Toomey. Which, arguably, she could do right now—just pull out the gun and shoot all three assholes in the back. But who would be the true asshole then? Bullets could pass through their bodies; a panicked stampede could leave people trampled; she could miss. No, here was not the place.

The crowd surges forward as one, and Mary Pat is spun halfway around so that she's involuntarily facing the courthouse again. The life-size dolls are hanging from the flagpoles and lampposts now with signs around their necks. One reads SEN. KENNEDY, another JUDGE GARRITY, a third MAYOR K. WHITE, and a fourth WILLIAM TAYLOR, a name she doesn't recognize. The men who carried the effigies stand below them with lighters in their hands. As the crowd bellows its approval, they light the dolls on fire.

It takes a minute. The flames dance along the edges of the effigies, some blue, some yellow. One of them—Garrity's—goes out, and they have to start again. But then . . .

The light from the flames washes over the crowd closest to the courthouse. It bathes them in red and yellow and blue light that floods their heads and faces like liquid. The air smells of lighter fluid and fury. The effigies twist on their ropes and burn.

The crowd chants, "Southie won't go!"

The crowd chants, "Niggers suck!"

The crowd chants, "We are one!"

For a moment Mary Pat's vision turns telescopic, and all she can see are the faces surging forward on necks that strain from the stretching, red mouths slick with spittle, signs thrusting into the air like pitchforks, legs of children draped down their parents' shoulders and chests. Moving through the thickness of the crowd and the thickness of its rage is like trying to squirm her way between freshly laid brick. Her lungs ache as if she chain-smoked half a dozen cigarettes in a row, and her head grows light.

Just when she thinks she might pass out, she clears the crowd. Pops out on the corner where West Broadway meets East.

Across Broadway, Frank Toomey reaches a cherry red Caddy with a white hard plastic roof. He chats easily with Johnny Polk and Bubsie Gould. He grimaces comically, and they share a laugh. He says something that makes both of them cock their heads. He nods several times so they'll accept that he means what he says. Then he gets in the Caddy and pulls off the curb. He U-turns and heads up West Broadway.

It's fucking agony as she waits to see what Johnny and Bubsie are going to do. They seem to be wondering themselves. Then they nod and walk three doors down to a bar.

Mary Pat runs full out for two blocks, hops behind the wheel of Bess, and stands on the gas. Bess putters out of the parking space. Begins to gain speed. Nears a stop sign. Mary Pat cranes her neck—nobody around—and blows the stop sign. She blows the next stop sign and reaches West Broadway with some momentum. At this point, all she's got are guesses. If Frank were heading home, he'd have taken a side street that ran parallel to Dorchester Street and worked his way over to his house on West Ninth. But he didn't. He drove up Broadway toward the bridge. Mary Pat lays all her chips on the table and decides he's heading into the city itself, downtown somewhere.

If that had been the case—and someone *hadn't* lit a car on fire and left it at the intersection of Broadway and E—she would have lost Frank Toomey for the night. But she reaches the intersection just as the traffic begins to snake around the burning car, and she catches sight of that white roof and cherry red frame as it passes the flames—*is everything on fire tonight?*—and keeps the car in sight until it turns right at the I-93 on-ramp.

She's three cars back by the time the Caddy exits at North Station and then crosses the bridge into Charlestown. The two cars between them pull over at City Square, so she plays it safe and lets Frank get way ahead of her. Too far ahead, it turns out, but she doesn't panic. Doesn't allow the fear to rule her. It's Charlestown—one mile square and not known for having covered garages. If he's staying in the neighborhood, she'll find him.

And she does.

Well, his car. She finds it parked in front of a barbershop across from the Training Field on Common Street. The barbershop is closed, its lights off. All around it are homes, some dating back to Revolutionary times, most to the early 1800s. They're row houses—either redbrick, brownstone, or clapboard—not an inch to spare between them. He could be in any of them. Or none of them. Could have taken a parking space where he found it and walked off around the corner. She thinks about looking for him on foot, but the only place more clannish than Southie is Charlestown. If she starts walking around looking in windows, word will get to Frank before she gets half a block.

But he'll come back for the Caddy, she hopes. She finds a spot with a clear view of his car on the far side of the Training Field, so named because it was where Union troops mustered and trained during the Civil War, and checks her wig and makeup in the rearview mirror. She settles in and tells herself she's not exhausted. She can't remember the last time she had real sleep; even in the motel last night, she got three hours tops. She pinches her thigh as hard as she can. Slaps her own face a few times. Smokes cigarette after cigarette . . .

She wakes around midnight with no idea when she fell asleep. She blinks half a dozen times, slaps herself again, and gets a clear look across the Training Field. The Caddy is still where Frank Toomey parked it.

Jesus.

Dumb fucking luck. Nothing more.

She resolves to stay awake even if she has to cut herself, but halfway through her next cigarette, her eyelids flutter. She gets out of the car. Stands in the clammy air, her wrists leaning against Bess's roof as she smokes. She spots a phone booth half a block up on the corner. Perfect angle on Frank's car from there, so she trudges up to it and steps in, closes the door behind her. She thinks of who she can call at this late hour—or at any hour anymore, she realizes with the pang of the exiled—and then she drops a dime in the slot and dials.

"Mary Pat," he says when they put him through to her. "How'd you know I'd be working the late shift?"

"Luck o' the Irish, Detective."

"We took three nasty automatic rifles off the street this morning."

"Did you?"

"We certainly did. Thank you."

"If you worked this morning, why you still at it?"

"I went home and slept," he says. "Came back, though. Everyone's doubling up. Half the cops in the city are gearing up for tomorrow. A lot of them were over your way keeping the peace tonight."

"I saw you at Auggie Williamson's funeral."

"Noticed you myself."

"Why'd you rush off?"

"We got a warrant we'd been waiting on. Had to serve it to a shit-head who killed his girlfriend, stop him before he could kill another one."

"That must have been satisfying."

"Not really. What I do feels a lot like sanitation work most days." He fails to suppress a yawn of pure exhaustion. "I heard you exchanged some words with Auggie's parents."

"Mmmm," she manages.

"I bet that wasn't pleasant."

"It wasn't."

He makes the same excuse she tried for. "They lost a son. Violently. They can't see straight."

"No." She sucks in a big wet breath that rattles in the confines of the phone booth. "They see fine." She looks out through the smeared glass at the Training Field where soldiers once prepared for battles to free the slaves. She imagines they were young, impressionable. Scared shitless. The grass of the field has turned nearly white in the summer heat—there's been no rain this summer; none—and under the street-lights and through the grimy glass, it looks like snow. She's never felt more lost.

No, she realizes, not lost.

Homeless.

She clears her throat and tries to explain something to Detective Michael "Bobby" Coyne, a perfect stranger when you get right down to it, but she feels the need to tell him something even she doesn't understand. She feels the need to be heard, whether she makes sense or not. "When you're a kid and they start in with all the lies, they never *tell you* they're lies. They just tell you this is what it is. Whether they're talking about Santa Claus or God or marriage or what you can or can't make of yourself. They tell you Polacks are this way and wops are another and don't even get us started on the spics and the niggers but you sure can't trust them. And they tell you that's the Way. And you, you're a fucking kid, you think, *I want to be part of the Way. I sure don't want to be outside the Way. I gotta live with these people my whole life.* And it's warm in there. So warm. The rest of the world? That's so fucking cold. So you embrace it, you know?"

"I know," Bobby says.

"And then you dig in because now you got kids and you want them to feel warm. And you spread the same lies to them, mainline them into their blood. Until they become the kinda people who can chase some poor boy into a train station and bash his head in with a rock."

"It's okay," he says gently.

"It's *not!*" she screams into the confines of the phone booth. "It's not. My daughter's dead and Auggie Williamson's dead too because I sold my daughter lies. And before she ended up swallowing them? She knew it. They *always know it.* They know at five. But you keep repeating the lies until you wear them down. That's the worst of it—you wear them down until you scoop all the good out of their hearts and replace it with poison."

She has no idea how long she weeps. Only that at one point, she has to put another dime in the phone, and still she can't stop crying.

Bobby stays on the line with her the whole time.

Once the sobs have become sniffles, she hears his voice through the earpiece: "Whatever you're thinking of doing, I'd like you to take a day off."

She can't speak yet. Her throat is filled with saline and mucous.

"Mary Pat? Please. Take twenty-four hours. Don't do anything. I'll meet you wherever you want. No badge. Just a friend."

"Why are you my friend?" she manages eventually.

"Because we're both parents," he says.

"I was. Not anymore."

"No, you still are. You always will be. And all parents know failure. It's the only thing we know for sure. So, yeah, your daughter, Jules, she had some failings that you passed on to her. Okay. But everyone I spoke to about her? They all talked about how kind she was. How funny. What a great friend she could be."

"What's your point?"

"You gave her those qualities too, Mary Pat. We're not one thing. We're people. The worst of us has good in him. The best of us has pure fucking evil in his heart. We battle. It's all we can do."

"I'm good at battle," she says.

"That's not the battle I'm talking about."

"About the only thing I'm good at."

"I bet there's a lot more you're good at."

"Now you're shining me on to keep me on the phone."

"You called me."

"So?"

"So I think you want me to talk you out of whatever you're planning to do."

She laughs, and he's chastened to hear that it's a dry laugh. "I don't want you to talk me out of anything."

"Then why call?"

"Because someday someone's going to make sense of this."

"What's 'this'?"

"What I'm about to do."

"*Don't* do it."

"And I want you to tell them what I told you."

"I don't want to hear it."

"I told you, Detective Coyne, that you can't take *everything* from someone. You have to leave them something. A crumb. A goldfish. Something to protect. Something to live for. Because if you don't do that, what in God's name do you have left to bargain with?"

Just as Bobby's thinking he should have started a trace on this call five minutes ago, she hangs up.

He sits there, staring at the phone, and remembers why he started doing heroin in the first place—when you're high on smack, the world seems gorgeous. When you aren't, it seems like a hopeless fucking mess.

Mary Pat hangs up the phone and leans back in the booth and watches with a kind of stupefied awe as Frank Toomey drives right past her.

She follows him back to Southie, once again taking the gamble that she knows where he's going, so she doesn't have to tail him tightly.

And he rewards her when he pulls over in front of his home on West Ninth. The street is so still, you could hear someone blow their nose from a block over. When Frank opens the door of the Caddy, she can hear the hinges creak.

Bess is already rolling. Mary Pat has her foot off the gas and is just allowing the creaky bitch to move via her own momentum. She waits to hit the gas until Frank closes the door to the Caddy and bends to lock it with the key.

This is it, she thinks. *This is the end. I run him the fuck over, slam it into reverse to finish the job if necessary, and drive away. I go as far as the money and luck will take me. Which, let's be honest, won't be far. And I die from police bullets or Butler crew bullets because I will not go to jail and I will not let those Butler vermin lay their hands on me.*

But Frank turns to see the car coming at him and drops to the ground. He rolls under the Caddy and almost makes it—he almost does—but the tires crunch one of his legs. From underneath the Caddy, his scream is sharp.

She screeches to a halt and gets out of Bess.

Lights come on—first in the next-door neighbors' house and then in Frank's. Frank has crawled out from under the Caddy and tries to get to one foot on the sidewalk. He's reaching into his jacket for a gun. But she's already coming around the front of the Caddy with her gun pointed at him, her wig sliding halfway down the right side of her head, and she fires. The shot goes wide, hits what sounds like a trash can down the street. Frank's hand clears his jacket, something in it for sure. She takes better aim and fires a second time, hears Frank shout, "Fuck!" He drops a gun and doubles over, and the blood spills from a hole in his stomach and through his fingers under the white street-light glare and down the front of his white pants.

He tries to charge her, even with the bullet in him, but the mangled left foot isn't cooperating. He makes the mistake of trying to put his weight on it, and he screams—it's more of a shriek, actually—and falls to his knees, ends up on all fours at her feet as she puts the gun to the crown of his head.

"Daddy!"

Mary Pat looks up to see the girl on the stoop. Agnes crouches behind her, holding the girl back. It's Frank's youngest daughter—Caitlin, the one who just had her first communion a few months back.

"Don't hurt my daddy," Caitlin screams. "Please, lady, please!"

Frank grabs at her legs. Mary Pat clubs him with the butt of the revolver.

Caitlin howls. "Don't hurt him!"

The next-door neighbor, Rory Trescott, runs toward them with a bat cocked. Mary Pat fires the gun once, aiming well wide of him, and Rory hits the deck.

Frank flops over on his side, blood pumping out of the hole in his stomach like a weak water fountain.

Mary Pat grabs his gun off the sidewalk and puts it in her waistband.

Caitlin Toomey comes off the porch as her mother swipes at her, trying to hold her back.

Mary Pat screams, "You keep her the fuck back!"

Agnes grabs her daughter.

Mary Pat sinks both her hands into Frank's greasy wet hair and gets a solid grip. She drags him across the asphalt to Bess—he's fucking heavy; it's like dragging a fridge—and her wig falls off as she does, lands in the street in a streak of Frank's blood.

"I know you, Mary Pat!" Agnes calls. "I know you!"

Mary Pat gets the back door open. She yanks Frank's hands—first the right and then the left—behind his back and cuffs them at the wrist. She shoves Frank onto the backseat like he's a rolled-up rug. Just pushes until he's in. She slams the door shut and runs around the side of the car.

"I know you!" Agnes calls again. "I know you! I know you!"

Mary Pat gets behind the wheel, drops the shift into drive, and pulls up the street. They've driven a few blocks when Frank groans from the backseat. "I'm bleeding bad."

"I know it," Mary Pat says.

"I could bleed out," Frank says.

"Well, shit, Frank," Mary Pat says, "wouldn't that just break my damn heart?"

29

Castle Island in South Boston is not an island, though it used to be. It's a peninsula, connected by a main road, Day Boulevard, that dead-ends in a parking lot, plus the two walking paths that lead out to the Sugar Bowl, forever tainted for Mary Pat as the site where Marty Butler used a bagful of money to tell her she had no children left walking this earth. Just as the island isn't an island, the castle isn't a castle; it's a fort. Fort Independence, specifically. The current structure, built in the mid-1800s on the site of two previous forts that dated back to Pilgrim times, is made of granite.

Edgar Allan Poe was stationed here at one point. The experience is said to have inspired one of his most famous short stories, though Mary Pat has never read any Edgar Allan Poe, so she holds no opinion on the matter. She knows from her school days that throughout its history—first as a Pilgrim stronghold, then as a British fort, next as an American one, and finally, as a historic monument in the possession of the Commonwealth of Massachusetts—no shots have ever been fired in a military action from its walls. But just like anything else in Southie, she thinks as she approaches, it was built to fight at the drop of a hat.

Frank has been passed out for a few minutes when she drives over the curb by Sullivan's fast-food hut at the end of the parking lot. Frank wakes with a yelp. He's disoriented and probably only half lucid from the blood loss. She can hear his handcuffs jingle a bit as he realizes they're attached to his wrists. She loops down the path along the north side of the fort. It's bumpy. Frank grunts a lot.

Bess is going to need all the help for what comes next, so Mary Pat steadily depresses the gas pedal as they go. When they reach the northwest corner of the walls, she comes fully out of her seat and stands on the pedal. Bess fishtails, and Frank falls of the backseat with a scream. Mary Pat grinds her foot into that fucking pedal and growls through gritted teeth as she wills Bess straight up the hill. Right near the top, the back wheels give, and she knows they're not going to make it. They're going to slide backward and probably sideways, and then they're going to tip and flip and roll.

"We're going out together, Frank!" she calls. Frank yells back something that sounds like "You crazy cunt, Mary Pat." But Bess, bless her ancient old-lady heart, finds one last breath in her engine, one last surge, and the back wheels catch dirt instead of grass and the car bursts over the top of the hill.

Mary Pat is not prepared for four bald tires at full acceleration to hit damp grass on a humid summer night, and they shimmy crazily all over the field leading up to the doors of the fort. She gets control of the car just before smashing into the doors, and the moment the car comes to a full stop, Bess expires. The engine shudders to a halt, and little metallic pings and gasps rattle around under the hood, and the frame shakes and surges like it's having a heart attack. Plumes of brown smoke shoot out from the back of the car and then spill from under the hood.

For a moment it feels like losing a pet. Mary Pat pats Bess's side after she exits. She tries to come up with the proper words, but all that finally occurs to her is a simple "Thanks" to the only car she's ever owned outright.

While Bess continues to pass through her death throes, Mary Pat picks the rusty old lock on the main door of the fort and pushes it open. She goes back for Frank, pulling him off the floor of the backseat by his hair.

She would have expected more rage from him. Tough-guy talk. Threats. But he's plaintive. Surprised, it seems, by her barbarity. When he hits the ground, he cries, "Come *on*! Please! *Please*, Mary Pat, I'm holding my fucking guts in here!" She hoists him to his feet and pushes him through the door in a wild stumble, which ends almost immediately when he puts weight on his mangled leg and falls down again. She lets him lie there for a bit, grinding his head into the grass.

The interior of the fort is an oval—parade grounds and storage rooms down below. Parapets and cannon slots up above.

She drags Frank into the first room she sees. The rooms just off the main parade ground are barely rooms. They have no doors, no furniture, nothing. They feel like prison cells, but she's pretty sure she's heard they stored gunpowder, armament, and food back in the long-ago. She drops Frank with his back to the wall to discover he's passed out again.

Pussy.

She removes the gun she took off him. A Colt .45 1911, almost identical to the one her uncle Kevin brought back from World War II. Uncle Kev would bring it out when she was a little girl and they went over to his apartment, and he'd let her sit on his lap with it after he'd stripped it and checked the chamber. He'd tell her he kept it for two reasons: 1) to always remind himself of the savagery man was capable of against his fellow man; and 2) in case the niggers came for them all some night.

In the end, he used the gun on himself, Christmas morning 1962.

She searches Frank. Finds a spare clip for the .45 in his pocket and adds it to her bag. She removes his coat, bunches it up, and presses it to his wound. He mumbles but doesn't wake, and she uses the duct tape to wrap the bunched-up coat as tightly as she can around the wound.

She gets a look at his leg and almost throws up. Jesus. No wonder he can't stand on it. The foot is pointing in the opposite direction, and the bones in his calf punch out through the skin like broken sticks. It gives her the idea, though, to pull off his remaining boot.

Where she finds a knife.

She considers it. Is this *the* knife? The one he drove up under her daughter's rib cage and into her heart?

She finds him looking at her. His breathing is very shallow. "You know you're a dead woman?"

She shrugs. "You'll be strolling—oops, sorry, crawling—into hell before me, Frank. Bank on it."

"Not if you get me to a hospital." His voice is friendly. Reasonable.

She jerks a thumb over her shoulder. "No car, Frank. It's dead too."

"Just walk down the hill to the pay phone by Sullivan's." A helpful smile joins the friendly voice.

"To . . . do what, again?"

"Call me an ambulance. Or call Marty."

She waits a bit before answering. Long enough to watch the hope flower in his eyes. "Frank," she says as softly as possible, "you are going to die tonight."

He opens his mouth to speak, but she cuts him off.

"There is no way out for you," she explains. "No threat, no promise, no bribe can buy you one more day of this life."

Until that moment, he'd thought he had a chance. But now he realizes—truly grasps—he's living in his own nightmare. Wide awake for every second of it.

He searches her eyes, and she allows him full access. Somewhere beyond the walls of the fort, a seabird cries out.

Frank Toomey's face grows dark and cold with outrage. "No!" He jerks at the cuffs on his wrists. "You hear me, bitch? No! You will—"

She slams the heel of her hand into his forehead, rams the back of his head into the granite wall. "How is it," she says as he tries to clear the tweeting birds from his fucking brain, "that you have any rage left in your soul for me? You took my child. You took my *child*, Frank. And the baby inside of her. You used her. Chewed up her life while she could have been living it and then plunged a knife up under her rib cage and into her *heart*? And you call yourself a human being?" She holds up the blade of his knife to his face. "Is this the knife?"

Frank stares at her with his dead eyes.

"Don't give me your fucking eyes," she says. "Like you're too cool for my pain. This is my pain." She slices his cheek.

"Jesus!"

"I said lower your fucking eyes."

He glances at his own blood on the knife blade and then looks down at his lap.

"You're only alive right now because I honestly want an answer— how can you raise children of your own? How can you know something of love and yet kill a child?"

"I've killed lots of people in my life, Mary Pat."

"I know. But a child, Frank?"

He makes a shrugging motion, his hands cuffed against the wall. "I don't think about it." The blood drips off his cheek in fat drops. *Plop. Plop. Plop.*

"About what?"

"About any of it. Killing someone, it's like shoveling snow—I don't like doing it, but if it's gotta be done, it gets done. And my kids have nothing to do with it. They're my kids. A separate thing. Your daughter—"

"Say her name."

"Jules," he says. "She was a problem. She was talking shit about telling my wife she was pregnant, and she killed that kid so—"

"She didn't kill him. She was with them when—"

He's shaking his head. "She used the rock on him. It was her."

She smashes her fist down on his shattered leg. The scream he lets out is like something from the animal kingdom, the screech of prey being eaten alive in the high grass. He topples to the dirt floor. Lies there with his mouth open, eyes wide with shock.

"She didn't use the rock," she says. "You're just trying to make shit up. You weren't even on the platform."

"Why would I make that up?" he gasps. Tears fill his eyes when he says, "Please don't hit my leg again, but why would I make that up? How's it serve me? And *of course* I was on the platform."

She doesn't say anything for a long time. She looks out at the parade grounds under the light of a half-moon.

"I think . . ." he manages as he works his way back into a sitting position, "I think she did it as a small mercy."

She looks back at him. *"What?"*

"Possibly," he says.

"Mercy from what?"

He doesn't say anything for a bit.

"Mercy from what?"

"I told them to fry him."

"Huh?"

"Throw him on the third rail," he explains. "Fry him. Show the rest of the spooks in this city what happens if they come down to our part of town." He looks at the blood slowly consuming his coat and the tape she's wrapped around it. His skin is the blue-white of mackerel. "Jules didn't like that. She kept saying let him go." He snorts. "We couldn't let him go. No. I told them, 'Fuck that. Fry him.' The boys, they listened—boys do that. They picked the kid up and were about to toss him between the second and third rail, and yeah, that's when she hit him. Which ended any idea that it was a fucking accident, thank you very much. He was dead the second he hit the ground."

She watches him steadily. Thinks it's odd how the worst of us look no different than the best of us. Like someone's son, someone's husband, someone's father. Loved. Capable of love. Human.

"And you couldn't forgive her, could you?" she asks. "For the mercy?"

He hisses against the pain for a moment. "If she was weak there, where else would she be weak? In a police station? On the stand? I'm sorry, Mary Pat, but you know there's a code down here. Live and die by it."

She reaches into her bag, comes out with her .38, and is about to blow his fucking brains all over the granite behind him when she hears a vehicle approaching.

The car pulls right into the fort. Doors open. Headlights sweep the parade grounds.

Marty Butler calls, "Time for a reckoning, Mary Pat."

30

Bobby's let it be known throughout Division that he'd appreciate being notified should anything violent connected to the Butler crew occur in the next week or two.

It doesn't take long.

Bobby shows up on West Ninth in front of Tombstone Frankie Toomey's house and listens to the witnesses—a neighbor, Frank's wife, and Frank's eight-year-old daughter—give their statements. Both the neighbor and Agnes Toomey conclusively identify Mary Pat Fennessy as the assailant and kidnapper. The kidnapping is problematic—by all rights, they should call in the FBI immediately and hand over the case.

Another day, perhaps, Bobby decides. Not tonight.

They find blood on the sidewalk and Frank's boot on the street. More blood there from the impact with the car and also streaks of it where Mary Pat dragged him. It takes Bobby a moment to realize what looks like a decapitated mop head lying in a puddle of blood is a wig.

Bobby calls in to headquarters from his radio, gets through to Vincent, and asks him to spread the word to anyone who has a source in Southie. Someone has to have seen a crazed blond woman driving a piece-of-shit '59 Ford Country, racing through the night with a gut-shot hit man in the backseat.

Bobby's back at the station when a beat cop working City Point

calls in that he saw a car racing up Day Boulevard about twenty minutes ago, filled with what looked to be Butler guys.

There's only one possible destination at the end of Day Boulevard.

Bobby says, "Heading toward the castle?"

"Well, it's a fort actually, Detective."

Bobby closes his eyes and opens them. Takes a breath. "Heading for
the *fort*, Officer?"

"Yes, Detective."

"Thanks." Bobby hangs up, speed-walks to his lieutenant's office.

31

Marty calls out a second time, "The more you make us wait, the longer we'll draw out the pain."

Frank opens his mouth to call back, and she puts the muzzle of the .38 to his nose. Raises her eyebrows at him. He shuts his mouth.

Judging by the strength of the headlight beams, the volume of Marty's voice, and the stray scuffing she hears as they mill around out there, she guesses they're pretty close. Maybe fifteen yards. No more. She counted four car doors opening and closing, so that means there's at least four of them, maybe six if they went full clown-car. But that would have been conspicuous, and Marty's not known to be conspicuous.

Four, then.

She can hear them spreading out, footsteps of varying distance on the dirt of the parade grounds. And one set of footsteps is growing very close.

She lifts Frank to his good foot and leads him toward the doorway.

The footsteps outside the doorway stop. The owner, she assumes, can hear them.

Mary Pat steps out with her gun to Frank Toomey's neck.

Brian Shea, caught by surprise three feet from Mary Pat, starts to raise his gun.

"No, no, no," Mary Pat says.

Brian takes one look at Frank Toomey—the mangled leg, the bloody coat duct-taped around his bloody waist—and lowers his gun.

"Drop it to the ground," Mary Pat says. "This is my only warning."

He looks in her eyes. Looks in Frank's. Drops the gun.

The other three are fanned out in a crescent about ten yards past Brian. Larry Foyle is the farthest away, taking up the left side of the crescent. Marty stands in the middle of the curvature, like one bad tooth in an ugly smile, and Weeds loiters to the far right. They all have pistols held loosely by their sides.

"You all right there, Frank?" Marty asks.

"Pretty far from that, Marty," Frank says.

"We'll get you patched right up."

"I know you will, Marty. Thanks."

"You sure about that?" Mary Pat pulls the trigger and blows a tunnel from one side of Frank Toomey's neck to the other.

For men used to casual violence, none of them seems to have prepared for this moment. Larry and Weeds just look shocked, mouths agape.

Marty screams, "Noooooooo!" as if his heart is breaking for the first time in his life.

Brian Shea reaches for his gun.

Frank drops to the ground, his body nothing but a bag for nonfunctioning organs, his soul already halfway to hell.

She shoots Brian somewhere in the middle of his body and hears him scream.

Marty is raising his pistol when she fires right at him—*Bang! Bang! Bang!*

She has no idea if she hits him, only that he's not there anymore as the other two return fire, the bullets hitting high on the walls behind her, Larry and Weeds running for cover behind the car and not taking much aim as they shoot.

She grabs the back of Brian Shea's collar. He's arching his back and kicking his heels against the ground. Making loud yips and yelps. She stays low, keeps his body in front of her as best she can, and pulls him back into the storage room with her. Once they're in there, he grabs her around the knees and slams his head into her stomach. She boxes his ears, one of her hands holding that heavy .38, and he lets go.

She pushes him into the corner and she kicks the ever-living shit of him. Literally *kicks*. Over and over, fast and dirty and indiscriminate. She doesn't stop until long after she knows he's no longer a danger.

"Is that all you motherfuckers *understand?*" she hisses at him. "Is there nothing else?"

He curls into a ball and she gives him a minute in case he might puke, then she comes behind him and pulls him tight to her, straddling him, her legs hooked over his. She tosses aside the .38—she emptied it out there—and reaches in her bag for Frank's .45. She pulls it out, flicks the safety off, places the extra clip on the dirt floor beside her. There's no way out for her, but there's only one way in. They have to stick their heads through that doorway if they want to get to her. She keeps Brian in front and points the .45 at the doorway.

"You just fucking killed him," Brian Shea says eventually, as if he can't comprehend the tragedy of Tombstone Frank Toomey's death. As if he's just been stripped of all the illusions he's held of a gentler world.

"Sure did."

"And you blew my fucking hip off."

"Well, if you make it out of here, Brian, you'll have a bad limp and a good story."

Outside, she can hear more scuffing sounds. Judging by the distance, she suspects they're over by the car.

"You just fucking *killed* him."

"Why are you shocked by this? You kill people all the time."

"*We,*" he says. "Not you."

Beyond the doorway, someone opens the trunk of the car.

She snakes her arm around Brian's abdomen and puts the muzzle of the big .45 against his crotch.

"The fuck you doing?"

"Were you there when my daughter was killed?" she whispers in his ear.

"I wasn't there," he says wearily. "I was called after."

She hears a thump on the ground outside, followed by the clack of metal against metal. To look, she'd have to move Brian off her and stick her head into the doorway, risk getting it blown right the fuck off, so she'll let them do whatever they're doing out there, thank you very much. But she admits to being curious.

"Who *was* there when my daughter was killed?" she asks Brian.

"Frank. Marty was in another room."

"So what happened?"

"I heard her and Frankie got in a fight, she kept coming at him, he whipped out a knife and, ya know."

"'Ya know,'" she says bitterly.

"Yeah."

She removes the gun from his crotch.

Outside, more scuffing, more metal sliding against metal, and then Marty's voice. "Grab the tripod."

The *tripod?*

Brian exhales heavily through his nostrils. She suspects it's his attempt at managing his pain.

"'Member in sophomore year," he starts, "when we—"

"Here we go. Memory lane."

He chuckles. "No, no, it was funny. We rigged all those toilets in the teachers' bathroom with—"

"Firecrackers," she says. "Yeah, I remember."

"We had a lot of laughs back then."

"We sure did," she says. "You think it'll save me?"

He says nothing.

She nods. "So why the fuck should it save you?"

His face grows flat again. "Marty can't let you live now. He loved Frank like a brother."

"Like a *brother*?" she says.

"Yeah. What else?"

"The way he screamed when I killed Frank? You tell me."

He gives it some thought, and his face grows panic-stricken. "You're sick." He spits on the wall across from him. "Fucking depraved."

She laughs. "You flood our community with heroin. Rent women out to fuck strangers for money. You molest children. Turn other children into worse versions of you. You rob. And you kill. But *I'm* sick. *I'm* depraved. Oh, okay, Brian."

From somewhere off in the dark, Marty calls: "Mary Pat, dear."

"Marty, dear!" she calls back.

His chuckle carries on the light breeze. "Let my friend Brian go and we'll let you walk out of here."

"No, you *won't*."

For a moment the only sound is the night.

"No, I suppose we won't." Another chuckle. "Can I ask you something?"

"Sure."

"That was a lot of money I gave you."

"Yes."

"Why didn't you just take it and go away?"

"And do what?"

"Make a better life for yourself?"

"I had my better life. Frank destroyed it."

"But *I* didn't," he says, all guileless innocence. "Yet you came at my whole organization."

"Oh, Marty," she says. "Oh, Marty."

"What's that, Mary Pat?"

"This is all you. All this sick fucking ugliness. You drive it and it drives you."

"I've lost you—what drives me, dear?"

"Fear," she says.

"Fear?" He hoots. "What could I be afraid of, Mary Pat?"

"Shit, Marty, that's between you and God, but I'm pretty sure it's a long, sad list."

Silence follows for quite some time. She can hear the distant water lapping softly against the shore.

Marty asks, "Do you know what I did in the war, hon?"

Whatever's coming, Mary Pat knows it's coming soon.

"I don't, Marty, no."

"I was a rifleman," he calls.

"Uh-huh . . ."

"More to the point," he says, "I was a sniper."

She hears the report of the rifle only after the bullet has punched its way through the bone and tissue of her right armpit. She pivots in an instant, a survival instinct as old as her body itself, and the next round turns Brian Shea's face to cherry pie.

He doesn't make a sound. He probably never realized he died.

She scrambles back into the corner of the room, and now the handguns go off, and she watches two more rounds hit Brian Shea's body—one through the chest, the other exploding his right kneecap.

"Cease fire," Marty calls.

Larry and Weeds stop shooting, but her ears continue to ring.

Marty calls to her again. "Do you know what you just received there, hon?"

She can't speak. She can't breathe. All her insides have seized up, like a large, cold hand is squeezing her heart as hard as it can.

"That was a 7.62-millimeter steel-jacketed bullet traveling twelve hundred miles an hour, Mary Pat. Once the shock and the adrenaline wear off, which should be any moment, your body will start to react to the damage. I suspect breathing will become difficult. Your blood will grow cold. It'll be hard to speak. Or think. But I want you to lie there and try. I want you to think about all your mistakes—first and foremost of which was an utter lack of respect for my generosity and my *friendship*. I want you to ruminate on that," Marty says, "because I am not going to finish you off. I'm going to sit here and enjoy a cigarette and the night air until you bleed out, you traitorous fucking cow."

The back of Mary Pat's throat suddenly fills with hot phlegm. She coughs it up only to realize it's not phlegm at all. It's blood.

Well, shit.

She's known from the moment Marty handed her the bag of money that she would not stop until everyone involved in her daughter's death answered for their sins. She never got to Marty himself, and that's too bad, but it's hard to get to the king. It's always been hard to get to a king.

But man, did she fuck up the king's court.

And now he's telling her to lie here. To bleed out. To wait for the rats.

Be nice to see Dukie again (even if she'll yearn for Ken Fen all the while). Maybe they can have a few beers and remember how much fun they used to have in the early days of their marriage.

"Hey, Marty," she calls, alarmed by how feeble she sounds.

"Yes, hon?"

She gets to her feet and the room spins and she falls sideways into a wall. "How did you come under the impression . . . ?" She steadies herself. Her lungs feel as if someone's dipped them in glue.

And Noel. Won't it be swell to see her Noel?

"What's that?"

"Under the impression," she repeats, "that I would ever take orders . . ."

She sticks tight to the wall on her left. Steps over Brian Shea and his missing face.

"I can't hear you," he calls.

"That I would ever take orders from a gutless . . . nothing like you?"

Coming home, Jules. Coming home, my baby girl.

She steps through the doorway into the half-moonlight and raises the gun. Actually gets a round off, maybe even two, before they return fire.

32

Desegregation of the Boston Public Schools takes effect on Thursday morning, September 12, 1974. The buses that transport black students to South Boston High School are accompanied by police escorts. The police wear riot gear. As the buses near the school, several hundred white protesters—adults and children—line the streets. Chants of "Niggers go home" give way to "Niggers suck" and "Hell, no, we won't go." Several protesters hold up pictures of monkeys. One brandishes a noose.

The bricks come from a construction site on West Broadway. Other people use rocks. But the bricks make the most noise and do the most damage when they hit the windows of the buses. The children on the buses discover the safest place during the pelting is under the seats, and the only reported injury is to a teenager who gets glass in her eye; she requires medical attention but doesn't lose the eye.

Inside South Boston High, the black students are met with something they've known forever at their own schools but didn't expect here—no white kids.

On the first day of school, not a single white student attends South Boston High School.

When word of this fact spreads through the demonstrators, their chant turns to "Vic-tor-y. Vic-tor-y."

• • •

A few hours before, at four in the morning, Mary Pat Fennessy's body is removed from the parade grounds of Fort Independence on Castle Island and transported to the Suffolk County Medical Examiner's Office.

Bobby, Vincent, and their hastily put-together squad of detectives and patrolmen arrive at Fort Independence about five minutes after Mary Pat's death to find Marty Butler and his men gathering their spent shells and preparing to leave. They don't put up any fight. The guns they used are legally registered. Mary Pat Fennessy fired at them after murdering Frank Toomey. Brian Shea was killed in what Marty calls "friendly fire."

Bobby arrests them and confiscates the weapons and the tripod Marty rested his rifle on, but Bobby has little doubt that the crime scene investigation will reveal events played out exactly as Marty says they did; he's acting too fucking smug for it to be otherwise. Bobby might—might—get the case into court, if only because Brian Shea died as a result of three citizens taking the law into their own hands. But the chances of that case making it to a jury are about as good as Brian Shea growing his face back.

At the medical examiner's office, they pull five bullets out of Mary Pat Fennessy's body. The kill shot was a 7.62-millimeter round to the center of her heart, but Drew Curran assures Bobby that another round from the same rifle which entered her body through the right armpit would have done her in within another ten minutes.

"It had to be a shot to the heart," Bobby says to Carmen a few days later. "Anywhere else? She would have just kept coming."

The day after Mary Pat's death, Bobby gets a call from Calliope Williamson. They catch up on a few things, and Bobby apologizes for not being able to make it back to the house after Auggie's funeral.

"That's okay," she says. "You're a good man."

Bobby thinks, *I am?*

"Is it true," Calliope asks, "that she helped you get the kids who killed my son?"

"Mrs. Fennessy?"

"Yes."

"Where'd you hear that?" Bobby says.

"Work. All the women used to be her friends are calling her a snitch, saying she betrayed her own."

"I heard you had words with her," Bobby says.

"I did, and I won't apologize for any of them."

"Not asking you to. Whatever they were, I'm sure she deserved them."

"But she also helped you catch my son's killers?"

"She did a lot more than that," Bobby says.

"I don't understand."

"The man most responsible for what happened to your son won't be able to do it to anyone else ever again."

"Because of her?"

"Yes. I'm not saying her intention was to get justice for Auggie—I don't think it was. But she got it just the same."

Silence as she processes that information.

"Are you going to her funeral?" Calliope Williamson asks.

"Depends when they hold it. If I'm working, no. If I'm not, yes."

Another long silence. Then:

"Maybe I'll see you there." She hangs up.

Big Peg McAuliffe spends the days after her sister's death trying to track down family for the funeral. Donnie, down in Fall River, says he'll attend and shares that he has a line on Bill, who's no longer in New Mexico but might be in Hartford. Big Peg reaches a few cousins and an aunt who say they'll try to make it.

It nags her that she can't remember the last words she exchanged with her sister. She knows the last time she saw her and knows what they talked about—Jules being missing. She knows she walked her to the door, but she can't remember their conversation. And it bugs her to no end; you should be able to remember the last words you ever said to someone.

Some of the people around Commonwealth shoot her strange looks, like whatever virus her sister caught in the last few weeks of her life might catch Big Peg too. It pisses Peg off, knowing what Mary Pat did to the family's rep. It's gonna take time, maybe a lot of it, to get their good name back.

She says to Donnie when he calls back, "I mean, yeah, they dealt with Jules harshly, but ya know, she played with fire and she got burnt."

"She was a kid," Donnie says.

That almost gets to Peg, but she swats it away.

"What're you gonna do?" Peg says.

"I know," Donnie says. "Can't fight city hall."

"It is what it is."

"No argument."

"And we all know how Mary Pat could get."

Donnie laugh-snorts. "She got that look in her eyes? There was no reaching her."

"None."

"So, Billy says he'll come."

"Yeah?" Peg lights a cigarette, surprised how nice it feels to know she'll see two of her brothers after all these years. "Be like a family reunion."

"Yeah."

"Yeah."

"So, all right, then," Donnie says to wrap things up.

"All right, then," Big Peg agrees.

They hang up.

Big Peg sits by her window for a bit, smoking and looking out at the projects. She spies a spot of pavement where she and Mary Pat used to play with jacks or do hopscotch or jump rope as kids. They were never the closest of sisters, but they had some good times. She can see the two of them out there; for just a second, she can hear their laughter and their small talk echoing off the project walls. A ferocious pang seizes her torso—heart, lungs, stomach. A bomb of desolation that explodes and ripples upward, eventually reaching her brain.

How did I lose my sister?

Where is Mary Pat's soul now?

How did things get so far?

She focuses on a pigeon across the way. It pecks at a window-sill. She has no idea what it's pecking at (some gum? another pigeon's shit?) but it keeps its head down. It does its job.

The chest pang passes, the shock waves wear off.

How things got so far, Big Peg reminds herself, is because Mary Pat meant well, but, let's face it, she was never much of a mother. Those kids ran the show in the house because Mary Pat spoiled them. Simple as that. Let them talk back to her, rarely beat them, gave them her last dime if they asked for it. When you spoil people, they don't thank you. They're not grateful. They grow entitled. They start demanding things they got no right to demand.

Like with the coloreds and the school.

Like with Noel and the drugs.

Like with Jules and another woman's husband.

Peg can't blame herself for Mary Pat's failings, can't go on a guilt trip because she walked the straight and narrow like a good citizen while Mary Pat wandered off the path and into the weeds and the swamp beyond.

And now Peg finally remembers the last thing she ever said to her sister. It was about their kids, and it feels like a prophecy when you look back on it.

You can't let them rule your life.

• • •

The day before Mary Pat is laid to rest, Bobby's son, Brendan, ends up in the hospital with his leg broken in three places. He got it skateboarding with his friends on a steep street near his mother's house. Tried to avoid a pothole, smashed into a Buick, went sailing over the hood. Broke his left heel, ankle, and fibula.

All clean breaks, luckily. Surgery goes off without a hitch.

Bobby and Shannon sit with him up the Carney. The cast looks bigger than the rest of him, a big white appendage jutting off his knee and hanging suspended at the other end from a metal U inverted over the bed. He's in good spirits, a little loopy from the drugs, and he keeps giving them this bewildered smile, like *How did I get here?* His aunts and Uncle Tim all visit, bring him toys, cards, books. Leave silly messages on his cast. They make so much noise in there, the nurses keep having to shush them. Finally, they shoo them out until only Shannon, Bobby, and Brendan remain.

Brendan snores softly, and Shannon looks across him at Bobby and says, "Our boy," and something in her voice breaks because something in Brendan is broken for the first time. He's rarely been sick, never had stitches or broken a bone. Never even got a sprain.

Bobby nods, keeps his expression even and supportive.

She looks beat. She was the one who brought Brendan in. Was here for two hours before Bobby arrived. He suggests she go home, get some rest, take a shower, at least, freshen up.

She's reluctant, but as Brendan remains sleeping and the night drags on, she gathers her things, kisses her son's forehead, and gives Bobby a small finger wave, her eyes wet and shaken.

When she leaves, the smile Bobby's kept plastered to his face since he got here—his cheerleader smile, his Dad's-on-top-of-it smile, his everything's-going-to-be-just-fine smile—drops. He imagines the black and purple leg underneath that cast, swollen and despoiled by swaths of black sutures. His son's flesh sliced open like a Christmas ham, so the surgeons could insert their instruments inside his body and fuse bones that had snapped like breadsticks. And while Bobby is grateful—ever so fucking grateful—that modern medicine is here to respond in this way, it nonetheless feels like a violation.

It could have been so much worse. Brendan could have soared over that Buick and landed on his head. His neck. The base of his spine.

It could *always* be worse. That was a mantra in Bobby's family growing up. And he agrees with it.

But he also must confront what he has grasped intellectually since the moment he first held his son in the maternity ward of St. Margaret's and is only now allowing to infiltrate his heart. Not because he wants it to but because that cast has given him no choice.

I can't protect you.

I can do what I can, teach you as much as I know. But if I'm not there when the world comes to take its bite—and even if I am—there's no guarantee I can stop it.

I can love you, I can support you, but I can't keep you safe.

And that scares the ever-living shit out of me. Every day, every minute, every breath.

"Dad?" His son is staring at him.

Bobby looks up the cast to his son's sleepy face. "Yeah, bud?"

"It's just a leg."

"I know."

"So why do you have tears in your eyes?"

"Allergies?"

"You're not allergic to anything."

"Shut up."

"Real mature."

Bobby smiles but says nothing. After a bit, he moves his chair closer to the bed, takes his son's hand in his. He raises it to his lips, gives the knuckles a kiss.

• • •

The funeral for Mary Patricia Fennessy is held at nine o'clock in the morning on September 17. It's sparsely attended. Calliope Williamson stands in the back and notices a large, fat version of Mary Pat standing up front with a group of unruly kids who all look in need of a bath. There's two old men in a nearby pew with thinning hair who have similar features to the fat woman and to Mary Pat.

Family, then.

Some of the nuns from Meadow Lane Manor attend but no co-workers. About another dozen or so mourners are scattered about a church that could easily hold a thousand.

Detective Bobby Coyne does not show up. She knows he would have if he could have—he's like Reginald that way, a man of his word.

Directly across from Calliope, in the opposite pew at the back, stands a handsome giant with kind eyes. He wears an ill-fitting suit and a tie with a knot that's bunched up and wrinkled. He keeps a handkerchief at hand and weeps silently but often.

She's seen him before—he used to pick Mary Pat up after work sometimes. It's her husband. She knows his name is Kenny, even though they've never been formally introduced, and that everyone calls him Ken Fen.

After the mass, she introduces herself on the church steps and expresses sorrow for his loss. Not just of his wife but of his stepdaughter as well.

He says, "You're Dreamy."

She shakes her head. "No one calls me that."

"I thought—"

"The women at work—about the only thing they remember about me is that I told them a story about my father calling me Dreamy when I was a kid. Never said anyone had called me it since, but they decided not to hear that part. Gave me the name so I'd feel more like their pet, I guess."

He sighs. "Well, I'm so sorry for *your* loss."

Her eyes pulse, as if someone just slid a metal skewer sideways through her heart, but she says nothing.

"A lot of loss going around," she says.

The other mourners are filing out. No one pauses to express their condolences to him. They walk around the two of them as if they have leprosy.

They remain on the steps long after everyone has gone, saying nothing. And it's strangely comfortable.

"Want to get a drink, Calliope?"

"I'd fucking love one."

They walk to the nearest bar past signs and graffiti that Calliope refuses to look at. She doesn't need to see the words to feel their ugliness. The ugliness is everywhere over here right now; it rides the air, it hangs from streetlamp poles. Hell, she can even taste it, like a pebble of tinfoil clamped between two teeth.

The bar is one that Ken Fen tells her stays open eighteen hours of every day to serve the men who work the three shifts at the electric plant. For ten in the morning, it's got a sizable crowd inside and two bartenders behind the bar, a waitress working the room.

They sit there for ten minutes. And not a single person acknowledges them. A giant and a black woman in a Southie bar and they may as well be invisible. The waitress passes them four times. Both bartenders catch their eyes. But no one takes their order.

On the waitress's last pass, Ken Fen once again raises a tentative hand to her and catches her eye. She blows right past him.

He turns back to Calliope and gives her a tired smile and raised eyebrows. "Good thing I brought my own." He reaches into his suit jacket and comes back with a flask.

Calliope matches his tired smile. "Me too." She reaches into her bag and comes out with her own flask, a gift from Reginald for their ninth—or was it tenth?—wedding anniversary.

They raise their flasks over the table.

"What should we drink to?"

"Our dead," Calliope says. "Of course."

"Of course."

They tap their flasks together and drink.

"One more," Ken Fen says.

"Oh, I'll be having more than one."

He chuckles. "Toast. One more toast."

She leans in again.

"To our living," Ken Fen says.

"To our living," Calliope agrees.

They drink.

Following the release of her remains by the Suffolk County Medical Examiner's Office, Julia "Jules" Fennessy's body is interred at Forest Hills Cemetery in Jamaica Plain. Per the last will and testament of her mother, the body is placed in a mausoleum atop a small slope in the southern corner of the grounds. Funds are dispersed from the estate of Mary Pat Fennessy every month to pay for flowers to be placed around the mausoleum door. Funds are also dispersed to satisfy an odd stipulation. Once every weekday, the assistant sexton, Winslow Jacobs, is tasked with spending half an hour inside the mausoleum with a transistor radio tuned to the local classical station, WJIB.

Winslow Jacobs has had some strange jobs in his time on this earth, but this might be the strangest. He ain't complaining, though—the head sexton, Gabriel Harrison, pays Winslow an extra fifteen dollars a week for the duty (which means Gabriel's got to be making thirty), and the truth is, within a month, Winslow has developed a fondness for the break in his day. Plus, the music grows on him.

As time goes on, he falls into the habit of talking to Julia Fennessy most afternoons. He tells her about his son, who works for a company paves road out in California, and his two daughters who are raising families of their own not far from where they grew up, and his wife's cooking, which won't win any prizes but tastes like home and that's good enough for him. He tells Julia about his father, who he's certain never loved him, and his mother, who loved him twice as hard to make up for it, tells Julia Fennessey most of what he can remember about his life in all its highs and lows, all its dashed dreams and surprising joys, its little tragedies and minor miracles.

ACKNOWLEDGMENTS

Infinite gratitude to:

My editor, Noah Eaker, who pushed me to be a more precise and more economical writer.

The earliest readers—Kary Antholis, Bradley Thomas, Richard Plepler, and David Shelley.

The later readers—Michael Koryta, Gerry Lehane, Mackenzie Pietzak, and David Robichaud.

My wife, Chisa. I wrote most of this novel in New Orleans while running a TV show during frequent COVID outbreaks and lightning strikes in the furnace of a Louisiana summer. Oh, and then a hurricane hit. Throughout it all, you gave me more love, support, and wise counsel than I could have ever dared hope for. This one's for you, babe.

ABOUT THE AUTHOR

DENNIS LEHANE is the award-winning, bestselling author of more than a dozen novels, including *Live by Night*, *Mystic River*, *Gone, Baby, Gone*, and *Shutter Island*. Born and raised in Dorchester, Massachusetts, he lives in California with his family.